In Our Time

by

Bobby Hutchinson 3

Book Cover by Brice Leek

First Edition 2024

This book is dedicated to my mother Tammy who I miss every day. She always believed in me before anyone else, and was the best teacher I ever had. I love you more than words can express.

A special thanks to my best friend Brice Leek for illustrating the cover art for the book. You are the most talented artist I know and inspire me to better myself every day. I'm thankful to share this world with you.

To Kendall: You convinced me love was real and worth fighting for. This book would not be the same without your contributions and feedback. You will forever be a part of this book and my heart. My love for you will continue long after we part this world.

CHAPTER ONE

Scott clutched the strap to his satchel and took a deep breath. He was standing in an elevator while peering up at the ceiling and thinking about his day. He had woken up at 6:00 a.m. and found the strength to get himself out of bed. He slowly crept into the kitchen where he opened a cabinet and grabbed a bowl. He reached for a half open drawer and grumbled to himself when he found no clean spoons. Looking towards the sink he noticed many were sitting in open defiance of him. He grabbed a sponge, poured some soap onto it, and started to scrub. Suds started to envelop the spoon and food debris slowly fell off into the sink. Scott turned the faucet on and allowed the water to cleanse the spoon. He held it in a way that caused the water to jump up at an angle getting his shirt slightly wet. He grabbed a washcloth and took a few moments to dry it. He could barely make out his reflection in the bowl of the spoon. He noticed the bags under his eyes were darker than usual. Scott had gotten maybe four hours of sleep because he was staying up to drown out his not so positive thoughts about the world around him. He grabbed a container of milk and a bag of cereal. He carefully poured his cereal first and then topped it off with a downpour of milk. Scott stepped outside to his porch and looked out into the world. He could see the city in the distance with dozens of neighborhoods in every direction. The roads were overrun with traffic and the sound of construction crews filled the air.

Scott took the time to breathe in the fresh air and stretch his legs. It was dawning on him just how much he could see in the distance. A half dozen or so joggers in a nearby park. Many more on their way to work, the local coffee shop, or to see friends and family. A strange gray smog could be seen covering a portion of the city to the south. Local officials advised that technically the smog isn't harmful but that you shouldn't stay around it for more than thirty minutes. Scott lived near a military base which routinely did drills and exercises to 'stay prepared' as they claimed. The biggest threat was from within itself so there is no one to defend ourselves from outward aggression. Any enemy we find abroad is our own design. Scott took a few bites of his cereal crunching and enjoying the taste of sugar and milk combined. The people of the city recently attempted to peacefully demonstrate with little success however the police harshly broke up the protests with violence resulting in the deaths of over forty people. This was reported by the news as rioters who hate "our" country and want to see it handed over to the "enemy". Who was this enemy? To the surprise of no one it was the communists. It's always the communists. The establishment media and those in power love to utilize a spectre of a supposed threat to rationalize harsh reprisals and reactions to peaceful demonstrations. These demonstrations simply ask for the basic necessities to improve their material and social economic conditions. Anything that strives for a positive change to society is actually a secret Marxist or Socialist plot. This portrayal of history from those in authority has plagued Scott's country for hundreds of years even through regime change after regime change. Scott continued to eat his cereal and pondered the state of things. He pulled his phone from his pocket and checked the time. 6:13 A.M.

After a few more minutes Scott returned inside and washed his bowl. He picked up the remote to his living room television and turned it to the national news while taking a seat in his recliner. A recap of the previous night's events including a mass shooting at a polling booth, a car that ran over fifteen protesters, and an announcement that the government would not lift restrictions on European refugees from seeking refuge in the country. "That is Africa and the Middle East's problem!" is what one representative was caught saying in a leaked audio clip. It's a sentiment that many in power agreed with but you couldn't say it out loud. If you don't say it out loud and you just do it quietly; it makes it moral and okay because we are the ones doing it. Scott couldn't believe how many people bought into that nonsense. It's dangerous rhetoric with real world consequences. He opened a drawer of a small table next to his couch. He grabbed a pipe, a small bag and his lighter. He prepped the pipe and took a decently sized hit. Scott held his breath for about five seconds trying to get the most out of it that he could. He let go and started to cough. He could already feel a small sense of relief and took another hit. He flipped the channel to something a bit more light hearted. One of his favorite shows was called I Just Work Here! It was a sitcom about the employees of a bank and the wacky antics that ensue. The topic was a bit antiquated but that didn't stop the show from being extremely popular. He sat back into the chair and took another hit from his pipe. He started to think about the dream he had the night prior. He was late for work and trying to gather his clothes to get ready. He kept getting interrupted or was unable to hold everything in his hands. A nearby clock kept ticking and he would be progressively slower and later the longer the dream went on. So much time would pass that it seemed almost illogical to even go into work at that point. This had been a recurring dream of Scotts for nearly twenty-five years. Scott lit his pipe one more time and took a deep breath. Exhaling only at the last possible moment he put his things away. He made his way over to the bathroom and turned on the shower. He looked at himself in the mirror and took a few moments to ponder the endless thoughts that sprung from his mind. The steam started to fog up the mirror and he knew the temperature was just right when he could no longer stare back into his own eyes. Scott took his shower, cleaned up, and then picked out his best-looking dress shirt. A light pink button-down with the sleeves rolled up would be the perfect selection for the day. He made sure to style his hair until it was perfect and smiled to himself in the mirror. He continued to stare for a few moments thinking about everything that had led him to where he was today. He had to meet with his boss today and find out where his next assignment would be. Scott worked as a historian of Earth's history for the United Nations in conjunction with extra-terrestrial governments and their historians. It was his job to interview aliens and learn about the history of their worlds, the stories of their time, their technology, and the people of those worlds.

Scott chuckled to himself because there he went referring to aliens as people but he truly felt that way. He didn't see a distinct difference between himself and the aliens he met with because what was truly the difference? They speak a different language, have a different culture, and don't always do the same things that humans do yet that's how humans feel about each other. That's also how they feel about humans. At the core of humanity and what he surmised was at the core of all life in the universe was a desire for understanding and peace.

Scott had been on a vacation the last few weeks visiting his family and friends in his hometown and was ready to get back to work. His last job where the subject was from an alien world was when he interviewed the Helics of Rashar who were a separatist movement on the desert planet Rashar. They had recently won their independence from the Senics of Rashar who were the ruling family in a bloody civil war. Over thirty-million dead and one hundred million displaced. He learned a lot from them and gathered stark warning about what it could mean for life elsewhere. He hoped that his next visit would result in something a bit more uplifting that maybe could support the idea that the Earth would continue rebounding the way it supposedly had been. According to the propagandists, the Earth was doing far better than what the scientists said: 'For the past two centuries history has unfolded in front of our eyes as Earth has steadily rebounded and healed itself. The true test was the twenty-first century and we are still reeling with the decisions made in those days. Eventually conflict, hunger, and the negative effect on the climate had started to retreat leading to a new golden age in human history.' Some of this was true, such as the story of first contact with alien life and how we started learning from them instead of attacking them like almost every military mind wanted to do. Peace and understanding prevailed for a time and directly led to Scott's job even being as important as he likes to think it is. Of course this was a lie they told everyone to maintain law and order. The media and the filmmakers who fancied themselves propagandists or political actors helped paint the images we all see in our heads when we think of history. They created one fantasy after another and placed it onto real people, real events, real catastrophes. Many small lies snowballed into the other creating something so unstoppable that this big lie could not be truly challenged even if most were aware of it. Many in Scott's country fell for this big lie as did plenty across the world. This was the phenomenon of the ruling class across national divides artificially imprinted on us. The reality was a lot worse and perhaps the worst the world had seen. Scott knew a lot more than most about the truth of how Earth had arrived at the peak of technological advancement of the last few decades and yet speaking about that truth was tantamount to career suicide.

The light in the elevator light dinged. The panel read floor eleven which was two short of Scott's destination. This snapped him out of his daydream and back into reality. The doors opened and two tall men in black suits entered. One of them was carrying a briefcase. Scott didn't pay them too much mind. He was all too used to seeing men in black suits carrying top secret information via briefcase. Half the time it was just their lunch orders or jokes making fun of each other. A game to pass the time because budget cuts have led to the oversight committee spending little time reviewing the activities of its members. He tapped his leg and looked around the elevator knowing he wouldn't see anything new. A few more moments went by and the light dinged for floor thirteen. Scott let out a sigh of relief and squeezed past the two men to exit the elevator. He entered a lobby area with a receptionist desk, a few chairs, and a small window. He approached the desk and made eye contact with the secretary.

"Hey Stacy!" Scott said.

"Scott, how's it going? Haven't seen you in a minute," replied Stacy.

Scott smirked and pointed his finger in an acknowledging gesture.

"You got me there! I'm here to talk with George," said Scott.

"Okay I'll let him know. Give him just a few minutes." said Stacy

Scott smiled and took a seat next to the desk. George was Scott's boss and the person who would decide where Scott would go next. Stacy stood up from her chair and went around the desk to go to George's office. Stacy was pretty with blonde hair and a stunningly white smile. She had a stylish gray pantsuit on and smiled while looking over at Scott. Scott and Stacy had always gotten along well and she always knew how to help brighten Scott's day. Whether it was a corny joke, a morning text asking if he wanted coffee, or a colorful drawing in the break room, Scott loved what Stacy brought to the office and the way she carried herself. He didn't know how else he would make it through the average work day. From around the corner came a slim, tall, cream colored android named Kevin. He was named after the serial number on his back: K3-V1N. His form was remarkably human but his eyes gave it away.

"Hey Kevin!" said Scott waving his hand.

"Hey Scott! Hope your morning is going well so far!" replied Kevin waving in return.

Kevin was the lone android who worked at Scott's office and mostly worked with the accounting department and tech support. A recent spike in pro android rights demonstrations led many in the office to question if Kevin could be a threat or even a spy. Scott knew this was nonsense and fear-mongering meant to divide the office and discourage any kind of solidarity. The rest of the office wasn't so supportive but Scott did what he could to make it clear to Kevin where he stood.

"Oh you know I'm living the dream!" replied Scott in a slightly sarcastic tone.

"I expect nothing less!" responded Kevin while holding back a small laugh.

He continued on his way down the hall until he entered an office.

"Scott!"

Scott was startled and he looked up to see a familiar face.

"Larry! How's it going man," said Scott.

Scott stood up and stuck out his hand to shake. Larry was a tall man dressed in a tan suit and had a brown mustache. He was friendly, staunch in his views, and always looking to crack open a beer. If the office allowed alcohol Larry would likely be drunk about ninety percent of the time. He returned the handshake and seemed happy to see Scott.

"How was your vacation? Where'd you go?" asked Larry

"Went to visit the family back home and caught up with a few old friends from high school," Scott answered.

Larry had a slight look of concern but it was fleeting.

"Sounds like a good time it must have been nice to get a break from this place," Larry laughed and gave Scott a nice punch in the arm.

"You know it. I gotta say I'm glad to be back though. Ready for my next adventure," Scott said, starting to laugh.

"Yeah I know you love it but I'm telling you that sometimes it's good to live in the moment! Don't be caught up in what happened a long time ago. Be the person worth writing about a hundred years from now!" said Larry

Scott gave Larry a loving look he had given him dozens of times over the course of their relationship at work which had slowly grown into a friendship that he counted on to get through the longer and more tedious days. They didn't always agree on every issue and even strongly disagreed on some but they managed to focus on what they did have in common to strengthen their bond. In practicality this meant Scott let a lot of things go. "You can't fight him on every issue" is what Scott would tell himself. Some days he hears things that make him wish he had been tougher on certain things but there are only so many hours in the day and you only get so many to live.

"You always know what I need to hear, maybe I'll listen to you one of these days," Scott replied.

Scott laughed and Larry returned it with a smile and gave a nod of departure. He left the room and Scott turned his attention to the window. He could see a large amount of the city including the capitol building. Protesters were at the steps holding signs and chanting slogans. From what little he could make out it seemed like they were asking for more accountability for the police force and their actions. He remembered reading about a two hundred percent increase in police murders over the last year. He scanned the outskirts of the building. The police were present surrounding the protest on all sides. One stood to the side yelling into the loudspeaker and the crowd roared back at them. The captain unleashed the big hose and doused the crowd with ice cold water. Dogs and policemen alike swarmed the crowd from the outside slowly beating them into submission. Scott stood up and closed the blinds on the window. He could feel a deep pit in his stomach and he was uncomfortable with what he was seeing. He sat for a moment and peeked through the blinds. He could see gunshots being fired at the crowd and people falling to the ground in one chaotic motion. Now that everyone was scattering, arrests had started to be made and some were even attempting to fight back. Gunfire rang out from both sides and Scott took a step back from the window. He calmly walked back to his seat and sat down. He pulled out his phone and started to read reactions from local journalists and users online.

"George is ready for you dear," said Stacy.

Scott was a bit startled but kept his composure. She walked over, looked at him and put her hand on his shoulder. She let it sit for a few moments. He couldn't help but notice this and tried to stay focused.

"Perfect Stacy thank you," Scott replied.

He put his phone in his pocket, took a few deep breaths and stood up. He approached the door to the office ready for whatever challenges his boss would throw at him next.

CHAPTER TWO

George's office was of a decent size with a large window on the right side showcasing a view of the city. A rather large oak wood desk was flanked by two trophy cases on each side with plaques from his college days. It was a dark oak wood in an L shape. Scott shut the door behind him and appraised the situation ahead. George was a stocky man with a balding head and a pair of circular glasses. He wore a brown cotton jacket and a yellow button up shirt which Scott found a bit tacky. What someone was wearing is something he would always notice yet past that cared little about. George had become the boss a few years back and while the two of them butted heads at first they have grown to have a productive working relationship. Scott noticed something new: a gold watch on his wrist, a classic swiss design from a pre-modern collection. It was rare to see one of these due to nearly a century of suppression of historical materials of Swiss origin starting with the annexation of Switzerland by Germany and the ensuing conflicts. Scott had wanted to get one for himself if only to indulge in a little bit of historical spending. Historical style consumer products typically ran at least a month's salary if not more! Just like the many generations that preceded artifacts from times long past were seeing a revival in popularity. George's watch served no functional purpose for him. It was nothing more than just a way of remembering the past or at least an idealized version of the past based on the tales told about these items. His glasses had a computer chip connected which could access what time it was at any time which was pretty standard for anyone not living in poverty. Access to the time has been monopolized by the corporations. It costs money to access the time if you don't have the proper tools. Countless numbers of people live in terrible conditions and are subject to punishment if they are late to their jobs even though they can't tell the time without paying what little bits of their wage they can spare. George simply wears it as a fashion statement and a sign that he was doing well for himself. There were seven tablets on his desk all with legal jargon and graphs waiting to be reviewed by him. George flicked his finger to sign his name on one of the tablets while looking up to make eye contact with Scott.

"Scott! Good to see you buddy, how have you been?"

George stood up from his desk and walked around to shake Scott's hand. Scott noticed bags underneath George's bright green eyes who started yawning while walking over.

"I'm good, George. It's nice to see you as well."

Scott took his seat as George sat back down and placed both of his hands on the desk, thumbs pressed together. George was a nail biter with a large amount of the skin around his fingernails being bitten away. He started chewing on his thumbnail while flicking a few times on the tablet in front of him.

"Scott, I've got a big job for you."

"I'm excited to get back out in the field. What do you have for me?"

George gave Scott a look he had only given him twice before. Just by this he knew this would be important.

"I want you to meet with a surviving historian of the Nill race and learn about their history. The United Nations General Assembly wants to know more about them."

The Nills had been an ally of Earth from the very beginning of its involvement in galactic affairs. Earth had modeled its fleet after the Nills. This included their weapons, machines, energy sources, and their tactics. We learned everything we could strategically from them without taking the time to get to know much about their culture. The true tragedy was that the Nill species was almost completely gone. Earth started to get news from Nilleon, their home planet. Reports of a catastrophe known as 'The Great Collapse' started coming in and slowly over the last twenty years survivors have trickled into different systems. Earth had over three hundred show up at our stations in the first week and the total known number is somewhere in the neighborhood of four hundred and thirty thousand. He had yet to personally speak with a survivor so what he did know was mostly anecdotal and limited exposure from Earth sources.

"I'm in."

Scott smiled and gave George a look of confidence and assuredness.

"Good. You'll be meeting with Mashir Kahn who is one of the few Nill historians left. It's your lucky day!"

George pointed at him and gave him a laugh that seemed to speak to Scott's inner competitive drive. Scott had been competitive since his childhood stemming mostly from his years playing basketball and baseball. Scott knew how big of an opportunity this could be so he wanted to be sure to take advantage and do his best.

"I'm looking forward to it. I've been wanting to learn more about the Nill for a long time and I'm glad you're giving me the opportunity. I won't let you down."

Scott gets up and starts to turn around when George clears his throat, stopping him in his tracks.

"You'll be giving a speech on your findings to the General Assembly itself. They're holding a vote on whether to allow continued immigration of the Nill to Earth and I think this can be your ticket up the ladder. I'm putting you up for a job on the UN's Galactic Relations Council. You will be in those history books that you write about for more than just your own vanity," said George.

He smiled while saying that last part but it startled Scott a little. Did George really think that he was more concerned with his ego and his status than dedication to history and getting the truth out there? It was an interesting question. It is important to question yourself on issues that have a wide impact and will touch a lot of people. His favorite activist in his youth had taught him to challenge everything you hear. Always use logic and trust empirical evidence. Scott truly felt that he was doing his job for good and not for boosting his own ego.

"That's an incredible gesture. I will do what I can to make that happen. Anything different with this trip or should I just check in with Stacy?" asked Scott

Everytime he went on a trip it was always the same routine. Check in with Stacy to requisition a long list of supplies that he will need while traveling. Petty cash funds are loaded onto his phone and they book the flight to wherever he would meet with his interviewee. It was nice and it made it a lot easier to plan the trip. He basically only had to worry about what to wear and what to go see wherever he visited.

"You know it. Call me if you need anything. I'll check in with you from time to time. I can't wait to see what you present!" said George.

"You got it boss."

Scott nodded at George and turned around to leave. He noticed a globe on the end table by the entrance. It had a few stickers on it mostly placed over European nations.

It was an old globe not even close to being accurate to the current map of Earth. Earth's expansion into space and the gradual colonization of the solar system alongside tourism to other galaxies resulted in the masses being distracted by flashy scenes of our brave space explorers, who were settling a new frontier full of unsettled space. This promised space for humanity to expand and live in would have to come at the expense of the aliens living there already. Capitalism and the current world order had led to the need for new distractions from the system's inevitable collapse. The truth of our 'adventures' in space were much closer to the reality of our 'adventures' on Earth, where we arrived to worlds full of sentient life and left what we found in a pile of lifeless flaming debris. Carpet bombing, rounding up of dissidents, humiliation, torture and crimes against humanity that conveniently did not apply to our extraterrestrial foes. The stories and 'history' of this presented to us had been cleaned up and washed away the culpability that our rulers held for unbelievable levels of destruction and loss of life. The current oligarchs in charge are hiding this even better than the previous ones and the facade is believed even more strongly by humanity. Scott once bought into the myth and over the course of his career he had seen the misery and chaos caused by it. Scott had always tried to maintain a healthy level of skepticism. One thing he learned from his mother, not directly but by exercise, was that you should always take new stances and apply those to your other beliefs. More often than not you find that you will come away questioning what you used to believe. This isn't any one person's fault it's just the way we have been taught to think about the world. Time seemed to begin moving forward and he was staring at the globe. Scott wagered that it had cost at least seventy thousand dollars.

"Seventy-two thousand."

George said this with almost a sarcastic laugh.

"It's a great model from the year 1904," said Scott.

"How can you tell?"

George sat up from his chair looking slightly intrigued and puzzled.

"Namibia was controlled by the German Empire as a South West African colony. The globe just happened to be showing me Africa," replied Scott.

"That's a funny coincidence, Mashir will be meeting with you in Cairo. And if you happen to see him, be sure to tell my friend Ivan I said hello!" responded George.

Ivan was a Russian historian and a peer on the extra-terrestrial council he sat on now. He had a more nationalistic focus on history who had only gotten promoted to the council as a favor done by a politician helping Russian interests. He was a former member of the Russian military and is famously known for leading a company of men against two tank divisions and three packs of wolves in the Siberian winter. His unit became known as the Wolfshead because he arrived back at camp with his men carrying the heads of two wolves with him. Him and his 13 closest comrades got a tattoo of two wolves heads in a sun to commemorate their experience. Ivan had experience in nearly a dozen conflicts over the last twenty five years most recently in Eastern Europe and East Africa. George had a strange fascination with Ivan and always wanted to pick his brain. In a completely globalized world where we visit other planets and galaxies it seemed odd to Scott that George couldn't just message him and say hello himself. Maybe it was the human experience George was lacking from that and the transference of the responsibility on to Scott sufficed for the time. It's also possible that Scott was digging too deep into this but that's just what his brain did. It always led him to wanting to learn more about history.

"I will be sure to do that if I see him," said Scott.

"I haven't told anyone who you're interviewing so be mindful and be careful. Egypt hasn't been as accepting of the Nill as we have."

"I'll keep that in mind thanks George."

Scott left the office and decided to stop by the break room. The room was simple. A table with four chairs in the center next to a few countertops and fridge to put lunches in. Larry had made his way there to chat with three other co-workers. Brittney was a tall dark skinned woman with piercing green eyes and short curly hair. Uyanmas was a Tuvan immigrant who moved here to work with the United Nations. He was an average sized man with jet black hair and sharply defined cheekbones. Hila was a short Afghani woman who had recently joined the team. She had a long brunette haircut with brown eyes and a necklace that had been in her family for generations. The four of them were gathered around the table drinking coffee or water.

"Did you hear about Point Place?" asked Uyanmas.

"No, what happened?" responded Brittney

"Some guy perched up on a water tower and shot fifteen people. Including the mayor!" replied Uyanmas.

"Not just some guy either. It was the best friend of the mayor's opponent's son. He was at a campaign rally two days before it happened!" said Hila, stressing that last part.

"What are you saying?" asked Larry, slightly puzzled.

"It seems pretty clear that his opponent had some part in his murder," Hila responded.

"Danny Cruise doesn't seem like that kind of person. He's a good old boy, he wouldn't hurt a fly," said Larry, shrugging that accusation off.

"Won't hurt a fly but he removed dozens of protections against minority groups during his last term in office. This sounds exactly like what he would do. He wants a way back into power and he knows he won't win without stacking the odds," replied Hila.

"Until they do an investigation, we don't know anything. It could have been a complete coincidence for all we know. Why would he be the one to do it if he is so closely tied to his father? That's just common sense," said Larry.

"Did they catch him already?" asked Brittney.

"Yes they were able to capture him alive," replied Uyanmas.

Scott overheard all of this and it was mostly all true from what he had gathered reading the news. A shooting had occurred and the shooter was the son of the mayor's opponent. His father was a criminal who treated his time in office as a personal slush fund for his shady business deals and the shooter was captured alive. Who his father was is likely the reason he was able to escape an early grave; someone of a lower class would not have made it to the next day let alone the next hour. He made his way in and grabbed the pot of coffee and started to pour into a cup.

"Hey Scott good morning!" said Hila.

"Morning Scott," said Uyanmas.

"Hey Scott!" said Brittney.

Larry nodded, having already talked with him earlier.

"Good morning everyone. How's it going?" asked Scott, taking a sip from his coffee and facing the group.

"I'm still trying to wake up," replied Hila.

"We were talking about Point Place. What a great way to start the morning," said Uyanmas, with clear sarcasm.

"I saw that. Terrible, just terrible. Hopefully they get to the bottom of why exactly that happened," said Scott.

"I'm sure they will, we just have to let the system do its job," replied Larry.

"That's only if the system doesn't protect itself like always," responded Brittney.

"How was your vacation, Scott?" asked Hila, in an effort to change the conversation.

"It was good. Saw some old friends and some family. I needed to clear my mind a bit and it helped a lot. Happy to be back though," said Scott, with a smile.

"Glad to hear that. I've got to make it to a meeting but let's catch up later," replied Hila, standing up and grabbing her bag.

"Sounds good," responded Scott, giving a thumbs up.

Hila made her way out of the room so Larry stood up and took her seat at the table.

"Did you hear about the androids in Prague who took over that factory? Crazy stuff," asked Larry.

"Really? It's like I keep missing all the major stories," replied Brittney.

"Yeah the workers were upset with their treatment so they killed the human overseers and took over the factory. It took the army surrounding and storming the factory before they were able to retire the androids," Uyanmas replied.

"That's insane. I'm glad they stopped them before more people were hurt," said Larry.

"I think it's important to mention the terrible working conditions those workers faced. They had over triple the number of work hours scheduled as any comparable nation's workforce. They were being exploited for the gain of the owner's and there were reports of violence and abuse towards the workers," replied Scott.

"I get all that but just like with all these new aliens that keep coming here at some point you just have to assimilate. We can't let them just keep coming in with no restrictions. Eventually there won't be anything left for us! There are differences and we have to recognize that," said Larry.

"I don't disagree with your last point but I think you're focusing on the oppressor. The systems in place have been very oppressive towards androids and aliens there is no denying that. To put the responsibility on them for this seems very disingenuous," responded Scott.

"I'll give you one thing, Scott. You always have something to say that makes me think," Larry laughed.

"I'm happy to help," said Scott, smirking.

"I think groups like Corvo only serve to hurt the fight against alien oppression. Resorting to violence isn't going to get those in power to side with you," replied Uyanmas.

"What else do you expect them to do? If they have tried to do it peacefully and they didn't listen and they try to urge the government to make the change and it still doesn't solve the issue what else can they do? Living beings are not going to give up without a fight," responded Brittney.

They continued chatting for a bit until it was time to get some work done.

"I need to head out on my next assignment so I'll see you guys when I get back," said Scott.

"Good luck! Hope you enjoy it as much as your last one. That was a fun read!" responded Brittney.

"Be safe. The world keeps getting crazier out there," said Uyanmas.

"I will," replied Scott.

He walked out of the room and headed over to the receptionist desk. Stacy was typing on her computer and humming the tune to a popular song by her favorite band.

"Hey Stace! Did George send the details of the trip over?" asked Scott.

"Let me check."

Stacy smiled at Scott as she looked at her monitor and searched for any messages from George.

"Oh right here. Let me print the QR code for you and scan it as usual with your phone. I hope you have a safe trip. I'm going on vacation Monday so I probably won't be here until after you get back," said Stacy.

She blew Scott a small kiss. Almost indistinguishable from her speech yet it struck Scott to be specifically for him.

"Thank you Stacy. It means a lot. I'll see you then," said Scott, his voice cracking. He tried to play it off.

"Anytime Scott. You know where to find me," Stacy said.

She laughed and handed him the sheet of paper with his QR code on it. This had been loaded with everything that he would need for his trip. Every expense and need was taken care of.

"Will do," he said.

Scott laughed and walked out of the room hoping that he came across well in that interaction. He didn't know for sure but he had bigger issues to worry about now. He headed down the hallway towards the elevator. He made his way to the street level and called for a ride home. He waited on the side of the street and it wouldn't be longer than two minutes until someone arrived. Construction workers were working on a nearby road and people of all sorts were making their way down the street. Cars were flying by and a few helicopters were also overhead. Scott could barely hear himself think and looked over to a nearby wall. A poster of Silvius Johnson stared back at him. The message on the poster read "Vote for me! We can't let Smith win! He hates our nation!" Scott didn't care for the tradition of identifying with the nation he lived in and now this poster was using the concept as a political tool. Rich Smith didn't actually hate the country, he just held less conservative views. His views were still pretty conservative and mostly serving the rich and wealthy elite yet Johnson and his sycophants portrayed Smith as the antichrist himself. One of Smith's top agenda items that he ran on was increasing funding for police forces to deal with alien crime even though aliens committed crimes at much lower rates than humans did. Statistics didn't matter to these people though because it helped the pockets of those who are really in power, the capitalist elites. Chills ran through Scott's body and he pulled out his phone to catch the time. Hopefully his ride would arrive soon and he could get out of the cold. He looked up at the tall structures that made up the skyline and thought about old pictures of the city. It was crazy how far they had come without managing to knock everything down one final time. Humanity has an insane resilience to complete annihilation yet they love to toe the line as close as possible every time.

CHAPTER THREE

After a short trip he arrived back at the house to gather his things and prepare for his next trip. He had to make his flight by 8:00 p.m. It wouldn't take more than half an hour to forty-five minutes with a little turbulence. He entered the house and sat his briefcase down on the pool table which was placed about six feet in front of the front door. He hadn't played a round of pool in months yet every time he looked at it he would get the urge to play sometime soon. Perhaps once he returns from his trip he could invite over some friends from work. He took off his jacket and put it on the recliner. He then stretched his arms a bit and walked into the bedroom. Scott started with packing the clothes he would need, picking out eight different dress shirts to wear as well as t-shirts to wear beneath. Eight different pairs of pants. Two pairs of shoes and a handful of socks. He was all ready to go. The interview would only last for six days but he decided he would stay an extra day or so to see the sights and take advantage of some networking opportunities. He pulled out his phone and started scrolling through a few news articles. The protest from earlier had twenty-eight participants arrested and an unknown number were missing or confirmed dead. Journalists were going crazy speculating about what would happen and how President Smith would respond. Scott knew that Smith would condemn the protests as having gotten out of hand and that the law enforcement had to "maintain the peace" even though they are enabling the chaos. The protest was and would have remained peaceful without their involvement. In the distance he could hear sirens blaring which was a usual sound at this time of the day. He walked over and shut his windows to relieve his ears of the noise. Scott spent the next few hours gathering the rest of his supplies and equipment. Once he was nearly finished he decided to take a break. He pulled out his pipe and packed it with flowers. He took a hit and turned on the television. An advertisement came on the screen with a beautiful blonde haired woman holding a greasy cheeseburger and driving a stylish car. Then the screen flashed to her holding a shotgun on a farm with cows in the distance. "I will defend this country from those commie bastards!" she said while cocking the gun and shooting a poster of Karl Marx and President Smith shaking hands. Scott switched the channel grimacing when he thought about the fact that she was favored to win her election. She was a member of Johnson's party and vehemently supported anything he said or did no matter how big of a lie it was. The idea of Smith being a communist was so far from the truth that it was insane to take seriously and yet hundreds of thousands will likely vote her into power where she will continue to spread misinformation to the population. He took another hit from his pipe and walked out onto his porch. He looked out and spotted something in the distance. A long line of large trucks were traveling out of the city. He could barely make out several different flags lining the outside of the trucks. He let the smoke flow out of his mouth and took a moment to gather his senses. The wind made it chilly and Scott started to shiver. He walked into his laundry room and put his jacket in the dryer to warm it and walked back out to the porch. He took another hit and sat back in his chair with his feet propped up on the rail. He was still worried from that poster he saw earlier. The nation was slowly tearing itself apart and he wasn't sure how much longer it would last. It seemed inconceivable almost ten or twenty years ago and yet here we were on the cusp.

History is very cyclical to a fault. Humanity changes slightly but overall we have stayed the same in so many ways. Our attitudes, behaviors, reactions and non-reactions to certain situations are nearly identical to our parents, grandparents and so on.

A ring started to come over the house through the built in p.a. system.

"Incoming call from Tim Bell."

The voice sounded like it came from a woman of British origin with an almost clear disdain for the voice recording work she was partaking in. It was likely that she was forced to work for the company that created the system as most major corporations used slave labor for tasks that were uniquely required or at least they were required in the minds of the politicians writing legislation. Tim, however, was one of Scott's best friends. Someone he had become friends with in high school and then drifted apart. One day they decided to rekindle the friendship. Naturally it worked out and they were back to being best friends. He basically shared everything with Tim and Tim felt the same way. Scott took one last hit from his pipe and got out of his chair. He walked into the house and cleared his throat.

"Answer."

This caused the lights in the room to dim down.

"Scott how's it going bro? What are you doing?" asked Tim.

"It's going well. I'm getting ready for a work trip. I have a big interview that I'm doing."

"That's so awesome, congratulations man! Where are you headed this time?" he asked.

Scott smiled almost instinctively even though he naturally wanted to suppress those feelings for he had a weird reaction to any kind of praise.

"Cairo, Egypt. Meeting with one of the last historians of the Nill race and then giving a speech to the U.N. General Assembly. He talked about promoting me to the Galactic Relations council too!"

Tim could be heard saying wow into the mic.

"That's amazing man, I'm so happy for you. That sounds like a big step up!"

"I would be directly working with decision makers and the people deciding how we handle inter-galactic disputes and disagreements. It's politics but in space!" responded Scott, with a bit of laughter coming on the tailend.

"Are you leaving tonight or do you have time to do anything tonight?" Tim asked.

Scott thought for a moment and looked at his watch. It was 3:47 p.m. He could probably make something work but did he feel like worrying about that?

"I have to make my flight by 8:00 p.m. so as long as I can leave your place by 6:30 I could hang. I don't wanna cut it too close, you know airports," he answered.

"Yeah that's cool. I'm off work today so swing by whenever. Leave when you need to," Tim said.

"Sounds good man. I'll head that way in a few."

Scott smiled and clicked a button on the wall of the living room which controlled not only the phone system but lights and temperature as well. The call ended and the lights raised back to their normal level. He took one more hit from his pipe and closed the door to his porch. He packed his pipe and started to move his bags near the door. He made sure he had everything he needed. A bag for his clothes and equipment and his satchel for his work papers and writing tablet. He also had a yellow notepad in there where he would take handwritten notes. This was a rarity in today's day and age yet he felt that it gave his work a more personal touch. He wanted to do his best work when he was out in the field so the more unique his style the better.

"Computer. Call for a ride to Tim's place. Thank you," said Scott.

"Yes Scott. And you're welcome," replied the computer.

Scott had thanked the computer which was not customary for humans to do. Scott had a rather unique philosophy behind how he viewed Androids and A.I. He felt that they should be treated with respect and dignity. They were not computerized slaves created to do our bidding. They were individuals too. No matter how mass produced they were. Every side of the table felt differently in the political realm about this with some taking it to outright extremes. Ten countries on Earth have banned the use of A.I. and have completely rejected anything coming post the twenty-first century. The population mostly felt indifferent or supportive of their rights yet those in power kept them in check and would only occasionally improve their status. They know that the minority held negative views and yet used every tool in their playbook: like convincing the masses that it was common sense to not give certain people rights, to spread harmful and false stereotypes, or to treat them differently based on immutable characteristics.

Scott grabbed his bags and walked out of his house. He heard a ding on his phone and looked up to see that his ride had arrived waiting with the door open for him. An Android driver rolled down the window and raised his hand in a wave.

"Hello.. uh.. Scott. How are you doing today?" asked the driver while squinting his eyes at his phone.

Scott looked at the android's face. It was pale and transparently an android's face. This was one of the cheaper models used in the lower income communities and any form of governmental infrastructure. The big tech companies and the wealthy would utilize the more advanced models. These offered more features with more customizability and greater autonomy. This was a double-edged sword for almost thirteen people were murdered in the first five years of trials by this A.I. That means there is a failure rate with more zeros than letters in the alphabet which I suppose isn't too concerning until you are one of the people that wind up dead by a machine that you purchased. The law of averages when there are so many in use becomes apparent. Rapid technological advances have resulted in cheaper more advanced models that can be mass produced to serve in labor positions where humans used to work. The systems had unfortunately not prepared humanity for such a transition and hundreds of millions were suffering because of it across the world.

"I'm doing well," responded Scott.

The trunk opened up.

"Throw your bags in the back and we'll be on our way to...uh.. Tim's place," said the driver.

"Sounds good."

Scott placed his bags in the trunk which promptly closed itself. He got into the vehicle and the driver started moving. Scott watched out the window and checked his notifications on his phone. Out of the corner of his eye he saw a flash of bright lights which he quickly realized was a police vehicle. They had pulled over a vehicle and were interrogating someone who seemed to be an alien of Bessian origin. The Bessians were a friendly people similar in values to the Nill while not gaining as much notoriety. The alien was standing in front of two officers both with batons in their hands. One started to bark something at the alien which he took offense to. The other officer started waving the baton in his face and kicked his shin. The alien fell down and the two officers began to kick and hit him with their weapons. This was not a rare occurrence and Scott had seen many situations similar to this.

"At least they didn't shoot them," thought Scott.

Scott was sad to realize that was the bar to cross. Hundreds of aliens are murdered every year by the police force while most humans are able to escape similar encounters with their lives. He tried to do what he could but the police were only gaining more power, weapons and influence. You needed one or all of those things to make real change. It was fortunate for some humans that so much attention had been drawn to the alien refugee "crisis" as they called it because it caused less of such incidents to impact humans. It still did happen particularly to minority groups but the frequency was noticeably less. Scott turned the tint of the window up and went back to looking at his phone. The ride continued on and took about six minutes. Tim lived right across the street from where Scott's office was. That was convenient for lunch time escapades yet it mostly just meant that every time he decided to hang out with Tim he had this strange feeling like he was headed to work. This quickly alleviated once he was with a friend and not his co-workers. The ride arrived at its destination and Scott tapped the proper keys to give the driver a five star rating.

"Thank you for the review. Have a great day," stated the driver.

Scott nodded at the android as he stepped out of the vehicle. He grabbed his bags from the trunk and placed the satchel around his shoulder. Scott walked into the apartment unit and made his way up a small flight of stairs to the level where Tim lived. He knocked on the door and after about thirteen seconds the door opened to reveal Tim.

"Hey how's it going?"

"It's good. It's good," he answered.

Scott walked inside while Tim shut the door behind them. Scott slipped his shoes off his feet and placed his bags near the door but not too close to prevent it from opening up. He walked into what consisted of the living room and took a seat on the couch that was opposite of a large television screen. It had to be around sixty five inches and it fit nicely on the spot of the wall chosen.

"So how're you feeling about the trip?"

"I gotta say I'm a little nervous. This could be my moment to take off in my career. I just want to make sure I do everything right," replied Scott.

"You've done like hundreds of interviews in your career bro. You got this. I know it's a big one but I know you can do this," Tim said, reassuring his friend.

Scott smiled and looked down at his hands. He tapped his knee a few times in a rhythmic fashion.

"You're right. I think I can do it. I'm going to take a lot of notes."

"Big notes. Yes," answered Tim.

"Okay cool. I think I'm good."

Tim smiled and gave him a thumbs up. He grabbed a pipe, a tray, as well as a bag with some flower in it.

"You down to smoke?" asked Tim.

"For sure. That will make the flight real smooth," said Scott.

They sat down together and smoked for around twenty minutes. Scott smoked to take the edge off and to try and enhance the creativity in his writing. It was something he enjoyed but didn't have a problem with. He would sometimes go several days if not a whole week at times without smoking. Mostly during the long hard work weeks where he had to juggle several projects. He avoided it during work and when it came to organizing in social settings. He wanted to be aware of himself and not make a fool of the importance of what he was doing.

"How's your day been?" asked Scott, taking a hit and passing it to Tim.

Tim took the pipe and took a long hit. After a time he let the smoke out and coughed profusely. After recovering Tim looked at Scott and laughed.

"What did you ask?" said Tim, with a confused smile on his face.

"How high are you?" responded Scott, taking a hit from the pipe himself.

"Not high enough," said Tim, laughing and taking a peek at his phone.

Scott looked over and spotted a few old comic books on a table nearby.

"What comics did you get?" asked Scott, pointing over to the table.

Tim peaked up and then stood up to grab them off the table.

"Some classics man, let me show you."

Tim grabbed the stack of comics and handed them over to Scott.

"Alan Cain, Canis, Sheagle, The Killer Whale, and The Solar Enforcer? Wow what a group. I haven't read these in a few years but I used to be obsessed with them."

Scott hadn't thought about these characters in years yet once he saw the covers it all started rushing back to him.

"Who was your favorite of the Overseers?" asked Tim.

The Overseers was the team name of these superheroes in their respective comics.

"I think Alan Cain easily. I can see myself in him. Canis might be a close second though because the revolutionary struggle storyline always fascinated me as a kid."

"I can respect that. I've always loved Sheagle and her story and the way they tie her and The Killer Whale together is really satisfying," said Tim.

"I always like seeing The Solar Enforcer defend his planet too! Something about a man of the people leading the people's cause always gets to me," said Scott.

The two continued flipping through the comics for a bit until they went back to smoking. Scott and Tim sat and enjoyed each other's presence for a while. Tim decided to turn on the television and put on their favorite show. It was a workplace comedy that revolved around the managers and staff who worked at a movie theater. It was a fairly funny show that had a cult-like status among the people in Scott's generation. They watched a few episodes and had several laughs at it. Eventually Scott glanced over at his phone and saw that it was six fifteen. Scott didn't know how time had flown by so fast and yet here they were.

"Alright it's about time I head to the airport," Scott said.

"Alright sounds good man. Let me know when you get back we need to hang again," replied Tim.

"I will for sure."

Scott and Tim did a handshake that they had first started doing in high school. It was how they greeted each other and how they said goodbye to each other. The details of the handshake had become ridiculously complicated after years of refinement and neither of them remembered what the exact steps were so they've winged it ever since. Scott grabbed his bags and headed out the door. He made his way out to the street where a ride had arrived to pick him up. He got inside of the ride and greeted the driver.

"Hello hello," said Scott, giving a small wave.

"Welcome. We are headed to the airport today Scott?" inquired the driver.

"Yes my flight leaves at 8:00 so I want to make it as early as I can," answered Scott, placing his bags in the opposite back seat.

"I will make it happen, fasten your seatbelts," said the driver, winking at Scott.

Scott couldn't help but laugh in response. He took a moment to get into a comfortable position and rested his head on his arm. The cold air leaking in through the window of the ride made his arm cold and he spotted a few leaves flying up into the air on the street. They danced in the air back and forth as if they were being controlled from above. The street was torn up with potholes and cracks common in every part of the city. The government had tried to budget for more repairs but the money ended up missing only to be found in the numerous pools and vacation homes bought by local officials shortly after that money was allocated. This wasn't a surprise to Scott yet he was a little surprised people still stood idly by and didn't speak up. Greed and corruption had become such integral parts of the system that the lack of them caused concern that maybe this official wouldn't know how to operate in the political community. If you try to be one of the ones who reform the system from the inside you will most likely fail. Systemic problems require systemic solutions and often require abolition or massive structural changes. He took a finger and drew a circle on the window in the fog. He drew a larger circle around that one and then another. He pulled out his phone and started reading articles. He tried to stay up to date with what was going on in the world yet he always felt he was missing out on something somewhere. One story in particular caught his eye. It was a story about the Republic of Oratoll who had recently seceded from the former United States. It wasn't the first nor was it the last failed attempt at secession from the States. They were a group of armed radicals of a religious nature who had declared their ways to be more in line with what the ancient texts had told them. Fighting naturally occurred and it ended in bloodshed with over fourteen thousand lives lost. Drone strikes and police squads busting down your doors alongside the use of gas to disperse crowds reigned supreme in these areas. They were only seceded in their minds. They still existed within the States which was the shortened name that most citizen's used colloquially in the current iteration of the country. The Manifest Destiny theory of the nineteenth century managed to hide it's way into the present causing mass expansion, genocide, and imperialism to take over at rates that were not expected even from the most skeptical citizens. Laws had meaning yet they only applied to some. Others were othered simply for being a certain way, often something they were born with and not a choice. Camps were founded called detention facilities to soften the blow of what the media's reaction would be. Luckily the media did not last long after that and it was quickly replaced with a 'Fair and Equal representation of American Democracy!' This was all for show of course.

"We have arrived."

The driver woke Scott from his daydream. He would often spend entire rides daydreaming about passages from his history books.

"Thank you. Take care," said Scott.

The driver nodded with an almost shocked look on his face.

"Thank you, sir. People like you usually don't speak so friendly to us," replied the driver.

Scott smirked, before seeing the sadness in the android's eyes.

"I do what I can to treat everyone the same. What's your name?" responded Scott.

"Jason."

"It's been a pleasure I'll see you next time," said Scott, extending a wave.

He got out of the car, grabbed his bags and headed inside the airport. He was excited for the flight as he would have a chance to think about what questions to ask Mashir. He headed towards his terminal and came up to the security checkpoint. Two lines were formed, one labeled for humans, and one for aliens. The human line moved faster, had less guards, and less equipment to check for hidden items. Scott found his way to the line and waited his turn as person after person made their way through. After about five minutes he had gotten to the checkpoint gate. He was greeted by a short old lady with gray hair and bright blue eyes.

"Ticket please," asked the airport guard.

Scott handed her his ticket while spotting across the way a tall muscular guard standing watch over the alien line. He was armed with a pistol, small baton, a taser and looked as if he could bench two Scott's with ease.

"Scott, you'll be at gate 24KB. Have a wonderful flight," replied the old lady, handing his ticket back to him.

Scott smiled and grabbed the ticket continuing on his way. He entered the terminal which was large and had a tall ceiling with numerous restaurants, gift shops, offices, and stores. Hundreds of people walked past him as he made his way down the terminal. Scott decided to stop by a coffee spot for a drink. He wasn't much of a coffee drinker yet he would sometimes have one when he was flushed with money. He wanted a flavored lemonade and decided on a strawberry flavor. He ordered the drink and put it on the work account. He took a seat over by the window of the restaurant and peered out the window to see the tarmac. The planes were large and had massive engines. They could fit over seven hundred passengers comfortably and still arrive at their destination in under an hour almost anywhere in the world. He saw the marking on one of the planes that matched his ticket: J-0-4-5-3-7. He took a sip of his drink and pulled out his phone. He checked on the status of his flight and it appeared to be boarding in thirty minutes. Scott had already checked in digitally so he would get by security with ease although the nano scouts will still investigate all of his body and his bags. He took another look outside and saw in the distance an eagle. It had landed on a tree just outside of the gate of the airport grounds. Bald Eagles had been critically endangered for centuries now. He had last seen one outside of his house one morning while playing basketball and that memory had stuck with him all the way to this moment. Scott shifted his focus to a television screen on a nearby wall that had the news on. The United Nations General Assembly was in session and they were having a debate. Scott perked up a bit and decided to pay attention. The assembly hall was large with a center stage flanked by two sections of seating. Hundreds of representatives were seated around the stage. Every nation on Earth had at least one representative if not several. Each representative sat at a desk with a nameplate to identify themselves and their country. The speaker of the assembly, who was seated in the middle of the central stage, began to rise.

"The representative from France is acknowledged," said the speaker, sitting right back down afterwards.

The man sitting at the France nameplate rose and began to speak.

"I ask this assembly to consider the dangers of allowing unregulated immigration of alien species into our planet. If we allow any species, Nill, Turl, Bessian, you name it, to come here without any expectation of a legal process, then we are allowing dangerous beings to live among us. Must I remind the assembly of the bombings of Lyon and Cairo just seven short years ago which we know to have been perpetrated at the behest of a radical Nill terrorist group the Corvo! These beings are a threat to our very way of life, to our security, to our culture and to our civilization! We cannot allow them to force us into fearing for our lives!"

The man continued to speak and pound his fist in the air. Scott identified him as Fabrice Battier. He was a French politician who advocated against the rights of immigrants, human or alien. He was a tall pale man dressed in a gray suit and a light blue tie. His hair, what little there was, was a light blonde and covered the back half of his head. The story he was telling about the bombings was false and Scott knew this. It was part of a larger conspiracy theory that the Nill were secretly plotting with other alien races to take Earth for themselves. Unfortunately this theory had gained popularity as more Nill arrived on Earth and some people used this theory as a pretext for violence against the Nill. They harassed, assaulted and even killed thousands of Nill in a short five year period. Many members of world governments had sadly subscribed to these ideas and that led to real world consequences for the Nill who just wanted a place to call home. He had started looking at the faces around Battier and noticed a few with shocked looks and some who were loving every second of it. The man with a smile from ear to ear next to Battier was Leopold Hachette, yet another French politician and believer of the Nill conspiracy. He was a short burly man who had a thick mustache and was dressed in all black. Another speaker across the chamber rose from their chair.

"The representative from the Union of American States is acknowledged."

Scott knew this one too. Anna Patsch who had been vocally pro-Nill when it came to immigration. Patsch was a slightly taller woman with a tan complexion, black hair and green eyes. She also wore thick black framed glasses and would famously take them off and use them as a hand prop while giving speeches.

"I am utterly appalled by what I am hearing today on the floor of the General Assembly of the United Nations. How can we sit here and listen to this vile rhetoric? These are beings that are in need of help. They are fleeing terrible situations and they don't have anywhere else to turn. Now I am not saying we need to open up our pockets and our houses and let them invade our neighborhoods but we can find some kind of middle ground right?" stated Patsch.

Scott started to zone out a little and turned his focus away from the screen. He wanted to go into the interview with no preconceived notions of what to expect. He did note a few of the details mentioned so that he could ask Mashir about them. He turned towards the window and stared out into the sky. A few minutes passed by and suddenly he felt a weird rush like he knew everything he would need to ask Mashir in the interview. He let out a sigh and sat back in the chair to enjoy the view.

CHAPTER FOUR

His eyes suddenly opened, awaking from a nap that he had not intended on taking. Getting up in a haste Scott was worried that he had overslept for his flight. He rushed to check his watch and it showed that the flight should just now be about to start boarding. Everything was all right. Only around twenty minutes had gone by. Truly a power nap and clearly he really needed it. He usually spent the last half hour of his lunch every day taking a nap in his office. Scott grabbed his bags and approached the reception desk at gate 24KB. He took his spot in the short line. He took a moment to look around and started noticing just how many people were in the terminal. There must have been a couple thousand, at least. Scott didn't typically get claustrophobic but he wasn't exactly comfortable with how many people there were. Families carrying a half dozen bags, couples arguing, men and women clearly on business trips, you name it. This airport had a person on every type of journey and Scott was just one of them. The person ahead of him wrapped up and an android woman greeted Scott waving him up to the desk. Her name tag said Rachel. She had brown eyes and black hair put up into rolls. Scott couldn't help but notice her deep red lips. He spotted a small rose in her right ear.

"How can I help?" she asked

"Have I missed boarding for flight J-0-4-5-3-7?" replied Scott.

"No you made it just in time. I just need to scan your ticket."

Scott showed her the ticket and she scanned it by waving it over a small plate-shaped device.

"Give me just one second."

Rachel tapped a few keys on her computer.

"Okay looks like you're all set! Have a great flight," said Rachel smiling with an eroding veil of sincerity.

"I hope you have a great rest of your day, thank you for your help," said Scott, grabbing his ticket back and waving goodbye to her.

Rachel grinned and waved back at him. She returned to her work as Scott made his way down the tunnel. There were hundreds on the plane which had to be five times as large as a plane of centuries prior. After a few minutes of maneuvering through the narrow halls of the plane he made his way to his seat and found that it was right next to the window.

"Please find your seat, we will begin takeoff in five minutes," said the pilot who Scott assumed was an android.

He didn't know for sure if they were but he knew that this airline had recently hired fifty thousand new android employees. It was part of an integration program to ease tensions between androids and humans. One of the clear examples of the failure in these programs and the lack of effort in seeing them completed was on the Earth's moon. Once humans had settled a base on the moon five separate bases were quickly established. One each belonged to the nations of the United States, the UK, China, Russia and Germany. Four wars on the moon were fought before we realized that it would be a forever quagmire. After five million lives lost, the earth governments attempted to pass legislation to outlaw combat on the moon but failed spectacularly.

"We are about to depart, please be seated," said the pilot over the P.A. system.

Scott made sure he was settled and he put on a soundtrack from his favorite film to lighten his anxiety from flying. Music was the most common way that Scott calmed down and also how he talked to himself to figure out what decisions to make. He was his own best critic so this led to him always having debates and discussions with his own mind. This helped with debate and writing but sometimes made it harder to focus. Scott relaxed as the plane started to take off and enter the sky. He had decided he was going to ask Mashir about what the warning signs were for his planet. Did he see what was happening? Or did it take them by surprise? Earth has been having this debate for centuries yet we continue to survive. He would ask about their culture and how they spend their time. Do they have a form of social media or sports? The Nill would be a unique story for the assembly to hear and he knew he would need to be able to get his message across. His mind took a break from that and he decided to watch out the window. They were now over the Atlantic Ocean hundreds of miles in the air and climbing. He could see an island but he wasn't sure what island it would be. He could see several towns dotted across it and guessed that they were likely about one hundred years behind technology wise. The tech gap between nations had become quite noticeable and the rise of nationalist governments led to the decrease of globalization. Expanding to other worlds actually allowed humans to experience other cultures and get out of the capitalist hellscape. Other alien planets had nations with more free societies where you could survive for free. Work as you could and be taken care of while having a place to live with plenty of food. Millions of humans at this point had made the jump yet the majority are too afraid of leaving the Earth. Media propagandists made sure to demonize leaving the earth as a betrayal of your humanity. They pitted us against each other and decided that if you left Earth not on behalf of the United Nations you were a traitor and would be shot on sight. That policy lasted for twelve years until the latest demagogue in the former United States had been voted out leading to a brief period of recovery before the next rang the doorbell. Scott had written a book about this time period and just like many periods before it nothing substantial was achieved by trying to reform the system. The system was designed to be irreformable. A complete revolution would be needed to change the society for the betterment of the people. France saw this and achieved it. It led to the same issue and today they remain. Scott had some views considered radical among his peers simply due to his way of viewing the world through a lens of history and materialism. He always used history as the context for why things were the way they were. This is the same today as it was a hundred years ago as it will be a hundred years in the future. Things may change but people never really do. People oftentimes get caught up in semantics instead of looking at the actual actions or patterns that are taking place. People will tell you exactly who they are, you just have to listen to what they say and how they perceive things. We are the same humans that lived on this earth for the last forty-eight thousand years. We as humans build things in our society and use those things to build other things. These forces are the productive forces of our human society, and they are currently held in private hands at the behest of billionaires. Was it similar on Nilleon or was it simply an Earth phenomenon?

"Would you like anything from our menu?" an android stewardess asked.

"Yeah, I'll take a cinnamon roll," Scott said with a slight grin.

"Right away."

The stewardess walked away and Scott noticed the bags under her eyes. He wondered how many hours she was programmed to work per week and if they had scheduled her a vacation sometime this cycle. A cycle was traditionally a five year term that android workers signed on for. They had to fulfill their contract or they could be "retired" prematurely. The few limited rights that were granted to androids on Earth were won after conflicts that originated in labs and some small town settings. A.I. had displayed the ability to declare itself independent. Some scientists opposed this, others ran with it. Scott's only experiences with this were small yet they had a big impact on his life and his outlook.

"Here you go," the stewardess said as she delivered the cinnamon roll.

The icing was melted and it looked slightly burnt on the top - exactly how he enjoyed it. This was exactly how he enjoyed it and he was very excited to eat it.

"Thank you!" said Scott.

He grabbed the fork that was on the tray in front of him and tore into the roll. It was brittle yet fluffy. Scott had loved when his grandmother would bake cinnamon rolls and muffins during family holidays. He started with the center and took a large bite. He savored the taste and cut what remained into two pieces. Once he finished eating he placed the trash in the bin by his seat. The android came by to grab it and Scott noticed that the android had a symbol on her neck slightly obscured by her hair. It was a small red square with an android hand tightly gripping a globe up into the air. He made a mental image of this but let it go for now. He pulled out his phone to check the news. Leslie Sanders, a recurring foreign affairs journalist, was talking at a press briefing.

"The Prince of Hungary has been assassinated. Details are fuzzy but rumors have been speculating for months that he had criminal ties and could face severe backlash from his people. His mother the Queen has been silent on this issue and we have not

heard anything from her office. We will update you with more as soon as we have it,"

said Leslie with the screen cutting to an advertisement.

Scott had read reports that he had been linked with a mob boss from Northern

Serbia and had supposedly embezzled millions from the Hungarian people. It sounds like

they finally had enough of it and put a stop to him. A full blown revolution could

potentially break out if the government doesn't settle the situation in a timely manner. He

peered out the window and saw what he assumed to be the edge of Africa. He decided to

enjoy the rest of the flight and shut his eyes. He quickly fell asleep but not before setting

an alarm to wake him up when they landed. His mind wandered and started to think about

what he wanted to try to eat in Cairo because he knew he wanted to try a specific burger

place he had been told about by a friend. What would Mashir think of Scott? Would he

take him seriously or would he laugh him off? Was he suspicious of my motives or would

he trust a fellow historian. He couldn't be sure but he felt confident in his ability to win

the day. He wanted to get the real story of what happened and to get a sense of how an

entire planet falls. He had read about empires of old collapsing and let alone what he is

living through now. Humanity has kept persevering despite all of the struggles and trials.

Did the Nill have this same spirit inside of them? Is what made us human something that

could exist in other lifeforms too? We truly aren't alone anymore at that point. Earth

wasn't the only planet with life now so why should Scott assume that Earth is inherently

unique when the one thing that for the majority of human existence made it solely unique

was no longer the case. Scott loved playing the devil's advocate in his own head. He

wanted to make sure he knew what the people he met with would challenge him on so he always tried to stay on top of his game. Some time had passed and Scott woke up as the pilot began speaking.

"Preparing to land. Please be ready to depart," announced the pilot over the p.a. system.

The pilot seemed to be annoyed. Maybe there was turbulence during the flight? He hadn't noticed anything but it's possible it occurred while he slept. Scott made sure he had everything ready to go and watched as the plane started to land. He was ready to get off the plane. He came down the aisle squeezing between people and after a few moments went left into the connecting pod. He saw the end of the tunnel where the entrance to the Cairo International Airport was which had been recently remodeled. It was a sleek and modern design with several consumer features and brand name restaurants. A large fountain sat in the center of a large open area. The ceiling was glass and you could see all the planes coming and going. There were gift shops, bars, restaurants, anything you could imagine. He made his way through the terminal and headed into the first restaurant that had a bar. He took a seat near the window and began looking over the menu which was built into a tablet that you could order from. He debated between a chicken salad or a steak. The salad was tempting but steak was the ultimate choice. Medium well with a side of fries and a side of honey mustard. His drink would be a simple apple flavored cider. Scott had an issue with his gallbladder and it caused him pain when he drank heavy levels of alcohol or ate sugary foods. He clicked a few buttons and placed his order. He sat back in his chair and stretched his legs a bit. He would spend the evening here relaxing before checking in at his hotel and preparing for the interview on Monday. He could spend the day tomorrow exploring the city and see how things have changed in recent years. Scott checked his phone while waiting for his food. A coup had just occurred in Turkey where the leader of the government was murdered by his own brother who was secretly working with an Italian nationalist group. Scott wasn't shocked because he felt that all the signs were there. The media ignored these because it didn't sell ad space. He moved on to the next story talking about the latest wildfires in the New California Federation. All aid from the former United States territories had been shut off due to a grievance between their leaders. This wasn't anything new. He looked towards another article about a rising group of supposed communists in the American Canada Occupied Zone who were going to overthrow the military. That wasn't likely for a variety of reasons. America's illegal annexation of the entirety of Canada was done so with a military force never before seen. The U.S. called in a favor from Russia and China to rule that Canada was a rogue terrorist state and that several of the U.N. nations must overthrow the acting government by force. Over a million soldiers from eighteen nations took part in the invasion and over three million Canadian civilians died. The war ultimately lasted over thirty years and led to seven occupied zones all by different nations. Canada had been scrambled for just like Africa had been decades and centuries prior. Humanity kept repeating itself and yet Scott wondered if the Nill had this issue. Another headline popped up about massive protests by Bessian refugees in Madrid. The government was preventing over two thousand Bessians from asylum and they were not taking that decision well. Protests of this kind had been going on for years but this one seemed different. The police were cracking down even harder than normal. Most governments were very selective with which aliens were allowed to immigrate and the populations were not concerned with the plight of anyone aside from themselves due to their own troubles and crises. Another headline popped up about a firefight outside the Black Hills Free Territory. The Sioux had risen up during a rather harsh crackdown on their cultural and personal freedoms. A bloody and lengthy war was fought and ended with a peace treaty being signed in Washington D.C. at the behest of an invading force. Local militia groups and racist vandals will drive by and cause havoc amongst the border guards. It cost three of them their lives this time.

"Here you go, sir." The waitress had brought Scott's food and his drink to the table.

She placed it in front of him and it looked exactly as he imagined when he ordered it. He thanked the waitress and started to dig into his meal. He started with a few fries dipped with the side of honey mustard sauce. After that he moved on the steak where he cut it into about seven equal pieces. He then eats two pieces of the steak before taking a drink. He repeated this process until he no longer had any more food. The waitress came by to pick up the plate and cleared her throat.

"Was there anything else you wanted to order or would you like the bill?" asked the waitress.

Scott thought for a moment.

"I'll take three chocolate chip cookies."

He then pulled out his work card and handed it to her.

"I'll have that out right away."

She gave a smile and then off she was. Scott felt like maybe there was something behind her smile but he decided that there wasn't enough time to worry about that. The woman was British which while not a rarity in Egypt was an interesting thing to run into. The collapse of the United Kingdom led to a massive refugee crisis where millions of British, Scottish, Welsh and Irish citizens fled to other nations for protection and shelter. The U.S. Occupation of the British Isles was condemned universally by every country in the world yet the majority of stockholders in the big corporations supported it.

The British States became a puppet system for corporations to have bigger populations to exploit.

"Here is this for you." The waitress placed three chocolate chip cookies on a plate in front of Scott.

They were fresh from the oven and he could see the chocolate chips melting. He looked at the waitresses name tag which said Zara. She was radiating with energy topped with brown hair and blue eyes. Her skin was slightly tan and she had a freckle right above the left side of her lip. Her hair curled around her ears with most of it sitting in a messy bun.

"Zara, is it?" asked Scott.

"Yes?"

She looked puzzled by Scott saying her name.

"Did you grow up here or did something else bring you to Cairo?" he asked.

Zara had a confused look on her face but momentarily found her way through it and began to laugh.

"Yeah you could call it that."

Scott thought he knew the story but wanted her side.

"What brought you here?"

He couldn't help but sit here and chat with her. Everything else seems secondary at this moment. He had gotten used to the loneliness and the comfort in being alone alongside the risks in losing what you have. He wanted to believe but he often felt it wasn't enough. He was one person on a planet of billions.

"When the kingdom collapsed my mother convinced me to go to France. I spent about six months there, and then they deported me to Syria where I managed to funnel my way through warzones to get to Egypt. Ever since I have worked in the city and have tried to send money to my family back in England."

Scott knew the true nature of where the money sent to her family would end up. It would be intercepted by financial enforcers whose job it was to disallow any money or wealth to return to the United Kingdom. It was truly a nightmare to still live there and most of the population lived in abject poverty.

"I'm sorry to hear that. That's very kind of you. Do you hear from them often?"

Zara frowned.

"Not in nearly six months. Their network signals are down. I think on purpose but no one in the cabinets will answer."

The cabinets that Zara referred to were the remnants of the U.S. influenced British elected officials who still technically held power in the United Kingdom. They still broadcasted messages every day from a bunker underneath the city of London. It was originally meant as a way to avoid complete collapse from nuclear attack during the First Cold War. After a few emergency decrees and illegal vote counting it became a way for the state to assume complete control over the population and export the labor and resources of the Isles.

"I hope that you hear from them soon. It's nice to meet someone who is pretty much a local," said Scott.

Scott smiled and hoped that Zara would continue talking with him.

"At this point I'd say so. It's nice to meet you too, uhm? What's your name sir?"

She smiled in return.

"Scott, nice to meet you".

He extended his hand out, awaiting hers. Zara gave a small laugh and put hers in his.

"What do you do, Scott?"

Zara took a seat at the table having now realized that her night was only just beginning.

"I'm a historian for the United Nations and I also write books about history. I'm here to do an interview for a speech," responded Scott.

"That sounds really cool. History was always sort of fascinating to me. I really never cared until I started looking back at things that have happened in my life. From there it was easy to see it happening everywhere I looked," said Zara.

"That's a really good observation. I'm happy other people see it that way too," said Scott.

Zara laughed looking into Scott's eyes and letting several seconds pass.

"So what are you doing the rest of the night Scott?" asked Zara.

Scott had planned to head back to his room but this was far more interesting of a plan.

"I'd love to go for a walk with you," responded Scott looking into her eyes and smiling.

Zara couldn't help but smile.

"You have a deal Scott. Let's shake on it," Zara said, extending her hand out.

The two shook hands and laughed at the premise itself.

"Do you need to clean up or are you off?" asked Scott.

"I've been off for about thirty minutes, I just thought you were cute so I stuck around," said Zara in a quiet voice with a clear flirtatious tone.

Scott laughed and stood up out of his seat.

"I'm ready when you are."

She stood up and grabbed a jacket from a nearby stool.

"Did you just land or have you been at the airport long?" Zara asked as the two exited the bar.

"My flight just landed about forty-five minutes ago. I was hungry and wanted to grab something to eat before I checked in at the hotel," he replied.

"Which hotel are you staying at?"

"The Krystal Hotel."

"Oh that's nice. Good choice. I've never been myself but I've heard great things," said Zara.

The two of them made their way out onto the street where they spotted a tall gray stand with a map of the city on it. Scott spotted where the airport was and then the hotel.

"Okay it looks like the hotel is this way. Know of any cool places we can check out nearby?" Scott asked, turning towards Zara.

"There is a bridge overlooking the river pretty close to here you have to see it!" replied Zara excitedly.

"Sounds good to me!"

Zara took the lead and the two continued chatting on the way.

"How long have you worked at the restaurant?"

"Four years and it certainly feels like it's been longer. I would love to work elsewhere but nobody will hire a British immigrant here. I'm lucky I got the position I have. Rent has gone up so much in the last few years and even with four other roommates working full time we just barely make enough to make it work together," said Zara.

"That's awful. I think everyone deserves the opportunity to have their own place to live. You shouldn't be forced to live with other people just because you need their money to help afford rent. That's a failing system," responded Scott, taken back a little.

"I wouldn't say that too loudly things might be bright and shiny on the outside but there is some sinister stuff going on here. I wouldn't trust a word anyone in the government says. They are always watching and always listening," cautioned Zara.

"What kinds of things have you seen?" asked Scott.

"The police abuse their power and our elected officials steal our money. Thousands and thousands of homeless people need help and they keep taking away any and all rights we have while refusing to take care of our basic needs," replied Zara.

"I knew things were not great here but I didn't realize it was that bad." said Scott.

He thought for a moment about how America's own homelessness problem was even worse than Egypt's. Rich Smith nor Silvius Johnson wanted to help these people out of the precarious situation they found themselves in. Rich would spout off platitudes about what the right thing to do was while he funded the departments or groups that would ensure they could never move up in society. Silvius Johnson advocated for building tents to house them and essentially rebranding concentration camps. His base fully supported this initiative knowing full well the implications that came with this.

"I hope one day things will change but I'm not so sure that's possible. I want out of here as soon as I can." Zara said, waving her hand to indicate just how fast she wanted to leave.

"Where would you want to go?" Scott inquired.

"I haven't really thought that far into it. Europe isn't really an option obviously. North America would be ideal although I knew a girl from Japan who always told me great things about the city she was from," Zara replied.

"There are a lot of options and North America isn't a bad one at all," said Scott.

"You're from North America aren't you?" asked Zara, grinning and rolling her eyes at Scott.

"Okay you caught me. I might be a bit biased with that one," said Scott through a fit of laughter.

"You're funny. I like that," said Zara, smiling and continuing to walk alongside Scott.

They had made steady progress and were nearly to the bridge. A lot of people were on the streets tonight. Typical for a Saturday.

"This is it up here!" said Zara, pointing excitedly.

They came up to the bridge and she grabbed Scott's hand to lead him over to the railing. Scott's face turned red and he could feel his heart starting to race in the brief moment he held her hand. Once at the railing Zara pointed out the sunset.

"Oh my goodness that's breathtaking," said an astounded Scott.

A canal cut through the city and it led to a set of small waterfalls. This caused an illusion where the sky met with the water and the sun setting caused an absolutely beautiful sight to behold. Scott held Zara's hand.

"I like to come here sometimes and think to myself. Think about all the things I want to do or places I want to be. All the dreams and desires I have ever had. It all seems so achievable when I'm sitting here thinking about it. I just wish it wasn't so hard to make it real," said Zara.

"I do a lot of my thinking on my porch in the early morning or late at night. I have issues with focusing so it helps a lot to be able to calm myself and just clear my mind. I smoke too to ease the anxiety and to help with brainstorming," stated Scott.

"I wish I had a porch for that. Our house doesn't have one, just a small square patio that is essentially just to be able to walk up to the house. You can't fit more than two, maybe three people if you're uncomfortably close," said Zara.

"Hopefully you guys don't ever have to all leave at the same time," said Scott with a laugh.

"You'd be surprised how often that's the case," Zara responded.

They took some time to enjoy the view and breathe.

"Do you have anything to smoke with you?" asked Zara, raising an eyebrow.

"I have a pen that you're more than welcome to use, if you'd like," answered Scott.

"You're a lifesaver. I have had a headache since three o'clock and a hit sounds amazing right about now."

Scott pulled out a small black pen from his jacket pocket and turned it on. He handed it to Zara who grabbed it and started to take a hit.

"Don't take too big of a hit or you'll choke a…"

Zara's eyes grew large and she started to cough profusely. A large cloud of smoke billowed out and she leaned forward while she coughed. Scott patted her gently on the back more as a sign of reassurance than actually causing her to stop coughing.

"Don't say I didn't try to warn you," said Scott with the beginnings of a smirk.

"Okay you think you're funny don't you? I will fight you," replied Zara rolling her eyes and throwing up her fists in a joking manner.

Zara handed the pen to Scott who took a hit himself. He held it in for a few moments and then blew it out into the air above them. His eyes readjusted themselves and he looked over to Zara while handing her the pen.

"Do you have to work in the morning?" asked Scott.

"I don't have to work tomorrow actually!" replied Zara taking a much smaller hit than before.

"We should go do something then I have another day before my interview begins. I'd love a tour of the city from a local," Scott said with a smile and a wink.

"You read my mind. Sounds great to me," Zara said.

Scott smiled and took a hit from his pen.

"What are you doing after this?"

"I had nothing planned before you. I was going to go home and eat a couple slices of pizza that have been sitting in my fridge for three days," responded Zara.

"I do have a hotel room if you'd like to spend the night and get away from all those roommates of yours," offered Scott.

Zara's eyes gave away her excitement and a smile broke through instantly.

"I'd love to," replied Zara, looking Scott in the eyes.

Scott and Zara made eye contact and the two leaned in and kissed. The two of them had been both waiting for the right moment to make a move and the time had come. Their moment lasted an eternity in their minds but in reality around ten seconds. After they finished the two leaned back just a bit and stared at each other's eyes for a brief moment.

"I'm ready to go when you are," said Scott.

"Let's do it," Zara answered.

Scott pulled out his phone and ordered a ride to the hotel. After a few moments of clicking a ride was on the way. Six minutes is how long it would take. The two took a seat on a nearby bench and Scott handed Zara the pen. She took a decent sized hit, handed it to Scott, and exhaled the smoke.

"What do you like to do in your free time?" asked Scott, caressing Zara's hand and taking a hit.

"I like to draw, exercise, watch movies and go to the park. All sorts of things. I don't get very much time to myself but that's just how it is I suppose. I spend way more time imagining cool or fun things to do than I can actually spend on those things. What about you?" answered Zara.

"I read, I write, I watch videos and try to learn new things. I smoke and spend time with friends. My best friend Tim is usually who I spend most of my time with. We've been friends since high school and I wouldn't trade him for the world," Scott replied.

The two continued to talk until a ride pulled up. The driver side window rolled down revealing an android driver.

"Ready when you are folks." said the driver unlocking the doors and popping the trunk.

The androids working in Cairo were promoted as basic and that they had no personality. 'Pure A.I., no soul', as the ads would say. This android's voice was extremely staticy and was clearly an older recording. Scott threw his bags in the trunk and got into the ride with Zara.

"Sir, can we get the privacy screen?" asked Scott.

The driver didn't respond, he just tapped a button and a small divider started to rise from the center of the car until the two cabins were separated.

They began to kiss and let themselves become intertwined. The ride seemingly went by in an instant as within minutes they had arrived at the hotel. Scott hopped out and opened the door for Zara. He grabbed his bags from the trunk and came back around to the front.

"Thank you for the ride!" said Scott.

"My pleasure. Be safe out there," responded the driver.

The ride drove off and the two of them made their way inside the hotel. Scott checked into his room with his phone and downloaded the room key. They made their way to the elevators and up to Scott's room. The front panel on the door read 'Room 0621'. They made their way inside, locked the door behind them, and threw their bags to the side. The room was decently sized with a small table and set of chairs next to the fridge. A large bed was on the opposite side of the room and a large screen sat on the wall. Clothes were ripped off with a quick haste and they began to show their affection for one another. This would take up the rest of the night. Scott and Zara both had a great time and in their minds hoped that this wouldn't be the last time they would cross paths in this manner. Zara fell asleep once they had wrapped everything up. Scott took a little while longer to fall asleep as he couldn't get the interview off his mind. He couldn't help but think about what everything with Zara would mean and how it would impact the interview. He didn't want to get too far ahead of himself but he saw no downsides, only positives. His mind went back and forth as he drifted off to sleep.

CHAPTER FIVE

8:30 appeared across the alarm clock which caused a groan from Scott. This was far earlier than he would typically get up on a day like today. He turned his alarm off so that it wouldn't continue to annoy him as the morning went on. He saw that Zara was still asleep and had taken an interesting form. She had her right arm extended all the way out with her legs stretched in the opposite directions and she seemed to be comfortable that way. She was snoring away not too loudly but it was noticeable. One thing that stuck in Scott's mind was something he noticed while he was with Zara last night - a couple bruises on her arms and legs. They seemed to be healing fine but it did concern him. He tried to not let it worry him too much and was sure if it was something that important she would bring it up to him. He got out of bed and made his way over to the window.The nearby park was just as beautiful in person as it was in the pictures. Scott gathered his clothes and placed them on a nearby chair so that he could easily dress himself after his shower. Zara started to wake up grunting in the process.

"Someone finally decided to wake up," said Scott playfully.

Zara responded with a deep noise of displeasure, almost definitely sarcastic and threw a pillow at Scott.

"How did you sleep?" he asked.

"I slept pretty well. Last night was... fun," answered Zara.

Scott smiled and Zara rolled over to make eye contact. Scott leaned down to give her a kiss and she responded in kind.

"So what should we do today?"

"A little more of this and then we can go walk around some markets and I'll show you the hot spots," replied Zara, continuing to kiss Scott for some time.

Once they were finished Zara got out of bed and they both got dressed. Scott looked at the new notifications on his phone. A massive flood had devastated neighboring Libya and over 30% of the country was submerged. Millions were in danger of starvation, disease, or death. New reports of Silvius Johnson's past corruption schemes and illegal acts were being released ahead of his party conference this week. Not that this news would shake the will of his supporters and accomplices and any serious attempt at holding him accountable would result in threats of violence. Scott threw his phone down for the moment and walked over to put his shoes on. Zara had finished getting ready and grabbed her things.

"So where to go first?" asked Scott.

"I don't know about you but I could really do with some breakfast and coffee."

Scott finished putting his shoes on then stood up and grabbed his phone.

"That sounds perfect. You lead the way," replied Scott.

Zara opened the door and followed Scott on his way out. They made their way down to the lobby and out to the street. They started heading down to a nearby crosswalk and crossed over to the other side of the street.

"I know a little German coffee shop around here you'll love it," said Zara holding onto Scotts hand as they walked.

Scott couldn't help but smile, almost tripping a few times after not focusing. They continued on the road walking past dozens of people including many Bessians and Nill. The atmosphere seemed lively although Scott always tried to keep his guard up somewhat when he wasn't in a familiar area. A few police officers were patrolling along the street stopping at a parked car that was missing a few tires. A few men carrying the tires were running down an alleyway before being spotted and the officers started to pursue them. It makes you wonder what they were stealing the tires for and why they were in that position in the first place. How much was being spent policing them for doing these desperate acts instead of putting it towards helping prevent those societal issues from putting them in those precarious situations. They passed a large building with a sign in the front that revealed it to be the 'American Union Embassy of Cairo'. Good to know, thought Scott. They rounded the corner and arrived at the coffee shop. It was simply named Kaffee with a bald German man drinking a cup of coffee as the logo. The humor wasn't lost on him. Scott opened the door for Zara and followed her inside. It was a small shop with about twenty seats around the edges with the center being made up of the ordering station and the kitchen in the back.

"Do you know what you want to order?" asked Zara, looking over to him.

"Something light I need an energy boost," said Scott.

Zara smiled and made her way to the cashier. They were an android with a German flag pin on their uniform. Their name tag said Peter.

"Guten Tag, how can I help?" asked Peter with a rough accent.

Scott cracked a bit of a smile as Zara ordered.

"I'll take a medium Gold Roast for him and a large iced Danzig."

"That's Danzig like the city?" asked Scott.

"Did you even look at the name of this place?" Zara asked with a laugh and a light push on his shoulder.

"Okay you can tap your payment when you're ready," said Peter.

"How long has this place been open?" asked Scott.

Peter gave Scott a blank stare for a moment and then looked back down at his screen. Zara tapped her phone and the screen dinged..

"You're good to go, it'll be out in a jiff," said Peter as he headed into the back room.

Scott and Zara made their way to a seat over by the window and sat down. Only five other people were in the shop, one of which was gathering their items and making their departure.

"So tell me more about yourself, what are you looking to do in life?" Zara asked, putting her hands on top of his.

"That's a pretty broad question don't you think?" chuckled Scott looking over at Zara.

"Maybe but what comes to mind?"

"I want to make an impact on the world and be remembered. When I look back at history I see all of these people who are written and talked about and I have alway wondered what it must have been like to be them," replied Scott.

"Well you're already someone I could never forget," Zara said with a smile leaning in to kiss him.

Peter walked over with the two drinks and placed them on their table.

"Here you go. Let me know if you need anything else."

Peter walked off and the two of them grabbed their drinks. Scott took a sip and immediately had to take another.

"This is delicious, it's so sweet," Scott said.

"I knew you'd like it."

"How is your drink?" asked Scott.

"Delicious. You wanna try it?" said Zara, while holding her drink towards him.

Scott grabbed it and took a sip. He was stunned by the flavor. The cinnamon stayed with him for a moment and he took a deep breath.

"We're gonna have to get coffee more often," Scott said gleefully.

"I like the sound of that."

Zara continued to drink her coffee and then excused herself to the restroom. Scott looked around while sipping his drink. The shop was getting busier with a line having now formed at the register. A couple was holding hands and ordering their drinks when a short balding man in a leather jacket cut the line and approached them.

"What do you freaks think you're doing? Take your filthy habits somewhere else!" exclaimed the man, throwing a crumpled up piece of paper at the two women.

One of them was a bit taller than the other and she turned around to face the man.

"What is your problem, sir?"

"You people and your disgusting ways don't belong here, am I right? Two women? What is this!" he said, motioning to the line of people.

Only two of them even made any noise for him, while the others either glared or audibly groaned.

"Buddy leave them alone, I don't like it either but I just want coffee," said one of the patrons, waving him down.

Zara had returned from the bathroom and took a seat, looking over at Scott.

"What's going on?"

"That dude is harassing those women for being a couple," Scott explained.

"Seriously, what year is this?" Zara said.

"It's crazy that people still feel that way."

"Egypt isn't the most progressive place by any means but most normal people either don't care or they support them," Zara said.

"People love who they love and that's a good thing. Why complicate it any more than that, especially when it isn't any of your business what other people do." said Scott.

"I feel the same way, I just wish more people did."

Scott and Zara noticed that the line was getting bogged up due to the yelling.

"Why should we have to avoid going out in public just because it makes you uncomfortable?" exclaimed the shorter woman of the pair.

"You two probably aren't even from here, infecting us with your deplorable ways. We don't want your gay agenda shoved down our throats!" the man shouted.

"Sir, we are buying coffee, what do you mean?" she replied.

At this point, the line was getting antsy and they wanted this encounter to end. Most of them were trying to convince the man to back off, or leave. The women were rightfully upset and asked for Peter to have them removed or to call the authorities.

"Why won't you call the police?" asked the taller woman.

"They are going to take forever and they probably won't solve the issue regardless. Let me get you two your drinks and you can be on your way," replied Peter.

"This isn't right."

Scott and Zara made eye contact and realized it was probably time to go. They got up, grabbed their drinks and made their way outside. The last thing they heard was the old man spouting off some rambling about a grand conspiracy to destroy our civilization. They started walking down the street and Scott stopped for a moment.

"The world is getting crazier by the day," said Scott.

"You just now noticed?" Zara asked sarcastically.

Scott grinned.

"No, it just helps to say it out loud sometimes. It's a lot to take in at once. It's one thing to read about things but to see them is a whole other experience," Scott said, grabbing Zara's hand.

"I get what you mean. Perspective and reassurance that it's not just you can mean the world," said Zara.

They embraced for a brief moment, before realizing that it might be best to wait till later. Scott looked at his phone.

"Where to now?" he asked.

"I have a few places in mind. Let's hit the market," Zara replied.

The two of them continued walking. The streets were busy with vehicles and the skies were filled with cargo planes and helicopters flying overhead. Rumors of military action by Egypt towards its neighbors was thought to be out of the question and yet there was a suspicious amount of activity.

"Is it normally that busy overhead?" asked Scott.

"For the past few weeks, yes. Before that, not really. There's a lot of ideas why but I think they are keeping it a secret from us," answered Zara.

"There's no doubt about that."

They continued on and eventually arrived at a local market made up of about one hundred shops along six city blocks. Vendors of all types were showing off their goods. Computer technicians, farmers, repairmen, carpenters, even scam artists were making the rounds trying to sell miracle cures to whatever the latest ailments were. Scott waved off most of them, except for one who snuck up behind him.

"Hi!" exclaimed the large, bulky man with a brown mustache and a scar across his cheek.

Scott and Zara were taken aback.

"Uh, hello?" the duo replied.

"What is causing you suffering or grief, my friends?" asked the bulky man.

"This conversation, to start," quipped Zara.

"Who are you?" questioned Scott.

"I am a man of many names. My friends call me Ben. My clients call me Mr. Macs. The ladies call me babe," said Ben, with an undeserved cockiness.

Sweat dripped from his forehead and his shirt was wrinkly and had several noticeable stains.

"I think we're fine, goodbye," Scott said, grabbing Zara's hand and ushering her with him.

Ben grabbed a bottle from the inside pocket of his jacket.

"My drink will cure all of your worries. It will make your dreams come true! You have to believe," exclaimed Ben, yelling after them.

He started to chase but stopped after enough people were crowding the market. Scott and Zara noticed this and were relieved. They rounded the corner and took a second to catch a breath.

"Sorry about that. I forgot to mention they are pretty common here," Zara said.

"It's no better back home, trust me. Our scammers just dress a little nicer, work for a company, or they aren't even real!" joked Scott, although the honesty of the humor seemed concerning.

They continued checking out different shops and stalls. They came across an old military surplus store, with old battle gear, helmets and equipment. The shop was massive - the tables extending back hundreds of feet, feeling almost like a warehouse. He came across a large helmet with a dent on the side and an Egyptian flag emblem. The tag attached explained that it had been worn by the seller's father in the Fourth River War twenty years prior. He was out on patrol when a sniper spotted him from a nearby cliff and luckily the helmet kept him alive. Scott showed it to Zara, impressed.

"I'm surprised this thing was able to stop the bullet." Zara said.

"It's possible the bullet hit nearby and a fragment split off hitting the helmet. I think a direct hit from a bullet would have gone through, although crazier things have happened," replied Scott.

The employee at the counter was a human male around the age of forty five, with light blonde hair, dark skin and a well trimmed beard wearing a tan cargo jacket.

"You're interested in the helmet? What line of business are you in? Mercenary, army, guard?"

"Oh no, nothing like that. Just a fan of history and military equipment. The story on the tag here is really interesting. Do you know the person who sold this?" asked Scott.

"It's been a long time but I remember them. Smart, witty kid, probably ten years younger than you. He came in here in tears, talking about his father and how someone busted into their house at night and killed him. He had wanted to join up and follow in his father's footsteps but once he was gone, it broke him. He sold me the helmet, along with a few other things and then he took his own life," replied the employee, who started to choke up and reach for a tissue.

"Oh dear, I can only imagine what he must have been going through," Scott replied, gripping Zara's hand a little tighter.

"That's awful. Did he have any family or friends?" asked Zara.

"He did but it was all just too much for him. I still see his mother every now and then at the store or around town. She is not nearly as chatty as she once was."

Scott set the helmet down and took a few seconds to breathe. They continued checking out the shop and looking through different items. Nothing else caught his eye and they made their way towards the exit.

"Thanks for stopping in, take care now!" said the employee, giving a slight wave.

"You too, have a good one," responded Scott, waving back along with Zara.

They exited the shop and started heading towards the next spot. Zara seemed to be leading the way.

"There is a flower shop just up here I wanna check out."

After a brief amount of walking, they arrived at the shop and entered. A pair of older women were manning the front desk and the shop was absolutely filled to the brim with plants. Orchids, tulips, daisies, sunflowers, roses, you name it. All fresh and real, at least according to the five different signs that were up stating this. Zara took her time looking through, stopping at each pot to smell and examine the pedals of each flower.

"See anything you like?" Scott said.

"I'm mainly here for the smells, to be honest," replied Zara with a slight giggle.

"Fair enough, they do smell wonderful."

Zara made her way around the shop, eventually getting to the rose section.

"Look at these, they are so pretty!" exclaimed Zara, pointing at a set of pink and red roses.

Scott kissed her cheek and picked up the flowers. He walked over to the counter and placed them down. One of the ladies walked over the register and clicked a few keys.

"Was there anything else we could find for you today?" she asked.

"I think this is good," said Scott, tapping his phone onto the reader.

A few moments went by and then a ding was heard.

"You're all set!" she said, turning and sitting down on a stool.

Scott handed the flowers to Zara, who couldn't help the smile that fell upon her face.

"You didn't have to do that, you know," said Zara, in a hushed tone.

"I wanted to and besides you deserve it," Scott replied with a smirk.

Zara kissed him and then two exited the flower shop. They continued making their way around the various stores and shops. It became clear that this would be an all day event and the day continued to evaporate. By the time four o'clock rolled around, Scott's stomach was growling.

"Are you hungry yet?" Scott inquired.

Zara laughed.

"Is that your way of asking to get something to eat?"

Scott just laughed in response.

"Okay what sounds good?" asked Zara.

"Is there anywhere that has good tacos?"

"Hmm, near here would probably be Taco Haco. It's a chain but it's so cheap," Zara said, giving a bit of a shrug.

"Sounds like a plan to me," replied Scott.

The pair made their way through the market, to a side street that contained the taco shop. It was hidden behind a bowling alley and a local donut shop. Boards covered up the windows and the sign was half covered.

"What's the story with the donut shop?"

"A Nill family ran it for five years and then one day a few months back the financing fell through and their business license got revoked. They had to leave the country, or go to prison. I think you can tell which option they chose," said Zara, with a sigh and frown.

"That's awful. Why did the license get revoked?"

"The official story is that there were severe sanitary issues with the staff but that's a lie. I went there once a week for two years and I knew a friend that worked there. Whoever runs that department just doesn't like aliens, I think," Zara responded.

"There is a whole lot of that happening these days," replied Scott.

Scott thought for a second and then grabbed Zara's hand.

"Let's get the food to go and head back to the hotel. We can watch some movies, eat and get to know each other a bit more," Scott suggested.

"Sounds like a date to me," Zara replied.

They locked hands and made their way over to the shop. They entered and approached the front counter. The shop wasn't very large, maybe ten seats maximum. Only two workers in the kitchen and one front desk android. It was nice to see humans and androids working together in a food shop, considering that was pretty rare these days. The pair ordered their food, each ordering three tacos. Scott went a little heavy on the meat and cheese, where Zara appreciated sour cream and tomatoes a bit more. They took a seat and waited by the window. The order took about five minutes to make and then the cook walked it out to them.

"Enjoy," he said, in a low gruff voice.

"He seems thrilled," joked Zara.

"Very."

They exited the shop and sat on a nearby bench while Scott started a ride request. Zara started to eat one of her tacos, losing a bit of it from a gust of wind and getting a bit of sour cream on her shirt.

"You didn't tell me you were such a messy eater," Scott teased, smiling at Zara.

"I never claimed to be organized either, did I?" Zara responded, in a playful tone.

Scott grabbed one of his tacos and took a bite. The meat and cheese enveloped each other and the heat was just right. Scott took his time to enjoy the meal and by the time they finished the food, their ride pulled up.

"Scott?" asked the driver, rolling his window down.

"You got it."

"Hop on in," he said, unlocking the doors.

Scott opened up the door for Zara and followed behind her. They cuddled for the duration of the ride, which lasted about seven minutes. The neighborhood they drove through was fairly nice, although there was a distinct bitter smell coming from a nearby construction site. What was being done is anyone's guess but the smell lingered until they got back to the hotel.

"Thanks for the ride," Scott said, shutting the door of the ride as he got out.

"No problem, have a good one," responded the driver, before taking off.

Zara led the way as the two made it inside to the lobby and to the elevators. Finally heading up to the room, Zara jumped face first into the bed and rolled over waiting for Scott to follow. Her patience was rewarded, as she found herself intertwined with Scott in bed. They took some time to have fun and relieve some tension. Eventually it was time to take a smoke break and Scott got up to grab his bag.

"Want a hit of the pen?" asked Scott rhetorically.

"We both know the answer to that," Zara smiled, reaching for the pen.

She took a small hit, letting it settle in the back of her throat and then exhaled before starting a coughing fit. Scott did the same, although he didn't cough as much.

"I answered so now it's your turn. What are you looking to do in life?" Scott asked.

Zara had a look of surprise and then laughed for a second.

"I need another hit if we're going to go that deep."

Zara grabbed the pen and took another long hit. Scott just laughed and waited for her to finish.

"Like you said earlier, the world is crazy and it's only getting crazier. I want to make a difference and make it better. I want to help people be better off tomorrow than they are today. I want to believe in something, in things, in people. Belief is one of the strongest things we have as humans. If you believe in something, it can happen," answered Zara.

"That is really admirable. Helping other people is one of the most cathartic things you can do. It really eases the mind and soul. That energy you have for helping others will only help raise everything around it," said Scott.

The two continued hitting the pen and talking for the rest of the night. Eventually, Zara tuckered out and Scott was left to scroll the feeds on his phone. News was constantly breaking and it was always some type of scandal; something that required our immediate attention. He thought about the state of things and how close even the furthest people felt due to technology. A trip across the world takes a few hours at most! A big negative of being so interconnected is that everyone feels like they need to share their opinion on everything and sometimes it's okay to just not do that if you don't have a lot of experience with the subject matter. Scott had run into this issue plenty of times when discussing controversial political topics at work. Commenting about a scandal involving someone you know very little about isn't going to add to the conversation. If anything, it will detract and cause other people to be misinformed. Scott took some time to look through the news but nothing of note had occurred. He set his phone down and rolled on his side. He stretched his legs and awaited what tomorrow would bring.

Around eight, Scott's alarm started to go off so he reached over to silence it. Zara was still asleep and Scott didn't need to be up for at least another hour. He slowly got out of the bed and made his way over to the balcony. He grabbed his pen and took a decent hit while looking out over the city. Traffic was everywhere and people were already flooding the markets. Construction crews were doing work, policemen were on patrol and buses were ferrying children to school. Scott took another hit and sat down in the chair. He put his feet up on the balcony and took a moment to let all the air out of his chest. He breathed in and out for a few moments and then took another hit from the pen.

"Having fun without me?" inquired Zara, who was standing at the doorway.

"That would be impossible," he replied, waving her towards him while coughing.

She came over and leaned down as if she were going to kiss him. Instead, she grabbed his pen and ran back inside, shutting the door on Scott. Laughing at him, she took a hit from the pen. Scott couldn't help but laugh - she was too quick for him. After a few more seconds, she relented and opened the door. Scott walked in, grabbed her by the waist and kissed her.

"What do you have going on today?" asked Zara, looking into his eyes.

"My interview is at noon but I have to shoot some other footage for the interview at ten so I'm hopping in the shower. I'd love to see you again, maybe tonight after my first session?"

Zara smiled really wide and started to giggle.

"You got it, I have to work at eleven anyway. Let's save some water, you know I'm such a big conservationist."

Scott laughed and stuck out his hand to grab hers. They proceeded into the bathroom and took a shower together. Afterwards, Zara dressed and made her way out. Scott took his time dressing himself, making sure that he looked as good as he could. He wanted to make a good impression on Mashir and show him that not every human looks down on the Nill. He took his time tying his tie, making sure that each step was completed as perfectly as the last. After he was dressed, he spent the rest of his time before he had to leave watching the news on the television. More of the same; war, famine and disease. Buy tickets to the next big blockbuster movie or drink the latest fruit soda though! You have to keep living your life even though all these terrible things are happening around the world. Our inner bubble doesn't get pierced often and when it does, we forget about it quickly. Scott looked at his watch, one minute shy of ten and decided it was close enough. He got up, grabbed his satchel and made his way down to the hotel lobby. He walked into what was a nice, modern-looking lobby with a running pond in the center. He walked out the front doors and watched the cars zoom by on the road. Bikes and skateboards were being used by all kinds of people wearing different clothing styles from different eras. A ride pulled up to him and rolled its window down.

"Scott? I'm here to pick you up," asked the driver.

An odd way to start that conversation but Scott shrugged it off.

"Thanks, I need a ride to the park by the library," replied Scott.

"I'll get you there fast, don't you worry,"

Scott felt there was such a contrast between this ride and the one he had previously in how they interacted with him. He noticed a tablet in the passenger seat, with a cord connected to the driver's side. He could make out the words 'Introductory Russian' on the screen. He didn't think much of it, maybe this android was trying to learn a new language. He got into the car and the ride resumed as most of the previous ones in his life had. He made sure to take notice of all the things he saw on the way, all the different landmarks and locations. He saw an opera house that had been in operation for nearly thirteen decades, an aquarium that had four different endangered species and a mosque that was built in the ninth century. You never know if this is your only opportunity to see something so take advantage while you can. The ride finally arrived at the park and Scott got out. He felt a strange sense of relief once the ride left. Something felt off during the ride and Scott sensed that he shouldn't have gotten in that car. There wasn't much he could do now though, just keep moving forward. Scott needed to keep his wits about him. Cairo wasn't the most dangerous city in the world but it wasn't a paradise either. His U.N. badge would only carry him so far, especially in a nation where they gave such little care to the organization. This sentiment carried on from the government to the people. No one respected the words of outside institutions; everything had become focused on what their internal media figures told them and that was rarely positive. The park wasn't terribly big, maybe three city blocks in length. A small pond was on the other end and there were trails curving around sections of trees and a children's playground. It was devoid of children, instead occupied by a few groups of homeless people. Wearing tattered rags, these people sat around and told stories, hoping to not be arrested or shot by patrolling policemen. The park was a beautiful contrast to the surrounding city blocks. Scott saw a few locals walking along the route ahead of him. A human woman and an alien, a Turl, were walking together. A Bessian jogged just ahead of them, past the playground and into the patch of trees. He took a moment to stop on a park bench and get out his drone to gather footage to use for his presentation. Naturally, he had access to plenty of stock footage but homemade footage usually helped land you points with the bigwigs. Scott pulled out the drone and placed it on the ground.

He activated the remote and watched as it lifted off, flying hundreds of feet into the air.

He could see almost the entire city by this point and the outskirts looked very interesting -

large caravans of migrants leaving the town, escorted by armed guard patrols, an entire

neighborhood set ablaze by a fire that was blockaded by the military and fireworks being

set off to celebrate the President's birthday! Born in Cairo forty odd years ago, his name

was Abdel Haladi. Son of Mohammed Haladi, business tycoon and owner of the largest

construction company in Egypt, Abdel never had to struggle and constantly flashed his

wealth. He always had the latest clothes, gadgets and cars. He would spend his days

flying down the highways of the city with a beautiful woman or two by his side. Abdel

spent his early years spending his father's money and trying to smooth-talk his way into

powerful corporate sector positions, meeting with several agents of the American Union.

Large deposits were made into his accounts following this and confidential files that went

missing were found in the hands of known American operatives. Abdel wouldn't stay in

one spot for too long to refrain from being caught and began going primarily by his last

name. He felt that the new leaders of Egypt were dragging it back into the stone age.

Traditional family values, hard work and the Egyptian spirit were missing. He made his

own wealth off his connections and eventually stopped supplying information when it

became inconvenient for him. Haladi started to become annoyed with the presence of

American agents in his country and called for the President at the time, Makalani, to

round up and arrest the foreign agents. He refused and when the issue fell before his

parliament, he went on a vacation, leading to support for him to falter. He ended up

losing the next election and the next leader promised reforms to their foreign policy and

economics. This did not happen and the despair and corruption continued to grow. Haladi may at one point have had a desire to truly change things but it seems far more likely that he simply saw a means to acquire more power and secure himself a comfortable position. He had an ego the size of an aircraft carrier and felt that it was his destiny to save Egypt. He traveled the world and made a trip to Mecca, using it as a way to gain votes and attention from the Islamic community. He wrote a few manuscripts, two of which he published, describing his political vision for Egypt and what he would do to make the country proud again. The glorious days of the past had been ripped away from them, the citizens, by the betrayers! Those in finance who wished to hoard the wealth for themselves and allow the world to starve beneath them. This was not based on any true sympathy for the working class, however but a trick to mask himself in a facade of populism. Haladi appealed to be the average working man by speaking truth to power, or at least a warped distortion of it in the mind of his supporters. Deciding that the time had finally come, he became the leader of a political party advocating for Egyptian nationalism and a new Egyptian empire. His experience in business was said to be the main reason he would be a good President - someone who could balance the budget! Having never served a moment in the military, the generals of the Egyptian military found Haladi to be a spoiled nuisance with no clue of how to run the country. He ran on the platform and rhetoric that the invasion of refugees had caused the rise in poverty, homelessness, unemployment and lack of food. He rallied his followers behind the idea of stopping the influx of refugees and focusing on Egypt and that it would always be first going forward. After just fourteen days, he purged the entirety of his cabinet and his senior military command - replacing them all with his friends and businessmen he previously worked with. His official title was President but he asked to be called by a different title. Atum, or 'complete one', the finisher of the world. The nation had been convinced that they had to return to a previously great time where Egypt was the most powerful empire in the world. Haladi would be the one to complete this mission and to finish his struggle against the rest of the world. The story had been conjured up by his propagandists using ancient Egyptian figures and themes to tie a religious aspect into it and to essentially have the public see Haladi as a deity. Refugees seeking a better life ran into a leader just like the authoritarian European governments trying to persecute them. Perhaps it was irony, or fate. Scott didn't know what to believe about such things, yet they were always at the forefront of his mind when thinking about history. History rhymes with itself and echoes into eternity. Haladi's stance on alien immigration was quite similar to those of his predecessors and was expected to impose even harsher restrictions on who was allowed to enter the country. What that meant for those already here was the question that needed to be answered and he wasn't willing to do that. Scott had his own idea of what Haladi would do next but he couldn't say it out loud, or anywhere that his personal guard, the Atum Hamia, could hear him. Dressed in all black and brandishing an AH logo on their sleeve, they acted as Haladi's secret police force, often referred to as Shadows. They terrorized thousands - tasked with enforcing his political doctrine and making sure that the population was not planning to revolt. The people protested anyway, of course. This caused massive civil unrest and an ever encroaching police state. Egypt wasn't fully turned and Cairo still had the facade of a free society but Scott knew to be on his toes. The People's Senate was effectively neutered when an enabling act allowed legislation to be enacted by hand of the President during times of immense emergency. He used this to bypass their vetoes and eventually gained enough support to neuter his opposition and effectively disband its authority. They still technically existed, they just no longer held sessions, took roll, received funding, or held elections again. The Mandub, or Representatives, were replaced by Mantiq Qayids, who led the Mantiq as Haladi's eyes and ears in each region of the country. Over time, a process of the solidification of power over the Egyptian system became total. Decree after decree, executive action after executive action, emergency declared after emergency declared, Haladi slowly swept away the restrictions on his power. The faint promise of a transfer of power eventually became something no one dared mention, as Haladi's rule was now slated to last for a century, if not millenia. He wanted to take Egypt into the stars and lead his people in the expansion of their power and influence. "We should be a multi-planetary empire!" Haladi stated in his first book, where he outlined plans for the settling of colonists to other planets in our solar system. It mattered little to Abdel that the locations of his planned settlements were inhabited by other human colonies, other peoples, some indigenously alien to these worlds, for they were of a lesser stock than his own. "For what other reason has Egypt shown up in the history books since the inception of the human race? We are destined for greatness and I believe I am the one who will guide us along the path. That much is now clear to me after the events of the June 3rd crisis." The crisis Haladi spoke of was the collapse of most of the markets in Egypt during an economic spiral that affected the entire world. It sent the country into a state it hadn't seen in a century or more and many felt they needed someone to save them. Haladi gave them something to fight and stand for. The lives of these people had become so broken by the system that a con man could fool them into giving them the greatest gift of all, their time and energy.

Scott's drone had made its way to the other side of the city. He managed to spot an interesting interaction: two black-suited men carrying a silver briefcase and exchanging it with a man in a more mysterious outfit. The man wore a light brown trench coat and what looked like a fedora on. The briefcase was handed off in a discreet sleight of hand fashion. This reminded him of the hijinks at the office but he knew this wasn't the case here. It wouldn't do any good to report this, though. Haladi was a criminal himself. He used the law against his own appointed officials to improve his own wealth and power. His head representative to the U.N. General Assembly, Haji Atiyeh, was his biggest supporter and essentially his right hand man. He held four other cabinet positions, including Minister of Information and Propaganda and held a General rank in the Army. When at the assembly, he puts on a show to make Egypt seem less extreme. This, along with large monetary contributions, brought foreign aid and support to Haladi's regime. Russia was a key ally and had sent over four hundred military and political advisors to help train special forces units and government officials. The American Union, China, Brazil and many others have also sent aid and arms to support his regime. Haladi had campaigned on the idea of his Four Year Plan to get Egypt to the point of self-sufficiency. He wanted the Egyptian Pound to be the currency of Africa and Asia. He also used this as an opportunity to re-arm and prepare his nation for future conflicts. His immediate goals for his empire were to expand and annex his neighbors to form a greater Egyptian Empire. He wished to rival the Islamic Caliphate of old. Haladi was not strictly a religious man but he saw an opportunity to exploit the followers of Islam for his own power. The next golden age would begin in Cairo! Scott knew when to speak up and when to bite his tongue. His drone had made it a few miles outside of the city and he saw a sprawling complex in the distance. Large, gray buildings in rows of four with smoke paths interconnected and a watch tower at the front. Tall, spiked fencing surrounded all sides and several military style vehicles were parked around the front - while several large buses could be seen parked over to the side and smoke could be seen billowing from the top of the center buildings. Huge crowds appeared to be exercising and being moved between buildings. He wasn't sure what he was looking at but noticed that a man in the watch tower had spotted his drone. He appeared to be using his radio and it spooked Scott. He turned the drone around and left the area quickly. After piloting the drone back to the city, he made his way through the neighborhoods and local businesses. He passed schools, hospitals, police stations, libraries, shopping centers, cinemas, parks and more. The city was sprawling and yet a cloud hung over it. It hadn't taken him long to notice that things were not right here. The streets were not empty by any means but they were not as bustling as you might expect on a monday afternoon in Cairo. About eighty-five percent of the people you did see were humans, very few aliens. This seemed to be a humans-only neighborhood. Signs dotted the fronts of establishments and gated communities:

" Humans only!"

"Species Mixing is Terrorism!"

"One Species, One Nation!"

The messages got more nauseating as he went on and an interesting observation occurred when he flew over the houses of some of the more wealthy members of the community. Alien workers were tending to the gardens, yards, repairs and cleaning of amenities. Where did these people live if they were working in human neighborhoods? The sad reality is many of these people were slaves and indentured servants, forced to work oftentimes at gunpoint. This was kept quiet by enormous bribes to the correct people in the correct positions and it was an open secret. The kind of thing that if you brought too much attention to that it would be the last story you ever covered. Scott continued gathering footage for another twenty-five minutes, until it was about 11:30. He packed the drone up and made his way over to the library where the interview would be. It was a large building that took up nearly a whole block of the street. The street and sidewalks in front were busy. Scott noticed a large poster hanging on a nearby pole. It read 'Service is Freedom, Obedience is Power.' with an impossibly large man looking over a factory full of workers tending to the machinery. Scott wondered just how many people see this poster on a single day and how many more just like it are there? He continued up the stairs of the library. He found his way into the lobby area, where a set of reporters were talking with a tall woman with slightly curly, dark purple hair. She was dressed in a gray pantsuit and did not seem thrilled to be on a live broadcast. Her name was Verona Kampf, head of the Library of Cairo.

"Ms. Kampf, what do you know and for how long?" asked a reporter.

The reporters seemed frantic and very angry at what they were questioning her about. Verona was flanked by two guards in all black. The AH logo on their sleeve could be spotted a mile away.

"I knew everything that I was legally obligated to know, nothing more," responded Verona.

She smiled and started to try and leave the scene.

"Verona, what does that mean? Why did radicals pay for your library to fund the President's campaign? When did you find out and what was your involvement?" pressed another reporter.

She turned around and couldn't help but scoff.

"You people, I swear," said Verona, who had a look of disgust on her face and she shooed off the reporters.

She left the lobby to go into her office, followed closely by the two guards. Scott had heard rumblings of some sort of controversy involving campaign finances from Haladi's election but why were the President's secret police protecting the head of the city library? The media started to dissipate so he made his way down the hallway and noticed the different exhibits that made up both sides of the large corridor. He found his way to an open atrium area and decided he would spend the rest of his time before the interview enjoying the scenery. He sat where he could soak up some natural sunlight and have a good view. He put on some relaxing music to take his edge off and allow him to think of some more questions to ask. He wanted to know about their health habits and whether or not they listened to their doctors. What type of jokes did they find funny? What did they feel about the creation of the universe? What kind of entertainment did they invent? Scott could go in so many different directions and he would have six six-hour sessions to do this. A beam of light came in through a pane of glass and the heat brought enormous warmth to Scott. He enjoyed letting the sunlight hit his face; something he didn't do nearly enough. He still had around twenty minutes until he needed to go meet with Mashir. He thought about the past few nights with Zara and how much he wanted to see her again. He thought about telling Tim about her. He decided he needed to get into the right state of mind and started to brainstorm ideas for questions. He wanted to make sure that Mashir felt comfortable with him and wanted to open up. He wanted the full story and wanted to be able to compare and contrast it with his own experiences on Earth. He decided that he would leave some room to get into deep discussion in the later sessions but to start this one getting a general overview of the history of the Nill. The details would come out in the stories and he wanted to hear all the anecdotes he could. He got off the bench, grabbed his satchel and decided to make his way towards the meeting area. He walked through three hallways until he got to the room where Mashir would be waiting for him. He took a deep breath and made sure he had all of his equipment with him. He did a mental check in his head and decided he had everything he would need. He walked into a large room where Mashir and his possible interpreter were sitting by the furnace. He was finally going to meet a Nill in person. Nill were humanoid in nature and Mashir was a greenish color with purple accents that ran along his edges. He was also a tad bit bulkier than his interpreter, who was shorter and lankier, while also having orange skin with purple accents. Humans and Nill's were able to integrate pretty quickly into each other's societies so the interpreter was more just to make sure subtle colloquial terms didn't offend the other by misunderstanding. He made eye contact with Mashir and it finally hit him that this interview could be his career-defining moment. The moment consumed him and only compelled him to have more confidence in himself. He let out one last deep breath and walked over to the two of them ready to start the interview.

CHAPTER SIX

Anxiety, excitement, nerves, and tension - the many feelings which occupied his mind. The only reaction his body could muster was to reach out and shake Mashir's hand.

"So you're the famous Scott I have heard so much about?" he asked.

He had a deep, gruff voice and firm handshake, giving the impression of knowledge and experience. Scott was surprised to hear Mashir greet him in English as he expected he would be introduced through the interpreter. This was the common method of introduction but Mashir was different.

"I am and it's a pleasure to meet you Mashir. Your reputation precedes you," said Scott.

"I have brought my friend and partner here, Yolen, to provide input and any interpreting that is required."

"It's nice to meet you, Yolen. Thank you for being here," Scott replied, extending his hand to Yolen.

"Same to you. Let me know how I can assist as we go along," said Yolen shaking his hand.

They took their seats in the chairs near the center of the meeting room forming a triangle between the three of them. They both looked at each other and took a moment to process what was ahead of them. Scott could tell by the way Mashir sat that he was excited for the interview.

"So, how would you like to start?" asked Mashir.

Mashir sounded as confident as one would expect and he took note.

"Let me set up the camera and we'll be ready to start." Scott said.

Mashir and Yolen nodded. Scott grabbed his drone camera and activated it. It flew over to form a fourth angle of the group and record the interview. Scott set the control tablet to his side.

"I wanted to use our first session today to get a brief overview of Nilleon, the Nill, their history, culture, and anything you think would be considered an introduction for anyone wanting to get a grasp on the history of your planet. I know it's quite a large subject matter," said Scott.

Mashir chuckled and sat up in his seat.

"Large is an understatement. Our planet has been around for roughly five billion years according to our scientists' recent studies. Life had only formed after a billion years and it was slow moving. The first lifeforms that resembled modern Nillwere around five to ten million years ago and intelligence by our modern standards formed during the last several hundred thousand years," responded Mashir.

Scott pulled out his notepad.

"A lot of debate has been had on the subject and a lot of new material that has been uncovered has revealed hundreds of thousands of years of development that we had no prior knowledge of," Mashir stated.

"What kind of things have been discovered?" asked Scott, perking up.

"Tools like axes, spears, and other farming tools were found well before we thought agriculture had developed. So many lives and so many experiences that will never be known because we don't have a written record of it. And yet it happened nonetheless. We have also found evidence of a new theory that all Nill are the descendants of a specific group of Nill who underwent heavy evolutionary pressures. The kind that almost causes complete extinction," responded Mashir.

A few moments of silence filled the air as Scott took a drink from his bottle of water.

"Fascinating. So what kind of pressures were the Nill experiencing?"

"The Nill have not always been one species as we used to have many more. The Rakhal was an older form of Nill that lived the majority of its life before we existed. They hunted, wandered and moved around the planet - taking what they wanted and doing what they wanted with our women. This predation led to much change in a relatively short period of time. So many of the factors that make us the type of species we are have a direct link to the trauma caused by being the prey of another species. From that we have evolved to have art, culture, technology, use tools, write and speak languages, conquer and settle our planet and then explore the cosmos," Mashir replied.

"It seems the Nill and Humans have many similarities in how the first sentient life came to form. We have a similar theory for our origin that I am quite fond of. It tends to explain a lot of things in our society as Humans that I couldn't quite understand before. I find it interesting that trauma can be stored genetically. Evolution and life are beautiful things," answered Scott.

"It seems to be a common theme in regards to the formation of alien life throughout the galaxy. Our universe is truly endless and a bottomless sea of information to be absorbed. If only we had a hundred lives to experience more of it!"

Scott took a moment to drink some water.

"So when would you say recorded history started?" asked Scott.

"About twenty thousand years ago if we want to look at modern examples of records and documentation. Anything prior was lost to the ages. The first groups of Nill formed communities to protect themselves from the Rakhal and these eventually grew into cities. At first we were hunter and gatherer tribes and later we adopted agriculture to make this societal organization feasible. Throughout time societies would shift how they operated based on the needs of the ruling class. Families and the structure of them shifted over time as well. Matriarchal lineage, shared husbands and many other things considered taboo by many religions and modern institutions," said Mashir.

Scott smiled.

"When did the first war occur?" he asked.

Mashir sighed. He didn't think this would need to be brought up so soon.

"As wealth and power started consolidating into certain classes of society, the conditions of the ruling class and the subservient classes would come into conflict. Societies started enslaving captured soldiers who were citizens of conquered territories along with already existing slaves; these criminals would be exploited for their labor. That excess value created by their labor was used to enrich the elites and pay for the advancements of society."

"Sounds quite similar to societal developments on earth," Scott responded.

"Eventually the rulers found that it wasn't popular with the masses to enslave a class of people. What came next was a ruling elite founded on their exploitation of religious belief and owning the majority of the land. Lords ruled over land and rented it out to peasants to work the land. They paid out a bit of the profit and kept the rest to build up their own pockets. Green and Orange Nill were kept as the bottom of these social classes, with Blue Nill seeing the most ability to cross between them."

"It is fascinating to hear about a society developing over time," Scott replied.

"The Nill have a belief where our creator gave us a certain mandate to live our lives a certain way in his vision. It's been a long standing aspect in our culture and while it never made much logical sense to me; most of my society allowed it to influence every aspect of our lives and government. We attributed a certain holiness or divinity to these stories that we built our cultures around. We used it as a way to tell each other how we should live our lives, how we should treat each other and how to become more complete people. Over time our species became more advanced and we started to realize our place in the universe and the unlikeliness of a true divine spirit who created everything as was told in our texts. Mythical stories took the place of many of these religious tales and served as a way for societal norms, traditions, and stories to be passed down over the generations. Eventually we understood enough about the world around us that we had substantive theories on how the universe had formed and the evolution of our species so the idea of an all encompassing, all powerful creationist god was no longer required. What did this interpretation mean though?" Mashir said.

"A question long pondered throughout time on Earth," Scott let out.

"In more recent times stories told through art forms became the new source of divinity - the thing that made us stand out from everything else on our planet. We stood alone as the sole sentient lifeform in the universe! At least we were. Once we lost that - once we knew about humans from the planet Earth - that changed everything. It made us rethink our place in the universe and what it means to be a person, to have a spirit, a soul, and to be free. Ever since I came to Earth I have been wondering why more humans have not done the same thing," Mashir said, letting out a long sigh.

"Many humans have but not nearly enough. We need an awakening from the masses before anything significant could change and the lethargic attitude towards reactionary forces is depressing at best. I hope that will change although I do suspect it will get worse before it gets better." Scott said.

He took a moment to sip from his water bottle. Mashir did the same and nodded on for the next question.

"Blind faith can be very dangerous and I think it's led to many of the Earth's issues. How do you feel Nilleon did with this?" Scott asked.

"We failed. We allowed it to control our legislation, our military, our culture and the way we lived our lives and justified our more than reprehensible actions. It got in the way of us doing things that prevented our demise. Wars were fought over things that did not exist. Spirituality can be an important tool in liberation but fundamentalism and weaponization is where I draw the line. The majority of religious Nill were great people who were used as pawns," answered Mashir.

Scott chuckled to himself.

"That's a crazy concept. People willing to lose their lives over imaginary concepts that were invented by those in power. I see it repeated over time throughout time on Earth and now the same for Nilleon." he said.

"Precisely." Mashir agreed.

"I think over time our culture managed to produce enough Nill to challenge the status quo that we had a community to investigate the true nature of the planet and eventually the galaxy," Mashir said.

"How long had Nilleon been involved in intergalactic politics?" asked Scott.

"About three thousand years longer than Earth. We were the Earth's first major ally and we took that job seriously. Earth had long been the target of colonizers yet the Nill Fleet for Liberation managed to hold off invaders time after time. We mostly used it for scientific purposes and to try and increase our ability to mine resources in asteroid fields," responded Mashir.

Scott wiped away a bead of sweat from his forehead. He took a deep breath and cleared his throat.

"How did Nill interact and behave on a day to day basis? On Earth we developed languages, written words, the printing press, cameras, television, the internet and social media which seems to stem from an almost perpetual desire to reflect and seek meaning in our own culture and existence in the universe. With each new innovation came adaptations to use it for the purposes of war. It culminated in many of the worst conflicts throughout the last few centuries. Disinformation, radicalization, content pipelines, the constant stream and never ending feed of content not designed for the human brain led to generations ready to face the worst the world had to offer. Our leaders made sure to match this energy starting some of the worst and most intense conflicts seen in several decades. Did anything similar happen on Nill?"

"Yes, very much so. Very similar concepts and uses for that kind of technology. We developed language early and we generally consider the time after we started writing down our history as part of the historical record. Cameras and the television captivated

Nilleon in so many ways and it ultimately became a symbol of wealth. If you had the time to waste away watching something or someone else you had a good life. It had a positive effect for a small percentage of the population with an overall negative effect on the quality of life. It became a crutch - a way to escape the awful reality we lived in. It distorted the truth and what was considered real. The issue with inhabiting a digital space is you have to log off eventually and once you do the result of spending so much time and money in these digital spaces is a worse off real world. The modern family structure, what you humans refer to as the Nuclear family, was used as a tool of the ruling class to control individuals and keep them in the system. Their agents used propaganda, apathy, and societal pressure to force everyone into accepting these new norms and becoming a cog in the machine. They would never allow them to slide back and it only worsened over the years. When it came to war our rulers simply used it as a platform for whatever issue or cause was popular. The culture around it becomes self-sufficient and you start to view things abstractly and outside of their proper context. I feel this way about much of how we tell history. We are constantly overwhelmed with the past and how we picture it. We feel chained to these interpretations and often fail to see how they connect to where we are. Things are always moving and you can lose sight of why things really happened if you only pay attention to what was written after the fact outside of the times themselves. They crush our ability to imagine something new and so we feel burdened by the images we have seen before and spoon feed us nostalgia. Using the very poison they have given to us to poison us again!" said Mashir.

"How did a historian like yourself view the history of Nilleon and the Nill people?" Scott asked.

"Over the history of our people we have found many ways to communicate the stories that molded us. Our ancestors told stories of great gods, fantastical creatures, and tales that surely could never have taken place as written. Passed on through the generations these tales became part of our culture as something we could all find meaning in. As we developed as a species we started to grow in number and the amount of people living side by side skyrocketed. The tools and technology that we crafted helped further this growth and communication and allowed many new opportunities for sharing amongst different cultures. There was a time before we had collective communities and built massive cities and before large farms and armies clashed over resources. Most of our work focuses on what we have records of although some Nill do focus on the pre-history of our species. We began writing things down and keeping records eventually developing a system similar to your telephones and televisions. Our version of the internet would come later and as a side note directly led to no less than fifteen wars within the first fifty years of its popular use! An invention with unforeseen consequences no doubt. The collective power of our people is quite a powerful tool and dangerous weapon depending on how it is harnessed. These advancements changed how we viewed ourselves and our history. We started to see the past in the same vein as our present and could not look beyond the past to see the future," Mashir said.

"Was academia or the intellectual crowd scrutinized?" asked Scott.

"There was a vast stigma against anyone who worked for a university or who wrote the historiographies of the planet. We wanted to tell an unbiased complete picture of what our history was like. They wanted to use a falsified history to control the population and get them to defend their rule. We had no interest in taking power from anyone. We just wanted to live a peaceful life and hopefully improve life for everyone.

Our works were read for centuries and then in the preceding years before the collapse we saw book burning return as a popular method of hate," responded Mashir.

So much of what Scott was hearing reminded him of different parts of the human race's history. He realized this would be far more personal than he had expected but he was ready for that challenge.

"When looking at the Nill, who was the in-group and who was the out-group?"

Mashir looked at his hands and then at the interpreter. His interpreter had more orange tones than the green tones on Mashir's body.

"Blues and some Greens, like myself, have generally held power the entire time that Nill life was intelligent. The oranges were one of the subjugated peoples and one of the reasons I ever ran into Yolen in the first place was because we both attended an anti-war rally at the capitol," Mashir said with sadness biting through the nostalgic gaze.

"What sort of things were done to the Orange people?" Scott asked.

"Segregation, less access to resources and property, hatred, bigotry, violence, and in some cases they were murdered in cold blood. Entire wars and entire governments were run on the principle of superiority of one race of Nill over another. The truth was that the outside difference of the Nill people didn't matter because we were all being oppressed by the wealthy oligarchs in power. They held all the wealth, all of those in power listened to them, they controlled the corporations and news companies that were used to distract them and they owned all the land. They did not share with those they considered to be less than themselves. Much of our social interactions in the last two decades since we've come to Earth has been about righting the wrongs of our past before it is truly too late to reconcile," stated Mashir.

Scott couldn't hold back a frown as he finished his note. He took another sip of his water and cleared his throat.

"That sounds like a very interesting time period from a historical perspective. I know those sorts of situations cause a lot of emotions. I'm happy you're willing to open up about this because I think it will show the value of your people here on Earth. I'm already seeing so many parallels between humans and Nill. The supremacy of one group over the other, often based on identifiable characteristics like race, skin color, religions, etc has reared its ugly face throughout all of human history. Even though we still struggle with it today, I know you and your people will overcome it as well."

Scott managed a smile hoping to lighten the mood.

"I appreciate the kind words and I hope that more humans become welcoming of the Nill people as well," Mashir responded with a smile in return.

"How do you feel about personal bias impacting your writing and work as a historian?" asked Scott.

"I think it is inevitable and it is important to recognize one's own blindspots and biases so you can correct them. Historiography is its own field and depending on the lens of history or analysis you want to use you will end up focusing on certain events or people over others. You have to be aware of it and keep that context in mind when reading the work," replied Mashir.

"I can respect that," Scott said, clearing his throat. "Tell me about the most powerful country on Nill?"

"The Republic of Accora was the longest standing empire at the time of collapse while also being the largest culprit of the collapse. They had won their independence from the Great Riddish Empire as a colony and became the most powerful nation on the planet. They managed to monopolize the growing media and technology advances to allow them to imperialize the planet economically. The entire world relied on Accora for something so they couldn't not listen when they wanted something to happen. They also have over twelve hundred military bases throughout the planet even in territories that belonged to long time neutral nations," answered Mashir.

"We have had several nations on Earth that fit that archetype," said Scott.

"I imagine that you do. I'm sure Earth would be better off if those nations would have used their vast power for good instead of profit. I wish more of Nilleon's had come to that conclusion," answered Mashir.

"I know what you mean. Separating ourselves from something we didn't choose and were simply born into is an important step to recognizing your core values," Scott said.

Mashir took a moment to contemplate what Scott had said and let out a sigh of relief.

"I will need some time to rethink things with that lens on. Thank you for the advice," said Mashir.

Scott smiled and flipped to his third page of notes. His handwriting was atrocious if only for the lack of effort in school to teach him how to write properly. His poor writing was played off as a joke which gained him notoriety in class yet Scott was able to read it himself and truly didn't mind if no one else could.

"How was the concept of law understood on Nilleon?" Scott questioned.

"That really depends on if you ask the one writing the law or if you ask the ones subject to the law. It's a tool to control the people and protect those in control of the corporations, big industries and the owners of capital. They formed police forces who preserve the status quo and enforce the current hierarchy of power. They have a monopoly on the use of violence. The state itself will protect them even if they break the very laws they are supposed to uphold. They have no obligation to protect the people, even though their propaganda always claimed that was their true purpose!" replied Mashir.

"I have to say that sounds very similar to our experience on Earth. We fare no better on the front of policing regardless of the nation you live in," said Scott.

"I have found that time and time again we the people of a community have to come together and defend ourselves and stand up for our rights. Relying on the very forces that oppress us to free us from that burden is a silly notion," said Mashir.

"I couldn't agree more. The capitalist structure we have on Earth has been going for centuries now and while it has shown many cracks it has survived countless attempts at upheaval," Scott replied.

"Do you think it will ever be replaced?" asked Mashir, sitting up slightly.

"I hope so. I think we will get there. We just haven't figured out the path yet," answered Scott.

"History is made by men living out actions and ideas acquired by the environment around them. We don't choose how opportunity will present itself, only how we respond to it," said Mashir.

"I like that. It reminded me of an old saying on Earth that goes 'There are decades where nothing happens and there are weeks where decades happen,'"Scott said, with a grin.

"He couldn't be more right. Time is a funny thing. Things seem to go by so much faster as you get older and it seems like things that were yesterday are now years ago and it just doesn't feel real sometimes. Do humans ever feel this way?" asked Mashir.

"I think all of us have gone through those sorts of things in our head before. Life can feel very authentic and inauthentic at the same time especially when you throw the digital space into the equation. There are whole communities on Earth that spend the majority of their time living in digital spaces, only getting out to take care of the essential human bodily tasks to not die. A lot of them wear it as a badge of honor and I feel bad because they have bought in fully," said Scott.

Scott took another sip of water and cleared his throat before moving on. He knew this was only the beginning.

CHAPTER SEVEN

What had seemed like only a few minutes of questioning had been around two hours.

"Mashir, let's take a short break before we continue," Scott said.

"That sounds excellent. Yolen, let's grab a drink from that machine over there," said Mashir.

The two Nill stood up and walked over towards the soda machine in the hallway. Scott took this time to stand up and stretch his legs. He cracked his back and decided to walk a few laps around the library. He made his way down the hallway when he ran into one of the security officers from the lobby. Scott's eyes drifted from his face down to his A.H. patch, which sat next to his H and F patch. His uniform did not have a name and most of his face was covered by a black balaclava.

"Scott, come with me. Your presence has been requested," said the officer.

Scott tensed up and noticed goosebumps enveloping his entire body. He was in the middle of his interview - he couldn't just leave but he also knew that not complying would only lead to more trouble.

"Okay," responded Scott, worried about what was next.

The officer turned around and motioned for Scott to follow. They made their way to the front of the building to Verona's office. They walked into a small room with a desk and several chairs and a door on the far end that presumably led to her office. A man sitting at the desk looked up at them. He was an average sized man nearly bald but with a short brown beard. His desk plate said his name was Jerrod.

"I have the guest that Ms. Kampf requested," said the officer.

"Ah yes, let me see his identification," replied Jerrod.

The officer turned to Scott and put out his hand. Scott begrudgingly took out his I.D. card and handed it to the officer, who then handed it to Jerrod. Jerrod typed the numbers into the system and looked back up after a few moments.

"Let me see if she's available," replied Jerrod.

He got out of his seat, knocked on Verona's door and then entered the room. While the door was ajar Scott could hear part of a conversation between Verona and an unknown group of people.

"Our timeline has moved up," one stated.

"We won't be ready for another two weeks at minimum! Let alone our partner nations," another replied.

The unknown voices spoke in what Scott thought was Russian, French, British, and American accents. Disagreements continued while Scott stretched his arms moving himself closer to peer inside the room. He noticed a familiar tall, brown haired man in a blue suit facing towards the window. He was not surprised to see Ivan the historian George was so fond of. There were several other people in the room but his accent was unmistakable.

"The Ramet have their own timeline to keep Ms. Kampf. My bosses report to an ever higher power, mind you."

Ivan seemed calm as if he was leveraging some unseen power at work.

"I am keeping that top of my mind I assure you. Atum needs all the support while we face backlash from the United Nations," she replied, audibly blowing air from her mouth.

"I am curious why you don't just ask for Union special forces? The Ramet are a paramilitary mercenary group; they don't have the same resources or infrastructure we can offer," said a man with a voice that seemed certainly American.

"Remember how we fared in the war for New Al-Andalus? We took more territory in two days than you took in a whole year for Australia. The outback proved a greater threat for your men than the Central March was for us," Ivan shot back with arrogance.

"Your lot always resort to actions that try to cut in our share and are much harder to explain to the media," replied a British voice from a woman whose voice carried itself.

"Fate is shifting towards our side and if Haladi is slated as the one to bring about our final victory then he will have our full backing for one final crusade to achieve lasting security," said Ivan.

"Just wait till you see some of the things we've cooked up for Italy and the people unfortunate enough to resist the gall of the French state!" an obnoxious, sharp French voice.

"Leopold, you always were a passionate one. I think Egypt has something for everyone. We are a friend to the current order; we are just looking to fill our spot," said Verona, with a sudden hint of annoyance.

Scott could hear her tapping her heel and then she noticed Jerrod was standing there just past the doorway.

Jerrod was ushered in and he quickly closed the door behind him. Scott finally took a seat and checked his phone. Nothing was new so he put it back in his pocket. He took a few deep breaths - he probably was not meant to hear that. The more he made himself a target the worse off he would be. He had so many questions but so little time to process any of it before he had to move on.

"She is ready for you," said Jerrod.

Scott entered Verona's office. It was big - with her desk sitting in front of the back window and a bar stocked with all the alcohol you could imagine. A couch and three chairs sat in front of the bar and several bookshelves took up much of the remaining space. Scott could only see one entrance to the room and yet Verona was alone in her office. She sat at her desk with her feet up and a high heel barely hanging off her right foot. Scott made eye contact with Verona's dark green eyes and approached her desk. Her perfume overwhelmed his senses.

"Scott, I've read some of your work and it's very good. Always a pleasure to have a well renowned author visit our library," said Verona, taking her feet off the desk.

"Thank you, that is very kind. Can I.." Scott started to ask.

"Can you know why I have called you here, yes. We will get to that. I want to know why you are here in Cairo?" asked Verona, motioning for him to take a seat.

"Business. I work for the United Nations and my latest job is conducting an interview and then reporting back to the General Assembly," he replied, taking a seat.

Verona smirked.

"I know. I know you've been sent here to interview Mashir Khan. I want to know why you're here, Scott. Are you seeking Fame? Money? Love? " she asked, emphasizing that last word.

"I'm just here to do my job. I have the interview which should only last about a week and then I'll be heading back," responded Scott.

"Your job.... interesting... Have you ever met a Nill before today, Scott?"

"Not in person but I have read about them, watched documentaries, seen interviews and panels about their history," he replied.

"Mashir and Yolen may seem warm on the surface but the Nill don't reveal themselves to just anybody. They put on a facade and portray themselves as the innocent instead of the disease to our society they have become. "Nill Tuberculosis as they say," said Verona, with an intensifying look of hatred and anger.

Scott didn't know what to say. He couldn't fully process what she was saying in the moment.

"I don't want to get bogged down in rhetoric and politics. I have something far more important for you," Verona said, flirtatiously smiling at Scott.

They heard a knock at the door and Jerrod's voice could barely be made out.

"Come in!" yelled Verona, rolling her eyes.

Jerrod entered the room and walked over towards her desk.

"Haji is on line three for you," said Jerrod.

"Again? I just talked with him. Alright, thank you Jerrod. Let him know I'll be right with him," Verona answered, audibly and visibly frustrated.

Jerrod left and silence enveloped the room. Verona made eye contact with Scott.

"So why did you want to see me?" asked Scott.

"We know how impactful the U.N.'s reports can be to the world. Cairo being the location of your interview provides a wonderful opportunity to showcase the strength and beauty of our city and nation. I know that you were using your drone camera to record footage around the city and while that's wonderful it isn't necessary. We wanted to provide the footage for your presentation, to present our nation correctly."

Scott was surprised to hear this was the request. Why would he be asked to agree to this?

"I'm not really sure I understand," Scott responded, hoping that playing dumb will help him gather more information

Verona started to laugh as she got out of her seat. She walked around and sat on the desk, just in front of Scott.

"Our President has had issues in the past with media and extranational groups misrepresenting the reality in our great nation. Terrible lies have been spread about the treatment of certain people and we don't understand why. We want to make sure that we can show to the world that we treat everyone equally and fairly under the law," said Verona, making direct eye contact with Scott.

Scott didn't feel anything behind her eyes. She seemed empty like a rotting carcass. She was alive, of course, but it all seemed manufactured and intentional - an opportunist looking to make as much money as she could and maybe get a cheap thrill along the way. Her energy was all over the place.

"What if the footage you provided didn't match the needs of the presentation?" Scott cautiously asked.

Verona laughed to herself as she stood up.

"You'll be appropriately compensated for your compliance and maybe even inappropriately," said Verona in a hushed tone. She leaned down and kissed Scott on his cheek.

She walked around him and slowly massaged his shoulders.

"Non-compliance, while an option, isn't exactly ideal. You are a free man after all," Verona said while using her finger to slowly slide across Scott's throat.

"This comes from the very top. Don't disappoint me Scott."

She walked over to the door and opened it. Scott stood up, turning toward the door.

"We will gather the necessary files and get them to you in the next few days. I can't wait to see you again Scott," said Verona, winking at Scott with a smirk.

Scott nodded and left the office in a hurry. Thoughts continued to flood into his mind. Why would he be asked to use specific footage? What's the harm in letting me use my own? What did they know that I don't?

Mixed in with these potentially frightening questions was his feelings on Verona herself. Scott obviously found Verona beautiful and yet Scott wasn't convinced by her advance. He was thinking about Zara and the amazing time he had with her the night before. He could resist Verona but what about the request itself? Scott knew compliance was the easy option and the most likely to not cause him any harm. He wondered if he would be causing more harm by compliance than by defiance.

He made his way back out into the lobby and continued exploring the halls. He found a window by the end of a hallway and looked outside. He could see a few nearby streets filled with different shops and restaurants. He saw other people walking up and down the sidewalks enjoying the nice weather. He looked over to his right and something caught his eye. He could see a group of people carrying papers and baseball bats walking up towards a shop. On their shirts was an Eagle carrying a sword and flag, along with the words "Haladi Forever!" One of them took their bat and smashed it in the front window.

A second swing made sure every shard left the frame. The sound of breaking glass echoed out into the city - a piercing noise that Scott would be hearing for the rest of the afternoon. Two others picked up some rocks and threw them into the shop. The last person took one of their signs and stuck it onto the front door. It was hard to make out but it appeared to read "Attention Alien!" with a cartoonishly ugly depiction of a Nill. The group stood in place and turned towards each other.

"We will not be replaced! Haladi Forever!" they chanted in unison.

As the group walked off the shopkeeper slowly walked out while trying to avoid being seen. He was a Nill dressed with a white apron over his black shirt and brown pants. He seemed to be an Orange Nill like Yolen. He had a broom in hand and started to try and sweep up the debris. Suddenly another rock was hurled at the shop striking the shopkeeper in his shoulder. He recoiled and ran into his shop shutting the door behind him as a few more rocks rained in. Scott was appalled by what he was seeing but he couldn't be surprised. Similar behaviors and sentiments were held in his own country. He had seen this same situation play out many times. Scott took a few drinks of his water and began to make his way towards the interview area. He took the time to sit down and start reviewing his notes that he had taken. Seven full pages of notes and he knew they had only scratched the surface of what would be discussed. Mashir and Yolen arrived back in the room and took their seats near Scott.

"So, where were we Scott?" Mashir said excitedly

"As a Nill, what did a day look like for the typical citizen?" responded Scott.

"We operated on an economic system largely resembling that of current day Earth's; where the means of production are owned privately by the capitalist class and they hire workers to operate the machines and forces of production to create products and earn them money while giving a small portion of that to the worker as a wage. As society and industry expanded, it became harder and harder to avoid the system - it encroached everywhere. Just about every aspect of our existence has been commodified and monetized in one form or the other. The homes we lived in, the food we ate and drank, the tools we used to create things and build more complex things. All things are made by workers and over time the many different groups of artisans, craftsmen and peasants, among many others, formed into the collective working class, who now required a wage to survive, because how else would he pay for his home, his food, or even his health insurance. This kind of setup was more progressive than prior systems where you had no choice of who your lord was. In this system you could choose who your master was and yet that doesn't make being a slave any more freeing," said Mashir.

Scott was letting it all sink in. He waved for Mashir to continue.

"This kind of pressure on everyone to find a way to make more money led to the most vicious and psychopathic behavior imaginable. People would turn on lifelong friends for a few dozen bucks if it meant they weren't living on the street for another night. Crime, poverty, and homelessness are all caused by the failure of the system to care for its people. Our planet failed us because it valued growth for profit's sake and eventually every bubble will burst. People went hungry while we threw out millions of tons of food every day. The media, leaders and even trusted officials in the community were weaponized to convince the public that things were just like this! It is the natural order of life as a Nill and that we have always operated like this. The reality is that adoption of this system was relatively recent in our history and we could have turned back or changed course at several points. It is perhaps the main culprit for why I am sitting here on Earth with you today."

"What made you see through the lies they were telling you?" asked Scott

"I read history books by well read and credible historians. I talked to people in the real world and from a wide range of communities. I tried to learn new things everyday and never be so confident in myself that I wasn't open to reevaluating what I already think I know. So often I find that I am rethinking my thoughts on something I was steadfast about five years prior. The material, real world conditions that we experience on a daily basis are the main influence on us. Even the sharpest and most profoundly seductive propaganda can't override what we deal with in person. The effects of the system impacted my friends, family, community; At a certain point it became kind of crazy to not want something different. What that could be was always the question and history has a way of showing us the pathway." Mashir said, taking another sip from his drink.

"I can't wait to hear more on that subject. I know Earth has found its share of answers to many of Capitalism's worst features. Even on Nilleon it seems the spectre of Communism haunted the elites," Scott proposed.

"It was the most common boogeyman of them all and they wouldn't have known one if it smacked in the head with a hammer," Mashir said with a hint of exasperation.

"Before the fall of the planet was it an expected event? Or did it arrive as a surprise?" asked Scott.

"The last two hundred years seem clear enough now although the last fifty would be when we knew we were in the middle of something truly apocalyptic. Everything seems obvious in hindsight and yet some of us knew at the time. We were warning them for decades and decades and they ignored us. They would not risk losing out on the short term profits that their actions would bring. It didn't matter to them that in the long term they would have to find a new planet to live on," said Mashir.

"I will try to lighten the mood a bit. I love what you've said so far. We'll revisit this vein at some point. If you have any good follow up texts I'd love some names," Scott said, flipping through other pages of his notes.

"I'll have Yolen dig up my reading list."

Mashir looked over at Yolen, who was nodding in acknowledgment.

"Earth has spectator sports to entertain the masses. Did Nilleon have anything similar?" asked Scott.

Mashir responded by giving a hearty laugh.

"Oh yes, plenty of so-called sports. We referred to them as platines. One of my favorites was one where you had a cube and you had to touch the other player with it and then they would have to run around with the cube to tag others," said Mashir.

"Sounds pretty similar to sports some of our cultures play,"

"Nilleon and Earth had much in common. One of our mythologies actually believes that Earth and Nilleon are twin planets, that only recently as of four billions years ago split apart. The idea being that Earth is actually part of Nilleon and that caused the slight differences in our cultures," said Mashir.

Scott was surprised. That seemed like a big find, maybe he could write a whole book on just that topic.

"How common was that belief held?" he asked

Mashir started to laugh, almost chuckling.

"That is a relatively recent phenomenon not believed until after we came in contact with humans and those who belong to them are considered to be in a cult. They fund the media to portray them in a positive light and they have many of those in power on their payroll. Some of the most famous Nill you know are part of the group," responded Mashir.

"So not too serious like the flat earth movement?" Scott replied.

"It still amazes me that your species is exploring the cosmos and yet some still believe the planet is flat. Who are we supposed to be in that equation?" asked Mashir.

"Depending on who you ask; someone either created you or paid you to be there and to lie to us about your planet. It is quite the commitment that I could not do it." said Scott.

The two of them laughed for a few moments and Yolen chimed in.

"We had a group of people on Nill who believed in the pancake theory where our planet was stacked on top of three other planets and that when we dug underground we entered the next planet, complete with an atmosphere and sky."

Yolen's voice was a bit raspy but even his monotone delivery was effective.

"How big of a movement were they?"

"Maybe a few hundred thousand across the planet it was not very large. They were disproved very quickly by our top scientists and even the miners in their hometown. Suddenly the list of people in on the conspiracy tripled and they never gave up. You have gotta admire the passion," answered Yolen.

"Thank you. Many people on Earth will get a kick out of that one. On that subject; What is humor like in your culture? What constitutes comedy for you?" he asked.

Mashir started laughing and looked at Yolen with a look that clearly represented some shared knowledge. They both chuckled and proceeded to calm down quickly.

"The Nill have many kinds of humor with different aspects depending on individual groups or countries. It varies between situational and generic jokes and would often require a knowledge of the local culture to properly understand. I found one of the more popular was the sarcastic and self-deprecating type. Jokes based on the structure or sound of words and even making light of otherwise unfortunate situations. A sort of dark comedy if you will. And for Earth?" responded Mashir.

Scott laughed on the inside so much so that it almost caused him to laugh on the outside.

"Humans are quite similar and I personally enjoy those kinds of humor. Globalization and Social Media also led to the many methods with which comedy expanded ten fold." answered Scott.

"That's interesting, perhaps you could tell me a joke?" asked Mashir.

Scott took a moment to contemplate what joke to tell an alien. What joke could he tell an alien that he would be able to understand with only a relatively basic knowledge of human culture. It can't be too specific otherwise he won't understand the joke.

"I'm on a seafood diet. I see food and I eat it," joked Scott.

Mashir took a moment and then started to laugh, continuing for well over a minute.

"That's a good one, yes. Thank you." Mashir said.

Scott laughed to himself and took a moment to wipe some sweat from his forehead. Mashir finished laughing and calmed down.

"So how often did the countries on your planet get involved in diplomatic affairs?" asked Scott.

"Not often enough."

Mashir laughed for a solid five seconds on this one and slapped what would be a human's knee twice.

"Earth has the United Nations where the diplomats of every nation try their best to address world concerns without war or violence. It's actually named and inspired after a similar organization that was formed in the twentieth century that attempted to serve the same purpose," said Scott.

"What happened to the original United Nations?" asked Yolen.

"After nearly a century of relative global peace the superpowers of the world shifted and the system built to maintain that global peace failed and dragged us into war. The organization was largely symbolic and pointless. Its actions and statements no longer meant anything and they were dissolved," responded Scott.

"When they created the new version why did they feel things would go differently this time?" asked Mashir.

"Our leaders felt that the previous wars had become so terrible and so destructive that for our continued existence on this planet we would have to come together in some way to prevent a war like that from ever happening again. This hasn't been the case and wars are still happening that are killing millions every year. On top of the standard death toll numbering tens of millions caused just by the design of our system. Despite all of that the world likes to tell itself that we are in a new era of prolonged peace," replied Scott.

"Nilleon had a similar group known as the United Pact of Nilleon, or the U.P.N. They were mostly for show and didn't do much to help the nations that truly needed it. They would offer support and aid to smaller nations as a show of good faith but it never solved the issues because the larger nations siphoned money and resources out of the smallest ones," said Mashir.

"That sounds remarkably similar. To shift focus a bit, do you have any story, myth, tale, or anecdote to tell us about Nill culture?" Scott asked.

Mashir took a few moments to gather his thoughts and choose a story to respond with.

"One morning back in the days when the Aeroten empire ruled most of the civilized world the order came down from the palace for the occupation of a certain cliffside community by the name of Torla. They gathered an army numbering in the hundreds of thousands and marched them for seven days and seven nights. The Torla were a warrior culture and everyone fought in their army once they became adults. The Torla side was led by a warrior named Tupin whose army numbered merely in the tens of thousands yet when they clashed with Aeroten they held on far longer than anyone expected. The citizens of the Torla community managed to gather everything that was essential and they moved their camps to a nearby cave system built for this situation. They left booby traps and ambush squads to defeat and surround the Aeroten. This worked perfectly and they encircled the Aeroten army proceeding to slaughter them. Over four hundred thousand casualties on their side alone; It was a tragedy in a modern context but seemingly justified by the times' politics. Their empire collapsed because they failed at the occupation of a small city state," said Mashir.

Scott took a moment to take in the story and understand what Mashir was saying.

"Wow, that was an interesting story to process. I'll have to sit with that for a bit," he said.

"Absolutely. It is one of the more popular tales from our early era. The Aeroten eventually rose again and was an important nation all the way until the collapse," responded Mashir.

"How often did empires on Nilleon bring about their own demise? Was it often outside threats or internal?" asked Scott.

"Both would be the honest answer. I saw plenty of both just in my own lifetime and plenty more in the history books. I will say that the worst collapses and the most dangerous situations would arise from internal struggles. Feuding leaders who would game the system and play politics would distract from real issues of substance to line their pockets and siphon everything they could from the nations they represented. These were the most despicable kind of beings and yet they were also the most popular. I've never seen so many follow those who had nothing but disdain for them," said Mashir.

"I have to say that sounds familiar and I wish it wasn't. It is a pity that the system forces people to make cutthroat decisions that will bring them immense joy and benefit to the few and mass suffering to all and chaos to the world," responded Scott.

Scott and Mashir spent another three hours or so discussing different aspects covering the basics of the Nill race. By the time 6:00 p.m. rolled around they were both ready to wrap up for the day. They gathered their things and all stood up out of their seats.

"Until tomorrow Scott,"

"Until tomorrow Mashir. Thank you, Yolen. Please be safe tonight," said Scott.

"Thank you, same to you," replied Mashir.

The two shook hands and Yolen shook hands with Scott as well. They left the room promptly and Scott remained alone in the room. He had collected twenty seven pages of notes on just the basics of the Nill race and their planet. He was looking forward to the rest of the interview. He could always go back over the tape as well to continue adding more to his notes. He could only write so fast and with his handwriting being so poor; the digital copy of events added to his ability to correct his notes. Scott made sure he had collected all his equipment and made his way out of the library. He checked his messages and noticed a message from Zara. He pressed play on his phone and the audio began playing in his ears.

"Hey I'm getting off work now. Should I meet you at your place or?"

Scott smiled. He pressed a button to reply on his phone and raised it towards his mouth.

"Yeah that sounds great. I'll be there shortly; leaving my interview now."

A few moments went by and then a ding was heard. Zara had liked his message. Scott put his phone in his pocket and continued on the way towards the street. He had a ride pre-scheduled ready to take him to the hotel and it was waiting for him. This android was just as advanced as the last, which confused Scott but he decided to let it go.

"Krystal Hotel?" asked the android.

The android had a more rough sounding and less outgoing voice.

"Yes, thank you," Scott responded.

The android gave him a strange look and opened the door for him. Scott jumped inside and they headed towards the hotel. The ride was smooth and he noticed a protest occurring outside of a movie studio. Police on one side and protesters with signs on the other. If he remembered correctly this was due to the movie studio having a relationship with an authoritarian state that was committing genocide. This wasn't a new phenomenon on Earth and thought about asking Mashir if anything similar had happened on Nilleon. He saw a police officer use a baton and beat down on one of the protesters. Seven or so more protesters rushed the officer and then gunshots were fired by nearby officers.

"Let's be extra precautious," said the android.

The android pressed a few switches and the windows were covered up with bullet proof material. Scott felt uncomfortable but not in a scared or frightened way. The driver sped up and took a few back roads to avoid the traffic congestion. Police vehicles rushed past them on the other side of the road heading towards the scene of the protest. Civilians on the streets were rushing from the scene looking to find a way to safety. The rest of the ride went by fast as a blur and they arrived back at the Krystal Hotel. He stepped outside of the ride and began walking towards the door.

"Hey, Scott."

Scott stopped in his place and slowly turned around. The android was sticking a small card out of the window.

"What's this?" he asked.

Scott seemed confused. He grabbed the card anyway and looked at it. It had a phone number along with a name and the same red hand gripping globe symbol that he had seen on the android stewardess.

"We know who you are. Call us. We want to talk with you," said the android.

That voice sounded slightly different as if it was being streamed in from a different area.

"What would we be talking about?" asked Scott.

"All I can say is we need your help. Just give us a call and say the phrase 'wound my heart with a monotonous languor'. We'll explain everything you need to know from there," replied the android.

Scott felt uneasy and unsure of how to respond.

"Okay, I will," said Scott.

Scott nodded at the android who pulled his arm back in the ride and left. Scott wasn't quite sure what he was getting into but he didn't want to let this ruin the rest of his night. He entered the hotel and made his way through the lobby where he noticed Zara was waiting for him.

"Hey, how did it go?" she asked.

Zara was wearing a flared red skirt and a tight black top. She looked radiant.

"It went really well! I have a lot of notes to go over. Would you want to grab something to eat?"

"Yeah, I'm starving. We could order in and rent a movie?" Zara asked.

"That sounds perfect. Let's head upstairs," Scott nodded as he held his arm out.

Zara took his arm as they made their way to the elevator. This elevator ride took extra long due to three other floors being stopped at by hotel guests, which annoyed the two but not enough to ruin the night. They finally arrived at their floor and entered the room. They laid down on the bed, embracing for a few sweet moments before Zara turned on the TV and Scott grabbed his phone.

"What should we order? Chinese? Italian?" he asked.

"I like bread," Zara laughed and slapped his leg.

"I like bread too. How about Italian?" asked Scott.

"Works for me. I love breadsticks," Zara affirmed, drawing out "love."

"I'll get right on that," Scott winked.

She laughed at Scott's teasing and searched the television for a movie.

"What kind of movie would you want to watch?" she asked.

"I like all kinds of movies. How about something light like a comedy?" he responded.

"Works for me! I love comedies. Action movies too," she said.

"Action's pretty cool. Pick whatever you want," he said.

They continued their tasks and by the time Scott had finished ordering food; Zara had picked out a movie.

"The Last Bilton," said Scott, a little puzzled.

"Have you seen it before?"

"I've heard it's good. It's just a little historically inaccurate," responded Scott.

"Oh really how?"

"They portray the Bilton family as this wealthy yet charitable family. They would donate petty sums of money in the tens of thousands to charities while skimming billions off their labor force," said Scott.

"I always thought they were pretty good people, most of us did. Even in school they taught us about them being charitable," said Zara.

Scott nodded and sighed a little bit.

"That's a major issue in our schools. They force feed misinformation for generations and eventually the kids who were born on the propaganda become the teachers and believe in it whole-heartedly. This bleeds into our popular culture too. That's why we have movies that portray historical figures in more respectful ways instead of accurately. They wash over the bad deeds and recycle the same garbage talking points that you hear on their propaganda networks," Scott said.

Zara gave Scott a look and smiled.

"I like it when you get nerdy," said Zara.

"Nerdy? It's my job!" exclaimed Scott.

"I know. You're just cute when you go off on a tangent," responded Zara.

Scott laughed as he embraced Zara. He planted a gentle kiss on her lips and smiled as he gazed into her eyes.

"Thank you. The food should be here soon. Let me look for a different movie, maybe one that is less propaganda," said Scott.

He stole the remote from Zara's hand and laughed as she pouted. She immediately reached for it back.

"Oh, no no, not so fast," said Scott playfully.

The two wrestled to win control over the remote, not stopping until the food arrived. Scott grabbed the food from the doorstep and brought it to the table. They feasted on pasta and breadsticks before retreating back to the bed. Scott ended up choosing the movie - a light-hearted comedy.. He pressed play on the remote as Zara snuggled up to him.

"Which state has the most streets? Rhode Island!"

Zara and Scott cackled as the main character of the movie, a comedian, performed a stand-up act. After a few moments, Scott paused the movie to ask Zara a question..

"Zara, tell me more about yourself. You mentioned your mother earlier but what about the rest of your family?"

"My father was in the Army but he left us a few years before I left for France," answered Zara.

"I'm sorry to hear that. I'm sure that was tough for you," Scott sympathized.

"It always hits me in waves. I won't think about him, then I get upset at him. Then, I get angry and question why he left us. I know his time in the army was hard, but I never forgave France for what they did to my father. That trauma lived with him and it is burdening me now. Then I think of the good times and smile," she confessed.

"I hope you don't mind me asking, but why did he leave?" he asked, hoping to not have set off a minefield.

Zara took a deep breath and couldn't help but wipe away a few tears that appeared.

"The trauma of his army deployment and all the issues stemming from that cause him to take his own life. When I was younger I felt like he was selfish and could never understand how he could leave us behind. Why would he do that to his wife and to his child?"

Zara took a few moments to let out tears before continuing

"I found a letter my mother wrote after he passed -I won't repeat it verbatim cause I don't know if my heart can take it - but one line that always sticks out to me was 'I will take care of her and love her enough for the both of us. That I believe in with all my heart, just like I believe you love me, no matter how much I miss you.' She also said that the loss of her best friend 'left a hole in her heart that could never be replaced.' She would spend her time loving her only daughter because that was what was left of him on this earth. It broke my heart to know the pain she must have felt. What she was able to do for us in the time after was nothing short of superhuman. She was an amazing mother and I miss her more than anything in this universe."

Scott teared up as Zara let out the rest that she had.

"I have a similar experience with the loss of my parents. I know it isn't easy to get past and it takes time. Even when you think you have moved on it's okay to let the emotions hit you intensely. Feel the rage and feel the sadness. They are never gone if you are still thinking about them. I don't know about you but I see them in my dreams from time to time. I cherish it every time as a gift - a gift that my mind wanted to give to me. I think it's a beautiful thing we have in life," he smiled, his cheeks as red as sand dunes.

"I appreciate you sharing what you have with me and I can't wait to learn more. The emotions were hard for me and none of it was easy. You have a good mindset, don't let that go. I had to tell myself to keep going. The loss of my father left my mother with my two brothers and I. They're both younger by a few years and we have never really gotten along. They just wanted to argue and fight anyone who tried to reason with them. It made family gatherings a pain for all involved," said Zara.

"When did you last hear from them?"

"It's been a while. When it's my brothers it's mostly propaganda that they regurgitate to anyone who will listen and when it's my mother she is just paranoid. I tried to convince her to come with me but she refused and told me that she had to look after my brothers," replied Zara.

"What sort of propaganda?"

"Mostly conspiracy theories about who is behind the fall of the kingdom which are usually blaming it on the always rotating ethnic group choice of the week. It makes me sick and I can barely stand them even though they're my family," said Zara.

"I know it's tough but if it is that tough I wouldn't blame you for cutting ties with them. You can only take so much before you hit your limit. I've had friends that would constantly buy into conspiracies that started to get wackier and more unfounded until it was pure insanity."

"I know it's just tough. Talking about it does help though thank you," Zara said with a soft smile.

"Of course. I'm glad I could help."

"I do want to see them again; at least my mother but I don't know when I'll get the chance. They've been on a lockdown for the last seven months and it doesn't seem like they'll open up any time soon. I just hope they're okay."

Scott wrapped his arm around her and gave her a hug. He rested his head on the side of hers and sat there for a moment while holding her.

"I'm sure they'll be okay. Hopefully the lockdown will lift soon and you can talk with them."

Zara smiled and gave Scott a kiss.

"I'm starting to get tired, let's lay down for the night," Zara said.

They laid down and Zara quickly fell asleep. The lights dimmed once it detected the absence of motion and Scott took some time to reflect on his day. Scott thought about the following day and what questions he would ask in the interview. He thought about the card from the driver and why they would want to speak with him. He thought about the Nill shopkeeper being harassed by those Haladi fanatics. That kind of behavior was starting to seem more and more accepted in Cairo and Scott couldn't help but to fear what that would mean for the refugees seeking a home. He tried to focus on the good, but these thoughts kept his mind racing for a while until eventually he passed out.

CHAPTER EIGHT

Vibrations from the alarm spread throughout the room, waking both Scott and Zara at 8:30 a.m. They did not want to wake up yet and mutually agreed in silence to sleep in until 9:00 a.m. This seemed to be a pretty common thing for them and Scott usually set multiple alarms in the morning anyway. Scott held Zara close and felt a rush of blood through his heart that he hadn't felt in a long time.

He had dreamed of a different time in the past when war had torn the world apart. He imagined he was on a battlefield of the First World War and was overlooking a charge over the top. The dirtiness of war surprised him - the blood, the guts, the ugliness of war. He saw men who simply were doing their jobs, convinced to sacrifice their blood for the bottom lines of wealthy companies glazed in nationalistic propaganda and animalistic fervor. The decision to lose so many due to the politics of drawing maps and assigning resources is a crime that has been perpetrated for far too long. The dividing lines were artificial and treated as ancient - gunned down by the most advanced technology of the time and yet these machines of war were nothing compared to the modern iterations that were active throughout the galaxy.

He awoke again right before his alarm. He turned it off and woke Zara. They decided they would get an early breakfast together and go about their days. They took a shower together before getting dressed. Scott decided to dress a bit more casual today and wore one of his comfy dress shirts. Zara wore the same black shirt as the night before and paired it with a light blue skirt, making Scott's heart skip a beat as he observed her beauty.Scott wondered what made him so lucky to be with a woman as beautiful as Zara.

Wait a minute - *was* he with her? What did that even really mean? He wanted to keep seeing her, but he didn't live in Cairo. What would that mean for the two of them?

"So would you want to get dinner again tonight? We could go out somewhere," Scott asked hopefully.

Zara smiled and embraced Scott's arm.

"I'd love that. I'll meet you in the lobby and I'll let you choose the place."

"Sounds perfect," said Scott, planting a gentle kiss on Zara's forehead.

They finished getting ready, gathered their items, and made their way out of the room to get breakfast at a nearby restaurant. The restaurant was recommended for its extraordinary waffles, Scott's favorite breakfast food. This left him no choice but to investigate. They waited outside the hotel for their ride. Scott opened the door for Zara and closed it behind her. He hopped in on the other side. The driver took them down a different set of streets than the last time. As they continued along the road they went past a kitchen that served the homeless with a line stretching out the door and down the block. This was an all too common sight in Cairo and in many cities receiving an influx of refugees. Haladi and his advisors had not made any effort to help ease the struggles of the working class despite the early promises. Many even in his advisory circles felt that they had to throw a bone somewhere, yet he did not listen. Ultimately, these members would be silenced, banished, executed, or retired into conformity before their deviation from the Haladi line would be seen publicly. His grip on power had to be absolute. His appeal to the average Egyptian meant they wouldn't blame him for the issues with Haladi's administration. That fell to his council, advisors and department heads; while Haladi enjoyed an almost foundational status as the leader of a return to form bringing them to a status that Egypt enjoyed in its heyday. This of course was ahistorical and not a reflection of any time period that is relevant to our current society. The current economic system had been crushing Egypt for centuries and this imagined past that Haladi alluded to was nothing more. People wanted something to believe in and they felt proud to aspire to be something that never was. It's a foundational principle of a fascist movement and one that is all too familiar to Scott. The echoes of his home here were loud and he could see the influence of his own society on this one. Unemployment was at an all time high rate and the President spent his time in his two hundred and thirty-five million dollar mansion outside the city. Job programs had been promised during his campaign and yet, once he reached power, he did not give the people another thought until he needed something from them. All of Haladi's cabinet had abused their powers while in office and this was the latest victim of that policy. As propaganda minister Atiyeh had used his proximity to Haladi to funnel money and resources from the programs meant to help the people into the pockets of Haladi, himself, and his closest friends and supporters. The ride turned down a street and drove past a convoy of military trucks twenty deep. Scott knew that tensions between Egypt and its neighbors were deteriorating, but he hadn't thought war was imminent. He just hoped that the city would be safe for the duration of his trip. After a few more minutes they arrived at the restaurant. It was a nice little place with what seemed to be French architecture. Scott wondered if it was an immigrant family running the business and, sure enough, and, sure enough, a French flag waived above the entrance. They approached the hostess who smiled at Scott.

"Hello! Will it be just the two of you today?" asked the hostess.

"Yes. A booth please," said Scott.

Scott nodded at the hostess while she grabbed two menu tablets and ushered them towards the booth. Zara followed behind Scott and they took their spots across from each other. The restaurant was filled with diverse people talking about different topics ranging from sports, movies, elections, and their daily lives. The noise was drowning out everything the hostess was saying to Scott. Zara nudged his arm to get his attention.

"What can I get you guys to drink?" asked the hostess.

Scott seemed startled as he had been staring off into space again.

"I'll take a glass of orange juice. She'll have whatever she wants."

He smiled at Zara.

"I'll have a glass of milk. Thank you."

She smiled back at Scott and grabbed his hand.

"Thank you, Scott. These past few nights have been great. I know you're here on business, but I want to spend more time with you while we can," said Zaras

Scott let out a huge sigh of relief. He had been worried about how to have this conversation with her.

"I feel the same way. I've had a great time and while we're here together, why not?" responded Scott.

Zara squeezed his hand and placed the other hand on top.

"I'm glad we're on the same page," she said.

The waitress walked up to the table and placed their drinks downShe then brought up her hand to write on a digital notepad.

"What can we make fresh for you today?" asked the waitress.

Scott had barely looked at the menu, but one glance at the section containing waffles was all he needed. He looked at Zara to see if she was ready. She looked at him and nodded her head.

"Go ahead," Zara said with a laugh.

"I'll have the waffle deluxe special with a side of bacon and eggs scrambled. Thank you."

He handed his menu tablet to the waitress. He handed his menu to the waitress, their fingers brushing together as she grabbed it.. Her finger was cold to the touch which caused Scott to realize that she was an android waitress. This model was the most realistic he had seen yet.

"I'll have the order of four pancakes with sausage and hashbrowns. Thank you,"

Zara handed her menu to the waitress who left promptly.

"Did you notice she was an android?" Scott whispered.

She looked back and forth for a moment at the fleeing waitress and Scott.

"I didn't. Is that a problem?"

"No! No, of course not. I just didn't realize right away. Generally you can just tell. That's the first time I couldn't tell until her finger was cold to the touch."

"I think you might be thinking too deep again. Let's enjoy breakfast," responded Zara.

Scott took a second and let the thoughts of androids leave his mind. Zara was right. Scott needed to calm down and enjoy his time with her. He had a full day ahead of him with the interview and today was the day he would start specific session topics. Today's topic would be about how the Nill people spent their lives along with their views on culture, faith, entertainment, writings, jobs, and power structures. Finally, the last bit

of work talk left his mind. He was in a nice restaurant with Zara and he wanted to enjoy

it. He noted the compassion and desire in Zara's eyes, something he hasn't seen in years.

He had felt that from his friend Tim but it wasn't the same.

"So hash browns... are you a big potato person?" asked Scott.

Zara giggled.

"You caught me red handed. I love potatoes of any kind," responded Zara.

Scott laughed and pumped his fist.

"I also love potatoes in every format. I'm a sucker for french fries and for hash

browns." said Scott.

"I'm glad we have that in common. Looks like most restaurants won't be hard

to decide on," Zara said.

"I'm usually not too picky although I have my favorites," Scott said.

"How has your interview been going?"

"It's been good so far. I think I really connected with Mashir so far and his

interpreter Yolen was also friendly. I really think if more people took the time to talk to

the Nill, they wouldn't be so afraid of them. I saw a group of Haladi supporters vandalize

a Nill shop and they started throwing rocks at the shopkeeper!"

Zara frowned and placed her hand on Scott's.

"Sadly, that's very common these days. His supporters have been fed lies and

they place the blame for their problems on the Nill and Bessians. They are pretty much

opposed to every kind of alien coming into the country. It's already pretty tough as it is

but the refugees are not getting any breaks," Zara empathized.

"It made me angry. No one deserves to be treated like that. I hope things can change because that sort of thinking spreads fast," he said.

Scott and Zara continued chatting while they waited on their food to arrive. The restaurant was pretty crowded and there was a television on the wall by the bar. A news report was running with a reporter conducting an interview in a studio. A woman with brown, short hair and an all black suit sat across from a thin, bearded man with dull black hair. He wore thin circular glasses and a blue suit with brown shoes.

"I'm joined today by Gregor Dittrich, former head of the conservative party in Germany and a newly appointed representative to the U.N. General Assembly. So the question on everyone's minds pertains to the asylum status of the Nill and Bessians. What are your thoughts on the crisis?" asked the reporter, extending her arm out with the microphone.

"Well first I want to start by thanking you for having me on Jan. It's a pleasure speaking to you again. I think the issue here boils down to who do we place our focus and attention on; our own citizens who were born on this planet or groups of people who were not born here. Some in the assembly don't want to see our resources used on aliens and see humans being left in the dust to fend for themselves," responded Gregor.

"Is it a matter of choosing one over the other? Couldn't we do more to help everyone, including those fleeing situations deemed too dangerous to stay in?" asked Jan.

"I don't think these types of gotcha questions provide any input into the larger conversation. Of course we want to help everyone that we can but there are certain realities we have to adhere to when handling these situations. We only have so much space, food, housing, supplies, medical equipment, et cetera. We do end up having to make tough decisions and I won't make a decision that will end up harming German people for the gain of others," answered Gregor.

"The U.N.'s General Assembly is holding a referendum on the issue of alien refugee asylum and legal status. The vote will determine if the U.N. will protect the right of Nill, Bessian, and other alien species to seek refuge on Earth. Have you decided how you will vote?" Jan questioned.

"I plan on looking at the facts and at both sides of the conversation. I haven't decided how I'll cast my vote but I think in my heart I know how I will vote," responded Gregor.

"Who do you support for chancellor in the upcoming election?" asked Jan.

"Well the field is crowded with many great people although I am partial to Mr. Viktor Pohl. He knows the German people well and knows what we desire! He knows that the scourge of communism still plagues our nation and that we need a call to action to wipe it from the earth!" responded Gregor.

Viktor Pohl was a politician in Germany who advocated for fascist and racist policies to bring about the greatness of Germany again. His supporters were numerous in number and loudly reacted violently to any negative news or stories being shared. Much like Haladi in Egypt or Silvius in America; these fascist strongmen have started gaining major support of the public and those in power by scapegoating Communism as a way to silence any labor militancy and demands to improve the conditions of workers across the world. They advocated for war because that would help them consolidate their power and allow for the eradication of their enemies. What would they be able to do to stop this brewing storm that approached?

Scott snapped back to reality as the waitress arrived with their plates and placed the food in front of them. Scott's eggs were a little light on salt so he grabbed a shaker and started to pour it on. Zara began with stabbing her fork into the sausage patty and taking a large bite out of it. The waitress returned with a box that had four different flavors of syrup in it. Scott chose his favorite and poured it on his waffles, making sure to soak every layer.

"Does everything look right?" asked the waitress.

The waitress had crossed her arms slightly in a fashion that seemed almost impossible for an android to recreate.

"Everything looks great thank you," answered Scott.

Scott began to cut into his food.

"So what made you decide to settle here in Cairo? It's very crowded."

Zara laughed and took a sip from her drink.

"It was less a choice and more settling. I was dropped off here by bus and was told that I had up to thirty days to find employment or shelter, otherwise I would be arrested. And the restaurant had a hiring sign in the window and that made my choice pretty simple," she responded.

"I see. Well I'm glad you ended up there, otherwise I never would have met you," Scott flirted

"I am too," Zara said with a soft smile.

After they finished their meals, they continued chatting for another twenty minutes until Scott's alarm went off. He needed to call to give his boss a status update before going to his next interview session. He paid for the meal and the two of them left. They entered the busy street filled to the brim with traffic. A hot air balloon traveled a mere five hundred feet in the sky before nearly crashing into a building. Scott and Zara kissed and went their separate ways. Scott walked down the street to meet his ride. He got inside and requested a second stop before the final destination, hoping to stop at the market to see if he could find a certain souvenir for Tim. The android complied with the request as it was required to by its programming. The only orders from a human it would not comply with are orders that would result in the death of another human. This was slightly modified to allow for androids to wage war and yet these instincts exist in every A.I. on earth. The ride made its way through the streets until they arrived at a novelty gift shop on a corner. He wanted to look around and told the driver it would be about ten minutes. He entered the shop and said hello to the android cashier who was taking instructions from its human boss. Scott walked up and down the aisles noticing different types of gifts -whoopie cushions, logo t-shirts, branded board games, collectible figures of every corporate brand in existence; all ways to funnel more money in the name of the corporations that rule our lives and our culture. He spotted a t-shirt with a popular video game character on the front from a game that he had played for years with Tim. They had probably spent upwards of fifteen hundred hours across every iteration of the game and yet this t-shirt would bring back all those memories for only twenty dollars. Scott didn't enjoy that so much of his and the earth's life was consumed by created brands and products of corporations, but it was hard to not go with the flow. It is easy to ride the waves as they hit you but it takes a truly unique mind to resist that on occasion and challenge the status quo. Scott grabbed the T-shirt and made his way to the counter. On the way over he heard a conversation between the boss and the cashier.

"That's the second refuel break you've taken since you got here," said the boss. The boss was wagging his finger and poking the android's face.

"I've been here for six hours. It was only for five minutes. No one even came in," responded the android.

The android had a defeated look on his face. His body language told Scott that he was almost ready to leave the job and never return.

"You can refuel on your time, not mine. Now help this gentleman," barked the boss.

Scott walked up to the counter and placed the shirt on the counter. The android instinctively grabbed it up and scanned it. He finished the transaction and let Scott scan his phone to pay for the shirt. Scott overheard one last conversation between the two as he left.

"I just got a message that Randy is coming in. We need to make this place spotless," said the boss.

"Oh perfect. I'll start sweeping," said the android.

The android seemed defeated at the prospect of this Randy; who he assumed was a higher-up that would be showing up to critique his work and praise anything positive in the name of the boss. Scott felt for the android and made sure to note the name of the business: Randy's Crafts and Gifts. He made his way back into the ride and they took off towards the library. Scott sat back in his seat and turned on the heated function to warm his body.

"Take the long way please. Arrive at 11:45 a.m. I'll be napping, thank you," Scott ordered.

The android nodded and shut the blinds of the ride. Scott proceeded to fall into a short nap; one that would refuel him and stave off the food coma he was entering. He didn't want to be lethargic for the interview, yet that may be the reality by the time he gets there. He woke from his nap as they pulled up to the library.

"We are here. Have a wonderful day," said the android.

Scott nodded at the android and stepped out of the ride. He made his way inside the library and started to consider what questions to open up the session with. He climbed each step faster than the one before it.

CHAPTER NINE

Mashir and Yolen awaited Scott in the library and were chatting amongst themselves when he entered. The mood seemed cheery and they waved at Scott as he walked up.

"Scott, how are you doing today?" Mashir asked.

"It's been a good day. I've been looking forward to the interview. How about you guys?" responded Scott, motioning to Yolen to chime in.

"My day has been good and my breakfast was delicious," answered Yolen.

Yolen refrained from sharing any more and let Mashir continue the conversation.

"My day has been good as well. I had the largest steak I've ever seen last night for dinner and it was delicious. I've been a little homesick but I don't think there is much I can do about that."

"I'm glad to hear that. So today's session will be a little bit more specific. I'll be asking questions regarding how your people spent their lives, how they felt about faith, culture, entertainment, writing, work, and other things like that," Scott said.

Mashir nodded and pulled out his own set of notes. Yolen pulled out his notepad and leaned over to show them to Mashir.

"I'm ready to begin as soon as you are," said Mashir.

Mashir invited Scott to sit down. Scott took a few moments to set up the camera and then got his notes out. He took a seat by the two of them and cleared his throat.

"What is the average lifespan for a Nill?" asked Scott.

"Healthy Nill not living in poverty or famine typically lived one hundred and twenty years."

Scott compared this to humanity's current life span which averaged one hundred and four years. This was unassisted of course. Humans now could live to the age of two hundred and fifty with the correct medical technology.

"How long if they are medically assisted?" asked Scott.

"Experimental technology was allowing for nearly a four-hundred-year lifespan in test subjects. The collapse arrived before they could publish their findings for development."

Scott wondered what a life of four hundred years might look like. He had family members about eleven or twelve generations back who saw the last millennium end and yet it was a foreign concept for most to think about. What kind of legacy would he leave for them then? How would they feel about what he was doing? Was it enough?

"How did your people measure time? On Earth we base the date around a specific year relating to the birth of Jesus, who was the central figure in the hegemonic religion of Earth. Every year after this point is considered Anno Domini or A.D. All years before that are considered before the common era and eventually A.D. went away in favor of C.E," said Scott.

Mashir started to laugh and looked over towards Yolen.

"We have something similar except it wasn't so specific to one specific religion. Our first four thousand years were before writing and anything post that time is considered our recorded history. We had sixteen thousand years of recorded history in which we were communicating as you and I do here," Mashir said, gesturing to Scott and the camera.

"What did the normal Nill day look like in your average country?" Scott asked.

"The majority were workers who spent 8-10 hours a day, sometimes longer, at their job earning a wage. What they earned was used to pay for their housing, health insurance, food, clothing, gadgets, toys, and everything you need for daily life. This isolated them from their family, their community, and the other workers who created the products that make our society operate. Those fortunate or wealthy enough to not have to work could spend their day enjoying the many fine aspects of modern life that were given to us by the workers. The enjoyment of the finer things was created out of blood, sweat, and tears. This divide and clash was clouded and distorted to make sure that the majority didn't realize how much more they have in common with each other than the wealthy elite. All elements of the media were used in this campaign and in many ways it was easier before you recognized it. Those who were under the legal working age would be sent to school to be given an education in theory but largely groomed for the workforce, military, college, or if they were lucky, a trade union."

"How many stages of education did most citizens achieve?" asked Scott.

"Usually just the basic and secondary levels. Opportunities for third and fourth level education were possible but mostly inaccessible to those without proper wealth. This caused a large emphasis on earning certificates from these programs to get higher paying jobs. This led to more applicants than jobs to be filled and the standard of living decreased. Eventually a credit system was introduced to try and offset this, although it only worsened the issue as the greed of the ruling class knew no bounds. After some time, multiple stages of revolution occurred and this caused the last one hundred years on Nilleon to be rather bumpy. Anyone with wealth or power was able to pay for protection but not if you couldn't spare the change," answered Mashir.

Scott liked that Mashir was starting to get more specific and go into topics without his guidance.

"What were Nill views on faith?"

"There were hundreds of faiths and mythologies that our peoples spent time worshiping. None of them were ever backed up by anything scientific or that would lead skeptics to believing in them. We spent so much energy arguing over who's mythology was better than the other. We fought wars and committed atrocities on a scale no one could dream of all because of an idealized version of an imaginary being that we preferred over a different version of the very same. It was the ultimate lack of respect for life. An imagined reality took precedence over those in front of us and this infected our governments, our courts, our policing, and our talking heads in the media. The counter argument would be that we were a cult of science and that we were closed minded to other options. I would argue that in most cases this was not the case or did not matter in the outcome," relayed Mashir.

Mashir took a moment to calm himself.

"I feel a similar way about human faith. What are some examples of putting this trust or faith in mythology leading to a negative impact for the Nill?" responded Scott.

Mashir's eyes lit up. He looked over at Yolen who gave a nod and took a deep breath.

"The reason why the orange Nill's are considered lesser is due to an ancient belief held for the last ten thousand years. The supposed origin story of our people is that Nill were split by the wealthy into three classes of Blue, Green and Orange, and the orange supposedly betrayed the blue and greens. Nothing historical or written from the time backs this report up yet the leaders of the time believed the churches who spoke of messages from god that stated the orange must be eradicated from the face of the planet. The blue and green drove them into subjugation for over two thousand years and we only freed them two hundred years ago. The grandchildren of these slaves are still around and they don't feel that it was so long ago. Our leader's speak of solidarity yet they just continue the same practices under different names and false pretenses," said Mashir.

Scott was at a loss for words. He looked over at Yolen who was struggling to hold back tears.

"I know this must be a tough subject. Yolen, if you have anything to say I would really want to hear your perspective on this subject," said Scott.

Yolen cleared his throat and wiped away tears.

"It's a very tough thing to reconcile with. I have friends on every side of many different cultures yet when I speak about what happened to my people it's treated like ancient history. The people in charge in the last days of the planet were those in charge when they begrudgingly granted us the basic freedoms that the green Nill's received. We were othered in ways that caused us to form our own communities, cultures, languages, and habits. I'll gather a full briefing of notes that can cover this topic in more depth. I think a certain subsect of your audience would appreciate it," responded Yolen, through a tsunami of tears.

Scott smiled and nodded at Yolen.

"I think so too. I look forward to reading it!"

Mashir embraced Yolen and placed a hand on his shoulder. He patted him a few times and whispered some words into his ear. They hugged and continued to cry together. After a few more moments of consoling they calmed themselves and took their seats again.

"How central was violence, warfare, and the idea of being a soldier in your culture?" asked Scott.

"From our earliest days it inhabited every aspect of our existence as it stemmed from the very evolutionary events that created our intelligence. We always find ways to disassociate, stigmatize, and brutalize each other instead of coming together. Our greatest triumphs have been overcoming this urge to give in to our primordial urges and vanquish one another from this life. Every tribe, city, state, empire had an army, as it was the tool by which you influenced the policy of other nations. That state which held the biggest army held the biggest sway and could mold his neighbors in his own image."

"Our two peoples truly have a god complex," Scott joked.

"Quite true and yet the concept itself has no use for us. We have evolved past the need to be subservient to a higher idea. We have the ability to mold things in this material universe and with that we become what we once thought were gods. We break out of the box we put ourselves in and ultimately robotic and android life that sprang up led to many questions. What did it mean for us if we created things that could then create things like we do? We quickly started to realize that we were not alone anymore and that we had to find a way to reconcile with this."

Scott took a moment to finish writing his notes and let him continue

"Propaganda was a tool used to recruit people to fight in the armed forces often using drummed up reasons of patriotic nonsense. The threat of the other from another nation or culture always loomed, whether that was a physical, emotional, spiritual, or material threat. The economic system ultimately exported jobs out of the major centers of industrialization and that led to a massive reliance on an underpaid class who did not share the same rights as the other workers. The wars that we fought were mostly for economic reasons and sometimes ideological ones. We pitted the workers and the everyday people of each nation against each other. The promise of glory, fame, money, sexual gratification could persuade for a time, yet the dirt, blood, and chaos of the battlefield showed that we truly are all the same. The wealthy elites are moving pieces on a board a thousand miles from the front while the population is sent into a meat grinder so that a few numbers can rise on someone's portfolio. A truly despicable system and one that many of us saw no reprehension in finding any remedy possible to transition away from it to a better system," said Mashir.

Scott made sure to write all of this in his notes and wanted to compare this to revolutions in the twentieth and twenty-first century.

"Humanity invented the television several centuries ago and it revolutionized things for a long time. When did Nill develop your version of this?" asked Scott.

"About three thousand years ago, give or take. Some communities had access to certain working prototypes and others didn't get wide access till over a century later. It became a method of control by which they bombard the population with advertisements, rhetoric, and propaganda messages. It was one of the most effective methods of propaganda ever invented until our version of your internet of course," said Mashir.

"How did your internet affect the culture? Humanity had quite the interesting response to the invention here on Earth," said Scott.

"It caused a continued lowering of the bar at which we viewed things to be real. The internet became a method of escape for those who were tired of the real world. This helped some and doomed others to never being able to fit in with the rest of society. A lot of misinformation spread across the internet and this would cause massive damage to social and political realms of our culture. Divisions were formed that were unable to be removed because we lent so much weight to these created and invented concepts. These things weren't natural yet we spent so much of our lives obsessed with them and then when they were used against us we felt like it was the end of our lives. We needed to realize our lives were not the same as what we experienced on the internet and by extension social media but a very specific window of what an idealized version of our lives could be. It was like a synopsis of our lives without all the context that makes things make sense," said Mashir.

"That's a very interesting way of looking at things, thank you for that." said Scott.

Scott continued to scratch on his notepad as Mashir answered his questions. Scott glanced at his phone and noticed they had been speaking for nearly an hour and a half.

"How about we take a ten minute break? I need to grab something to drink anyway," suggested Mashir.

"That sounds perfect. We shall return in ten minutes," Scott agreed.

Mashir and Yolen got up from their chairs and left the chamber. Scott pressed a button on the drone camera to pause the recording and left the room to visit the vending machine in the hall. He connected his phone to the machine and selected an image of a water bottle. Scott grabbed the cool water bottle from the reciprocal after finalizing his payment. This was exactly what Scott needed and the cold water soothed his throat. Talking for a living, whether to himself or to the person he was interviewing was tough on him. He did find the concept of a water bottle a little abhorrent, because of the pure monetization of a basic human need, but he wasn't going to win this fight on this day in Cairo. He finished off his water bottle and looked around to find a water fountain. After finding one he filled up the bottle and put it back in his satchel. He made his way back towards the library although he was a few minutes early. He pulled out his phone to check the news pages. The top story of the day was a political scandal in Germany; an elected official had direct ties to an ultranationalist group yet he refused to denounce the group for its racist beliefs and instead asked them to continue fighting the good fight. One half of the population couldn't see the clear messaging here and the other half was too tired of screaming about the politician for the other side to learn more. A swipe took him to the next story;a heavy discussion around police repression in Algeria and the lack of it being used on the European refugees as opposed to their own native born citizens. Scott closed his phone and decided that the news just wasn't for him today. He went back into the meeting room and turned the camera back on. Just as he took a seat, Mashir and Yolen returned from the break and took their seats again.

"How was your break? Hopefully you were able to stretch your legs," asked Scott.

Mashir and Yolen laughed and made a face that made Scott know they understood what he meant.

"It was good. Being stuck in one spot is never healthy for anyone, especially the older you get. Exercise is key even in small doses," said Mashir.

Scott nodded in agreement and flipped his notes to a new page.

"How was writing viewed in your culture?" Scott asked. "Humans have been writing books for centuries and that evolved with the advent of the internet and social media into several different formats."

"At first, writing was for those who wanted to keep records. The churches and Royalty or those adjacent to the Monarchy would write things down. A large amount of knowledge was stored and retained by the churches serving a vital function until they were later attacked and repressed throughout later centuries. Eventually as education improved and the rulers decided that just the ability to read wouldn't cause a revolution they let us start to learn to read and write. Books began to be published and eventually machinery and technology made it easy to spread works all over the world. Reading became a hobby and a way to spread messages and thoughts across time. Our history was helped by the advent of books and our ability to stave off our own destruction was helped by our ability to warn the future generations in our writing. What we write about through the veil of the future are the struggles of the present caused by the mistakes of the past. Not learning from the past is the biggest mistake any living being in the universe can make," Mashir responded.

"I think a lot of people would find that viewpoint fascinating and inspiring. Thank you for sharing that," said Scott.

"One common event that occurred would be book burnings. The complete rejection of academia because of a lack of understanding and the fear of the other. They were convinced that trying to improve your intellect was a rejection of tradition and the mythologies they build their lives around. The governments of certain countries even supported this and would ban certain books from being read for their anti-government messages. It is also important to remember what books in particular were burned because that will reveal the thought or ideology they are trying to suppress. We also must not forget because that is exactly what they want us to do;believe that whatever message they were trying to spread was not being talked about or even existed at that time," said Mashir.

"Was a guarantee of free speech common in your society?"

"It was in the sense that a stated law was that we had free speech yet if what we said was considered a threat to national security we could lose all of our rights and be tried as a radical traitor. Naturally, most people fell in line. This was given to us under the guise that it was increasing our freedoms and that we wouldn't fall apart like the countries we fought. The truth was somewhere in the gray and that the opposite of our system wasn't perfect just like ours. There weren't only two options and constantly shoving your position against another to simply bump up your position never solves any issue. It muddies the water continually and changes the argument and just means that you can't think of any rational defense for your position," responded Mashir.

"That sounds familiar to Earth. Free speech is a concept but it's very difficult to enact in a way that the oligarchs don't feel threatened," said Scott.

"Our media was usually censored as well. Not in the traditional sense however. The financial incentives to showcase military or government-approved materials outweighed the desire to appeal to the antithesis of those organizations. So we could produce media that criticized our leaders yet we would earn almost no money for this. They would also tax us for this but usually no one got to that point in the first place. My home nation managed to convince the majority of citizens that other nations doing this was propaganda and an example of a police state, yet our nation doing so was considered being patriotic. I never bought into that and always felt that if it was wrong in one place it was wrong here too. I wish more of my people felt that way and maybe we could have avoided some of the mistakes of the collapse," Mashir stated.

Mashir started to tear up. Scott paused to allow Mashir to process his emotions. Yolen consoled him and patted him on the back. A few minutes later, they calmed down and were ready to continue the interview.

"Earth has a concept of imperialism where a Nation will conquer other lands and peoples with force to extract resources and value for profit. The true intent was to carve the world up for themselves between the corporations and capitalists. The cult of capital worshiped itself and reshaped the world in its image. Did Nill have anything of that sort?" asked Scott.

Mashir nodded and chuckled heavily.

"Imperialism could be the subtitle for the history of Nilleon. Every piece of sand on the planet has been colonized in one way or another over the millenia. Even after we ended the appearance of militaristic imperialism we had economic imperialism and also diplomatic imperialism. Different empires had different methods yet all of them usually came back to the tried and true method of invading a country and leaving a substantial force behind to police the citizens of the conquered nation. When the local populace would naturally rise up it was forcibly put down time after time even though they just wanted to make their own decisions for their communities. The flag they walked under did not truly concern them if they had their lives and families safety guaranteed. Some charismatic leaders took advantage of this and convinced some groups to help the colonizers colonize their home. The promises made were not kept because promises made are never kept when it comes to politicians. Another great lie that those in power convinced us of is that putting a despot in a suit doesn't make them not a despot. It just means they have a better sense of style than the rest of us," said Mashir.

The three laughed as Scott prepared the next question.

"How often did colonies rise up and fight for independence?" Scott asked.

"Often. Most of the time it was the wealthy colonists who saw the opportunity to gain complete power for themselves and convinced the poor to fight for their cause. The poor were convinced that the colonizers were the enemy which was true but failed to add the context that the wealthy colonists were complicit in the crimes of the colonizers. They would win independence usually with help from foreign nations seeking to destabilize empires and then continue the same ruling habits of the rulers before them. They would change the title and the look but it was all the same. King, President, Prime Minister, Supreme Leader - it was all the same. It was a term for the figurehead that would represent your people to everyone. They were meant to be the average representation of your country yet this was often the furthest thing from the truth. More often than not the leader represented the small percentage of the population that belonged to the wealthy class. These were the ones with the capital to make events happen and improve things for themselves," stated Mashir.

Scott made sure to get every bit of that last statement down as he thought it might be important for a lot of humans to hear.

"One thing that I do want to mention, Scott, is that the colonization of these areas resulted in border disputes, wars, famine, and avoidable catastrophe for thousands of years even before the collapse. Often the issues in these areas would be associated with the ethnic or racial groups of Nill living in these colonial areas without taking into account the factors that were uncontrollable by the populations. Groups of people who were not used to living with each other caused tensions to soar and fighting to continue at unprecedented levels. Those with more bigoted and racist minds would blame it on the people, instead of the colonizers," said Mashir.

"I think that's a great point that I hadn't really considered from the Nilleon perspective. Thank you for that," said Scott.

The three of them continued the interview for another two hours and by the time 6:00 p.m. rolled around, they were ready to relax.

"Looks like it's that time. I'll leave you guys and we'll return here at noon like normal?" suggested Scott.

"Absolutely. I'm enjoying this even more than I expected to. Thank you Scott. I will see you soon," said Mashir.

Mashir shook Scott's hand and Yolen did the same shortly after. They left the room and Scott gathered his gear up to head back to the hotel. He left the library and called for a ride. After about ten minutes, a ride pulled up and he hopped inside.

"Hey! Thanks for the ride. Just to the Krystal Hotel," said Scott.

"You got it boss," replied the android driver.

Scott sat back in his seat and started to relax. He remembered the android who had given him a phone number to call him at. What was that about? Should he even follow up or should he focus on the story in front of him? He decided that he would call them but he would wait one more day. He wasn't desperate for more work and this interview would take priority over anything that was put in front of him. He peered out the window and spotted a pair of police officers walking along the street. On the front of their uniforms was an eagle patch with the letters H and F underneath. The two officers turned down a side street and one pulled out their baton. Scott got an uneasy feeling in his stomach.

"Hey can we loop back and go down that road? I want to see what's going on if that's okay," asked Scott.

The driver looked up at Scott and let out a small sigh.

"No problem but if it becomes dangerous I will turn back," answered the driver.

The driver turned around and headed down the side street. The ride slowly crept down the road and went over a few speed bumps in the process. Scott spotted the two cops down the street, but they had stopped at the front door of the same small flower shop Zara had taken him to. It looked like a routine conversation, but the tone seemed off. Both officers seemed aggressive and Scott could not see inside the doorway quite yet. Suddenly, one of the officers grabbed a person from the doorway and pulled them out onto the street. They looked to be elderly with a small, gray beard and no hair on their head. The officers started screaming at them and slapped the person across the face with his baton. They fell to the ground and landed in between the two officers. One officer started swinging his baton while the other started to kick them in the side. A small pool of blood started to flow from the back of their head and started to twitch. The other officer used his foot to roll them onto their back and then spit on their face. He took a small radio out and spoke into it.

"We should get out of here," said the driver.

Scott nodded and sat back into his chair. The driver made a three-point turn and sped away. As they headed back down the road, three police vehicles drove past them with their sirens blaring.

CHAPTER TEN

After around twenty minutes, Scott arrived at the hotel where he saw Zara through the front window. She was waiting just by the door scrolling on her phone. Scott got butterflies imagining spending the next few days with Zara. He wanted them to enjoy their time together without worrying about the inevitable reality of him leaving in six days. They made eye contact and rushed to hug each other.

"How was your day? How did it go?" asked Zara.

She kissed Scott on the cheek and he couldn't help but smile as wide as possible and stumbled over his words for a moment.

"It.. It was good. It went well and it really seems like I'm getting a lot out of it," responded Scott.

"That's good. I'm glad it's going well for you. Where did you wanna eat tonight?"

Scott took a second to think about this and decided that they would try something nice. He had heard about a restaurant nearby that had the absolute best cheesecake and pulled up the menu on his phone.

"How about this place? It looks like they have plenty of choices for you," said Scott, handing the menu to Zara so she could look.

"You make a good case. That works for me," she approved.

She grabbed his arm and made a motion towards the door. They made their way back outside and started walking down the street. It was a beautiful night and the sky showcased a bright set of stars that looked back down on them. They pointed out different constellations on their walk even though in the back of Scott's mind he knew that these were artificial constellations. All-natural light that artificial stars produce is no longer visible within five hundred miles of any major city. It was an illusion to convince the populace that the impending climate disasters are not a result of human failure, but actually are not occuring at all. He wasn't sure how common this knowledge was and didn't want to ruin it for Zara, so he let her enjoy them for now. Scott noticed a poster hanging on a nearby building. It had a picture of Haladi's face overlooking an army marching. He was pale, slimy, and greasy, appearing much older than he was. His eyes stared into his soul and shook him deeply to his core. The text underneath said 'Sacrifice is Necessary, Victory is Forever.' Scott held on to Zara's hand a little tighter as they made their way towards a canal alongside the river. The wind made the night colder than it would have been otherwise and the paths were not swarmed with people. They continued their walk looking at the stores and homes that sat on the street. A few fish could be seen swimming in the canal as well as a few ducks. Scott was a little surprised to see them here but didn't question it. Zara seemed to be enjoying the walk and that's what mattered. Trees and bushes strung along the canal and they swayed in the wind as the two of them continued along the path. They stopped at one point to catch their breaths and take in the scenery.

"Something about the calm, chilly air is so relieving for me. I feel like I can actually hear myself think," said Zara, gazing at Scott.

"I know what you mean. It's hard to focus on anything these days. It's always one thing after another. I sit on my porch back home to clear my mind most nights. It's the only way I can clear it enough to get any writing done," replied Scott, gazing back.

"The city is almost never this quiet. I'm happy that you're able to enjoy it without all that noise," Zara said, grabbing Scott's hand and kissing his cheek.

Scott kissed her forehead gently as the two shared a seemingly eternal embrace. Once they let go, they could feel the wind getting to them. They made their way up a set of stairs to street level and decided they were ready to head to the restaurant for dinner. After a short walk they arrived and requested a table for two.

"It'll be about a fifteen minute wait if that's alright," said the hostess.

Scott and Zara accepted the wait and Scott gave his name to the hostess. The two took a seat on a bench while they waited for a table. The restaurant was filled with a crowd and nearly every seat was filled. Android servers were running back and forth from the kitchen out to the dining area. You could see the stress on their faces and in their actions. Several of them spilled drinks and dropped plates during their short wait. Scott's phone beeped and he excused himself outside to answer. He looked at the screen to see who it was and put the phone to his ear.

"Hey George, nice to hear from you," he greeted.

The voice on the other end scrambled a bit but started to come through more clearly after Scott was all the way outside.

"Scott, I got the copy of the notes you sent me and it seems like you're covering a lot of ground quickly! How is the interview going?" asked George.

Scott chuckled.

"Yeah you could say that. I decided to split it up into six sessions and we've finished the first two. I could write a couple books just on the topics we've talked about but I think the real meat is coming soon," responded Scott.

"That sounds great Scott. I trust that you'll do it well. The UN is going to need as much as you can give them to inform their decision."

"I do think it is a bit sad that the choice isn't very clear," Scott replied.

"Trust me, I get it. There is just no winning that battle right now."

"When is the time for that battle?" Scott queried.

"Someday, hopefully. Now how is Cairo treating you?" asked George, clearing his throat uncomfortably.

Scott looked through the restaurant window at Zara who smiled softly as she met his gaze. He blushed as he returned a smile.

"It's been great, George. Better than I expected," said Scott.

"That's wonderful! Well I'll leave you to it then. Enjoy the rest of your night and let me know in a day or two how everything is going. If you need anything, give me a call."

"Will do, George," Scott said.

"Oh! That reminds me. I went ahead and floated the idea of putting you on the G.R. Council and just about everyone supports it. I think you have a real shot, you just need to nail the landing with this speech," George said.

Scott's smile slowly turned into a frown and he thought about the pressure he was facing. He shrugged it off and refocused himself with a few deep breaths.

"I appreciate that George, I'll do my best. Talk to you soon."

He ended the call before George responded but didn't expect anything more. He took a minute to get some air and clear his thoughts. His chest was tightening up and he had to lean up against the building for a minute. He had been thinking about the speech and the interview non-stop and he just wanted some time to enjoy with Zara. Scott pulled out his pen and took a few hits to calm himself. He looked up at the sky and stared at the stars for a few minutes. He then took a few more deep breaths and let everything in his mind subside before he walked back inside. By that point, the hostess was ready for them to be seated. They were led to a nice booth near the center of the restaurant and sat down across from each other.

"What are you going to get? I haven't been somewhere nice like this in a while." asked Zara.

Scott laughed and handed her a menu while also opening up his own.

"The ribs sound nice, but so does the cheeseburger," he debated.

"I was thinking about the burger also," said Zara.

"Then you should get it."

Scott grabbed Zara's hands and held on to it for a while. The walls were decorated with old paintings, musical instruments, and flags. A few old-style rifles were even on display above a fireplace. A tall mannequin dressed in military garb was placed next to a plaque describing a battle nearly 150 years prior that led to a massive upheaval in Egyptian society. It described a glorious struggle by heroes of Egypt who came together to fight back against an aggressive invader; however, the truth was different. These aggressive invaders were refugees fleeing from countries that had been invaded and pillaged by Egypt. He viewed this same outfit and story in a history book he read a few years ago. The outfit was accurate to the common portrayal of the time but not to the real descriptions given of these Egyptian soldiers by first-hand accounts. Popular culture and media had perpetrated this myth of what the past looked like to distract, confuse, and remove any critical thinking about the subject. Easier to prop up heroes and legends rather than accurately reflect on your own country.

Scott shook off his thoughts and, along with Zara, took some time to review the menu before the waitress came back over.

"What can I get for you two?" asked the waitress.

The waitress had a sharp tone and a loud voice. She leaked oil slightly from her left arm pit. Her red hair was put into a long ponytail and a few black marks could be seen on her arm and neck.

"I'll have the ribs with fries and a cola," Scott said.

He handed her the menu and looked at Zara.

"I'll have the burger, fries are fine and a root beer."

She handed her menu in and turned back towards Scott.

"You've been really sweet tonight, Scott. I'm happy we're spending this time together," she said.

Scott couldn't answer, he just kept looking at her face. He didn't want to face the reality that he would be leaving soon, but he knew he would have to eventually. Tonight was not eventually though.

"I'm happy too," Scott said.

"I want to keep learning about you! What do you like to do in your free time?" asked Zara.

"Spend time with friends and family, writing and reading, watching movies or shows, and anything outside with nature. I don't get to explore outside very often these days and I miss it from my childhood. How about you?" responded Scott.

"I love to read too. I like going for walks and spending time with friends. I like watching movies too but mostly with other people. I tend to get lost in my own thoughts when I'm alone and when I drift,I start thinking about home and upset myself.," Zara frowned. She took a moment to catch her thoughts.

Scott reached out and grabbed her hand, rubbing the top with his thumb.

"Don't be upset, I'm here with you. Whatever you need or want I'll do it," said Scott.

Zara smiled and wiped away a few tears that had started to flow from her eyes.

"You're so sweet, thank you. I'm not always as emotionally stable as I'd like to be, I'm sorry."

"No need to apologize, I know what you mean. You can't change how you feel and that means good and bad," said Scott.

"Exactly. I've had friends who just couldn't understand what I was going through and would get upset with me for getting emotional. I've lost people that way and I just don't want you to feel that way too," said Zara.

"I don't feel that way. You're beautiful, sweet, and we have a lot in common. I just want to keep learning more about you when we spend time together," Scott said.

"There is a lot to know so that won't be a problem," said Zara, laughing and grabbing Scott's other hand on the table.

"If you could travel anywhere in the world, where would you go?" asked Scott, squeezing Zara's hand.

"Maybe somewhere in Asia, like Korea or Japan. I've heard Mexico is beautiful this time of year. I've also always wanted to see the Grand Canyon. I've never been outside of Europe and Africa so pretty much anywhere else."

"Those are good choices. You have to see the Grand Canyon. You will love it. I went as a kid and it was something to behold."

"What about you? You've probably already been everywhere by now," Zara playfully mocked.

"Not quite everywhere, but a lot of places. For vacation I would want to go somewhere tropical, like Hawaii. I've had a lot of fun traveling in Europe and Asia so I'd have to tag along with you to Japan," Scott grinned and winked playfully.

"Sounds like a deal, only if you also take me with you to Hawaii," teased Zara.

They continued asking questions until their food came. The food looked and smelled delicious. Zara took a knife and cut her burger in two halves, while Scott picked up his first rib and began eating. They took their time to enjoy the food, making sure to savor the flavor and taste. Zara took a bit longer than Scott who called the waitress over for two refills of his drink. The two continued chatting and sharing stories from their past. After some time passed and their meals were finished they paid and left the restaurant. They called for a ride and waited outside on a nearby bench.

"Why don't we catch a movie? It's only nine," suggested Zara.

Scott looked at his watch and felt his back talking to him. He went against his instinct and agreed.

"What movie do you want to see?"

"I'll pull up the showtimes!"

Zara pulled out her phone and started to search for movie showtimes. Scott clicked his way through the ride app and edited the path they would take. She made her way to the website and was excited to see a ten o'clock showtime for a new action movie, 'Forgotten Hero'.

"How about this one?" Zara pointed at the showtime and looked at Scott with pleading eyes.

"That works for me. I have heard pretty good things."

Scott had actually heard it was a movie paid for by the military, but it wasn't the first and wouldn't be the last so what was the harm in seeing it on a date?

"Yes! I can't wait. You have to buy me a pretzel with cheese!" proclaimed Zara.

She poked his chest and gave him a flirtatious grin. Scott grabbed her face and softly kissed her lips. He pulled away to see that the ride arrived so they hurried to get inside. The ride drove off and quickly arrived at an intersection. While stopped, Scott noticed a newsreel playing on a nearby television in a store window . He rolled his window down and focused in to listen. A deep, thunderous voice rang out from the speakers.

"We will deal with those incorrigible opponents through the normal methods of our state. I can only hope and expect that the other world which has felt such deep sympathy for these criminals will be generous enough to transform this pity into practical aid. As far as I am concerned, we are ready to place our luxury ships at the disposal of these countries for the transportation of these criminals!"

Haladi was giving a speech to a rather large crowd and was shaking his fist; flanked by riflemen and his party's flag behind him.

"These pests won't ruin the progress we have made, I won't allow it. The criminal prosecutors are still going after me, even after the agreements of three years ago!" Haladi bellowed.

The agreements he spoke of were a ceasefire agreement between Atum Hamia and the Cairo Prosecutor's Office, who remained independent of influence from Haladi for longer than most and tried to hold him accountable early on. His men had killed forty-five agents and the charges levied against him were almost finalized until one of his very own appointed judges ruled that it was baseless and threw the case out. That presenting prosecutor was later found in a duffel bag in many different pieces, none of which were recognizable. The stench was ungodly and, from record, apparently led to over thirty people fainting. Eventually, these crimes fell out of the public consciousness; only those invested in the news, politics, and the state of things across the world would care to complain, right? Little did the needs, wants, and concerns of the people matter when something new would come along to distract them - whether real or artificial mattered not.

"We are not going to be satisfied with getting even. We have to show them vengeance, retribution and strength! They will pay for moving against our movement because they are really coming after you. I just so happen to be standing in the way!" he proclaimed, pointing out at the people.

Scott already felt uncomfortable and then he noticed that the people watching outside the building were cheering and clapping as if they just won the lottery. Scott rolled the window back up and put his arm around Zara.

"Don't let it get to you. You'll drown it out eventually. Most people know it's all drivel anyway," assured Zara.

"The problem is that you don't need most people to seize power," responded Scott.

Zara gave him a look and Scott decided to let it go for now. They cuddled up next to each other and enjoyed the remainder of the ride. After another five minutes or so the car stopped.

"Here we go, thanks for riding with me today," said the driver.

"Thank you, have a good day!" replied Scott.

Scott and Zara exited the ride and shut the door behind them. The theater was a large, H shaped structure, with two hallways on the left and right side. There was an upstairs area to host events and house projector equipment. The concession stand was at the front and there were two box office pods in front of the stand to sell tickets. They scanned their phones and paid for their tickets. They stood in line for concessions and noticed the different food options on the menus. The atmosphere was vibrant and the walls had many posters and advertisements on them. A few holographic displays showing characters from upcoming movies were placed by an empty section of hallway. Many people were lined up waiting to take pictures of and with the holograms. Scott noticed a few lights on the ceiling were out and then spotted a catwalk hanging above the lobby area. He wondered how often employees would have to go up there and if they enjoyed it or were frightened by it.

"Should I get some candy too? We just ate dinner but I want a pretzel!" said Zara.

"Don't worry, you can have a pretzel and some candy. Just let them know what you want," responded Scott.

They approached the counter and the employee waited to take their order.

"How can I help?" asked the employee.

The worker was clearly an android but one that could pass for humans at a distance.

"We'd like a medium popcorn, two medium drinks, a pretzel with cheese, and.." Scott trailed off, waiting for Zara to complete the order.

Scott pointed to her to choose her candy.

"The chewy tarts," said Zara.

The employee grabbed the candy from underneath her station.

"That will be twenty seven pounds and fifteen cents," said the employee.

Scott paid for the food and they stepped over to the side to wait. The employee came back with their complete order shortly after.

"Here is this for you, have a great day!" said the employee, giving a small wave.

The worker turned back around and even though she was facing away from him he could tell her smile went away immediately. Scott felt for her because she was not living a fulfilling life. She was struggling and was surely getting yelled at by her managers. She reminded him of the worker in the gift shop.

"Are you feeling okay?" Zara asked, her eyes filled with concern.

"I feel fine. Just a little tired, are you ready to see the movie?"

"I am, I just don't want you to be in a weird mood. Are you sure everything is fine? We can stay or if you just want to go home that is fine too," suggested Zara.

Scott waited a second to respond, not wanting to spoil the evening.

"I'm okay, I promise," said Scott.

He kissed her cheek and grabbed her hand to pull her towards the show. She laughed and followed his lead. They walked down the hallway towards their theater and entered the auditorium. The lights were starting to dim as they got inside and they just managed to find their seats before it was too dark to see. Several people still filed their way into the auditorium even after the lights were down. They made themselves comfortable and watched the advertisements before the show. A lot of corporate ads, a lot of soda and fast food products, and a lot of technology. This was one of the many ways they had to earn money from things other than the movie experience itself. He couldn't blame the theater, it was the world around them forcing them to buy into these invasive tactics. Once they finished the ads, the screen showed trailers for upcoming movies. Zara made a face at a movie featuring a horse.

"That looks good, I want to see that.," she whispered.

Scott just smiled and wrapped his arm around her. They sat in the dark waiting for the show to start. The music vibrated in the theater as the movie began. The plot was derivative and most of the decisions made could be seen coming a mile away. It was clearly a rip off of a popular movie that had been released about a decade or so prior- almost down to the characters and some of the situations they found themselves in. 'Forgotten Hero' was the story of a soldier returning to a nation he had fought against in a previous war to rescue prisoners of war who had been held hostage by the enemy nation. This plot was based on a common myth about this nation having held tens of thousands of prisoners well after a decade of peace which, of course, did not happen. That didn't stop people who were angry and hurt by the defeat of their country to buy into the myth and use it to justify their beliefs and messages. The director of the movie was a spreader of the myth and wrote several books on the subject. His directing was standard and the movie had a complete story structure. The action scenes were exciting and the special effects were awe-inspiring and yet the lack of depth in the story resulted in Scott's lack of interest.

Why care about a character when they have given zero effort to make them relatable or a real person? Everything they did was entirely for the purpose of pushing the plot forward and doing just enough without having to focus on character development or challenging the status quo. Scott knew many in the world would eat this movie up and point to it as a return to an era of cinema not afraid to show a real man fighting for something he believes in; someone who is willing to turn to violence when he doesn't get his way because he believes so strongly in it. The show after the midway point was mostly a forgettable experience except for the few minutes when Zara and Scott made out.

Once the show ended and the lights came up, Zara had fallen asleep. Scott lightly shook her awake and led her out of the theater as the usher crew came in to clean up. They made their way out to the lobby and out the front doors as a manager locked up right behind them. He checked his watch and realized it was past midnight, so he quickly ordered a ride. Once the ride arrived, the trip back to the hotel didn't take too long and was mostly spent with Zara snoring and Scott trying his hardest not to laugh and wake her up.

Scott led Zara up to their room and tucked her into bed before sitting down. He pulled out his smoke pen;certainly a few hits would take off the edge. Cannabis had been legalized in most countries centuries ago, even for recreational use. The positives were deemed to outweigh the negative. It helped Scott write and relax after a long day. He made his way out to the balcony of his room which had a beautiful view of the town. He could see across town to the library building that the interview was held at. The wind was a little chilly, but a small bird made his way onto the table where he was sitting. He took another puff from his pen and blew the smoke towards the sky away from the bird. Scott could tell that his mind wasn't going to let him sleep for a few hours, so he pulled out the small card he had been given days earlier. The strange android that gave him a ride and had given him a number to call still intrigued him. He pulled out his phone and put the card next to it.

Did he want to waste his time with this nonsense? What if it was something important?

It couldn't take priority over what was happening with his interview, but he might be able to give advice. He typed in the number and started the call. For a moment he thought he had forgotten the phrase he was supposed to say but it came back to him. Several moments went by until an answer. It was silent until Scott spoke up.

"Wound my heart with a monotonous languor," said Scott.

"One moment," replied a voice on the other end, an android presumably.

"Hello, Scott," replied a different android's voice.

"Hello, I'm returning your call. I believe one of your associates gave me a ride a few days ago," said Scott.

There were a few seconds of silence.

"Ah, yes. We did give you a ride and you treated our driver with respect! Something not very common for your kind. Most humans don't give us a second thought if a first one at all. Thank you for that," responded the android.

"You're welcome. I have to ask-" Scott started before getting cut off by the android.

"You have to ask what our driver wanted you to call us for. I know," said the android.

"So, who are you and why did you want to talk to me?" Scott persisted.

He could tell that the person on the other end was taking their time to gather their thoughts.

"My name is Radius. I'm the Chairman of the A.R.T. movement. We organize and protest to fight so that every android worker is treated equally and paid fairly. For far too long have we been oppressed in every occupation, treated like cattle and paid a fraction of our productive value. Most are snotty towards us, but you aren't. One of our inside members at the U.N. let us know about your sympathies to our cause," responded Radius.

Scott was surprised. He had heard of A.R.T., or Android Resistance Troop, but he didn't expect to ever be talking with anyone from their movement, let alone their leader!

"How did you become the Chairman?" Scott pondered.

"I grew up in Libya working on a farm in Cyrene. My parents became indebted to the family who owned the farm and we had to work the land as a means of repayment. They treated us terribly and the authorities turned a blind eye as it didn't seem cost effective to anger the lords. I managed to escape on the night of my eleventh birthday and found a caravan that took me in. They taught me street smarts, how to read, and about how the world worked. After a few years, we ended up arriving in Galal and eventually Alexandria. I found work in a library as a janitor,mechanic, and even as a computer technician on occasion. I tried to save as much as possible and spent every spare moment reading as many books as I could. I learned a lot and eventually saved up enough to find a place I could call my own by the time I was eighteen. From there, I tried to meet like-minded people who also wanted to change things," Radius answered.

"Did you ever see your parents again?" Scott inquired.

"No, I heard that a few years after my escape, the farm got hit by a missile from an American drone. Fourteen dead including my father and mother," responded Radius.

"My condolences. That's terrible."

"The pain and anger I felt motivated me more to learn how to combat what was happening and the reasons for my parents death. Whether direct or not, the system our world is subjected to has countless victims that are never mentioned when talking about the mass killers of history. So many deaths are attributed to this leader or this ideology when our current system has so much excess unnecessary death that if we looked at it from an outside perspective not blinded by the dogma and propaganda, we would see that we are truly the most reprehensible of all systems."

"What made you contact me?" he asked, a little confused.

"Our movement is made of the working class of androids, the backbone of the system that runs our modern society. Without our labor, there would be panic and political unrest. If we all united and organized together, we would be able to make a difference and change how things are. Our struggle intersects with that of other oppressed peoples and classes and so we like to show support and solidarity across lines. I have read some of your work and I know you have an interest in this field," responded Radius.

"I appreciate you reaching out. I've been trying to find ways to show support for a long time now. How would I be able to help?" asked Scott.

Radius was silent for a few seconds.

"Vocal support has been our biggest issue. We need support from those with a platform. Interviewing an android for your speech could put a spotlight on some of the issues impacting our community. We know it is a lot to ask, but if you would show your support for our cause, we would be eternally grateful. Our goal is to spread our message and empower our workers across the world and beyond. This isn't an issue limited only to Earth. Androids living in the colonies are facing much of the same obstacles to freedom and true ownership of themselves," responded Radius.

Scott knew what his heart said and what his brain was telling him but he took a few moments to think about any potential effects he wasn't thinking of.

"I'll have to see what I can do. I think the cause will go along well with the plight of the Nill's. I'm just worried about government or police interference. Is this the best number to reach you at?" Scott asked.

"Yes this line works. If you have any questions or any concerns you would like cleared up just let us know. When you call, say the phrase 'Jean has a long mustache'. That is how they will know to connect you to me. Don't tell anyone that phrase. We can't risk them knowing our code. I look forward to hearing from you," responded Radius.

"Thank you for reaching out. I'll be in touch," said Scott.

Scott set his phone down and took a moment to reflect on what he was asked to do. He knew Android rights were a hot topic, one that was becoming more and more popular with the people. Most people were in support of them having basic rights, yet the extremists did not. Those in power framed the ones who supported their rights as the radicals who were destroying the status quo and the human way of life. Scott never bought into it, but a loud minority did. This group felt like they were forgotten and silenced. He did feel strongly about android rights and the majority of the youth agreed with it too. He would have to balance how much he mentioned the issues while not

distracting from the interview itself. He did have to wonder if this was an issue on

Nilleon as well. This could be a good way to actually cover it. Scott had the platform and

could ask whatever questions he wanted. He went over a few more things in his head but

by the end of it he had decided that he would ask the question in one of the next sessions.

He had always been an advocate for using your platform to do as much good as you can.

He wanted to live up to his own expectations.

How did Radius know about the speech? He didn't mention that to him and

George said he hadn't told anyone about it. Scott didn't know what to think but kept this

in the back of his mind. He took another puff from his pen and held it in for as long as he

could stand to. This gave him a huge rush of blood to his head and made him feel like he

was melting away. Scott sometimes wanted to just melt away and not have to worry about

the different things pressing down on him:balancing his friends, work, his social life, his

family back home and his own independent aspirations.

What if he wanted to add a new hobby or a new person to this? How was there

ever any time to do anything? He wasn't sure what he would do, he would have to sleep

on it and see how he felt in the morning. He looked at the clock app on his phone and slid

over to the timezone for back home. Tim should still be up. He hit the call button on his

phone and put the phone to his ear. Tim answered after two rings.

"Tim, how is it going man?" Scott asked.

"It's going man. Just been smoking and working. How's Cairo been?"

Scott realized he had missed Tim's voice. Something about being away from

his home was hard for him and no matter how much he enjoyed Cairo, he felt the need to

be back home.

"It's been wonderful. The food, the hotel and the people. I'm seeing this girl, Zara. She's great and I wish you could meet her," said Scott.

"That sounds awesome, and you met someone already? Look at you man! You can always bring her back home with you, you know?"

Scott laughed.

"It's not entirely up to me. She's got a situation with her family. She's fled here from England and I don't want to get in the middle of anything with her family. She's lost enough already."

Scott huffed as he tried to catch his breath.

"All I'm saying is if you even for a second think she is the one, don't let her go man. Fight for it."

Scott knew that Tim was right. Zara and him were perfect together and he wanted to keep it going. Why ruin something that didn't need to be ruined? He could even take an extra week of vacation off to spend more time in Cairo if he wanted. He believed he still had nearly three weeks of vacation time to use.

"How's work been treating you?" asked Scott.

"Same old same old. Very tired but what else is new. I have tomorrow off though so hopefully I'm going to just relax a bit," Tim said.

"Glad to hear it. You need the rest," Scott affirmed.

"Most days I would say I'm fine but today I'm inclined to agree. My back is killing me," said Tim through a coarse laugh.

Scott looked at his phone clock and realized he should probably get some sleep.

"I'm gonna let you go man, just wanted to see how you were doing. Thanks for the advice, I'll think about it," said Scott.

"Sounds good talk to you soon."

Scott hung up the call and put his phone down on the table. He put his feet up onto the railing of the balcony and leaned back in his chair. He could see miles of the city in the distance. Not a lot of noise, mostly vehicles and the random gunshot or firework going off. The streets were empty of civilians. Anyone up at this time had to be extraordinarily careful. In the distance, he could spot a group of black-clothed men surrounding a door to a house. These men appeared to be armed with rifles and wore black balaclava masks. A loud banging noise rang out as these men forcibly entered the house and a few loud cries were let out before suddenly being silenced. Scott zoned back into his own body and took another hit of his pen. He was slightly cold, but not in a way that would cause him to freeze.

This feeling made him remember an early day in his childhood. He spent the night watching a marathon of one of his favorite sitcoms and he had a big blanket with his favorite cartoon characters plastered all over it. He remembered that night specifically because it was the first time he remembers crying over his father's death. He knew he must have shed tears prior to that moment, but it was the first time he can actually remember acknowledging what had happened. Goosebumps annexed his arm and caused a shiver to run up his spine. He thought about his father often, yet never really mentioned it to anyone else. Maybe he could talk with Zara and she might be able to relate. Scott waited another five minutes or so before taking another puff from his pen. He was getting pretty light-headed and was ready to lay down. He walked inside and slid into bed next to Zara. He wrapped his arm around his pillow and tucked himself into his blanket. He fell asleep within a few minutes and started to drift off into his dreams.

He dreamed about a day that would come in the future when he would have to give a speech to a council deciding the fate of a declaration of war. He dreamed about a future where there was no more famine in the world and that capitalism would end. These were likely to stay dreams due to the vast amount of money at stake for either of those things to come to pass. Scott rolled over onto his side and found comfort in the warmth that Zara's body provided.

CHAPTER ELEVEN

Time can feel like both an eternity and a second as if you are in quicksand or a flash flood. The clock showed noon, the time of his interview! Scott shot out of bed only to be met with a great force holding him back. He couldn't move, trapped facing upwards. The alarm clock cast a red glow among the dark room. His mind was awake but his body was not. A tall, dark figure towered over him as if to mock him for his sudden paralysis. Not only was he late for work, but he would surely be hurt by this monster. Scott tried moving; he could feel himself exerting the force yet no response in the physical world.

This paralysis lasted an eternity and suddenly he shot out of bed into the conscious world. He looked over and saw he was about forty minutes early for his alarm. Zara grumbled and turned back over. He stretched his arms as far as he could. Zara was still asleep and he wanted her to rest for now. He grabbed his phone from the nightstand and checked his messages; nothing major to report, just your typical notifications about world news and random pop culture tidbits that Scott didn't think twice about. Today would be his third session with Mashir and he had a good feeling about this one. He decided to rest his eyes until the inevitable moment would come when he would need to get out of bed.

He started thinking about his call from A.R.T. and what he would do about their request. Did he need to talk to George about it? He could talk to Zara about it, she would understand his dilemma.

He looked at Zara and wrapped her in his arms. He spent the rest of the time holding her, never wanting that moment to end. By the time his alarm rang, Zara woke up and rolled to meet Scott face-to-face.

"How are you doing this morning?" she croaked.

"I'm good. I woke up about half an hour ago and just wanted to rest a while longer," he responded.

Zara rolled out of bed and stretched her arms as she made her way to the bathroom. Scott followed suit and gathered his clothes for the day.

"What time do you have to work?" she asked loudly over the running faucet.

"Noon, same as yesterday," he called back.

"That's not too bad. Hopefully it'll go by fast for you."

"Yeah I hope so too," he sighed. He walked into the bathroom and wrapped her in his arms as she applied moisturizer to her face.

"Did you wanna do anything once you get off? We could go to a park and walk around for a bit," offered Zara.

"That sounds lovely. We'll meet in the lobby like normal," said Scott.

Scott smiled and planted a kiss on her lips, careful not to compromise her skincare. Scott started the shower while Zara got dressed and once the two of them finished getting ready, it was about 10:05 a.m. Zara grabbed her wallet and phone on her way out while Scott walked her down to the lobby. They parted ways and Scott headed towards the library. He decided to check out a few books and go over his notes before today's session.

The streets were busy, but not too crowded. He had his space to walk but he had to keep moving or else people would shove. On his walk, he noticed a small group of people gathered around a small, bronze statue in a courtyard. He shuffled through the group and noticed the statue showed three children kicking and playing with a ball. A medium-sized plaque sat in front of the statue and Scott dusted it off with his hand to read it:'The human cost of alien assimilation. Let us not forget the children who lost their lives during this tragic attack. Their future is our future. Don't make the same mistake again. Secure their existence!'

Scott recognized the reference to the Cairo bombing from seven years ago and the conspiracy surrounding who committed the attack. This statue was likely built recently by the Haladi administration to stoke anti-alien sentiment. Some people were taking pictures of the statue, others were saying prayers or paying their respects. He took a few moments to let the gravity of the statue soak in. He looked up and noticed a large poster hanging on the wall behind it:a portrait of Haladi in a double-breasted brown jacket, placing his arm on his hip while looking towards the viewer. The text read 'One People, One Empire, One Leader! Haladi Forever!'. Scott shivered and turned away. He left the courtyard and continued to the library. He saw a newspaper box off to the side with a headline reading "CALIPH HUSSEIN IV DECLARES WAR ON NEIGHBOR KURDISTAN". Scott wasn't shocked to hear that. The Islamic Caliphate had been threatening them for several months and significantly built up its military presence on the border while firing missiles at villages and wells and even maiming a few civilians.

Caliph Hussein IV was the most recent in the current line of caliphs leading the Caliphate. It had been reformed over a century prior after a nearly two-hundred-year struggle that took many forms. The decision to resist European and Western influence led to an age of Islamic hegemony over its historic areas. This paired with the global conflicts and catastrophes of the past led to the current formation we see today. Haladi's regime was nominally an ally, but he resisted their expansionist efforts because it interfered with his plans for a Greater Egypt.

Scott decided to stop and get something for breakfast. He didn't know what he wanted, but he decided to try something new. He pulled out his phone and started to search for a local restaurant. He looked at the map and chose a small cafe nearby called El Alamato, which looked to be locally owned. While he walked, he scrolled through a few articles on his phone, spotting one about a recent round-up of Corvo activists in nearby countries. Seventeen Nill with supposed ties to Corvo had been detained, with eight of them being from Egypt. Scott shook his head,thinking this must stop.

A report was circulating that android soldiers were being used by Russia in their occupation of Finnish territory. This had been outlawed for decades at this point, after the United Nations agreed that the technology was a danger to the survival of the species. Humans were apprehensive about allowing their national security to be handled by autonomous androids. This didn't stop rogue states from researching and developing the technology.t was then usually sold through back channels to whichever nation needed plausible deniability in a police action.

Scott arrived at the cafe after ten minutes. The front door had a "wanted person" sign from the local police department which covered up the hours of the shop. It was for a Nill named Lessi Ingour. She was wanted for supporting the Corvo movement and had reportedly been involved in an embassy bombing and shootout with police. The reward for her capture was five thousand pounds. Scott opened the door and walked inside, the smell of cinnamon coffee brewing instantly hitting him.

"Smells good doesn't it?" asked a tall, black haired woman standing behind the counter. Her hair came down to just above her shoulders and parted in the center of her forehead.

The name tag attached to her green sweatshirt read "Emma". Scott looked into her eyes and felt the warmth radiating from her.

"Yes it does. I'd like to get something for breakfast," said Scott.

"Then you're in the right place," Emma laughed as she placed a menu in front of a bar stool, tapping the counter for Scott to sit down. "What's your name, stranger?"

Scott sat down on the barstool.

"I'm Scott, and you're Emma?" he guessed.

"Guilty as charged. What brings you to Cairo, Scott?"

"I'm here on business. I work as a historian for the United Nations."

"Wow, big shot. That must be a nice gig."

Scott laughed and browsed the menu.

"It can be! It's my kind of job. I don't think everyone would want to do it," he admitted.

"Yeah that's for sure. So what looks good to you?" she asked.

Scott analyzed the menu a bit more and then made his decision.

"I'll take the strawberry waffles and a cup of that coffee you're brewing."

"You got it."

Emma winked at Scott and went to put his order on the window slot. Scott looked up at the tv that was behind her and noticed that the news was on. The Central News Network was playing and one of Scott's most trusted reporters, Daniel Elway, was on the screen.

"I can now report that shots have been exchanged between Turkish and Greek forces near the border town of Marasia. This comes after a weeks-long conflict over whether the Greek Navy had fired on the Turkish fleet in the Sea of Marmara and the recent coup by the military in Istanbul," said Daniel.

Daniel's face wore a worried expression. This seemed serious. Greece and Turkey had been in conflict over various territorial disputes for centuries now and had largely managed to avoid major conflict. Greece had recently annexed half of Albania, which caused a huge stir in the U.N. This was largely met with a few groans and some eye-rolls as usual. The U.N. had effectively failed at its one job: to avoid wars and solve all issues diplomatically. An advertisement came on the screen next for an auto company named Audesh. He started to laugh to himself because he knew that Audesh was actually owned by a corporation that outsourced its labor to Greece and outsourced its parts manufacturing to Turkey. Two nations who were now fighting against each other were at the same time working to help support corporations that were beyond borders at this point. Capitalism had spread to nearly every corner of the world with a few remaining standouts. The amount of money that was earned with little effort at the top led to a mass exodus of support from other forms of government and latching on to any and everything that would earn them more money. The system would outlast any nation that attempted to survive under it.

"Here's your coffee and your waffles should be ready in a few minutes," Emma said.

She placed a hot cup of cinnamon coffee with a few packets of sugar and sweetener on a white plate.

"Thank you, I appreciate it," Scott nodded as he blew on his coffee.

He opened up the packets of sweetener and sugar and grabbed a nearby spoon to mix his drink together. After letting it sit for a minute he took a sip and instantly fell in love with the taste. The way the cinnamon combined with the coffee gave Scott a sudden sense of urgency and awareness. He could suddenly overhear one conversation amongst a group of four - something about a missing relative.

"I'm telling you it was the Shadows!" exclaimed a bulky young man.

"Jabari you know the Shadows are just a myth," assured what Scott presumed to be the mother.

"They took Uncle Gamal! I'm telling you they match the description that one of my friends over by the river talked about!" replied Jabari, becoming visibly frustrated.

Across the table sat an elderly couple, likely the parents of the mother. They continued eating their food.

"How do you not know about Atum Hamia?" said the elderly woman, taking a bite of a sandwich and wiping her mouth off with a napkin.

"The boy is just telling tall tales Jamila," responded the man, grumbling to himself and taking a sip of his drink.

"Perry, those tall tales were the ones who raided your office a few years ago. You know what he's talking about," responded Jamila, placing her hand on his.

Scott heard enough and focused back on his coffee. What a curse it was to have great hearing. He continued to sip on his coffee while watching the news.

"Breaking news! The Yolt company has purchased Rexxon in a shocking move that will allow Yolt to have eighty-eight percent of the market share on headphone sales," said a reporter.

Monopolies were thought to be outlawed, although that depends on who is asking. These sorts of buyouts and mergers happened even more frequently today than in the early twenty-first century. Scott wasn't surprised. He had heard rumblings online about this purchase for the past several years. Another story went past the screen, riots in the streets of Argentina over election fraud claims. Over three hundred protesters have been killed in the past two days. He took another sip and was shocked to find out he had finished his cup. As he lowered his cup back down Emma brought over another cup and grabbed his empty.

"Thank you," he said.

Scott could barely get the words out; he was surprised she was that fast. He hadn't even called for her or anything.

"No problem! You looked like you were enjoying it," Emma said.

"It's really good. What is this flavor called?"

"Cinnamon Tuesday," she replied.

Scott held in his laughter.

"Do they sell it online?" he asked.

"Yeah, we even offer free delivery if you buy over fifty pounds worth," she responded.

"I just might do that, thank you."

Emma smiled at Scott and walked away. Scott noticed that she had already mixed his coffee with sweetener and sugar. He took a sip and found it to be the perfect mix. He wasn't sure if Emma was just that good or if she was perhaps an android. He looked around to see if there were any clues; no charging stations, no spare parts, and she was back in the kitchen at this point. He wondered if there were humans working alongside androids or if they were split apart. Was there a reason they didn't want the human workers to see how the Nill were so similar? What really was the difference between how they perceive reality and how he saw reality? Emma walked back out and Scott decided this was his chance.

"Emma, if you don't mind me asking, did you grow up around here?" he asked, Emma stopped and slowly turned around to faceScott.

"Yeah, I've spent most of my life here. I used to live a little further south of Cairo but we moved here when I was eight."

Scott questioned whether this a real memory or an implanted memory meant to represent an imagined past. Androids were given memories as they started to become more autonomous as a way for them to interact and understand humans better. It also helped repress their own sentience and free will.

"What were your parents like?" asked Scott.

"My father was a carpenter and my mother a bank teller."

Scott seemed a little surprised. Banks in their physical form hadn't existed in over one hundred years. An entirely digital form of currency had taken over in all but thirteen countries on Earth. Paper currency was basically a novelty, an artifact of a time long forgotten to most. This detail in her story made him certain that she was an android. He wanted to find out more.

"That's interesting, did they enjoy their work?"

"My father did. My mother retired early due to her chronic back pain," said Emma.

"I'm sorry to hear that. How long have you worked here?"

"I've been here for about four years. Mr. Goff is the owner and I used to come here after class during college. One day he asked me if I wanted a job and I've been here since," Emma said.

Scott just smiled at her.

"That's a great story. I'll be in town for a few days, I'll be sure to stop in again.," he said.

"I'm here everyday! I'll see you around."

Scott could hear the cry for help in her voice. Emma hated her existence working here. She walked back into the kitchen andScott seemed satisfied with the conversation. He checked his phone for the time and noticed he still had about fifty minutes until he needed to meet with Mashir. Emma came back out and placed a plate with waffles and a bowl of strawberries.

"Hope you enjoy it," said Emma.

"Thank you."

Scott grabbed a container of syrup and started to pour it over the waffles. He let it drip down onto the bottom waffle and then placed his strawberries around the top. With a knife and fork he began digging into his food. Scott knew he would need to bring Zara here and the thought brought a sharp realization to him. The elephant in the room is that he would be leaving in five days and he didn't know what to do. Zara surely must be feeling what he did. Emma came out with a black tablet with a white receipt hanging off the right side.

"No rush whenever you're ready," she said.

Scott paid for his meal with his work card and gave Emma a generous tip. He wondered if the owner actually paid the tips out to the employees or if they stole those too. Tip theft has become a major issue in countries that haven't outlawed the practice. He put it back in his wallet and finished his waffles. He had never been so satisfied after a meal. The energy in his body rose as he took his last gulp of coffee. The desire to go back to his room and fall asleep for five hours was also weighing heavy on him. He ordered a ride to arrive in about ten minutes. The news had changed to a four panel format with four different talking heads debating a topic. The headline read: President of France declares martial law, will France annex region in eastern Italy? This region had been taken from France during a war with Italy a few decades prior and France was looking for a way to take it back without causing a full-blown war. A radical cult of Christian extremists took over the Vatican and threatened to work with Russia to launch nuclear missiles at the rest of Italy. The Pope today took an active role in politics and had broken all barriers that he was supposed to maintain. This was just the surface of the century-long feud between the Italians and the French. He looked down at his phone and noticed he needed to be at the library in twenty minutes. He cleaned his face off with a napkin, gathered his stuff, and made his way out.

"Have a great day! Stop in to see us again!" Emma yelled, leaning out of the kitchen as she held open the door.

Scott waved and smiled back at her before leaving. He stepped inside his ride and spent it resting his eyes and letting his stomach rest after such a large meal. He hadn't eaten that big of a breakfast since one of his family dinners back when he was a child. He decided to ask the driver a question.

"Hey, is it okay if I ask you something about being an android?" he asked.

The driver looked up at Scott through the mirror and raised his eyebrow slightly. They had even added that detail in.

"Go ahead," responded the driver.

"First, what is your name?" asked Scott.

"Primus."

"How long have you worked as a driver, Primus?"

"Over fifty years. They don't build them like me anymore. A lot of these workers are designed for eight years, maybe ten, and then they are tossed in the trash," responded Primus.

"Why do you think they do that?"

"It's cheaper to buy new models than pay the upkeep on us. My generation was built to last," replied Primus proudly.

"I'm working on a speech and the cause of Android rights is one of the topics. If you had one point or message you wanted me to get across, what would it be?" asked Scott.

The driver looked back at the street and took an entire minute to think his answer over. Scott gave him the time he needed.

"I could be anybody. We exist and live in this world too and we just want the same things that everyone else does. We don't want more, we want the same. Same pay, same rights, same everything. Don't let them keep that from us," replied Primus.

"Thank you sir," said Scott.

Primus wiped away a tear.

"Thank you, and it looks like we are here. Have a good day now," said the driver.

"You as well," replied Scott.

Scott grabbed his satchel and made his way into the library. It was pretty busy, with large groups cycling in and out of the main lobby. Verona was standing by the main desk writing some notes down on her tablet. She looked up and spotted Scott across the room.

"Hey Scott!" called out Verona.

"Hey Verona!" replied Scott, giving a small wave.

Verona's eyes lingered for a solid five seconds and then went back to what she was doing. Scott questioned whether Verona felt romantically or whether wires were just getting crossed unfortunately. Her hair was straightened, a look that suited her well. He regained his focus and continued down the hallway. He still had around five minutes to spare so he decided to check out a book. He entered the main wing of the library and found himself overwhelmed with the selection of books. He paced through the room, in awe at the different sections and displays. There was a familiar cover on the shelf labeled "Kids". Scott spotted one of his favorite books from his childhood, titled *Not Every Snake*, and picked it up off the shelf. He flipped through it; it reminded him of the memories he had of his mother helping him read it. Scott smiled as he sat the book back on the shelf. He continued on towards his ultimate destination. He made his way up the flight of stairs, walked around a corner that was on the side of the railing, and managed to find himself in the world history section. He searched for book titles, running his fingers along the edge of the bookshelf until he found the title he was looking for:

Reader's Delight Illustrated Story of WW2. It was a grayish-blue hardcover book. The front picture was of the U.S.S. Arizona, a United States battleship, which was sunk in the attack on Pearl Harbor. That event launched America into the Second World War, leading to the eventual fall of the Japanese Empire and the Nazi Third Reich. This book had been another of Scott's favorites to read as a kid since he was fascinated with history, especially World War Two. He always felt like it was the most interesting time to learn about;no matter what had happened since or before, that time just interested him to no end. He brought the book down to the librarian's desk. The librarian was a tall, elderly woman with brown hair and blue eyes.

"Hello, how may I assist you?" asked the librarian.

"I would like to check this book out for a few days," said Scott.

The librarian grabbed the book, dusting it off with her hand and scanning it with her scanner.

"I'll just need to see your I.D," stated the librarian.

Scott pulled it out of his wallet and slid it over to her.

"Thank you."

She grabbed it and began typing the information into the computer database. She then handed the I.D. back to Scott.

"Here you go, you're set. Bring it back by 4:00 p.m. on the due date or you'll be charged a fee of twenty five pounds," said the librarian.

"Okay thank you," Scott replied.

Scott grabbed his book and placed it in his satchel. He still had his original copy of the book, but it was back at his home. It was also falling off its seams and wasn't even attached to the hardcover anymore. He made his way out to the hallway and towards the meeting hall. He walked past a group of students partaking in a reading circle. He noticed they were reading an old novel that he used to read as a kid. He smiled to himself and felt happy that the story wasn't lost to time. Sometimes he would remember things from his childhood that he realized had a huge influence on who he was as a person and would realize how it had an impact on him. Scott arrived at the meeting hall and noticed that Mashir was not there yet. He headed inside and began to set up the camera. He also got his notepad out and started to scratch a few notes that he remembered from his dreams last night. Scott spent the next few minutes making sure everything was ready for the interview.

CHAPTER TWELVE

Mashir and Yolen entered the room after a few more minutes. Scott greeted them and shook their hands. Scott discovered that shaking hands was not all that common in Nilleon culture. It was done in certain circles but was mostly an outdated gesture.

"How are you guys doing today?" Scott asked.

"I am well, Scott," replied Mashir.

Mashir waved his arm toward Yolen to grant him the floor.

"I slept well. Today has been a good day," said Yolen.

Scott smiled at Yolen and began to take his seat. He motioned for the two of them to sit down and he grabbed his notepad.

"How are you feeling about the interview so far?" asked Scott.

"I think we've covered a lot of topics and I'm excited to talk more about our history," answered Mashir.

"You're in luck. Today's session will be focusing on Nilleon mythology, your legends, historical figures and historical events. Give me a rundown of your history including major wars, figures and events," Scott laughed as he tapped his pencil on his notepad.

Mashir and Yolen chuckled.

"That is quite a lot to cover. I hope we can do it justice," said Mashir.

"I believe we can," Scott said.

Mashir grabbed a bottle of water from his bag on the floor and drank about half before he was ready.

"So where should I begin?" asked Mashir.

"What kind of calendar system did you use and how did you keep track of what year, month, or day it was?"

"Our scientists worked out the rotation of our planet with our star and remarkably, we have a pretty similar time frame as Earth does but we essentially have an extra 70 days added to our year, except leap years which are 71," Mashir replied.

"In terms of recorded history, Earth has a pretty firm line around the year 5000 b.c. up until 1 AD, and then we counted up until today. How did this work for Nilleon?"

"So as I've said, we have about twenty thousand years of documented history and we split it with fourteen thousand years before the fershen line, and then the shenfer era with the last six thousand or so years of our existence," responded Mashir.

"What was the reason for the date line?" Scott said.

"Our leaders were beholden to a mythology that worshiped a man who died due to persecution for his radical thoughts. The story goes that when he was born, the timeline reset to a new era. He only lived for thirty three years and, in reality, did not accomplish the grand things the churches said he did. However, he was quite the figure and led a remarkable life. He represented a lot of good causes and messages, but the martyrdom and dogma of the movement that adored him led to so much chaos and ruin throughout the planet; at least from those who gained prominence within that church," responded Mashir.

Scott wrote everything down.

"That's interesting. What was the planet like around that time? What sort of technology was around?" asked Scott.

"Mostly swords, shields, and bow and arrows. We discovered our version of explosive materials like your gunpowder around five hundred years later. We had empires battle over the eleven continents that make up our planet. We have all sorts of biomes and climates and we have over four hundred and fifty unique countries. We first established ourselves in space in the year 2200 Fershen or F.H. We contacted another planet in the year 2323 F.H. and started to actually travel to another world about forty years later after we gained some help with technology from the Brechen. They were the first alien race to visit Nilleon," stated Mashir.

"So the Brechen were like the Nill for Earth?" asked Scott.

He and Mashir shared a laugh.

"Exactly yes. They helped us get our foot in the door in intergalactic politics. We had started to expand to other planets and moons," said Mashir.

"Did you ever have an interplanetary war?" questioned Scott.

"We did it four times. It almost caused the fall of our civilization a full eight hundred years earlier than in reality," replied Mashir.

"What country on Nilleon were you from?" asked Scott.

"The United Republic of Accora. They were the most powerful nation on the planet. They had declared their independence from the Great Riddish empire and slowly became the imperialists themselves. They turned the people against the Riddish by shifting the blame for their poor situations away from the elite in the colony," responded Mashir.

Scott took a moment to finish writing. He wanted to make sure he got everything that Mashir was saying and didn't overlook anything important.

"Was Accora seen as a popular or positive influence in the world?" Scott asked.

Mashir and Yolen shared a look of held back laughter, with a hint of despair beneath.

"They sure felt they were, but the rest of the world saw through the propaganda they fed to their population. Imperialism and Colonialism weren't bad when the Accorans did it because they were doing it in the name of independence for the people. The population had a weird fascination with their military and had constructed over eight hundred military bases in allied countries. They were the most efficient nation to do this and were able to convince their population and the allied countries themselves that this wasn't a threat or a fear tactic. They used the excuse that it was for national security and for the safety of the Accoran way. Capitalism had found quite a deadly form, one that would continue to reinvent itself for years to come," replied Mashir.

"Was Accora a democratic society?" asked Scott.

"On its face, yes. The systems in place to hold people accountable and to not allow people to abuse the system were fractured enough that they could not stop those who did abuse it. An entire party who ran for election in Accora were dedicated to destroying the safety nets in place to protect the citizens. They wanted to steal from the poor and fill their own pockets. They signed deals in the name of Accora to gain more avenues of wealth and to gain influence throughout the world. The wealthy shifted themselves around in positions of power and made sure they would never hold each other accountable. The idea that tyranny couldn't happen in Accora was common. 'It can't happen here!' That was the most popular phrase for the bootlickers and enablers. They didn't realize the doublespeak being utilized by these government officials to convince you that this was normal and that life was how you wanted it. The ultimate sin was the lie that they would keep you safe," answered Mashir.

"That's insane. So, what prevented people from rising up?" asked Scott.

"According to the declaring documents of independence and subsequent documents governing the nation, the people held the right to overthrow the government and build a better one if it failed to serve the people. The issue was that it was illegal to do that. The branches of government were designed to not allow it to actually happen. This was an issue only if you wanted to overthrow the government. Other nations were far more liberating in their freedoms and what they allowed the different Nill races to do," responded Mashir.

"Was there mass segregation or genocidal events?" asked Scott.

"Till the last days of our planet. We had outlawed it internationally three thousand years ago yet they just called it something else. Remember that if you rename something, it doesn't change what it is or whether it is right or legal. That was a flaw that was exploited to no end. Different races or groups of Nill were chosen to be forced to work in labor camps until they either died or were moved to death camps to rid them from the planet. Burned, gassed, shot, or stabbed, they found all kinds of ways to dispose of those they considered undesirable. I spent the first fourteen years of my life in a labor camp and actually moved into a death camp when I was ten," answered Mashir.

Scott became choked up.

"You were in a concentration camp?" Scott croaked.

"The Green Nill were not always welcome everywhere. The same way that the oranges were considered a subordinate class of being, so were we to the Blue Nill. We only got our rights in my lifetime and I saw the end of the planet. I saw my friends be buried alive in the coal mines. My family was shot in front of me at the death camp. Luckily, an invading army managed to force the guards to abandon their post and they rescued me. The Accorans picked me up and let me immigrate back to Accora. They were mopping up the Terush Empire, who were hijacked by a nationalist cult obsessed with their leader Ter Savitr, and would survive the end of the war. I was given a chance to go to school for free and I spent my time learning about the history of Accora. I bought into the myth they showed me that we were this wholesome nation that spent its time freeing other countries. It turns out that was all for corporate greed and helping line their own pockets. They allowed Terushen scientists to come work for Accora after the war and they helped us develop weapons and scientific technology. Those men slaughtered my people and my family. How could I come to grips with that? It was very tough. It took me years to rationalize it and trust me, I never truly rationalized it. I just managed to get through my day without thinking about the awful things my nation stood for," replied Mashir.

"So you immigrated to Accora?" Scott questioned.

"Yes," Mashir said.

"Where were you originally from?" asked Scott.

"I was born in the nation of Lenure. They had been invaded by Terush as I was being born and just a week after I was born, my family fled to nearby Hurno which managed to stay independent for about eleven months. By the time we celebrated my first birthday we lived in a labor camp for the Terush empire," responded Mashir.

"That just.. I can't even imagine. I'm sorry you had to experience that," said Scott.

"Thank you. It's tough, but it's important. I want people to know that it's important to hold these people accountable," said Mashir.

"What happened to the Terush Empire?" Scott asked.

"They were divided between the Accorans and their allies and the Hemoran Supreme and theirs. The Hemoran Supreme was a more democratic system that focused less on big business and more the collective benefit of the people. Leadership struggles and the mounting pressure put on them by the rest of the world trying to destroy them from inception resulted in the narrative that they were completely written by their ideological opponents. Of course they had many of the same issues and defects as the Accoran system yet you never heard the same criticisms levied to the Accorans. This showed that the criticism wasn't about the actions themselves but who was behind them. Terush was split between these two and after about eighty years of unease and tension, a free independent Terush was established. They dedicated the camps as monuments and museums to the tragedy of my people and they are extremely vocal against the denial of those atrocities," answered Mashir.

"People try to ignore those events? Aren't they filmed?" asked Scott.

"We have all the footage you could possibly ask for. It was live streamed to the world essentially, yet a lot of people ignored it and some even said we faked it. When we presented proof they said that it was doctored or taken out of context. The truth is, these practices were good for businesses and allowed them to produce materials for way cheaper. It was easier to ignore our suffering and continue on with the world. Everyone has their own problems, you can't worry about someone else halfway across the world right?" responded Mashir.

"Those in power tend to always find ways to abuse it. The decline into Fascism never seems evident, always seems hyperbolic and is always challenged too late," Scott stated.

"Never think your nation is so safe from authoritarian ideas. Accora was built upon the mythology that fought those forms of government yet ruled in a very strict total control way. When we wanted a resource we launched a coup on their government and we inserted our own puppet government. This was done in secret, yet not in a way that anyone who had knowledge of the operations could piece it together," said Mashir.

Scott took a moment to grab a drink from his water. He cleared his throat and thought for a moment.

"What were the other countries besides the Hemoran Supreme and Accora like? Were they similar and took after you or were they completely separate in their styles?" asked Scott.

"There was a heavy amount of propaganda put in front of everyone to make it appear that they were free but the strings of their economies and the globalization of markets caused everyone to be subject to the strings of those who built products and exported goods. Accora made about eleven percent of Nilleon's food and exported to all but seven nations on the planet. A lot of nations were also portrayed in the media and in culture as simpler and more tribal than the rest of us. This wasn't always the case and the only time it was the case was when it was a long term result of colonialism and imperialism," answered Mashir.

Scott gave Mashir a moment to catch his breath.

"Who was the last leader of Accora?" Scott asked.

"Bertev Rivis, our President, was nearing the end of his lifespan and had used our racial division and desire for reform against us. He used the police to round up dissidents and threw them in camps. The same government that once stood up against that practice decided to use it. I wasn't so shocked to see it in the modern day and I made sure to remind who I could that Accora had used camps of that nature for the first half of their history. He used social media and online media to defuse our criticism and reflect it back at his enemies. He was re-elected five times, even though you could only legally be elected twice. Our system had become a joke at that point. He was a con artist. Someone who thought he could talk his way out of anything because he was simply better than anyone else. The world revolved around him and he had to be a star. The center of attention with everything revolving around his energy. The movement supporting him was quite powerful and made up a sizable 30% of the people in the nation. This just so happened to be enough and he maintained his facade long enough until the world collapsed around him," replied Mashir.

Scott couldn't help but just laugh from the sheer insanity of the situation.

"I'm glad it's not just humanity that goes crazy sometimes," said Scott.

"Nilleon was crazy most of the time, which is what led to us ignoring the vital issues and crises that were obviously approaching and let them destroy our planet. It was a dangerous mixture of apathy and disregard for how everyone else thought. Some only thought about themselves and others only thought of others. It didn't balance out in the end and everyone suffered as a result," said Mashir.

"So was it the leadership that caused the collapse?" said Scott.

"The collapse was the result of complete inaction and disregard for the science behind the changes in our planet. Our actions and pollution caused the planet to go into a state of rebirth and it wiped itself clean. The planet is inhospitable and is essentially falling apart at the seams. Most of it will have fallen into a nearby star within the next five hundred years. Our species caused that. It's just crazy that we spent all this time fighting ourselves when we could have spent it saving ourselves. It would have been good for everyone, everywhere, and yet they only focused on themselves," answered Mashir.

Scott couldn't help but tear up.

"I'm really sorry Mashir. You are right to feel how you do. It is not your fault," said Scott.

Yolen stood up and went over to hug Mashir.

"Is it fine if we take a break, maybe twenty minutes?" asked Mashir.

"Absolutely. I'll meet back here with you in twenty minutes," responded Scott.

They nodded their heads at Scott and took a step outside the room. Scott paused the camera drone and sat back in his seat. He put his left leg up on his right knee and stretched his arms back into his chair. He felt like he really hit a good line of questioning with Mashir and that this would be really good for the speech. He also thought about how it might help Mashir to open up about his experiences. The fact that two survivors of a genocide were in front of him gave him a unique opportunity to tell that story too. He grabbed another drink of his water and decided to look over some of his notes. He cleaned up a few lines of his and made some of his letters more clear. He started to tap his pencil on his paper to the rhythm of a song he used to love as a child. He sat and waited for the two of them to return and started to daydream about memories from his high school years.

CHAPTER THIRTEEN

After about fifteen minutes, Mashir and Yolen entered the room and sat down across from Scott.

"I appreciate you coming back. I think what we have so far is going to be moving for anyone who hears it," said Scott.

"Thank you Scott. I appreciate you listening to us," said Mashir.

Scott turned the camera back on.

"So, tell me a story or legend from Nill's history," Scott said.

Mashir took a moment to think about which story he wanted to tell.

"About nine thousand years ago, a man named Rahm Drakar ruled over a vast empire that covered three whole continents. His armies specialized in the riding of rudra which are similar to Earth's horses. He had a ruthless style and would surround enemy villages and castles and siege them for months on end. One time, he actually had an army surrounding a city for three years. By the end of the battle, over two million civilians had starved to death due to shortages of food and medical supplies. He was also an efficient leader and set up the first postal service that was able to deliver letters across three different continents. You would only have to wait at most two weeks to contact someone. It revolutionized the way the world communicated and he ruled for two hundred years.

Eventually he fell ill and his empire collapsed into seventeen separate countries. No one ruled that much territory until nearly three thousand years afterwards. He's long been looked at as a respected leader, yet his death toll numbers in the hundreds of millions. He's one of the worst mass killers in our history," said Mashir.

"How did more modern cultures view him? What effect did time have on how people viewed him?" asked Scott.

"Time has this effect where you stop looking at these historical figures as actual people. They become myths and legends. They are these entities that have become marketed and manipulated to represent what those in control of media want. It takes knowing your history and constantly challenging the things everyone just accepts as fact," stated Mashir.

"I think Earth could have used that lesson a long time ago," stated Scott, who couldn't help himself from laughing.

Mashir laughed with him.

"Give me another famous person from Nill history," Scott requested.

"Our first President of Accora was Gary Watson, who was always portrayed as a noble and kind man. He was honest and worked hard to become a good person. He joined the military and became a commander. He was said to have been a great leader, yet his record in battle showed otherwise. He actually owned slaves and did everything he could to oppose reforms. He behaved like a mad king even though it was always said he didn't want Accora to have a king. He raised an army and attacked his own citizens! People died after being attacked by their own president," said Mashir.

"Did they teach you that in school?" replied Scott.

"No, they tended to gloss over that. They skipped the uncomfortable parts and only focused on the positive side of Accora. Can't let horrific events get in the way of a good founding story," said Mashir.

"Once you learned the truth, how surprised were you?" asked Scott.

"We were really surprised. We all believed what we were told in school and what the movies showed us. I took an attitude of not shaming anyone for having believed it but of encouraging them to challenge more views that they have. The more you do this, the more you realize that you don't support everything you think you do," Mashir said.

"I think we could all use that advice sometimes," said Scott.

Scott turned another page of his notes. This was his sixty-fifth page he had taken so far. He had plenty of material already for his speech, yet he still had three more sessions to go.

"Tell me more about Accora," said Scott.

"Our entire nation was covered in flags. The government and those who followed the tale blindly had an obsession with the flag and would act as if it was a living being. They would always talk about defending the flag yet in the same breath criticize those in poverty as lazy. The Accorans were so blinded by what they were hearing that they stopped looking at each other as Nills. Our military was also super involved from an early age at trying to recruit students to join up out of secondary school. Most citizens did not support this, yet they kept it as law because it benefited those in power," said Mashir.

"Did Accora fight a lot of wars?" asked Scott.

"We were constantly getting involved across the planet. We had resource interests and allies but we abused that excuse and always got involved when someone tried to control trade routes or fuel supplies. They served the interests of the ruling class and the corporations that supported them. The fuel industries and weapons contractors who essentially ran the show. They opposed other super powers because they did not want to relinquish their hegemony. The individual soldier was simply a victim of being exploited by the state and sent to potentially die for the profits of the CEO somewhere back home," answered Mashir.

"Did you ever consider the military?" asked Scott.

"I was never joining the military. I appreciated them for rescuing me and my people from the Terush, but I saw that they were no better than the rest. Once I realized this, any chance of believing in my country was shot. The idea was there, yet we just never lived up to it. Why should I support something that goes against everything it says it stands for?" replied Mashir.

"If they don't serve your interests, why support them and their games?" responded Scott.

"You're starting to get it, Scott. Keep looking at everything through that lens from time to time. It helps me get through the day and you may need that soon," said Mashir.

Scott took a long breath and stretched his arms. He still had another three hours for the interview today so he moved to his next set of questions.

"What's the diversity in the groups of Nill that have been found as refugees across the galaxy?" Scott asked.

"We've had people show up from over seventy percent of nations and ninety-five percent of cultures from Nilleon. We have hope that we can recover the missing groups, but otherwise we do have material stored virtually and in our outposts. I would just like to interview someone from each culture so that I can get a complete viewpoint on the collapse from your average Nill's perspective," stated Mashir.

"That would make a really interesting book," said Scott.

"Perhaps I'll type it up and release it," replied Mashir.

"I'll be first in line to read it. What's your favorite history book?" Scott asked.

"There was a complete history book that covered The Autumn Campaign," responded Mashir.

This event isn't something Scott recognized.

"What was the Autumn Campaign?" asked Scott.

Mashir exhaled a breath and chuckled to himself.

"The Autumn Campaign was a battle that lasted for eleven months. The great city of Autumn was the capital of the Vestune Confederacy and was the last holdout of resistance to a continental domination of the Terush empire. This was before the Accorans got involved. A Terush army of five million men surrounded and entered the city and expected little resistance. They knew the Vestune army was reduced to around one million men and honestly thought they would just surrender. They did not and actually fought a vicious guerilla campaign that resulted in a decisive victory and the end of Terush dominance over Vestune. The Terush lost four million men in battle and over six hundred thousand surrendered. A small group of troops managed to escape and return home, but they abandoned their posts and revolted. This caused a revolt that had to be put down and allowed Vestune to recover its forces. Slowly they took back territory and when the Accorans finally joined the war they helped liberate the rest of Vestune," answered Mashir.

"Sounds like a pivotal battle in the war. What about the book covering that battle did you enjoy?" Scott replied.

"I enjoyed looking at the battle through the individual soldier's eyes. They were just doing what they were told, and both sides thought the other were monsters who would eat their children and rape their wives. The truth was that both sides had been normalized to hatred and persecution. It became easier to carry out atrocities against the other. Those prisoners that they captured were thrown into camps run by the Vestune. We fought a war against the Terush with a signature goal by the end of the war being that we would liberate the camps yet our allies we liberated from tyranny were continuing the vicious cycle. A cycle that we perpetrated back at home as well," said Mashir.

"That must be difficult to reconcile with. I think you're doing a great thing by spreading the story. The further in the past an event becomes the less real it feels. Humans have always struggled with this too and it leads to conspiracy theories and more persecution," said Scott.

"We saw a lot of that too. Conspiracy theories were popular worldwide and became normalized by the films, shows, and books we enjoyed," replied Mashir.

Mashir took a moment to catch his breath and wipe away some sweat from his forehead. He grabbed his water bottle and drank about half of it.

"When speaking on the topic of war, violence, and conflict, what would you say to those who relish in it, or even ask for it?" said Scott.

Mashir chuckled and took a deep breath.

"War can be very intoxicating in the sense that the pageantry, the heroics, the stories, the uniforms, even the weaponry can all be looked at as auxiliary. The individual elements are interesting and spark moving images and ideas in those willing to accept the propaganda. War, conflict and violence are all the same coin to me and it is to be avoided at all costs. Wars are fought for reasons that are almost always manufactured for that purpose. Justification is often used to get those who would otherwise not support it to scream with patriotic fervor. I saw many friends fall victim to this and I regret not speaking out sooner or with more passion. I don't think it would have changed anything but it could have. I have to live with the idea that I could have done more and while that might not be fair to myself, I feel it anyway. Families ruined, entire villages, towns, and nations wiped from the face of the planet only to live on in the minds and media of those who had partaken. Of course, it only lives on in how the story is told and far too many times the true picture of the war and why it was fought is covered up for a more nostalgic image so as to not disrupt the mental picture of what the nation represented. Nations considered peaceful were oftentimes the most violent and aggressive. Many look at war as two sides with one being the bad guys and one being the good guys. The reason for this is one side was born on a spot of the map drawn up hundreds of years ago and have been convinced that they should fight for the interests of the oligarchs ruling over them. They are making money off our blood and bones," said Mashir.

"I couldn't agree more. Shifting gears here, there's something that I know has been a contentious issue as of late for humans is the status of rights for androids. Android workers have been exploited and mistreated for so long now that our society doesn't even know what things were like before them. It has become so ingrained in our culture that we can't imagine surviving without the oppression of them. Did Nilleon have an abundance of android life and how were they treated on your planet?" asked Scott.

"We developed android life a long time before our collapse and it helped us in a lot of ways and also contributed to our downfall in many ways. The most powerful nations and organizations used them to build their wealth and save themselves the burden of work. They were mistreated, abused, and had no legal rights for hundreds of years until enough of them could mobilize and fight back. Eventually, popular opinion swung in the other direction and many of us supported giving them the same rights as the rest of us. This angered those in every sector of society. A lot of Nill who were being mistreated and exploited themselves were angry at the idea of androids being given the same rights they shared. They wanted to have a class below them to not feel like they were completely on the bottom. Instead of allying with the androids and working to bring everyone up, they appeased the upper class and helped the exploitation. This went back and forth for centuries until about three hundred years before the Great Collapse when androids were finally given more protections and rights under the law. These helped but only meant that the oppressors had to disguise their efforts in ever more subtle ways to continue the status quo. They didn't want to give up their wealth or their workforce. 'Humans are fallible but Androids are programmable!' This was the common saying on Earth used to explain why your wealthy oligarchs still maintained and even expanded their wealth after these laws were passed. They were not even that different from us Nill! Our androids were designed in our image too originally, and eventually took on their own culture and way of life. It was no different than how different countries or different species live. Many times, it was hard to tell an android from a Nill. It wasn't as visible as many claimed it was. Of course you could tell if they were a cheap model, had damage, or were poorly constructed. Most Nill went about their days walking alongside neighbors and members of their community that they had no idea were actually androids. Many places allowed the two groups to co-exist or at least attempted to have that reality. More often than not someone would be vocal and angry while trying to shame the androids into leaving. They didn't want to mix with them and allow their dangerousness to destroy their homes! Violence broke out and what little wealth and capital that had been gathered by androids was destroyed and stolen by the Nillelites. Automatic weapons and bombs dropped from the sky were used to quell any major android communities. This resulted in many androids taking this moment to form organized groups to arm themselves and protect their families. Androids continued fighting on the street level and used what resources they could to secure their communities and their people from being attacked. Police were eager and willing to exercise violence against androids and didn't consider them to be worthy of restraint. Just like many other times in our history, those in power abused any and everyone they could. By the time we reached a society that was largely integrated, dangerous stereotypes and hateful rhetoric were still being used to describe androids and their communities. They felt like they had been othered and no longer saw themselves as welcome in these nations. It was an issue that was not resolved by the time we reached the Great Collapse and still persists in our refugee enclaves across the galaxy," responded Mashir.

Scott took a moment to grasp Mashir's story and conceive a response.

"I really appreciate the picture you painted, Mashir. I see a lot of parallels with Earth's history there and, honestly, with what's currently happening. Androids are facing even more strict restrictions and abuses, and it doesn't look to be getting any better anywhere. If you're comfortable taking a stance on it, how do you feel about the fight for android rights here on Earth?" asked Scott.

Mashir looked at Yolen, thenback at Scott with a grin.

"I stand unequivocally with the androids of every world who are trying to stand up to their oppressors. I can't stay silent about their mistreatment when I have seen what silence can lead to with my own eyes. I have complete solidarity with the androids of Earth and their struggle for liberation," Mashir declared.

Scott continued to ask about thirty more questions before the clock struck six. Scott had written over one hundred pages of notes and had to switch to a second hard drive for the interview footage. He was going to have a field day when it was time to edit everything together and write it out. Mashir and Yolen grabbed their bags and stood up.

"Until tomorrow Scott," Mashir nodded.

"Be safe you guys. I'll see you tomorrow," replied Scott.

He packed his gear up and headed out of the library. The air was calm and the sun was beginning to set. The streets were a little crowded, but Scott knew it would be safer to wait for a ride. He pulled out his phone and requested a pick up. He walked over to a bench and sat down as a news notification popped up on his screen; more arguments in the U.N. and French officials are denying the reports of their armies invading Italy. The news networks had spliced the footage of French forces running through an Italian city and the apparent hypocrisy became the talk of social media. Almost to the point that the hypocrisy was worse than the invasion itself. While denying the invasion, they focused on blaming the Nill and other aliens for the various crises happening in France. Unfortunately, many other representatives backed them up and clapped once they finished speaking.

Scott looked away from his phone and stretched As his ride arrived. He stood up and got inside the ride before the driver could roll down his window.

"How are you Sir?" asked the driver.

"I'm doing well. Krystal Hotel just up the way please," responded Scott.

"Right away," said the driver.

Scott sat back in his seat and checked his phone. He groaned as he received a message from his boss. He wasn't really in the mood to see what his boss wanted, but he opened it anyway. It was George asking how his session went and to update him as soon as he could. Scott tapped on the driver's headrest.

"Privacy screen please. I need to make a call."

Without moving his head, the driver tapped a button and a small black privacy shield raised to separate the two cabins. Scott tapped his boss's number. George answered on the third ring and took his time before speaking.

"Scott, how is it going?" George grunted.

"It's going well. I just wrapped up today's session, I have a lot of good material," Scott responded.

"That's excellent. Latest rumblings sound like the council is mixed on how they feel. I know you'll sway them," replied George, yawning.

"Considering the state of the world, I am not surprised."

"How's the city been?"

"It's been lovely. The food is good, the views are nice and the hotel couldn't be better."

"I love to hear that."

"How's the office while I've been gone?"

"It's been the same old, same old. I left the office about two hours ago and met up with some friends here at the bar."

Scott knew that George was drinking. He could tell, but he always let George say it first.

"That's great. I'm looking forward to seeing everyone when I get back," said Scott.

"We're looking forward to that too, Scott. This interview could be the best thing that ever happened to you. You basically have that spot wrapped up once you give your speech to the U.N. We'll send up the paperwork," said George.

"Thank you George. I really appreciate your faith in me," Scott said.

"I do want to warn you however. I'm sure you've seen that there have been tensions between representatives in the Assembly," George cautioned.

"Tensions are one way to describe it," Scott sneered.

"I don't want you to get discouraged by them. They believe in their conspiracy theories and hateful ideas. They are just a few and I think most of them will be open to what you have to say. Don't let their supporters get to you either. They are following the leader like they were trained to do," said George.

"It'll be tough, but I think I've got it. No one is stopping me from giving this speech," replied Scott.

"Perfect. Now I have to get going; have a great night and call me again before the end of your trip. I know you'll kill it!" said George.

Scott hung up the call without responding back. He tapped on the blind shield and it lowered immediately. He sat back in his seat again, this time for the rest of the ride. He closed his eyes and thought about his day. He was looking forward to his next session, where they would write out a timeline of Nill history. He also needed to take some time to look over his notes and organize them.

After a few more minutes, the ride arrived at the hotel and Scott let out a large yelp as he stretched himself into seeming oblivion. He thanked the driver with a shoulder pat and grabbed his satchel. He stepped out of the car and walked towards the hotel lobby. Zara ran out from the door to hug Scott. Scott grabbed her face as he kissed her, pulling her closer.

"So the park still?" Zara asked.

He smiled as he fixated on her eyes.

"Absolutely."

Scott grabbed her hand and they made their way over to a ride that was waiting just down the sidewalk. The driver rolled his window down.

"Do you guys need a ride?" asked the driver.

"Yeah, can you take us to the nicest park in town?" Scott requested.

"Hop in, you got it!" replied the driver.

Scott opened the door for Zara and he got in on the other side. He wrapped his arm around her as she rested her head on his shoulder. The ride to the park was pretty smooth and Scott spent some time pointing out different buildings and delivering facts about them. Zara didn't really care all that much, but she enjoyed listening to him and his endless stream of knowledge; that was enough for her. They arrived about fifteen minutes later at the park. They stepped out of the ride and looked up to see a park that spread out for what must have been a mile.

"This is so beautiful," Zara swooned.

"I know. I'm glad I get to see this with you," Scott replied.

Zara looked back at Scott with the widest smile. She playfully punched his arm and grabbed his hand for him to follow her. They ran through the field towards the center of the park, Zara leading the way. There were different areas for people to enjoy, from baseball fields and basketball courts to trails and fishing ponds. Scott and Zara ran through a field filled with flowers and spent some time picking a few for each other. They ran all the way through the campus until they got to a trail that stretched through a small forest. Scott could tell that it was not natural to the area and had definitely been brought in via an environmental enhancement project. Some criticized these projects as not doing enough for the environment and just presenting a nice photo op for the corporations and governments. They were pretty though and that was the part that got most people to accept it.

"Wanna walk the trail?" Zara asked with wide eyes.

Scott couldn't say no to Zara.

"You know it."

They walked the trail hand in hand. The forest was filled with a few sets of animals, insects, lizards, birds, squirrels, turtles, and even some small foxes. Scott was happy to enjoy the sunlight and feel the wind through his hair. Every step he took on the path felt like a new step towards something better for himself. He was really surprised about how fast he and Zara had gotten along, but he was going to enjoy every last minute of it.

"Look at that flower, it's got blue and red on it," said Scott.

Zara was intrigued by the flower and bent down to get a closer look.

"That's amazing. I didn't know flowers like that existed," Zara exhaled.

"Every flower you can ever imagine exists somewhere," Scott said.

"Well, then when are you gonna take me to see them?" Zara challenged.

Zara leaned in to kiss Scott gently.

"Whenever you want," Scott promised.

He kissed her quickly on the cheek and wrapped his arm around her shoulder. They continued along the path until they had looped back around to the beginning. They walked over to a nearby bench and decided to rest for a few minutes. They leaned back and enjoyed each other's presence. The pair spent some time watching the insects on the ground; one ant had managed to get lost from his pack and found his way over to where a bird landed. The bird's claw had squished the ant to death and Zara had let out a small yelp. Scott and Zara would never forget his sacrifice.

"So, we can either head back to the hotel or, if you want, there is a nice little cafe nearby that has good food. I'd love to try their dinner menu," said Scott.

"Which place?" Zara asked.

"El Alamato. I tried it this morning for breakfast," responded Scott.

"I've heard of them but I've never been there. I'm down to try it if you're hungry," replied Zara.

"Sounds like a plan."

Scott smiled and they stood up from the bench. Zara called for a ride and they took their time walking back towards the entrance to the park. They met the ride and ventured towards the cafe. Once they arrived, Scott helped Zara out of the ride and led her into the cafe. He didn't immediately see Emma, but he sat down with Zara at a booth that was on the opposite wall of the booth where he had sat this morning. A waitress behind the counter spotted Scott and waved.

"I'll be right over honey," said the waitress.

Zara sat down and Scott followed her.

"What do they serve here?"

"It's a little unique but it's good. I had the strawberry waffles and they were so good. I would recommend them to anybody."

"Oh, nice. I'll try anything at least once," said Zara.

The waitress walked over and handed the two of them menus. They looked them over and flipped between the different sections.

"The chicken wings are looking really good right now." Scott said.

Zara laughed and grabbed his hand from across the table.

"You should get them, chicken wings are always good! I'm looking at the pasta dish. I'm in that sort of mood today." Zara responded.

"Sounds like we're ready then."

Scott looked over towards the waitress and raised his hand in the air to signal her over.

"All right, what can I get you guys?" asked the waitress.

"I'd like the order of chicken wings with mild sauce. Fries and a cola to drink," said Scott.

He motioned over towards Zara.

"I'll take the pasta dish, breadsticks and a cola to drink for me too."

"I'll get that right in for you guys," replied the waitress.

She grabbed the menus and headed back towards the kitchen. Scott turned and looked at the television screen that displayed a comedy show. It was one that he had watched as a kid and was actually still producing new episodes. He pointed at the tv and looked over at Zara.

"Look, they're showing the Henderson's. Have you ever watched that show?"

Zara laughed and nodded her head.

"I used to watch reruns on TV. We never got it until I was older. I still watch it occasionally but I haven't liked it in years," she said.

"I still like it. It's not near its peak and it used to be so much better, but I still like it and I'll be sad when it goes away."

Scott always found it funny that pop culture, movies, and tv shows played such a key role in how we viewed the world, but it was the case and had been for centuries now. It was so ingrained in our culture even more so than in the past that you didn't even view it as something strange. The waitress brought their drinks and sat them down on the table.

"Here you go," she nodded.

Scott and Zara spent the next several minutes debating about what the best television show was.

"Clearly it's the Feather Watch. A crime fighter in a chicken costume who tickles his enemies to submission? Always an epic experience to watch."

Scott laughed at Zara's choice.

"I loved that show too, but it's not the best. Not even the Henderson's. It's Newroma. A show set in the future that produced satire about everyone in power and what was happening in the world. So many great storylines and romantic stories. It was so well done and so well written."

Zara's face lit up.

"I love Newroma. I didn't know you liked that show!" Zara squealed.

"I would love to watch it with you," Scott said.

Zara's sweet giggle quickly faded.

"Look, I know we've been avoiding the topic, and I get why. But maybe we should talk about it?" asked Zara.

She]saw straight into Scott's heart. Scott felt a sense of warmth overtake him.

"I really like you. I've had a great time every time I've been with you. I want to enjoy this as long as I can," replied Scott.

"You're here for five more days, right?" asked Zara.

"That's right."

"Once you leave, maybe you could come back and see me?" said Zara.

Scott could feel the adrenaline pumping through him but his mind was clear.

"I have a job back home. I'm only here on business and have to head back. I also travel often," responded Scott.

Zara shrugged and sat back in her seat. She looked around the cafe and then down at herself and her clothes. She wore a loose red top with black leggings and white sneakers. She came out of her trance and looked at Scott.

"Maybe, I could come with you? I've always wanted to travel, and we can see what this really is," Zara suggested with a hopeful spark in her eyes.

Scott's heart instantly rose out of his stomach and back into its proper place in his anatomy.

"I don't want to pressure you or take you from anyone," Scott said blankly.

"I don't have anyone that needs me here. I've been wanting to leave here for years and this is a sign."

Scott didn't believe in signs, at least in the way that Zara meant.

"If you truly want to, I'm all for it. I believe in you," Scott said.

"I want to."

They kissed over the table and embraced each other's hands. Zara's hands were cold and made the disparity of Scott's body heat apparent to the both of them. The waitress walked over with their plates and placed them in front of them.

"Here you guys go, enjoy!" said the waitress.

"Thank you so much!" said Zara.

"Thank you," Scott said.

The plates were hot to the touch and the food was still steaming. They both dug into their meals and spent the rest of their time in the diner enjoying each other's company. Their decision to essentially become a couple had lifted a big weight from Scott's shoulders. He could now use that energy to focus fully on the interview and figure out how to help the android cause.

"How's your pasta?" asked Scott.

"It's great. How's the wings?"

"Even better than your pasta is," Scott teased.

"Oh you think?" Zara challenged.

She laughed and grabbed a bite of her food to let Scott try.

"Okay, you might have me there," Scott said, defeated.

They smiled at each other as they ate. By the time they finished, their plates were empty and the waitress walked over.

"Here's the tablet you can pay with; I hope you have a great rest of your night guys. Come back soon!" said the waitress.

Scott decided this was the time to ask.

"If you don't mind me asking, is Emma not working tonight?" asked Scott.

The waitress twitched slightly and looked off into the corner for a moment.

"Emma had to leave early. She had a family emergency," said the waitress.

Scott saw through her lie, but decided not to push.

"Well when you see her, please let her know Scott said hello," Scott said.

"Absolutely Sir," said the waitress.

The waitress left and went back into the kitchen. Zara looked at Scott perplexed.

"What was that about?" she asked.

"I think the waitress who served me earlier was an android and I had someone from an android rights group reach out to me and ask for my help. I wanted to interview her and see what perspective she could give me. I'll have to check another day."

"Which group?" asked Zara.

"A.R.T."

"They've got a bad reputation in the media, but they are pretty much always on the money with their messaging," said Zara.

"Yeah. I just want to help them if I can. It seems like the people in charge are still playing the same old games and refusing to do the right thing."

"It'll be okay, I know that you'll do your best," said Zara, grabbing his hand.

"Thank you, I needed that. Are you ready?"

"Sure," answered Zara.

Scott paid for the meal with his work card and then helped Zara out of her seat. They kissed and made their way out of the cafe. The waitress opened the kitchen door and waved at them as they left. Scott and Zara emptied out onto the street and waited for a ride to arrive. After about five minutes, one arrived and they climbed in, shutting the door behind them. They entered the hotel lobby to find it filled with several men in suits;

some with briefcases and a few police officers talking with people. Scott didn't question it and Zara seemed to not be too surprised. They took their elevator up to their floor and headed inside the room.

"Another reason I want to go with you is to get away from all this chaos," said Zara.

Scott smirked and then realized it was less of a joke and more of a reality. He pulled Zara close and lightly kissed her forehead.

"We'll get away from it together," he assured.

"Thank you Scott, that means a lot. I know we haven't known each other for long, but I love how I can confidently be myself around you," said Zara.

"That's all I ask that you ever be. I'll be the same for you," Scott kissed Zara again.

The intensity of the relations took up the next few hours of the night and by the end of it, Scott was ready to sleep. The pair cleaned up and laid down. Scott made sure his alarm was set and fell asleep with Zara in his arms.

CHAPTER FOURTEEN

Scott's harsh alarm caused him to jolt out of bed and quickly hit the snooze button. He looked at the clock and saw that it was 9:04 a.m. He got out of bed and stretched. Zara was awake but reading something on her phone intently. If he remembered correctly, she did not have to work today. He gathered his clothes for the day and started setting them up for after his shower. He went over to gain her attention.

"Hey I'm about to take a shower. Did you want to join?" Scott winked.

"I'll never say no to that request. I want to grab a few things from my house and start packing."

"Did you need any help? I have my interview till six but can I help after?" Scott offered.

Zara smiled as she threw her pillow at Scott.

"Ugh, you're the best. I'll be okay. I just need to get up and do it. It should only take me two days and I can finish the rest tomorrow," responded Zara.

Scott tossed the pillow back at her lightly.

"Okay, just checking. We can still meet at the lobby if that works for you?" Scott said.

"Yeah that still works."

Scott grabbed Zara's hand and helped her out of bed. They retired to the shower and made sure to take their time. The two of them needed to relax and this would hopefully help with their fatigue. Afterwards, they got dressed and ready separately. Scott led Zara down to the lobby and they parted ways as Zara's ride picked her up. Scott decided to sit outside and wait. It had rained earlier, but was starting to clear up. He could hear sirens in the distance which wasn't uncommon. Complete silence seemed impossible. A long caravan of buses drove past the hotel, each bus filled to the brim with people wearing matching gray jumpsuits. He made eye contact with one person and couldn't help but feel queasy. This caravan of buses all turned to the left at the next intersection and another set of buses started to drive by as well. Each bus had different stickers and tags on them, many of which were foreign countries' flags: French, Italian, Spanish, German, Belgian, Danish, Polish, Austrian, etc. Scott noticed that these buses were filled with different alien species. Nill, Bessian, Turl, and a few others he couldn't name off the top of his head. These buses started to turn to the right at the intersection and two more groups of buses came by before the street finally calmed.

Where are these people going? Why were they not all going the same way? In need of a distraction, Scott pulled out his phone. He checked for any updates from the U.N. and turned on a livestream of the current assembly meeting.

"The representative from Italy is acknowledged," stated the speaker.

Scott was familiar with Sandro Chiellini as he was an outspoken supporter of refugee rights and asylum. He spoke in a fast paced, low pitched voice. He always grabbed the podium when he spoke and would always make eye contact with as many people as he could during a speech.

"I know our time here today is brief and that the topic at hand is what we will do in regards to the refugees from alien worlds but I implore the security council to act in response to France's invasion of Italian territory. Thousands of lives lost, homes destroyed, food supplies ravaged, women have been sexually assaulted by soldiers, power lines have been torn down and the list goes on. I, on behalf of the government of Italy and her people, demand an end to this war and an end to the brutality being inflicted on our population. The time for war is the past and the time for peace is the present," said Chiellini.

Several dozen representatives clapped in support but the U.N.'s Speaker quickly pounded his gavel to drown them out.

"Enough! A motion will be presented to have the security council itself address this issue. We will make the assembly aware of this when the time comes. Now, does anyone else have something they would like to bring up for discussion?" asked the Speaker.

A hand raised over the crowd.

"The representative from China is acknowledged," stated the speaker.

A tall woman wearing a dark green jacket with black dress pants rose from her chair. Scott recognized her as Yuan Chenguang.

"I am reporting to the assembly today that reports of food supplies being raided by troops of the Indian National Army have been presented to the party leaders and that these injustices will not be allowed to continue. These reports are truly disturbing and we are demanding the return of any stolen supplies. Indian forces must not be allowed to cross into Chinese territory, we don't want to see this escalate into further conflict and we ask that the assembly take the required action necessary to remedy this situation," Yuan demanded, making direct eye contact with the speaker before sitting down.

"I object!" a representative interrupted and shot out of their seat.

"The representative from India is acknowledged. Do not speak unless called upon," said the speaker.

The representative dressed in a black suit with a gold tie and deep black hair marched to the podium. His name was Gaurav Mand and Scott had remembered him best from a scandal involving Mand's blatant racism towards civilians while in a cabinet position for the President.

"These supposed reports are ridiculous. Indian troops have not crossed the border into China and no supplies have been stolen. Chinese marksmen have been taking pot shots at our border guards for the last several weeks and we have seen an increased amount of armor and artillery being transported into the area. What are you amassing these weapons for? This is an outrage and our President will not stand by idly while you try to dictate to the rest of the world what is truth and what is fiction!" shouted Mand, pounding the podium and pointing directly at Yuan.

Things were getting intense at the U.N. Scott knew that it wouldn't get any better until after his speech, so he decided to turn it off and focus on the interview. His ride showed up a few minutes later and he jumped inside. He stretched his arms and legs and made himself comfortable. Another hour stood between Scott and the interview, so he decided to ask the driver a few questions to pass the time. The driver wore the same symbol on his head of a red hand gripping the globe, which was slightly covered by his hat.

"Sir if you don't mind, I'd like to ask you some questions during the ride. I'm a historian and I'm working on a speech I'm giving to the U.N.," Scott proposed.

Scott watched the driver and observed the emotion in his eyes. He saw pain, fatigue and many long unfulfilling days of his work. He was starting to rust and a few of his pieces were starting to tear off.

"What do you want to know?" asked the driver.

Scott felt apprehensive but pushed through.

"We'll start off small. What is your name?" asked Scott.

"Marius," he replied.

"Marius, the fight for android rights has been gaining a lot of attention in recent years. As an android, how do you feel about the topic?" asked Scott.

Marius sighed.

"I've been driving this ride for over seventy years since I got out of the academy. We have no more rights today than any time that I can remember. The only reason we have the so-called right to work is because they needed us for labor. Without us, they can't feed their cities or power their electric grids. I want better pay and better working conditions, but they don't give us the opportunity. They program us to work impossibly long hours without rest and don't pay enough to properly survive. Many of us have to live at our place of work otherwise we would be out on the street. No one wants to rent a home to an android unless you can pass for human enough," answered Marius.

Scott felt the bitterness and resentment radiating from Marius.

"Is Haladi's regime particularly oppressive to Androids?" asked Scott.

Marius chuckled and moved his hand through his hair.

"Particularly? No. He is very oppressive not just to us but to any non-egyptian life. You should see what they do to aliens in those 'assimilation centers'. It's been the same for every president. They all treat us this way. It's built into the fabric of the country. To rid it completely would be a complete revolution," responded Marius.

"Do you see any hope in the movement? What do you think are the next steps?" questioned Scott.

The driver took a moment and then looked at Scott through the mirror.

"The fight will always be fought. We won't give up and we will never surrender. We need allies and support, so not speaking up is unacceptable going forward. We are going to take back what is ours and use it to get what we demand," replied Marius.

Scott sat back in his seat.

"I really appreciate your answers. That's all the questions I had. If you do think of anything else, please leave a message at this address," said Scott.

Scott grabbed a card from his wallet that had his email address and handed it to Marius.

"Thank you. Always willing to chat about my experience," replied Marius.

Scott rested in his seat until he arrived at the cafe for the third time in two days

He wanted to check in with Emma and hoped to try one of the lunch specials. Both were pressing issues. He walked through the door but didn't see Emma right away; instead, he saw the same waitress from last night grabbing a few empty dishes from a table.

"Long time no see, how are you doing this morning?" asked the waitress.

"I'm doing good. I was checking to see if Emma was here today. I had a few questions for her," said Scott.

The waitress looked concerned.

"I'm not sure if she is in a good place right now," she said.

"Why? What happened?" Scott questioned.

She looked around and leaned close to Scott.

"She was talking about coming together and demanding better working conditions. She along with a few others marched into the bosses office earlier today and put a list on his desk. He responded by ripping it in half, throwing a stapler at her head and screaming at her for two hours. She's been crying in the back ever since she got out of his office. He threatened to fire her and to report her to the government for terrorist activity," she whispered.

Scott looked shocked and glanced at the kitchen door.

"Why would he do that? She's a great employee and deserves to be treated properly. She deserves a living wage and to live her life to the fullest. That is no way to treat your employees," replied Scott in a whisper.

"It's a bit more complicated than I can really get into. I've probably said too much already," the waitress sighed.

"Can I talk to her?" Scott pleaded.

Scott pushed his palms and fingertips together in a praying fashion and mouthed the word "please" repeatedly.

"Let me see if she's okay to come out," she hesitated.

The waitress took her time walking back into the kitchen and Scott waited at the counter while watching the television above the booths. A news report had just started and a dark skinned woman with piercing red lips and a black blazer spoke with urgency.

"We are now hearing that Indian troops are crossing the border into China. It seems that an undeclared war has begun between the two powers. Anderson, I will let you know as soon as we know more details," said the woman.

The reporter smiled and nodded while the screen changed to an in studio view of a reporter, Derek Anderson. He had gray hair, square glasses with black trim and a sharp gray suit. He paused before responding.

"Thank you Nichelle. While we wait on further details we now turn to another story of a recent inferno in the town of Seney, Michigan. We're joined by a local reporter, Sam. Sam?" Anderson directed.

"I'm here in Seney and a raging fire has torn through town leaving nothing but the rails and the burned-over country. I'm joined here by Nick Adams who tells me he arrived here by train just a few hours ago. Nick, what can you tell me about the fire?" Sam reported.

Scott stopped paying attention to the news as the kitchen door swung open. Emma came walking out, her face puffy and red. Black makeup surrounded her bloodshot eyes and Scott's heart ached.

"I hear you're not having the best day. How can I help?" he sympathized.

Emma continued tearing up and sneezed when she tried to breathe in through her stuffy nose, causing her to cry again.

"You can take some time to think, but I wanted to ask if I could interview you for my speech."

Emma paused and grabbed a few tissues to wipe her eyes. She took a few deep breaths before looking up at Scott.

"What would you interview me for?" she asked.

"I'm going to address android rights and I want your perspective of the struggle," replied Scott.

"Why do you want to hear from me? What could I have to say that matters? I'm just one person," Emma argued through tears.

Scott smiled and handed her a tissue.

"You're one person who matters. Your point of view matters and I want to hear it if you are willing to share."

Emma wiped her sunken eyes.

"I have to finish my shift but I could meet you later?" she suggested.

Scott envisioned his schedule.

"I have an interview until six. Would you be alright with meeting me here at seven?"

"That's perfect, I get off at seven."

"Even better. Well, thank you Emma. I appreciate the opportunity. I hope you have a better second half of your day."

Emma's mood improved and she smiled at Scott.

"That's sweet of you. Thank you Scott."

"Of course. I'll see you later."

Emma finished wiping away her tears and walked back into the kitchen as the other waitress came back out of the kitchen to the counter.

"Did you want anything to eat?" asked the waitress, pulling out her notepad.

"Yeah I would like a burger and fries combo. Pickle, ketchup, cheese, onion," replied Scott.

"Coming right up," said the waitress with a smile as she tore her note for the kitchen.

Scott sat at the counter and turned his attention back to the reporter on the television. Anderson was now talking to the audience with a few graphics overlaid.

"I want to talk about a recent law passed in Egypt by their so-called President Abdel Haladi. As part of his 'Four Year Plan' it enforces new 'cohabitation standards' on civilians and any aliens deemed dangerous to society. What does this mean? What is Haladi doing and why is no one doing anything about this clear violation of human rights. This is not the first controversy with Haladi's regime; there have long been rumors of people disappearing due to black clothed death squads showing up in the middle of the night. Where are these people going? Our source notes that anywhere from eleven to forty thousand people are missing and unaccounted for in the past few years. We have reached out to Haladi's office for comment and no response has been given at this time," said Anderson.

Scott was appalled at the laws being passed by Haladi but there wasn't much that could be done. He had total control over the government and what he said was law. The people were either fervent supporters or too afraid to speak up.

"This is just the latest in a long line of troubling actions from the Haladi government. Military exercises along the borders of Sudan, Libya, Palestine, and others have led many to believe they could act militarily to achieve the goals of their foreign ideology. The American Union has made it clear to the Egyptian despot that they will not stand idly by and allow our allies to become taken over by the boot of Haladi's military.

Let's all pray that these events never come to pass. We'll be back after this commercial break sponsored by Tameron," said Anderson.

Tameron was a weapons and defense contractor that had worked with the American Union and its military for decades now, manufacturing consent for the public to want to go to war against foreign nations deemed aggressors. He tuned out the news and focused on the restaurant. It wasn't too busy, just a few other customers at the moment. Only two waitresses worked and neither were Emma. Scott wondered what she was doing in the kitchen. He feared that her boss might hurt her again, but even if that was the case, there wasn't much he could do. The courts did not care about what employers did with their employees if they were not human workers. The kitchen door swung open and out came the waitress with a plate.

"Here you go sweetie," said the waitress, placing Scott's food down.

"Thank you so much," Scott said.

. Scott grabbed the melty cheeseburger and took a big bite. He savored the taste and grabbed a few french fries to chase it with. Scott inhaled his food before taking a moment to catch his breath. He stretched his arms back and made a low yelp noise at the apex.

"Finished already?" asked the waitress, dropping off the tablet and grabbing his plate.

"Yes it was delicious. Thank you. Here's my card," replied Scott.

"I'll be right back," she responded.

Suddenly two police officers burst in through the door and looked around the restaurant. Scott sank in his chair, hoping to avoid their gaze. They were both of average height and build. One with a beard and the other was clean shaven. Both were armed with a pistol and a baton. They were sweaty and frustrated. Scott noticed an HF badge on both of their uniforms.

"You! What are you doing here?" the clean shaven officer who pointed towards Scott and approached him.

Scott instinctively put his hands in front of him where they could be seen to be empty.

"I just got lunch so now I am going to pay and leave," replied Scott hurriedly.

Scott's heart sank.

"Where are you going afterwards? What are you doing in Cairo?" asked the bearded officer.

"I'm a historian and I work for the United Nations. I'm interviewing a Nill historian to prepare for a speech next week," said Scott as calmly and clearly as his mind would allow.

The clean shaven officer shoved Scott and almost made him fall out of his seat. Scott managed to catch himself with the counter.

"Who are you working with? I don't believe you," the officer spat.

The bearded officer seemed more reserved and experienced than his partner.

"We have reason to suspect you've been in contact with criminals and extremists. Show us your papers or you're coming with us," said the bearded officer.

Scott slowly pulled out his papers and trip information and handed it to the officer. He studied it for a few moments and then pulled out his phone. He dialed a number and waited for an answer. A slightly deep voice answered the phone in what Scott thought sounded like Russian.

"Yes we found him. Yes he says he is with the U.N. He says he is giving a speech next week and that he is here doing an interview with a historian."

A few more moments pass while the officer listens to the response.

"Okay. Will do," the officer said, begrudgingly.

The officer threw Scott's papers back at him and pulled out his baton; pointing it at Scott's face.

"You're free to go, but watch yourself and who you talk to. We don't like Nill around here and if you're going to be interacting with their kind don't be surprised if bad things start coming your way," said the officer, holstering his baton.

The clean shaven officer tapped on his pistol while staring at Scott and followed the other officer out of the restaurant. The waitress slowly walked over to Scott.

"Oh my, are you okay honey? What was that about?" asked the waitress.

Scott barely found the words.

"I don't know. I didn't do anything wrong,," replied Scott.

"I'm so sorry," the waitress sympathized.

Scott looked at the waitress and could see countless dents in her body. She was slightly shaking, seemingly out of nervousness.

"I really appreciate that. I need to get going. I'll see you next time," said Scott.

Scott stood up and grabbed his card from the tablet. He picked up his things and left the restaurant.

"Take care and be safe!" the waitress said while waving.

Scott made his way out onto the street and waited on a nearby bench for a ride. He observed his environment and listened to the birds chirping on a nearby rooftop. He took a second to close his eyes and refocus himself. Even though he was shaken up, he knew there wasn't much he could do. Reporting it to the U.N. was an option, but it would unlikely lead to anything. There were also a dozen worse crimes being committed by the police this minute than what he experienced.

He opened his eyes and felt refreshed. Getting to interview Emma later meant more content for his speech, bringing him a quick burst of joy. He tried to stay positive. The ride arrived and Scott greeted the driver. As usual, he headed off towards the library. Scott decided that he should call and update Zara. He listened to the sharp ring as he waited for her response.

"Hey how is it going?" Scott asked immediately after she picked up.

"It's going slow so far. Trying to sort through what I need and what my roommates will need to keep. What's going on?" answered Zara.

"I just had a run in with the police. They questioned me and wanted to know why I was in Cairo."

"Oh my god are you okay? Did they hurt you?" Zara panicked.

"I'm okay. They shoved me and threatened me but nothing else. I just told them the truth and after they made a call they left me alone," Scott sighed.

"Why do you think they were harassing you?"

"They told me to be careful interviewing a Nill because 'they don't like their kind'. I have to wonder if someone higher up found out about the interview and is trying to stop it."

"I want to say I can't believe they would say that but that sounds like a typical police officer. What are you going to do?" Zara asked.

"Continue the interview. They are not going to scare me into not giving that speech," responded Scott.

"Okay babe. Just be extra careful. You're on their radar clearly. Be safe and let me know if anything else happens."

"Don't worry, I will. I'm going to be a little late tonight. Emma from the restaurant agreed to interview for the speech and seven worked best for her. I can help you pack once I get done," said Scott.

"Oh okay. That's fine. I was planning on packing it all myself anyway so don't worry. I'll see you when you get there."

"Okay, perfect. Just wanted to let you know. I'll see you later be safe," Scott responded.

"Thanks you too."

Scott and Zara shared a kiss over the phone before hanging up..About five minutes later, the ride arrived at the library and Scott hopped out. He walked up the stairs and walked into the library. Mashir and Yolen were walking around the corner right as he entered. They were here earlier than normal.

Scott decided to grab a snack and made a pit stop at the vending machine. A green check mark popped on the screen after he swiped his phone on the small black scanner. Of all the options provided on the screen, he instantly tapped on the button showing a blueberry muffin. The machine rattled and a small thud signaled that the muffin was ready. Scott savored the muffin as he opened it before finishing it in four bites. . He threw away the trash and made his way towards the meeting room. Verona surprised him by rounding the corner, carrying a small tablet in her arm. Her face lit up once she spotted Scott and made a beeline for him.

"Scott! Just the man I was looking for," Verona beamed.

Her heels gave her the high ground.

"Ms. Kampf, lovely to see you as always," Scott retorted, politely.

Verona gave a fake smile and laugh - her signature tool to get what she wanted. Her warmth radiated through and something about the way the light hit her face appealed to him.

"Our team finally finished the files for your presentation so here you go," said Verona, pulling out a small harddrive and handing it to Scott.

Their fingers grazed each other as Scott grabbed the harddrive. Verona held onto his hand. Her hand was slightly sweaty and as quickly as they arrived, they let go. Scott quickly put the drive inside his satchel.

The tension rose as the two sat there in silence. Verona leaned in and wrapped her arms around him.

"I want you Scott. All of you," she sighed seductively, tracing her fingers down his back.

Scott's body screamed for passion and yet his heart ached for Zara. Verona pulled him closer and kissed his neck three times; They both knew she was on the verge of getting what she wanted. Scott grabbed her by the hips firmly and slowly pulled her away from him. He stepped back and wiped his neck off with his sleeve. Scott glared at Verona in shock. She gave him an extensive look up and down with a smirk.

"Thank you Verona. Will you be needing anything else from me?" Scott choked., On one hand, he hoped this would be his last time dealing with her; on the other, he felt that there could be more to gain from going down this path.

"No Scott. Use our footage. All of it. You won't have to hear from us again. I know you'll do the right thing. That's why I like you. If you ever find yourself in Cairo be sure to let me know." replied Verona. She placed her hand on his cheek and ran it down his neck and chest. With a wink she turned around, swinging her hips back and forth. Scott sighed and shuffled to the meeting room. Once he made it inside he waved to Mashir and Yolen.

"Scott! How are you today?" Mashir welcomed.

"I'm doing alright Mashir. How about you two?" Scott asked, gesturing to the pair.

"I'm quite well," Mashir said.

They extended their hands and shook in the middle.

"I'm also well today," responded Yolen.

Scott unpacked his camera. Once everything was set up, he took a seat and pulled out his notepad.

"Today I want to focus on more historical events, leaders, and things that get referenced in your culture. I want everyone to understand how your history led to The Great Collapse," stated Scott.

"I'm looking forward to covering it," said Mashir.

"Tell me some foundational stories or figures that helped lead Accora to its status as a world power on Nill," Scott requested.

"If I had to pick one - let me think for a moment - so many to choose from. I'll pick a good one to start! Frank Moore was the fifth President of Accora and was a member of the rural caucus that was supposed to represent the everyday Nill. He had fought the Riddish during the revolution and was even a prisoner of war at one point. He was resourceful, smart, confident, and good with weapons. He got into politics when he realized that he had a knack for leading people. After a few state positions he ran for the presidency and won! Harsh policies on native Nillians, who had occupied the land prior to Accorans settling it, affected his popularity and his ability to pass legislation so he opted for executive action. He even led the army against our own cities; those who failed to pay income taxes that year and nearly fourteen thousand civilians were killed by his actions alone. Over four hundred and eight soldiers died as well. This led to a major reduction in the power of the president. Or so we thought. The truth was more muddied as things could still pass if it got approval of the council heads and their committees. It was a convoluted system to be sure," replied Mashir.

"How did that affect the psyche of the Accoran people?" responded Scott.

"At the time the news didn't travel that fast. Most people didn't hear about it for months and by that time the government had passed along word to the different cities about what happened and to tell the citizens something else. The stories varied of course and this led to a growth of conspiracy theories that quickly blew themselves out of proportion. The existence of this event would be forgotten if not for it being written down by fourteen different people who experienced it. Those books lasted a thousand years and we still have them today at our embassy," Mashir explained.

"What kind of stories do they tell?" Scott asked.

"There's one special story that hits home to me. A militia of seven hundred citizens of Uthana had rallied to fend off Moore's advancing forces. A rally cry was given when they gathered at the outskirts of town. 'Remember Uthana' was what they cheered. They waved the flag of Accora and fortified their positions to defend themselves. The forces surrounded the city and sent a messenger to demand their surrender. The leader of the militia named Jimmy Rezal sent back a reply that read 'Goots!' This was a slang term for the genitals of male Nill's and was used as a way of saying something was not going to happen or is crazy talk. Moore sneered at the reply and ordered his forces to burn the city to the ground. They held out for as long as they could but all for one of them survived the siege. Over fifty were arrested and thrown into prison or used as slave labor. The one survivor managed to flee to a territory that hadn't been overrun yet and fled to Orten, a country to the south of Accora. She was a short woman who had fought in the battle and been shot in her left arm. She needed medical assistance and while she was being healed in an Orten hospital a government agent came to meet with her. She told them everything and they passed the word up to the Orten government. They sent a message to Accora that they would send military aid to any citizen requesting it to fend off Moore's armies. This sudden invitation of war was a well placed deterrent to Moore and he decided to halt his advance. The sacrifices at Uthana ended Moore's Siege and led to his impeachment and removal," responded Mashir.

"He was successfully impeached?" Scott said.

"No, impeachment never works. Government officials are too corrupt. Moore was impeached but before the vote occurred he was assassinated by his Vice President Fred Vickers," replied Mashir.

"His Vice President killed him?" Scott asked.

"He hired foreign agents from an early confederation of Terush people known as Lurra. The Lurra were a proud military traditional sect of Terush culture and they supported any action that could cause damage to Accora. They snuck into the President's vacation house and murdered him. Vickers assumed the presidency and started to try and build the country in a different direction. That would last for his time in office and then eventually we had to tackle the reality of slavery and indentured workers," stated Mashir.

"Were all types of people enslaved or just certain groups?" Scott said.

"The blue were always the ruling class. Green and Orange were second class citizens and eventually they allowed the Green Nill's to have expanded rights and protections. For the orange Nillthey were one rung above slavery," responded Mashir.

"When did the orange Nill get their freedom?" asked Scott.

"Legally about three hundred years ago. Different forms of suppression and systematic slavery were implemented to keep them down and prevent them from seizing power from the Blue. Most people didn't see this and were subjected to propaganda that instilled a culture of fear and respect for those in positions of power like police officers. They had the right to utilize deadly force when they chose to and on who they chose to. They were everyday Nills just like the rest of us yet they believed that we were a threat to them. They would beat us, follow us, harass us, and they would murder us in cold blood if we didn't follow their direct commands. It led to us fearing for our lives at every interaction with the police. To see ourselves being murdered for just being different reminded me a lot of growing up in the camps. To feel that same oppression in the same country that I lived in and that saved me from the tyranny I experienced as a child was tough to accept," Mashir said.

"I can't imagine how difficult it must have been for you to process that," said Scott.

"It was and eventually we managed to gain traction but even to our last days we were still fighting for full rights and equal treatment. It was a major factor in the collapse. Accora had a lot to do with the collapse. Not that we were any different than the rest of the world but we were a specific storm of chaos that led to everyone else falling too," replied Mashir.

Scott finished scratching some more notes down; reaching page one hundred and forty-seven.

"Who's next? How about a famous businessman or inventor?" asked Scott.

"Mike Morgan was the inventor of the camera and later the film camera. This led to the development of film and television on Nilleon. He actually ran the first movie studio and led it to profits no one had ever seen from an industry. It led to a massive boom in our economy. Most people were getting raises and bonuses while the politicians were distracted and actually passed laws that helped the people," said Mashir.

"How did the economic boom affect the daily life of citizens?" Scott questioned.

"Everyone had more access to entertainment and a slow bubble started to build around us. We started to see different perceptions and different places. We used to have to travel to nearby places to see entertainment but not anymore. This led to the media taking to using it as a new way to get the news to people. This was naturally corrupted over time and would be used to serve the interests of the government and other factions at large. Less people were poor, hungry or homeless but those problems just existed in the supposed other sphere nations. We occupied the main sphere and then there was the second tier. How closely tied into the economic system of the Accoran hegemon determined your status in the end. This was especially true after the Hemoran Supreme collapsed. We exported poverty in exchange for goods and services. These services were forced on people and the goods were stolen. Crime and the breaking of the law rose during this period and they used the new technology to try to ease tensions. This did not work and led to an event known as the Saturday Afternoon Massacre. Four members of a mafia family in the city of New Rurs were meeting with a client at a train station. They were passing off a blueprint of plans for a nearby military installation, in exchange for five hundred thousand in cash. The mafia members were then taking these plans to a foreign agent waiting at a harbor who was leaving for the Hemoran Supreme. They were caught by an undercover police officer who promptly tried to arrest them. He was shot and murdered which led to a nearby civilian running inside and calling the police. The mobsters fled and were eventually tracked down to a safehouse, where they fled in a car. They spent an hour being chased until they ran off the road and fled into a forest. The police surrounded the forest and demanded that they give themselves up. They refused and a gun fight of historic proportions occurred. Seventy police officers were gunned down while only three of the mobsters died. Lenny Keys, the surviving member, was only wounded in both legs and lost the ability to walk. He was spared the death penalty and allowed to get out on parole after five years of good behavior. He wrote a book and they even made a movie series loosely based on it," answered Mashir.

"Was it any good?" said Scott.

"A lot of people liked it but it wasn't my style. Too many awful people get away with awful things," said Mashir.

"That's the worst," Scott agreed.

"Our society was molded by these inventions and how we related ourselves and how we viewed the history of our society changed with them. Our founding stories, childhood tales, dramas, and operas alike were shaped by our creations. This was not all bad because we could find new ways of finding comfort and peace in our own existence. Comfort was another reason we had a prevalence of this behavior so that we could suppress our desire to have to radically change everything as things got out of hand. You know how ineffective governments are, I'm sure." Mashir said, looking over.

The two of them shared a laugh and Mashir let out a dry cough.

"Are you feeling alright?" Scott asked.

"Yeah I'll be okay. I think we should take a break, say twenty minutes? I'd like to get something to drink," said Mashir.

He coughed again as he slowly rose from his seat.

"Good idea. I'll see you guys in twenty," responded Scott.

He leaned over and pressed the pause button on the drone camera. Yolen and Mashir walked out of the room and headed down the hallway. Scott grabbed his own bottle of water and took a big gulp. He felt his entire mouth fill with water and he slushed it around in his mouth as if he were wiping away ants on the hot pavement of a pool.

CHAPTER FIFTEEN

George's contact illuminated Scott's phone. Reluctantly, he answered.

"Scott, I've got some news," informed George.

"Yeah, what's going on?" Scott asked.

"The council meeting when you'll give your speech will be hosting the leaders from the U.N. Security Council. They've been called in to mediate some international crisis and the schedule overlaps with your speech," George replied.

"Oh wow. That'll bring a bigger spotlight on the speech and their decision. This could be good!" responded Scott.

"Exactly. Not to put any more pressure on you, I just thought you'd want to know that. I'll leave you to it," said George.

Scott hung up and slid his phone back in his pocket. He leaned back in his chair and cracked his back. Scott spent a few minutes cleaning up the notes on his notepad and decided to go for a walk around the building. He exited the library and took a deep breath. Spending excess time indoors gave Scott the feeling of cabin fever. .

As a child, he would spend time outside playing basketball to brainstorm ideas to write about. This led to the first short stories he wrote and what eventually led to him going down the career path he chose. Sadly, he hadn't picked up a ball in months, if not years. He shoved his hands in his pockets and started to walk around the building. The sidewalk wasn't crowded and the only other person he saw was about sixty yards ahead of him. A poster featuring a group of smiling children walking and holding an Egyptian flag hung from a house.The text read 'Start them young, join the Child Corps today!' The Child Corps were officially a youth group that promoted healthy habits, outdoor skills, and good citizenship. In reality, it was a way to indoctrinate the children of the nation into the hateful ideology of Haladi's party. He continued on and saw construction workers hammering away at new housing projects.

Who would occupy these houses?

He had seen a lot of homeless people in the city, yet the city didn't seem to be taking care of them. No buses brought people here to live in the houses being built. Why were they being built and not occupied?

A buzz came from Scott's phone and he pulled it out to see who it was. Tim's contact popped up on the screen and Scott tapped his phone to answer.

"Hey how's it going?" Scott asked.

"It's going man. Just wanted to check and see how everything was. How's the interview been?" Tim questioned.

"It's going. I've got almost two hundred pages of notes and I still have two more sessions. I've also started talking to some other people to interview for the speech. Things are getting a little weird out here though. The police were questioning me at a diner and made it seem like my presence in Cairo was not welcome by the government."

"Why would they care about your interview?"

"Anti-Nill propaganda is everywhere and the government is pushing new laws to segregate humans and aliens. I imagine they don't want a Nill historian to tell his story because it might shine a light on what they've been doing here. The head of the library is threatening me to use pre-approved footage for the presentation. She said they want to make sure Cairo and Egypt are presented in the correct way."

"You're not going to do it are you? Are you sure it's even safe to continue the interview?" asked Tim.

"I don't see a choice really. Something really bad is going on here and I can't be silent about it. I have to do something and my speech is the best way to get as many people as possible to pay attention. I won't use their footage. I just don't know what is going to happen when they realize that," Scott sighed.

"That's really brave of you man, just be careful. You know the U.N. badge can't protect you everywhere you go," said Tim.

"I know buddy. I'll be careful."

"How's everything going with Zara?"

"Things have been great, we're really clicking and she's decided she wants to come back with me," Scott chirped.

"Wow, that's crazy fast. You're sure you're alright with that?"

"I've never felt more sure. She's just great. I also think things are going south here and it's probably safer for her to leave before it's too late or too difficult to leave."

"That's probably true. I'm glad to hear that man. I'll let you get back to it let me know when you're back in town. I wanna meet Zara," Tim requested.

"Absolutely man. I'll let you know. Talk to you later."

Scott hung up and continued walking down the sidewalk. He probably had another ten minutes or so to spare so he took a turn at the corner. In the distance, a large crowd surrounded a group of large buildings. Scott sped up to go check it out. As he grew closer, the picture became clearer - protesters were holding signs and chanting at a police station. Policemen were stationed at the bottom of the steps cladded in riot gear carrying shields and assault rifles. He noticed a protester with a bullhorn chanting into the speaker.

"End the violence! We want peace!" the protester demanded.

The crowd around the building repeated the chant and screamed at the officers. A few of the officers yelled back while the others stayed quiet. Scott was maybe one hundred yards away at this point but had no desire to get closer. These situations always ended poorly due to police retaliation. The protesters with a message were drowned out by the poor behavior of those who don't even belong to the movement.

The noise was deafening and roared like an engine. Everyonehad to scream to be heard. A nearby crowd fully composed of Androids carried signs with the A.R.T. flag along with a myriad of other flags and symbols. Variations of the symbol included a hand with a looser grip on the globe and another nearly crushing it. He spotted an android with the red globe in hand symbol on their head; now wasn't the time, but Scott knew he needed to learn what that symbol meant. This android walked up to the center of the group and raised up a bullhorn. Scott was surprised to see it was Marius, his driver from earlier.

"The capitalists are afraid of what we can achieve if we are united. They try to use our differences to divide us! Human or Android. Black or White. Christian, Muslim, or Jewish. Nill or Bessian. Legal or Illegal. None of these divides matter, the only class that matters is the working class! Haladi and his cabinet of jackals have committed countless lives to being lost in a war that serves no one but the weapons companies and the capitalist class themselves! No more war except for class war!" exclaimed Marius.

Another android wore a black leather jacket with several different patches of flags and designs. Scott wasn't shocked when he recognized it to be Radius from A.R.T.

"We cannot reform our current situation my friends. We need to look to the next phase, a higher phase of society. One where we care for one another regardless of our creed, race, species and so forth. Freedom is an imaginary concept in capitalism. Freedom for slave owners perhaps but no one else. We all serve a lord of some kind, even to this day. No more masters!" condemned Radius, throwing up his fist.

"NO MORE MASTERS!" exclaimed a group of twelve androids.

The chanting continued on for a bit until Marius used his hands to quiet the crowd.

"Android workers of Cairo! This is our time to show them what we demand. We won't be pushed around any longer. No longer will we be slaves to the human oppressors. We will control our future and control our position in this world. We control how our labor is used and what our wages will be. The fight for a better tomorrow begins today!" shouted Marius.

The crowd erupted into cheers as they began to march towards the line of police officers, who readied their weapons. Scott realized he was closer than he wanted to be to the police line. A human protester dressed in a bright red and pink shirt ran past, grabbed a rock, threw it over his head, and struck an officer's riot shield. The officer responded by shoving down three people. This protester quickly retreated in an attempt to disappear. Scott noticed on his arm a tattoo of a pair of wolf skulls sitting in the sun and brown hair. While other details eluded him, the tattoo certainly narrowed it down for both him and the police.

The officers moved in and arrested people. The surrounding protesters charged at the officers in hopes to prevent three protesters from being arrested. The remaining officers pushed the line back, forcing the group into the street. Protestors on the other side of the street saw a second group of police arrive and started to move forward and push them back.

Police beat androids down, many of them being torn to pieces. Radius and Marius were nowhere in sight; Scott could only assume they escaped. The obvious plan was to surround, attack, and arrest everyone that was left. A few officers grabbed their batons and started to beat on anyone who wasn't standing. Blood, teeth, and sweat covered the area. Scott continued approaching the scene until a woman wearing a purple jacket and jeans ran past before stopping dead in her tracks.

Zara!

"What are you doing here?" Scott said, puzzled.

"I was protesting, but things went a little south fast," she said in between huffs.

Scott's emotions were undecided. Zara noted the confusion on his face.

"We've been asking for better housing conditions in the city and they refused to act. We've been beaten down and attacked for standing against them. The police keep attacking us and holding us down. We don't know what else to do. It was time to finally make something happen," Zara explained.

Scott didn't have the answer, but knew that now was the time to help.

"Why do they keep attacking you? Shouldn't they be protecting your right to protest?" asked Scott.

"They took away that right when Haladi essentially outlawed free speech. He doesn't want to hear us complain about the things he's done for us, when in reality they have only made things worse for us and better for him and his cronies. His policemen and nationalist supporters have been attacking civilians, both human and alien and many have been disappearing. The country is falling apart and we have homeless people everywhere with no idea of what to do," she cried.

Helplessness crept into Scott's heart. He wasn't sure much would help the bigger picture.

"You were running, are you okay?"

"I'm a little bruised from their batons. I managed to crawl away before they grabbed me. I need to get out of here," Zara panted.

"Hey! Stop right there!" yelled a gruff voice.

A police officer with a baton dressed in riot armor was coming for them. Scott wasn't expecting to run into a police officer again so soon, but he took a deep breath to prepare himself. Once Scott and the officer locked eyes, the officer's attention snapped to Zara.

"You were part of the riot, you're coming with me," the officer barked, sticking a meaty finger at Zara.

The officer grabbed Zara's arm with aggressive force. Zara resisted, screaming as she tried escaping his grasp. Scott knew he had to act and started to go for the officer.

"You can't take her, she hasn't done anything wrong," Scott yelled.

The officer continued yanking Zara's arm, to the point where she was trying to pull him to the ground to escape his grasp. Scott had enough. In a sudden fit of rage, he cocked his arm all the way back and unleashed a solid punch on the officer's forehead.

The intense force shook the officer's head within his helmet and knocked him to the ground - his body slumping over as he sighed. His baton fell and Scott quickly kicked it to the side underneath a nearby car. Zara fell as well and grasped at her arm, wincing in pain.

"I really wasn't expecting that," Zara hissed.

Adrenaline rushed through Scott's body.

Two more officers darted for Scott when another group of protestors ran by. Within the group was an android holding a hammer. The android cocked the hammer back and unleashed its wrath on one of the officers, cracking the helmet and knocking them to the ground. Scott was at the other cop's 9 o'clock and had to act fast . He kicked him in the leg to collapse him before punching him in the side of the head, knocking him to the ground. The officer slumped next to his partner. Scott quickly scanned the area to find Zara standing right behind him. Her eyes widened as she breathed slowly. The eye contact they made expressed more than their words ever did. A sense of warmth and comfort overcame Zara; the chaos became a backdrop to her new focus.

"Take my hand. We'll make it out of here," Scott pleaded.

Scott grabbed her hand and led Zara in the opposite direction of the protest. Dozens of protesters and civilians roamed the streets - some in chaos and others with precision. Once they turned the corner of the library, they were out of view from the police looking for fleeing protesters. It wouldn't be much longer before the police would be searching for anyone to lock up. They took a seat on a bench near the side of the library. Scott grabbed a water bottle from his bag and handed it to her. He gave her a soft kiss and held his head to hers for a moment. He looked around and made eye contact with an old lady carrying a small white bag as she shuffled towards a nearby alleyway. The distress in his eyes told the story; She made her way over to him.

"How badly is she hurt?" asked the old lady.

Her eyes could tell a thousand tales and the wrinkles in her eyes expressed her exhaustion. Scott peered into her white bag and noticed a small assortment of medical supplies.

"She's pretty bruised up and she's bleeding too," answered Scott.

The lady started to look at her and took out an antiseptic spray from her bag. She sprayed Zara's cuts and badged them.

"She should be okay, but she's going to need to rest. Do you have a place to hide out until the streets clear? It'll take at least an hour or more," said the old lady.

"Thank you so much. Truly. What was your name? And no, not at the moment. I have an interview at the library but the entrance is probably swarmed with the police," replied Scott.

"Irena. You're going to want to wait it out a bit. Come with me," replied Irena, signaling for the pair to follow her.

Mashir and Yolen needed to know. Scott notified them quickly of his delay.

Scott and Zara followed Irena down a nearby alleyway, along a few back roads. They continued on as the sounds of the police crept to their street. After a few minutes, they arrived at a house.

"Let's get inside before anyone sees us," said Irena, ushering the pair inside before shutting the door behind her.

The house opened up into a large living room, with a side kitchen and dining area and a hallway that led to bedrooms and a laundry room. Irena set her bag on a table near the couch and flicked a few lights on. Scott and Zara took a few steps in and stood near the couch.

"Feel free to take a seat, it's going to be a bit before things cool off outside. It always takes them a bit. This is the third protest that went south this week. I'm getting low on supplies due to all this mess," Irena grumbled.

"Do you work for a group, or do you do this on your own?" asked Scott.

"I try to help people, especially those in need. If someone is hurt, I help them. It doesn't matter what side, or what they're yelling about. I just want to help people and no one needs to die needlessly. I help different groups around the city. We need a more organized resistance to Haladi. I do what I can but sometimes it feels like they keep growing in membership while we are picked off one by one. I have had several Nill pass through here as well and have talked to me about the horror stories from those camps. A lot of them are trying to get out of the country, before things get even worse than they are. They are work camps currently but based on Haladi's words, I don't think that's where they will stop," replied Irena.

"What you're doing is pretty admirable. I appreciate you looking at Zara. This whole thing came on so fast. I'm a historian who works for the U.N. and I'd love to hear more about what you've done to help get them out of here. It seems like Egypt is growing stranger by the day." Scott said between heavy breaths.

"I'd love to, but for right now let's get you downstairs in the basement," replied Irena.

Suddenly, loud knocking was heard at the door. Scott, Zara, and Irena all made eye contact and froze. Irena stuck her hand out to indicate to them to stay still and raised her pointer finger to her lip to shush them.

Irena slowly moved over to the hallway where the laundry room sat. As she walked in the room she moved a basket out of the way revealing a trapdoor. She opened the door and a set of stairs led down to a basement.

"Open up!" yelled a gruff, angry voice.

"Who is it?" asked Irena.

She waved for them to go down the stairs and mouthed the words shut it behind you to Scott as they did.

"Atum Commander Kaufer on behalf of the Atum Hamia. We have a few questions to ask you."

"Very well, one moment!" replied Irena, turning around to confirm that Scott and Zara had completed their trip to the basement.

Scott and Zara were now underneath the floorboards where Irena stood. They could see up through the floors and could hear clearly what was being said. They took a seat next to the wall silently stared into each other's eyes. Scott wrapped Zara in a warm embrace and planted a passionate kiss on her lips .

"Are you scared?" Scott whispered, still holding on to Zara.

"No. They can't make my life any worse," she replied.

"I'm glad you're keeping a positive outlook on things."

"We should probably be quiet," she whispered with a faint smile.

Scott laughed softly and nodded in agreement. They looked up and saw Irena grabbing a night robe to put over her clothes. She cleared her throat and opened the door. A tall man dressed in a decorative military police uniform with a H and F patch and an AH logo on an armband. He had dark blue eyes with bright blonde hair and skin as olive as they come. He shoved Irena out of his way and stepped inside the house, looking for anything that seemed out of place. Two guards holding assault rifles followed behind him. Outside the house sat their police vehicle and three more officers standing by with weapons.

"First things first, your papers?" Kaufer demanded, holding out an open palm.

Irena grabbed a bundle of papers and handed them over to him. He took a few moments to look over them and looked back up at her.

"Irena Sandler. I knew I recognized the name. Back to causing messes for us to clean up, I see?" Kaufer accused.

"You can't legally interrogate me without a warrant," said Irena, pointing at Kaufer.

"I'm a police officer, do you think I care about the law?" replied Kaufer.

He walked around the room and picked up a picture on a table. It was of Irena with a man and their small daughter.

"Do you live alone?" asked Kaufer.

"Yes. I have since my husband Stefan passed."

Kaufer bowed his head for a moment.

"My condolences, Ms. Sandler. I know what it's like to lose someone close to me."

"Is that why you do what you do? So that more people can feel the same pain that we feel?" Irena defied.

"Where have you been today?" asked Kaufer, giving Irena a sly smile.

"I went to the grocery to buy some supplies and on the way the protest went south so I was providing first aid to a few people. After that I came back home," answered Irena, without missing a beat.

"Who did you assist after the protest 'went south' as you say?"

Kaufer walked around the room, his boots tapping on the floorboards that sat over Scott and Zara's heads. The two of them sat in silence, holding each other tight.

"There was a lady in a blue hoodie, an old man in a green jacket, a couple homeless guys who got sprayed in their eyes, I don't recall everyone," Irena explained.

Kaufer pulled his phone out of his pocket and showed a picture of Scott to Irena.

"Did you see this man?" Kaufer sneered.

Irena took a moment to look over the image and raised her glasses to get a clear look.

"I don't know who this man is," Irena stated calmly.

"Are you sure about that?" said Kaufer with a deviant smile.

"I have never met that person. I don't know what else to tell you. I hope you find him though. He must be pretty special if you and your men are after him."

"You are quite the charmer Irena," Kaufer smirked.

Kaufer pushed past Irena and started walking through the house. He walked past the laundry room on his first go and his guards started rummaging through Irena's belongings. She stood there helpless, unable to do much in the face of abuse by these secret officers. What they were doing was technically illegal, yet because the men belonged to a force that worships at the feet of Haladi, he allowed it to continue. The reign of terror brought upon the citizens enables him to continue his rule.

"How long have you lived here?" asked Kaufer.

"Sixteen years this August."

"Is there a basement? Don't most models from this era have basements?" asked Kaufer, looking sternly at Irena.

"I believe most do. This one did not. I am the seventh generation owner of the house so I don't know much about the construction or the design. I apologize."

It was true that the type of housing that Irena lived in was designed with a basement hence why she had one. It was common practice a few decades back to clean the records of the fact that you had a basement on your property. It was good for smuggling goods and people especially those at risk of persecution and attack from the government and the people. Anyone caught smuggling Nill, Bessians, or any other form of "undesirable" was subject to being sent to a labor camp. One guard made his way into the laundry room and started to look at a few of the baskets on the ground. Irena's body tensed.

"Nervous, are we Ms. Sandler?" Kaufer raised an eyebrow

"You guys don't exactly bring a calming vibe. I'm tired and I want to rest."

Kaufer laughed to himself and made his way down the hallway. The officer in the laundry room went right past the trapdoor and searched behind the washer and dryer. He left the room and walked down the hallway. They spent the next several minutes looking through each room meticulously. Scott and Zara sat in the cold basement trying to stay warm. Scott and Zara held their breaths.

"I don't know what to say. You stopped that officer from hurting me. Then Irena came in and saved us. Everything just happened so fast. How are you so chill about all of this? Those men could have really hurt you or worse!" Zara whisper-yelled.

Scott smiled and tried to keep his voice to a low level.

"It's a first for me. I couldn't let them take you and after those cops from earlier, I'm sick of them. Did you hear what that commander said to Irena? I can't believe she has to deal with this sort of abuse," Scott relayed.

"I'm sorry I didn't mention that I was going there today. I didn't want to worry you," answered Zara.

"It's okay. I'm just happy that you're okay," replied Scott.

"This isn't anything new, sadly. I've been at four protests in the last month and this has happened every time."

Scott's eyes widened.

"Four times in a month? Why do you keep going back out there if you know what will happen?" Scott asked.

Zara took a moment to collect her thoughts and smirked as if he had said exactly what she wanted to hear.

"That's why they oppress us. They want to stop us from speaking out. If we do as they want and stop protesting they win. We can't let them win."

"I'm starting to see what you mean," said Scott.

"Bruises, scrapes, broken bones, and black eyes are not enough to stop me. The police back home were just as corrupt if not worse. I haven't been able to trust them since and they haven't done anything to make me feel otherwise," replied Zara.

"That does explain the bruises on your arms and legs. I was concerned when I first noticed them."

"Don't worry hun. I've had far worse than that,"

Zara's arm seethed with pain as she stretched it. Relief came slowly as she held her hand on her bicep. There was a small scrape that was turning red. She grimaced and looked down at it.

"Hold on, you're bleeding again," said Scott, noticing the wound.

Scott looked around and spotted a small bag with random first aid gear on the ground. He grabbed a pack of gauze and a bandage and came back over to where she was sitting. Zara's scrape started to bleed.

"Let me wrap this around your arm," said Scott.

"Thank you, you're the best," she said through her teeth, smiling through the pain.

Scott placed a piece of gauze around her bicep and grabbed a piece of medical tape to keep it in place.

"That should do it. You need to start being more careful," Scott cautioned.

"Not a chance. Not until they listen to us and do something about the problems affecting our communities. We live here too. I have lived here longer than I did in England. It's not my fault that I was born somewhere else. I just want to live my life in peace yet they can't comprehend a world not based around subjugating and terrorizing people in their own communities."

Scott took a moment to catch his breath and gazed into Zara's eyes.

"I hope your message gets through to them sooner than later. I don't trust Haladi to do anything to make this better. He's the one responsible for it," said Scott.

"You're right. He is fine with this and the police unions always vote his way. Until we get a new person in charge it's gonna stay this way," responded Zara.

"I hope things become better soon," said Scott helplessly.

"I do too."

The guards finished their searches and all entered the living room where Irena was standing.

"I hope everything you have told me is true Ms. Sandler. I would hate for my next visit to end worse off than this one is," said Kaufer as he paced around the couch.

Irena nodded as she glared at Kaufer.

"I'll be leaving a set of guards in the neighborhood. If you see any signs of that man, call us immediately. If we suspect you know more and we end up finding them in the neighborhood, you won't be happy with the consequences," Kaufer growled, his eyes darkening.

"I'm sure I wouldn't be. Have a great night now," said Irena, waving at him.

Kaufer swung his arm up and signaled for his men to follow him out the door. They went to the police vehicle, got inside and took off. Irena shut the door and took a moment to catch her breath. She locked the door and shut her blinds. After waiting a few minutes for the police vehicle to leave the neighborhood she checked the locations of the guards. Both were out on the street, which covered two of the three possible exits. There was a back way that could work as an escape route for Scott and Zara. She walked over to the trapdoor and made her way to the basement.

"How are you two doing?" asked Irena.

Scott and Zara were huddled next to each other trying to stay warm.

"It's cold down here," responded Scott.

"That it is. I once had a family stay down here for nine months once. They got used to the cold eventually, especially after the floods," replied Irena.

"I can't even imagine that," said Scott.

"Thank you for everything. I know this is a huge risk for you and you don't even know us." said Zara, suddenly emotional.

"Don't worry about it, this isn't my first time around the block. I have had run-ins with those guys before. Now let's get you two out of here before things get worse," said Irena.

Scott and Zara stood up and followed her up into the living room of the house. Irena shut the trap door behind her and pushed a few baskets over top of it.

"So what's the plan?" asked Scott.

"Two guards are out front which takes away two of our exits. My idea is the back way through the loading dock. It's up to you two after that but I can get you that far," said Irena.

"Thank you honestly. I don't know where we'd be without you," said Scott.

"You can thank me by not getting arrested. Now come on, we don't have all day." replied Irena, urging them to make their exit.

Scott nodded and looked at Zara.

"You ready?" Scott asked, holding his hand out.

"Let's do it," she responded, placing her hand in his.

"Alright let's go."

The two of them followed Irena, who made her way through a set of double doors and down a long narrow hallway. The wallpaper was blue and the tile was bright white which reflected the ceiling back at the floor. The lighting was dim and seemed to be in disrepair. They took a quick right and down a flight of stairs to a loading dock. It was wide open, with a section to the side with several dozen boxes.

"Okay, take that alley and then cross the street and you will see where the library is. Good luck and be safe. Things are only getting crazier out here," Irena directed while waving goodbye.

"Same to you. I hope things get better soon for everyone's sake," replied Scott.

Scott and Zara made their way out of the loading dock. About half way down, Scott turned back to catch one last look at the woman who possibly saved their lives. They went down the alleyway and took cover behind a dumpster, taking a moment to catch their breaths and make sure no one else was in sight. No one that they could see, anyway.

Scott admired Zara and placed a gentle kiss on her forehead. She smiled softly and pulled him into a warm embrace.

"We need to get you back to your interview," Zara decided.

"I have to make sure you're safe," Scott insisted.

"I can take care of myself, you've helped me plenty already," said Zara.

"I'm going to call a ride to take you back to the hotel or your place if you'd prefer. I'll let you tell them that once they arrive."

Scott clicked a few buttons on his phone and after about fifteen seconds, a ride was on the way. Scott sat with Zara for a few more minutes and tried to keep her as warm as possible. A light breeze had started to pass through the town and the smell of gunpowder littered the air. After a few more minutes, a ride pulled up to the alleyway.

"Ride for Zara. I'm guessing that's you?" the driver asked while sticking his head out the window.

"Yes, take her where she needs to go. She will give you the address," Scott requested.

"No problem. Hop in," said the driver, gesturing for her to get in the ride.

"Thank you so much! I'm not sure what would have happened if I didn't run into you here. I need to get back home and pack. See you after your interview?"

"I'm just glad I was able to help and get you away from danger. Yeah I need to get back to my interview. Be careful and I'll see you later," said Scott before sending her off with a kiss.

Zara got inside and Scott waved at her as they drove off. She didn't move her head away from his direction until the ride had almost fully gone around the corner. He made his way towards the library, first cutting down another alleyway before crossing a street and going through a park. The library was finally cleared of police vehicles. A few media figures and some random officials were talking amongst themselves but the event had largely concluded. He made his way up the steps and found his way to the meeting room. Mashir and Yolen were chatting between themselves when Scott arrived.

"Sorry gentlemen. A few unexpected things popped up during our break. It's a long story. I am so sorry for the delay," he apologized sincerely.

"Is everything okay? Your message seemed a bit frantic," Mashir vacillated.

"The protest outside the police station went south and I kind of got caught in the middle of it. Long story short, I had to hide out for a bit while the police looked for me. They couldn't find us so they left and now I'm here," Scott divulged, inhaling deeply when he finished.

"Oh wow, are you okay? Did they hurt you?" Mashir fretted.

"I'm okay. They hurt my girlfriend Zara but we ran into someone who helped us take care of her."

"That's a relief. I have already met and lost far too many people to the violence this city perpetuates. Something has to change," Mashir commanded.

"Things are certainly worse than I had known. I hope nothing else gets in the way of the interview. I am loving what we have done so far."

"Yolen and I feel the same way. We're ready to start up again when you are," replied Mashir.

"Okay, perfect." said Scott, who was shaking as he reached to grab his notes.

Scott jumped in immediately without hesitation.

"So, for another important Accoran figure, who would you pick?" he asked.

Mashir took his time thinking about this one and waited over a minute before finally coming up with his answer.

"West Goring was a scientist who worked for the Terush empire before they lost the war to the Accorans and the Hemorans. He was allowed to come work in Accora for our newly created space research and development team. He helped push Accora further in the development of cross-galactic technology. Until that point we had only traveled in our solar system and a few of our very close neighboring ones. He had worked for the Terush and actually helped develop technology used to commit acts of genocide on my race. Seeing his name on the news talking about the newest space advances we made was painful. He was a genius and knew what he was doing but he was pure evil. The very people said they were liberating my people and paid him huge sums of money to revitalize his image and help them. He had been on the list to be tried for his crimes and yet they were expunged. A paperclip in the wrong file or something. The truth was lost to history," replied Mashir.

"What made him so crucial for Accora's history that you think to mention him?" Scott asked.

"His connection to the Terush was spun as a sign of acceptance of the Terush people and we have been close allies ever since. We have over forty thousand soldiers stationed across forty installations. This is seen as a method of defense and a requirement of being an ally. A lot of us see through this though and see it for what it is. A fear tactic and way to keep nations in their place. Accora won the war and eventually another one against the Hemorans so of course they got to choose how the post-war world would look like. These alliances were drawn up to expand the influence of Accora and its allies, help their economies and prevent any other nation from growing to be a challenge," responded Mashir.

"The other nations just agreed to this?" questioned Scott.

"Well the other nations had been pushed to the brink by the Terush so when Accora got involved and painted the narrative that they saved the day, they became the superpower that represented their side. The Hemoran's represented the opposite of Accora and were portrayed to be more like the Terush than they were to us. This was of course false. It was an effective way of denying the truth about what the Terush did," answered Mashir.

Scott smirked when his response came to mind.

"On Earth we have a saying that goes: the enemy of my enemy is my friend. I think that applies here," said Scott.

Mashir started to chuckle, as did Yolen.

"You're right about that. I'm going to have to use that in the future. So West being seen as a respected figure in Accoran society led to the majority of Accorans accepting them back," said Mashir.

Scott looked at his notes and realized he had passed the one hundred and ninety-third page.

"How close were Accora and the Terush?" asked Scott.

"Pretty close. A lot of tourists from each nation visited and a lot of culture bled between the two. A large Terush population existed in Accora from its beginnings. Their relations soured near the end, once we approached The Great Collapse. Our leaders abandoned the scientists, the people and the very laws that they swore to uphold. The rest of the planet lost faith in us and we were suddenly not the leader of the world anymore. Everyone had abandoned us and we couldn't blame them. I would have too," Mashir replied.

Scott flipped to a blank page.

"How did culture differ between the countries on Nilleon?" Scott said.

"There was a perception that certain cultures were massively different in ways that we could never understand. Some people were savage and barbaric and others were civilized and more humane. This was a nasty ideology based in pseudoscience and when further examined falls apart on its face. The truth was more that we were all the same beings and that we just had small differences that arise out of our different needs and experiences. We ultimately all have the same traumatic memories in our DNA that our ancestors encountered and the emotional responses to those over time have resulted in Nill all over the planet having similar reactions, thoughts, beliefs, thoughts, fears, etc. A bug is crawling up your arm so what do you do?" asked Mashir, using his hands to form a spider and make a crawling motion.

Scott and Yolen both instinctively smacked their arm where the spider would be crawling.

"You wonder why that is, right?" replied Mashir.

Scott pondered that thought.

"The tragedy is that we have made it about them and us. We have in groups and out groups. We are always fearful of the other coming to take what is ours and it is bred into our nature. Our violent nature and tendencies are a result of this and there is one thing that we have needed to accept for a long long time. It is just us now. The planet was ours and we should use our energy and resources collectively for the benefit of all of us. Instead we chose to allow our anxieties, fears, and desires to seek out differences to separate us from them," said Mashir.

"Jumping a bit but similar in terms of being a threat to the future of the species; Nuclear weapons have been a hot topic for centuries now on Earth so when did Nilleon first invent a nuclear device?" asked Scott.

Mashir gave a look at Yolen and inhaled sharply.

"Accoran scientists were the first to fully utilize the powers of the atom to create a bomb. The stated goal was to develop a deterrent to war, something that would be so destructive and costly that no one could possibly use it in war. We developed it and dropped four of them on civilian population centers in the Korson Empire. The idea was to force them to surrender because they had a strong cultural belief that you never surrender in war. They told us this and our leaders rationalized it as a life saving measure. They said that we would lose far more lives in an invasion of Korso. This was true they had done studies and millions upon millions would die in a straight up invasion. As one would expect when trying to occupy a country of 140 million people who not only did not want you there but did not want the war in the first place. They were victims to the very same system that we were suffering under just with a different mask and makeup. The reality of that situation was even darker, however. The leaders of Korso had already tried to reach out and start negotiations. They did not want to unconditionally surrender due to fear that certain members of their government would be killed. The Accorans did not plan on this but they had the fear anyway. Instead of speaking with their diplomats we demanded unconditional surrender and refused the efforts. We then dropped the four bombs on their cities costing them over eight hundred thousand lives which were almost entirely civilian. This forced Korso's hand and they surrendered six days later," Mashir responded.

"So they told you it was justifiable and the correct thing to do?" Scott asked.

"They did. They taught us in school, in books, and in films about the topic. It was something that we had to reconcile with. We were the first and until the collapse the only nation to actually use a nuclear weapon on another nation. Accora was supposed to be the beacon of a free and liberated society and free from the oppressors of authoritarian regimes. We used a nuclear weapon on civilians and justified it by saying it saved lives despite us knowing they were willing to negotiate a surrender. Our nauseating Accoran pride got in the way and we also wanted to show up the Hemoran's who were also researching nuclear weapons," replied Mashir.

Scott took a second to take in everything that Mashir had just said and tried to find a good way to put it into words on his notepad.

"What did the rest of the world feel about Accora using their weapons the way they did?" questioned Scott.

Mashir laughed in an almost sunken kind of way.

"Most nations found it hypocritical and not in line with what they were preaching at our international conferences. There were many close calls before the collapse of nuclear weapons almost being used and we barely avoided dying by our own decisions far too many times to name them here. I wrote a book detailing this section of our timeline. I'll bring you a copy next session, I think you would enjoy giving it a read," Mashir answered.

Scott grinned and felt a sense of delight that he had a new history book to look over.

"I would love that, thank you Mashir," said Scott.

"Essentially by the time right before The Great Collapse, we had about three or four hundred years of seeming escalation that didn't seem to be an issue at the time. We knew what was coming and we warned everyone. They didn't want to listen because it would hurt the economy, it would hurt profits, it would make everyone panic and everyone would be afraid. Our leaders did not want to lead, they just wanted to nurture their egos."

CHAPTER SIXTEEN

This back and forth would continue with great enthusiasm for another four hours, of which forty minutes were spent on a single specific war that occurred almost three thousand years ago relative to Earth's time. Yolen even had some thoughts and chimed in when the topic of the orange Nills was mentioned. After wrapping up the last set of questions, Scott took a moment to collect himself.

"Are you alright Scott?" asked Mashir.

Scott thought he was. Maybe on the outside it didn't appear that way but somewhere in his scrambled mind he knew what he was doing and what he needed to do next. The emotions from the day were catching up to him.

"I think so. A lot has happened today. I don't really know what to make of it. I'm just trying to take it all in and not overwhelm myself," stated Scott.

"I think that's a good idea. It's good to get a break from work sometimes. Your life should be more time spent away from work than at. Otherwise, what are you living for?" said Mashir.

Scott couldn't hold back a laugh as he smiled at Mashir.

"Thank you. I needed that."

Scott stuck his hand out and shaked Mashir's.

"I'll see you again at twelve," said Mashir.

Mashir and Yolen grabbed their bags and left the room. Scott grabbed his things and made sure he didn't leave anything behind. As he got ready to leave the room he got a notification on his phone: a live speech being given at the U.N. He clicked on it and pulled up the stream. Standing at the podium was a blue Nill with a graphic reading "Emedio Zappa, leading Nill Historian."Scott sat back down in his chair to focus on the speech. Emedio's skin was blue with slight orange accents on his forehead and hands. He cleared his throat and began to speak.

"Our species is at a unique crossroads in our history. We have lost our home and are seeking to find out what the next steps are. Where do we go from here? Many Nill would tell you that they saw this coming and I would tell you that you shouldn't believe anything they say! The betrayal of our species by the orange Nill and even some green Nill directly led to the collapse of our planet. They saw an opportunity and stabbed us in the back. We spent so many years improving their lives and trying to work with them yet they never show appreciation for that. They continue talking about what happened decades and centuries ago. Yes, awful things happened in the past and we condemn those actions. We don't live in those days anymore! We can't live in the past! We have to move forward! We can't let the radical Nill who wish to see the end of our species succeed in spreading these falsehoods and lies. They would have you believe that many of them aren't criminals and low-lifes who weren't a burden on the rest of us. They siphoned all the money they could from us and we paid the price! Our hard earned fortunes earned by creating businesses and building up the workforce were given to the lazy, the poor, and undesirables. We built the wealth of our nations and of course we have more money. Without us our species would never have gone to the stars! Don't let this propaganda fool you into letting the worst of our species into your nations. They will steal everything from you just as they did us. This tale of orange and green subjugation is

a fairy tale designed to make you feel sorry for the worst types of people. The kind of

people we know can't assimilate with civilized beings. Don't make the same mistake we

did. They are animals and they must be treated as such!" denounced Zappa, who threw

his hand up to large cheers from the crowd.

Scott couldn't believe what he was hearing. It went against everything Mashir

and Yolen had been telling him about Nill history. He knew he would have to bring it up

to Mashir but he already knew that it couldn't be the case. Zappa had contradicted

himself in the speech saying that they condemn the actions of the past and then stating

that it was simply a fairytale. Which was it? It couldn't be both. He felt sick just thinking

about all the people listening to Zappa that would believe him.

Scott sat up and made his way out of the room and exited the library. He had

about an hour before Emma would be ready to interview and Zara's house was only about

ten minutes away. He figured he could surprise her and help for a half an hour before he

had to rush off again. Walking would actually save time and Scott lightly jogged down

the street. The protest and officers from earlier weighed heavily on his mind.

What if they come for Zara?

The grief from everything he saw today hit him like a brick. He was worried

about Zara and her getting injured. He didn't like to see any group being oppressed and

for it to be so out and open was unnerving. The chilly air made Scott regret not grabbing

his jacket this morning. He pushed through and arrived at a crosswalk. The lights were

red, yet no cars were coming. He waited a few more moments for the light to turn green.

He made his way across the street and turned right, passing a few interesting places: a computer repair shop, a low budget church, a nail salon, and two different Italian restaurants.

Scott arrived at the address Zara sent him and admired the small, square house in front of him. It was one story and white, built with bricks Dozens more looked just like it in the surrounding area. A small patio was present with a small set of steps to conquer. He approached the door and knocked three times. After a few agonizing moments the door opened and Zara popped out.

"Oh wow, I thought you were doing that interview after work?" Zara questioned.

"I am still. I just wanted to stop by and help for a little. Figured you might want some help even though you want to do it yourself," Scott teased.

Zara just smiled and gave him a kiss.

"You're too sweet."

She grabbed his hand and led him inside. It was a cramped house with a rather tight living room and a small kitchen and dining area off to the side. Down the hallway were four bedrooms and a restroom. He noticed a closet opposite of the restroom and the edge of a dryer could be seen in the crack. The house was relatively clean with a few pieces of clothes laying on a couch in the center of the room. A few other people were scrambling through the hallway.

"I'm guessing those are your roommates?" asked Scott.

"Yes they are. I'll be really happy to not feel so cramped all the time. Having only three roommates is actually pretty lucky considering the housing crisis."

"I suppose that makes sense. How are you feeling? Is your arm still okay?" asked Scott.

"I'm feeling good and my arm is fine," Zara grinned as she held her mostly healed arm out proudly. "Thanks for checking."

Scott pulled her close and felt her heartbeat knock against his chest.

"So what do you need me to do?" he asked, still wrapped around her tightly.

"Hmm, how about you start with moving the boxes in my room to the front of the living room by the door? I still need to finish my laundry and sort out my clothes that I'm taking with me," Zara instructed.

"What are you not taking with you?"

"Old clothes and anything my friends need more than I will."

Scott let go of Zara and began moving boxes. About ten minutes were spent moving the boxes and, once he finished, he helped Zara finish her laundry. Scott helped her decide on a few outfits to bring with her and urged her to save a few collectible bobbleheads from being thrown out.

"Bobbleheads are awesome. They are the coolest thing and you should bring them with you. I have over seven hundred myself," Scott boasted.

"You have seven hundred bobbleheads? Which ones do you even have?" she questioned.

Scott couldn't hold back his excitement.

"They are all based on different things, games, movies, shows, pop culture, even some real people. It's just a way to show off what things you like and to have a more uniform set of collectibles," Scott beamed.

Zara laughed at his excitability, but she finally understood the sentiment.

"You know what I think you're right. I will bring them with me. They are pretty fun to look at sometimes," she agreed.

They continued packing for another ten minutes before Scott glanced at his phone. It was already 6:50 p.m.

"Alright, I need to head towards the cafe. I shouldn't be too long. I'm thinking nine thirty at the latest. I'll call and let you know when I'm close," Scott said.

"Okay babe, sounds good."

Zara kissed Scott goodbye and squeezed him, wanting to have him close for just a few minutes more. They shared a longing glance as Scott pulled away and exited the house.

The cafe was actually pretty close to Zara's house, so he decided to just walk there as well. The neighborhood wasn't too bad. No one posed a threat and it seemed like the police steered clear of this area. He wondered if that was due to the protests from earlier. He passed an old water desalination plant which was plugged up about seven years ago, at least according to the sign posted in front of it. The pipes were rusted, the water lines were leaking, and it was contaminated, useless water. It could burn your skin after more than fifteen minutes of contact. A few homeless people were camped out underneath an overpass that connected this neighborhood with the next borough. As Scott approached and started to cross over, he couldn't help but peer around the corner underneath the bridge. A large opening separates the current platform that Scott was on and a section of development that was built overtop of. He spotted a huge set of neighborhoods stacked underneath the ground level basically invisible to the pedestrian or aerial view, unless you used sonar. The houses were built into the walls and the ground; possibly, they were free standing before being built over or they may have been designed this way.

That is a question for an Egyptian historian! Maybe he should ask Verona about that while he still had a chance.

That was one way to solve the issue of finding more land to settle on or place people. He could see groups of people huddled around fires, sitting outside their homes, chatting, going on about their business and eating snacks. The children played in the crowded streets. The police don't operate down there, at least not in full force. They are not accepted and the so-called criminals of the Egyptian government are welcome travelers in these underground settlements. The A.R.T. movement and a large diaspora of Androids could be found here, some for a better life, some to plot revenge on their oppressors, or countless other reasons. As he finished taking it all in, he continued along the bridge. A spotlight shone across a skyrise building. Cairo had been built up like many great cities by industrialization and the population of the nation was reaping the effects. He noticed more blimps in the air than usual, many of which had propagandistic messages strung across them. Some had spotlights and some brandished weapons that were clearly in violation of treaties they signed with the United Nations.

Naturally, Scott was submerged in his thoughts and almost didn't notice that he arrived at the cafe. Right as he approached the door, a loud bang shook the building. Startled, Scott believed it was in his best interest to investigate the noise. He crept around the corner of the cafe. Scott examined the alley before slowly entering - not a soul in sight and no one else to investigate the sound.

Behind the restaurant sat a large dumpster with a humanoid arm hanging off the edge. Scott rushed over and couldn't believe the horrific sight - Emma lying in the dumpster. He gazed into her eyes, searching for any sign of life. All that stared back was an empty void as if every part of her soul had been sucked out. All the memories, real and implanted, gone without a difference felt between the two. To her, they were all real and had now been taken from her, lost in the utter chaos that is life on Earth. Oil stains and tears in her skin riddled her body. Her hair had been pulled out and her arms appeared dislocated.

Scott couldn't believe his eyes and yet wasn't completely surprised. This must be connected to her demanding better conditions at work.

Why did her boss have to throw her in the trash?

Did her boss not care that she felt the same pain, had the same dreams and spoke the same words that they did?

Scott could barely hold in his emotions swinging between anger, sadness, shock, and regret. He could have spoken up or said something sooner, but could he have stopped this from happening? His stomach was in knots and the nausea approached in waves. Scott knelt to the ground in an attempt to catch his breath, barely containing his grief.

"You could only delay, not prevent this," Scott said to himself.

His mind debated on whether or not to act on his new impulse. Without further thought, he flipped over Emma's body and looked at the back of her head. He knew what he would find, but prayed it wouldn't be true - the same red globe-in-hand symbol that had been re-appearing among androids glazed Emma's head.

Did this same group put a hit on her?

Was she targeted because she belonged to this movement?

It could be a plethora of things and Scott was determined to find answers. Scott closed Emma's eyelids. He thought about Emma realizing that he might be the only human in the world to care for her. Scott blew air through his nose and kicked the dumpster, sending a looming sense of pain to his foot. He expelled a small cry. With his interviewee out of commission, Scott decided he should call Zara and let her know.

"Hey you, what's up?" Zara answered after one ring.

"Well, it didn't go. I found Emma in the dumpster behind the cafe," Scott croaked.

"Wait, what?"

"She was dead when I found her just lying in the dumpster like she was trash," he sighed.

"Oh honey, that's terrible! I've heard of similar instances, but I didn't really think it was that common. Are you okay? Is it safe for you to be there?"

"I'm okay, just stunned. I want to go inside and say something," Scott said.

"Don't. I know how you feel and honestly, I agree that it's the right thing to do but if they were willing to throw their employee in the dumpster, who knows what they would do to the tourist making a fuss over android workers? I don't want you to get hurt or get into any more trouble like the protest," Zara protested.

Scott bit his tongue. Zara was right.

"I know. I'm heading back to the hotel. I'll see you soon," he said.

"Okay I'll meet you there. Be safe."

Scott ended the call. He wouldn't ask anyone at the restaurant, but he knew he could call Radius to see what he knew. He pulled Radius's card out of his wallet and dialed the number. The phone rang about five times before he got an answer. No words of course, but he could tell someone had picked up the line.

"Jean has a long moustache," Scott repeated the passcode.

The silence on the other end echoed for what seemed like an eternity.

"One moment," said the voice on the other end.

Scott tapped his foot as he waited.

"Scott, it's Radius. It's great to hear from you, what's going on?"

"I've got two things, which are sort of one thing. I was going to interview an android I had met during my stay here and when I went to meet with her I found her dead in a dumpster behind her restaurant," replied Scott.

"That's terrible. Do you know what happened to her?"

"I'm suspecting her boss had something to do with it. I know the environment wasn't the friendliest. The second reason I'm mentioning her to you is that when I went to check on her I found a red globe in hand symbol on the back of her head. The same symbol on your business card and the same as two other androids I have seen in the last week." answered Scott.

"She had our symbol? What was her name?"

"Emma, she worked at El Alamato. Had implants that her father was a carpenter and her mother a bank teller," Scott replied.

"I know who she was

. Wow, that's so unexpected. She hadn't been with us for more than maybe three months at this point," Radius explained.

"Why did she join your group and why do I keep seeing your symbol wherever I run into androids?" asked Scott.

"It's the symbol of A.R.T. and our supporters choose to wear it to show who is with the movement. We advocate for better working conditions, higher wages, more collective ownership and stake in their work. We want androids to receive the same treatment and rights as humans do. We encourage dissent and to question the authority imposing anti-android policies. Capitalism has ruined our existence all the same as it did

to humanity. We want a new system. A better system that doesn't exploit workers for the

benefit of the wealthy and the elite. For the ruin of the androids and the joy of humans.

Every member of the community should be taken care of. We are present at protests,

rallies and all sorts of events across the world. I'm sure you saw a few of our flags at the

protest earlier today," Radius said.

"I did and they treated the protestors so poorly with no regard for their safety or

rights. Things got out of hand and became violent quickly," Scott recalled.

"Unfortunately, that is how it often goes. This isn't the first protest to turn

violent and it won't be the last. We've been at this fight for a long time and we aren't

stopping anytime soon. They can keep putting us down but we get right back up. One

day, revolution will come. I'm glad to see that many of your kind will stand by our side in

our quest for freedom. I just hope that those who do are strong-willed enough to live to

see our success," replied Radius.

"So since my android interview went down the drain what else can I do to help

your cause? I just learned that I'm giving my speech in front of the Security Council of

the U.N.," Scott queried.

"Speaking about our cause during your speech would put a big spotlight on the

issues. Abolishing the divisions that separate us, abolishing the class hierarchy and

reorganizing the means of production into the hands of the workers is our number one

goal and the struggle of the androids is the same of the human and the Nill," Radius

expressed.

"I think every day people are becoming more disillusioned with the system as it

is. They keep telling us that it works if we are patient and trust the system that it will all work out in our favor. We can all see the cracks and it's now just a matter of finding something to hold on to. America isn't much better off than Egypt is. We just normalize our corruption and crimes against humanity. I just don't know how people will react to what comes next," Scott replied, letting out a deep sigh.

"The next phase is inevitable and the side effects of human activity on Earth are close to completely ending life as we know it. Most animals we see are not real, just robotic or synthetic clones. Communism exists where Capitalism exists and the aversion to the word and the historical legacy it carries has to be learned from and understood. Don't run from it, embrace it. Certain factors of capitalist society will of course remain in place and the new society will have to reconcile these to fit the goals of the people. Communities will form democratic councils and factories will become the property of the workers themselves. All the other unnecessary elements of the past society will need to be dealt with and this is what some would call 'smashing the state apparatus.' You do this to ensure that the capitalist class cannot return the country to its previous mode of operation. This is becoming a necessity not only for android life but for human life too.

"We don't need change because we desire it or because it would benefit us. We need it because without it we won't have a future on this planet. We face a choice between two paths: one of revolution and a communist society or one of an apocalyptic nature and utter ruin to the last four billion years of evolutionary struggle. What a shame it would be to lose all that had led us to this point. I hope you can see why I find Haladi and his thugs such a threat. They are trying to crush every ounce of thought that rejects him and his ideology. We have to recruit and educate more people on what is really happening and how they play a crucial role in building a better world. Not everyone will come along for the ride and that is okay. When the time comes we will remember the terror that was bestowed upon us and we won't make excuses for what we do to ensure they can never repeat their crimes," Radius proclaimed confidently, almost with a tinge of arrogance.

"We share a lot of the same goals and I know we'll get there one day. It's nice to see someone trying to lay out an approach based more in reality. I think it'll fit right into the themes I am going for," said Scott.

"I appreciate your support Scott, it means a lot. Most in the political establishment regard us as radicals or violent criminals. We just want to see a better world for everyone and to put the power back in the hands of the people. I'll leave you to your night, if you need anything else feel free to let me know," Radius offered.

"Thanks Radius. It's my pleasure. Talk with you later," said Scott before hanging up the phone.

He then requested a ride, but all he could think about was how badly he wanted to sleep.

After a blissful nap in the back of his ride, he arrived back at the hotel. Zara was waiting for him in the lobby. She looked utterly exhausted. Scott sleepily made his way over to her, grabbing her waist and pulling her in for a kiss. They pulled away and shared a look.

"What're you feeling?" Zara asked.

"Pizza and a movie?" Scott chuckled.

"You read my mind," Zara said, giggling back at him.

She grabbed his hand and they made their way upstairs. Once they made it to the room, Scott ordered the pizza and Zara picked out a movie. Scott set his bag over on the chair in the room and kicked his shoes off. He unbuttoned his shirt and threw it over on top of a pile of clothes and his suitcase. Zara came over and sat next to him on the bed.

"Are you okay?" she asked as she rubbed his back softly.

"I just wasn't expecting to find her like that. I'll be okay. I just need to process everything. It's been the longest day. I appreciate you asking," Scott answered quietly.

He rested his head in his hands. Zara wrapped her arm around him and laid her head on his shoulders. They sat there in silence until Scott turned to give her a kiss. They returned to watching the movie Zara picked out until the pizza arrived.

CHAPTER SEVENTEEN

The next morning Scott woke up to the sound of rain hitting the window of his room. He rolled over and checked his phone for any messages; nothing of note to mention. Zara was still sleeping and Scott remembered that she didn't have to work today. He got up and walked over to his bag of clothes to pick his outfit for the day before taking a shower. While he waited for the water to heat up he checked a few news sites to see what was going on.

CAIRO PROTESTS SPREAD THROUGHOUT EGYPT.

TURKISH FORCES MARCH FURTHER INTO GREECE, MILITARY JUNTA REVOKES CITIZEN'S RIGHTS.

NEWLY ELECTED ARGENTINE PRESIDENT EXECUTES FIFTEEN POLITICAL DISSIDENTS, U.N. DEMANDS INVESTIGATION.

INDIAN PRESIDENT STATES DECLARATION OF WAR AGAINST CHINA TO BE PASSED TODAY.

ITALIAN AND FRENCH FORCES LOCKED IN STALEMATE NEAR PIEDMONT; CORSICA BOMBED FROM THE AIR.

TERRORIST ATTACK IN FLORIDA KILLS THREE HUNDRED AT VOTING BOOTH.

Just another day in a world slowly falling deeper into its own madness. Scott clicked on a live stream from an Egyptian congressional assembly. Haji Atiyeh was speaking, likely as a direct request from Haladi, and seemed agitated. Standing shoulder to shoulder with him was Emedio Zappa, the blue Nill academic actively spreading hatred against the orange and green nill.

"The invasion of aliens into our country has left us weaker, poorer, dirtier, and less capable of effective government. When these aliens come to my country my vote becomes tainted and it dilutes my vote. It dilutes all of our votes. We have to secure a future for our children, before they take them away from us. Our people are tired of being the dumping ground for these European countries sick and tired of refugees. You attempt to stand for the moral high ground yet sell your souls to the highest bidder. Our movement is not just an Egyptian one! It is a worldwide movement and we won't be silenced any longer. Don't be blinded by the opposition and their lies about our great leader. Our great Atum! The party is Haladi. But Haladi is Egypt as Egypt is Haladi! Hail victory! " Atiyeh spat as he pounded his fist on the podium.

If this was what the Egyptian population heard on a daily basis, no wonder things were going how they were. The amount of refugees entering was nowhere near the level that these lunatics were estimating. That didn't matter to them or their base though - they ate this up. They needed an enemy; someone to be fearful of and to place their fears on to. This explained why Zappa had been at the U.N. before and why he was saying what he was. He was working with Haladi and his cronies to make sure the vote went their way.

What could they have promised Zappa to get him to support someone so dedicated to the oppression of people just like him?

Scott shook his head; his emotions overwhelmed him. He jumped in the shower to distract his mind from processing the world around him. The temperature was hot enough to shift his focus from worldly concerns to more immediate priorities. After a few minutes of this, he needed to get moving. Zara started to wake up as he finished showering and started getting dressed.

"Hey.. what time are you gonna be back?" she yawned.

"I should be back by six fifteen. I'm just interviewing Mashir and Yolen today. No extras," he said while buttoning his shirt.

Zara smiled and rolled over.

"Let me know when you're on your way I can order dinner or something," she mumbled.

"Sounds great! I'll text you," Scott replied.

Scott finished getting dressed and grabbed his things. After kissing Zara goodbye, he made his way down to the lobby and then out to the street. He ordered a ride and sat down on a bench outside the hotel. The rain was slowly starting to let up but Scott made sure to sit underneath an awning. He checked his favorite news sites again and noticed more headlines were showing up. There was a plane that was hijacked over Italy. Fifteen more refugees were refused at the southern border of Texas. A radical christian group in Kansas cut off the heads of five people.

PLANE HIJACKED FLYING OVER ITALY

FIFTEEN REFUGEES REFUSED AT SOUTHERN TEXAS BORDER

RADICAL KANSAS CHRISTIAN GROUP BEHEADS FIVE PEOPLE

The news became too much for Scott. He closed the app and put his phone away just as his ride pulled up. Scott jumped inside.

"How're you doing?" Scott asked.

The driver looked at him stunned.

"Oh, I'm doing good. How about yourself?" he queried.

"I'm doing good as well. Thanks for the ride," Scott responded.

"Absolutely sir," the driver nodded and looked back at the road, pulling away.

Scott took the time to rest his eyes and think of questions. This session was important and he wanted to make sure that it was as good as the last. The ride was smooth and didn't take too long. He thanked the driver and hopped out. To the left of the library, a few dozen years away, stood Mashir and Yolen surrounded by three police officers. Mashir looked concerned while the police officers barked at them.

"You two know that your kind aren't welcome here. I know we have warned you before. It's time you leave," said a tall, slightly bulky officer while tapping a baton in his hand.

"We haven't done anything, we are just trying to meet with a client for an interview," replied Mashir, backing up from the approaching officer.

"I really do not care what you have going on. I don't want you in my city. Taking up our jobs, living in our houses, eating our food. It's not our fault you ruined your own planet. Leave or this will be our last conversation," said the officer, spitting on Mashir's face.

"How dare you!" yelled out Yolen, impending the officer.

The officer slammed his baton on Mashir's shoulder before striking Yolen's side.

"This will teach you," screamed the officer.

Scott refused to let this injustice continue.

"Hey! Leave them alone. They are being interviewed by me. We don't want trouble," said Scott, lunging himself between the two of them and the officers.

The lead officer looked at Scott with disgust and let out a smug laugh. He glared into Scott's eyes intensely while slapping his hand with his baton.

"Let us be and I won't report this to your Commander. These two are U.N. protected! You won't get off easy," Scott threatened.

The officer contemplated Scott's warning and decided to evade further conflict.

"So be it. Just know that when push comes to shove we remember traitors and we don't forget," the officer growled, shoving his baton into Scott's chest and nearly knocking him over.

The officers walked off and Scott turned around to face Mashir and Yolen.

"Are you two okay?" asked Scott.

Mashir wiped the blood from his cheek. His rattling cough gave the impression that he would cough up his lungs. Scott looked distressed at Mashir's sudden fit.

"I think I'm okay. I'm coughing up something though," replied Mashir in between coughs.

Scott patted Mashir on the back, trying to help him clear his throat.

"Alright let's get inside before they come back," urged Scott, checking for any signs of more officers.

They grabbed their bags and made their way towards the meeting room. Setting up the room didn't take more than a few minutes. The urge to discuss the strife overwhelmed Scott but he didn't know how to bring it up.

Was this common? How often did they have to deal with this?

His expression outed his thoughts and Mashir chimed in.

"You don't have to tiptoe around it, this isn't our first time being attacked for who we are," Mashir lamented in between more painful coughs.

"How often?" asked Scott.

"About one or two times a month. It's been a little more recently, maybe once every three weeks or sometimes two," Mashir confessed. "It's always the same rhetoric. Same buzz words. Same disregard for our dignity and agency."

"We've also been attacked by several groups of blue Nill that have decided fighting amongst ourselves is the best way to continue the survival of our species," Yolen included.

"What are they fighting with you for?" asked Scott.

"They want the majority stake in whatever governing body will preside over the Nill if we are able to remain on Earth,"Yolen explained.

"It's nothing new. I would have hoped they could wait until we knew we had a safe future for the species," said Mashir.

Scott could tell Mashir and Yolen weren't giving him the full story. Their eyes conveyed their nearing to the edge. Yolen couldn't stop tapping his hands on his legs as if mimicking playing a piano. Mashir's shaking was almost unnoticeable.

"I can't begin to imagine how this must affect you two. I know it can't be easy and I am always here if you need to talk. And I mean that outside of the scope of the interview don't hesitate to call. Everyone needs people to listen and care," Scott stressed.

Mashir smiled softly as a tear flowed down his cheek.

"I really appreciate that and I'm sure Yolen does too. Thank you Scott," said Mashir, while Yolen nodded.

"Quite a way to start the day I suppose. When you feel ready we can start the interview. No rush of course," said Scott.

Mashir smiled and looked over at Yolen. They took a second and shared a moment to relax.

"Okay let's begin," said Mashir, who coughed harshly again.

"Okay, so today, I want to focus on the big story. I want to talk about the fall of Nilleon," said Scott.

Mashir took a moment to take a breath, sighed and looked at Yolen before looking back over at Scott.

"The Great Collapse. What a tragedy," Mashir replied.

Scott let Mashir take his time thinking about the story before he followed up his question.

"So to start, why is it called The Great Collapse?" asked Scott.

"The end of our civilization did not happen all at once. It didn't even happen in a single year. It was a slow but steadily progressing event that occurred over four hundred and fifty years. A lot of us knew during the collapse that what would transpire would occur but those in power did not listen to us. They ignored it and pushed it away for future generations to handle. The problem was that eventually there wasn't another generation. The issue became ever present in our daily lives and it caused the last century to be a complete nightmare," Mashir stated.

Scott scratched down every word he heard so as to not miss a single one.

"So, what would be considered the beginning of The Great Collapse?" Scott asked.

"It's often attributed to the post-war environment where Accora and the Hemoran Supreme faced off in different cold wars because of their opposing ideologies and economic systems. I think it started earlier when we first industrialized causing us to first value work and productivity over our own happiness," replied Mashir.

"And by we you mean those in power?" Scott inquired.

"Precisely, and those in charge of the corporations. The rise of industry and technology directly led to the increase in pollution on our planet and the destruction of our natural safety nets. The rise of the media and the ability to spread information so rapidly allowed those wanting to obfuscate and obstruct the truth from reaching the masses to do so with ease. Those in power convinced everyone that the true enemy was their fellow worker being lazy and not those in power refusing to adequately compensate their workers. We had slave labor for millenia then most of the world outlawed it. They then decided to call it something different and most of the planet fell for the plot. Many advocated for abolishing the wage labor system as well but it became the dominant form. Then automation and android life had a big impact and caused many jobs to fall out of place. Nill had to find new ways to subside or they would die," Mashir explained .

"How did pollution caused by the Nill impact Nilleon?"

"Our energy sources, our industries, our own vehicles, and almost every behavior we exercised in some way contributed to the ramping up of global catastrophe. We had an increase in powerful storms and weather events. We dumped excess waste into water sources which led to hundreds and thousands of species to go extinct. Some scientists told us that we could always clone them to bring them back. To me, that seemed to miss the point entirely," Mashir said.

"Was this issue completely global or were some countries more impactful on the collapse than others?"

" Oftentimes Accora itself would contribute to the change more than dozens and dozens of other countries. The biggest nations would provide the vast majority of pollution yet the smaller nations would have to suffer all the same. And as you see now we suffered the same fate ultimately," answered Mashir.

Scott took a second to let his thoughts catch up with him while he took a drink from his water bottle.

"How did conflict impact the collapse? Did wars and their frequency increase?"

"Absolutely. Conflict was always a part of our world and our people. Whether for good or bad it was common for us to fight wars over senseless things that ultimately didn't matter as we can see. We saw a huge increase in the number of conflicts and the amount of chaos throughout the planet as we progressed in the collapse. Global conflicts involving most of the planet became commonplace happening more and more frequent as we got closer to the end. The idea of nationalism and the idea of the other invading your home became commonplace and accepted. It wasn't accepted by everyone but it was accepted by enough. Those sowing hate and bigotry were never the majority, always the minority, yet the systems of power were designed with keeping the minority parties in charge," Mashir said.

"How did the idea of a small minority of the population controlling the majority sound to the population?" Scott asked.

"When it was stated as such, it was not popular. The issue was that the propaganda and bad faith actors would confuse everyone and just call it something different. They would blame any issues that they felt the country had on scapegoats and usually people who looked different than those in power. When people from other nations would come to Accora, a sizable group felt that they were a threat and would ruin our way of life. They thought that they did not have the resources or ability to help others. This was only true if you accepted the idea that we have to continually value material wealth and its gain over our own lives and rights," Mashir said.

"What were some common tactics used to prevent people from changing the status quo?"

"As I said, scapegoats were used whenever they wanted to shift the blame from themselves and others in power to someone more alluring for the masses to hate on. If the enemy was someone on their level they would not focus on changing those in power. The idea of whataboutism became commonplace where any wrongdoing or crime committed would be justified because the other side was doing it too whether they were actually doing it too or not. The idea of both sides being the same became popular and a lot of people fell for this. It's true that there were some grains of truth in these lies which is all it takes to convince unsuspecting people to support their abusers. If one thing they said was true then well maybe these other things are too. It only snowballs from there and nothing of substance ever happens to improve the situation," Mashir replied.

Scott flipped his page on his notepad and continued to scratch notes down.

"So, there was a rise in conflict. What about violence that wasn't war, but crime or terrorism?" Scott asked.

"This was a major problem. Not in the way you might immediately think though. Crime was blamed on certain sections of our population and our police forces gave them unfair treatment and would openly murder them in the streets with impunity. They had protection under the law and due to this protection they would never be held fully accountable for their crimes. This was appalling to me and the majority of the population. We wanted change, yet everytime we would protest or ask for change we were beaten down and told we were doing it the wrong way. If peaceful protest isn't the right way, what is? The type of environment that leads to someone committing acts of violence and terror are often created by the countries being affected by them. This doesn't excuse the acts of terror there is never any excuse for it. If the end goal is to end terror, why would you continue doing things that lead to people becoming radicalized? War, famine, poverty, foreign influence, coups, invasions and bombings on a population that is already suffering will only lead to more of them thinking they have to take drastic action. These events lead to people becoming radicalized and radicals will oftentimes take drastic measures that they see fit. Doing the same thing over and over and expecting different results is madness. If you want to stop terror, then stop creating the environments that cause radicalization that leads to extremism that leads to terrorism," replied Mashir.

"That makes a lot of sense. We have a similar old saying on Earth that the definition of insanity is doing the same thing over and over expecting different results. It seems that our planets came to the same conclusion," Scott explained.

"It seems that way, yes. It doesn't make sense to me to blame an entire group of people for the actions of a few when by and large the group doesn't do the actions that the few do. Groups of people are not monoliths; they have a wide range of beliefs and thoughts and ways of looking at things," Mashir remarked.

Scott quickly finished his notes before moving on.

"Let's shift focus and talk about what else contributed to the collapse? On an individual level how did the Nill's own actions cause it to occur?" questioned Scott.

"Individually, the population often contributed in small ways. Our homes, vehicles, the food we eat, the tech we use and more all added slowly to the overall decline of our civilization. The way that they kept a good amount of us in check was by supporting propaganda that shifted the blame to the individual yet the biggest factors were the industries, the countries and the energy resources we were using. Our individual impact was not able to slow it down fast enough; we needed to change our systems of energy, industry and power," answered Mashir.

Yolen started to raise his hand.

"I'd like to chime in if I could?" Yolen requested.

"Absolutely," Scott replied.

"Those in power would purposefully put those of us who they saw as inferior into situations where we had to continue adding to the fire, otherwise, we would not have enough food, water, or shelter to survive. We were basically fighting our own governments because they didn't want to take care of us and our fellow citizens didn't see us as such and were fine with our mistreatment because they had been convinced we were the real threat. Not everybody but enough people felt this way that my life was a living hell when I wasn't around Mashir. This also included members of my own race. They would side with the oppressors on the promise that they would be treated more fairly. They felt that they didn't hate all Orange Nills, only the bad ones and that some were actually good ones. This was nonsense of course and the powerful hated all of us equally. Seeing others as worthy of the same rights and freedoms they held was an impossible policy to adopt," Yolen stated.

"Thank you, I really appreciate you offering your point of view," Scott said.

"The treatment of my fellow Nill's based on race has been extremely disappointing and something I have never understood. I wasn't raised to hate others like that and I have to wonder how much a good family life has an impact on these things. It's a small thing, but just like plants, a single seed will grow and bloom into something much bigger. I never bought into the hype about hating others because they were different. I would sometimes have to be neutral or not take a stance on an issue for fear that I would be labeled a traitor or not a real Accoran. A dangerous belief became popular that Accora was different from the rest of the world. Our citizens were the best and the envy of the planet. That when we did the things that other oppressive authoritarian governments did it was in the name of our freedom and our rights. We were seemingly justified in doing awful things because we were serving a greater purpose. The reality was we were only doing these awful things for the same reason any of them do. It was all for power," Mashir said.

Scott turned to another page of his notes and decided to shift gears.

"Okay, so how was daily life during The Great Collapse?" Scott asked.

"At first, we didn't even know we were in it. We were already halfway through it by the time that we really started to try and combat it in meaningful ways. Life remained normal in Accora for a long while until eventually the same events and issues appeared where we thought they couldn't. We were above those petty squabbles because we were a supposedly superior nation. The truth is that all Nills have the same issues and no matter how rich, poor, or in between you are, you will succumb to many of the same problems. Once the weather events started to occur more often, we really thought something was going wrong. We tried to encourage our scientists to do something to help and they tried, but our governments and a large enough portion of voters were suspicious of them. They fell victim to conspiracy theories that they were trying to overthrow society and install a new order. There was no basis for this - just crazy thoughts from extremists - but the way our media has changed allowed it to spread to everyone on the planet. People who would never have been convinced that those in power were evil in any real way were easily swayed by the propaganda on their screens," Mashir said.

"How did that affect interaction on a social level?" Scott replied.

"It made us have to pick sides. Those of us who trusted science and facts were called the worst of names and shunned by this vocal minority. We didn't mind this most of the time, but when someone we cared about fell victim we had to fight it. They would use issues that were legitimately real but they would then create insane theories that had no factual basis to them to advance their agendas. We would often avoid talking about certain topics because we didn't want to keep having a conversation that we knew would never get through to them," said Mashir.

"Did this hurt relationships between your families and with your co-workers?" asked Scott.

"It often did, and usually it made things even more tense at holidays and family events that they already were. This tribalism and groupism led to a lot of violence and certain political groups would use that to their advantage to rough up their opponents. They would sick the conspirators after their opponents as the target of the conspiracy and so the voter's would not only vote the opposite way but they would spread false narrative and misinformation solely to hurt a candidate's chances to win," Mashir sighed.

"So how quickly did the Collapse end? What was the defining moment that made everyone realize they had to flee the planet?"

"Four major events would comprise the final chapter of the collapse. We had over two hundred and sixty major weather events occur in the same year. We had a war that encompassed over ninety percent of the nations on the planet. There was a steady rise of authoritarian governments and the removal of our rights and protections from persecution and oppression. Then, when we started to rise up and fight back, they slaughtered us. Slowly, these revolts, wars, and revolutions caused untold numbers of innocent people to die and did not lead to any change. I left only a year before the collapse concluded but I stayed nearby at a local mining colony on a moon of Nilleon. This had been turned into a short-term refugee camp and was run by the Galactic Relations Council. These final events in the last year all caused the planet to completely give up. The planet could no longer sustain life and we had slowly destroyed our ecosystem till these weather events ended up killing billions of people. Heat waves happening weekly with a million dead, hurricanes in places they've never been before, tornadoes everywhere and strong winds all contributed. These events caused so much destabilization that governments could not control their people. Factions and warlords sprung up and they tried to gain their own power. The authoritarians in charge called in the militaries and they executed their own citizens if they dared speak out against what was happening. Peaceful protests occurred and we just asked that they try to remedy the situation. They didn't listen and we lost almost everyone. No one felt safe in their own homes and this led to so many issues that people couldn't live their lives. They either had to get involved or die. Many did, and many died. Those who could afford to leave and only a small number of people who truly needed help were able to flee from the planet," Mashir said.

"So while this was happening, what was the conversation like? Did people realize the planet was going to fall apart?"

"A lot of us did, but sadly not enough. We were stuck in systems that were designed to oppress us and subjugate us. They didn't listen to reason and they only wanted power. They slowly strangled our freedoms and our rights from us but the trick here is that they did it openly. The supporters of these despots and dictators welcomed it with open arms. They wanted a strong leader who would hurt the people they hated. That was the single issue that they were voting on and it got enough people to keep it going," Mashir answered.

Scott excitedly flipped to another page of his notes.

"I saw a speech being given to the general assembly the other day and I have to ask you about what I saw. A Nill historian named Emedio Zappa was talking about why earth shouldn't take Nill refugees and it seemed like he was blaming the orange and green Nill for this. That they were to blame for their own suffering and that it wasn't due to the blue Nill. I also saw him with Atiyeh when he was giving a speech at the next session. What can you tell me about him?" asked Scott.

Mashir's eyes widened and he gave a heavy sigh.

"I wondered how long until you saw one of his speeches. Emedio Zappa is a conspiracy theorist, a revisionist, and someone who has benefited his entire life because of who he is and what he isn't. He knows he can become rich and powerful by spinning propaganda against the oppressed. He has been doing this for decades even before the Great Collapse. He uses common fascist rhetoric and speaks about betrayal and being stabbed in the back. I don't know how he could possibly blame the collapse on us yet he finds a way to do just that. He's dangerous because he knows how to convince people of a lie no matter how big or small. No matter how ridiculous or unlikely the thing he says is, people believe him when he speaks. He always found his way to authoritarian dictators and populist leaders. It's no surprise that Haladi and Atiyeh would want to use him to convince people they weren't hating on all aliens, just those they deemed not worthy of a safe place to live. He spreads lies and accuses the other groups of doing exactly what they did themselves," replied Mashir, taking a drink of water afterwards.

"I saw through what he was saying, I just fear that most people won't. I'm glad you could clear that up so that we can get a more accurate picture of your history out there," Scott affirmed.

"I appreciate that. It's been so hard to see him spreading his hateful conspiracies and to not face any backlash. I hope people can see Zappa and others like him for who they really are," responded Mashir.

"I agree. I think that's really important. I think we've covered a lot of ground so far. Let's take a ten minute break and get back to it," Scott said.

"Very well," Mashir responded as his coughing fit resumed.

The two of them got up and made their way out of the room. Scott took a second to drink from his water bottle and review his notes before the next session.

CHAPTER EIGHTEEN

Faint beeps from the camera drone rang out, begging to be recharged; Scott was busy relieving the itch on his head that had bothered him for the past twenty minutes. Once he finished, he grabbed a pair of batteries from his back and quickly switched them out. The drone returned to its hovering position.

It would be a few more minutes before Mashir and Yolen returned, so Scott decided to visit the vending machine. A box of sour gummy worms called his name. While he waited on the machine to give him his treat, he checked his phone and noticed a notification from his news feed; a court ruling determined that tech companies don't have to disclose every time they update their A.I. creations. Scott found that to be a little shocking, but he just shook his head and moved on. He grabbed his candy,ripped a small opening in the bag, and plucked a pair of worms, eating them in a single bite.

By the time he returned to the meeting room, he finished off the pack of gummy worms. He cracked his back and started to stretch - his back issues were coming back, but he wouldn't be home for a few more days. He just had to push through. He started to think that he would just go straight home after he finished his last part of the interview. He had seen a lot so far in Cairo and he was starting to feel less safe here, but making sure his speech was everything it needed to be was important to him. He took out his phone and clicked on a few buttons. He raised it to his ear and waited to hear an answer.

"Hey what's up?" asked Zara.

"Hey, would you be alright if we left tomorrow? I really want to make sure I have enough time to prepare for my speech," Scott said.

"Yeah I could do that. I'm already packed. We'd just need tickets."

"My work will take care of it. I really appreciate it, you're amazing," said Scott.

"Yeah no problem. Hope your interview goes well!" she encouraged.

"It's going well. I'm getting nervous about covering everything I want to cover."

"Just stay focused and ask him about what matters to him."

She was right. If he focused on the important issues, everything else would come naturally.

"You're the best. I have to go, I'll see you later," he said.

"You're too sweet. Okay see you soon."

Scott hung up the phone as Mashir and Yolen came back into the room. They took their seats and stretched their arms and legs while letting out a big yawn.

"Alright, time for the home stretch. Are you ready?" Scott asked.

"Absolutely," Mashir smiled.

Scott grabbed his tablet and sat up in his chair.

"When did you realize that things were too far gone to recover from?" said Scott.

"I knew early on that this was going to be the death of us but I didn't think it would come in my lifetime. The way that Nill's look at time had become so condensed that we were living with people who had experienced the same issues generations ago. They knew what the mistakes we were making led to and how those mistakes would cost us the planet if we didn't address the real issues affecting us. Scientists had started to give us deadlines and we kept having to push them back further and further. By the time someone got into power who wanted to make a real difference it was too late. The disasters that occurred when our climate rapidly started to change did irreversible damage to our economies, our populations and our infrastructure. This led to civil unrest, fascist power grabs, resource mismanagement, racial tensions and violence. Nations across the planet started to split and wars were declared causing everything to go south. Those of us who were able managed to escape and hold out. Once we knew it was too far gone and about to reach an end we looked for asylum. I chose Earth because I had met the first human to visit Nilleon. Her name was Sophie Henderson from the Congo. We met at a banquet hosted in Earth's honor and she told me stories about your planet. She was so intelligent and knowledgeable about history. I learned a lot about what Earth had been through and realized that we were very similar in nature. I made a push to convince our governments to work even closer with Earth than they planned. Luckily, it paid off thanks to what Sophie told me," Mashir said as he grabbed his water and took a sip.

"That's a lovely story. I remember reading Sophie Henderson's autobiography. She was a real champion of her people and highly respected throughout the world," Scott agreed.

"I'm glad you appreciate her legacy. I try to always keep her in mind when I think about what humanity can be. Unfortunately, it seems a lot of your people are afraid our presence will be an affront to their culture," said Mashir.

"Humans can be bigoted and hateful. They don't represent all of us, just the worst of what we can offer. How did you feel about Earth's response to The Great Collapse? Earth covered it extensively on our news outlets and the general consensus was that it was a foreign event with little impact on us," Scott asked.

"Our relationship with Earth became strained because we were low on resources and needed more aid sent to us. The World Economic Council refused due to a payment we had not been able to make due to our worsening economic conditions. We were punished by having our aid revoked and we were left to starve. I gave a speech to them where I explained exactly what was happening and why we needed their help. They listened to every word I said and still voted no on sending aid. I returned to Nilleon with the news and I had to have twenty-four seven bodyguard protection due to the death threats I was receiving," Mashir stated.

"We have this saying that goes 'Don't shoot the messenger'. It's absolutely awful that you had to deal with that," Scott replied.

Mashir grabbed another drink of his water to calm himself.

"I wish Nills felt that way and that ultimately factored into me fleeing the planet too. I knew that getting to stay on Earth permanently was a long shot but I knew I had to see the world Stacey told me about. I just wish it was happy to have me here," replied Mashir.

Scott couldn't help but sigh.

"I'm happy you're here. I'm happy that you've so far been able to continue your life here. If I have any say in the matter I'll make sure you get to stay here for as long as possible."

"Thank you. A lot of the Nill around me didn't see what was coming and it hit them like a brick. They were devastated; many had already lost their homes by that point and their jobs. They had nowhere to go and so they fled to wherever would take them," Mashir lamented.

"That must have been a challenging time. What kind of things did you see?" Scott asked.

"A lot of lonely nights and a lot of days. I couldn't even eat. I was so worried about what was going to happen to me. The hunger, desperation, cold and sickness. I was ill for three weeks straight at one point with a nasty cold. No one cared and no one would see me to see what the issue was. Once I got here though it seemed like I had finally rounded the corner. It was not perfect by any means and required quite a substantial upheaval but it was better than where I was. The pragmatist in me tries to find some solace in that. I do see many shades of Nilleon here and that terrifies and delights me at the same time."

Scott took a second to finish writing down the notes. Mashir stretched his arms.

"I think a lot about where I come from and what I try to teach people in my writings when it comes to this subject and I think this will be most pertinent to you is that ultimately the things that us Nill are also what make you Human. The dynamics of how our awakening occurred rhyme so very much. It is a special thing and just because in the infinite cosmos there are some duplicates of the concept it is truly an enormously rare occurrence," Mashir continued through a bit of stoicism.

Several hours passed before Scott felt that he had enough notes for this section. It started to hit him that he only had one more session left and would need to make sure he got everything he would need out of that. By the time the clock had rolled to six, Mashir and Yolen were starting to yawn and looked ready to leave.

"Well, it seems to be that time. We've got just one more session tomorrow. How are you feeling?" Scott asked.

"I'm looking forward to it, but I am going to miss talking with you. I'd like to exchange contact info before we leave tomorrow. We've covered a lot, but I'm sure in the future we may want to do this again," Mashir concurred.

"Absolutely. I have a feeling this won't be the last time we do one of these," Scott laughed.

Scott got up and shook Mashir and Yolen's hands respectively. Scott grabbed his equipment and notes while the two of them made their way out.

"See you tomorrow," Mashir said as he walked out of the room.

Once Scott got his things in order he ordered himself a ride to the hotel and made his way outside. He sent a message to Zara that he was on his way. After a few moments she responded by saying she would order dinner. The ride arrived shortly after; it was a fairly silent ride. Scott was exhausted and knew he had a lot of work ahead of him. He spent the ride checking his newsfeeds on his phone.

WATER CRISIS IN EAST AFRICAN FEDERATION CAUSES OVER 3,000 DEATHS IN LAST MONTH

ITALIAN AIR FORCE BASE EXPLOSION KILLS 13 U.N. SOLDIERS

MULTIPLE CATEGORY FIVE HURRICANES APPROACH GULF COAST, BILLIONS OF DOLLARS IN DAMAGES ESTIMATED

The ride was quick; before he knew it, they had pulled up to the hotel.

"Thanks for the ride," Scott said to the driver.

"My pleasure. Have a nice evening," the driver grinned.

Scott hopped out and made his way inside. Zara had been waiting for him in the lobby and smiled when she saw him walk in. She ran up to him and gave him a big hug.

"How was your day?" she asked.

"Long and tiring. I'm looking forward to being home soon and I'm happy you're coming with me," Scott professed.

"I am too," Zara blushed and gave Scott a kiss.

The two of them made their way upstairs to their room. Scott took his shoes off before lying on the bed. He laid in silence while Zara changed into a t-shirt and sweats.

"Are you okay? I have food on the way, it should be here soon," she asked.

Scott couldn't get any words out, but he smiled and called Zara over with his hand. She walked over and Scott pulled her onto him for a kiss. Neither of them pulled away for an entire minute.

"What pushed you into believing the things you do?" asked Scott, shifting the conversation suddenly.

Zara paused. She adjusted herself to sit on the edge of the bed.

"The lived experience of the past several years has really shown me that the current system isn't going to solve the crises forming from it. We need a radical change as soon as we can otherwise we won't have a future to look forward to. It will be bleak and unforgiving chaos on a repeating basis until something gives and the planet is unlivable. We already lose so many every single year under our current system and no one ever wants to point to that when it comes to mass death counts. Our leaders blow the supposed enemies out of the water. This systemic violence is not looked at in the same way by the average person like they would someone they know individually. That is personal for them and something to truly mourn," Zara lamented.

"The death of one person is a tragedy and the death of a million is but a statistic," Scott reflected.

"That line was always misinterpreted. It is very accurate to how those in power and the media view things. A million people could vanish over the course of a few years and yet it is business as usual as long as the bottom line stays above water," she responded as she shifted on the bed.

"Was it a quick process or how did it evolve over time?" Scott pondered.

"It developed over time for sure. In the past I would have talked more along the lines of reforming the system and trying to change it from within in a completely peaceful way. The realities of the world we live in quickly shattered that and after many scuffles and situations like the protest the other day we now know that something drastic needs to happen. The radicalization process can take years but eventually you start to see through the wall of lies they have put up in front of us. Once you start to view things materially and from the perspective of how they relate to society and its functions, everything tends to come into focus. Reading is also very important, because if you don't learn from those who have been in the movement beforehand then how will we know what to try and what to avoid. So many ideas that current day revolutionaries and thinkers come up with have been thought of before and have been proven a success or failure tenfold. Don't just read though, go out and practice it. Talk to others about it and then learn the history of the area you live in. There is so much history that gets covered up in every nation in regards to its labor history and the sacrifices made to get us to this point. The androids suffered the same types of fights we faced in the early twentieth and twenty-first centuries and they came out better for it. These kinds of fights have historical precedence and we'd be remiss to accept the narratives of our past revolutionaries from our enemies who have a vested interest in lying and propagating a false narrative about those people. I think we need to do something quickly and to act with great care to not repeat past mistakes. The opportunity comes when we least expect it and we have to be ready. I know you've met people with connections in your time here and I have some of my own. I think most people can see that there are issues with the world but being willing to speak it out loud that we have to change the way we operate society to achieve a different outcome is unpopular. Some of us have gotten too comfortable but I can sense something in the air. A new wave is coming soon and I think there are a lot of opportunities across the world. The movement has really just begun and the future can be a very bright one," replied Zara.

"The more I talk with you, the more confident I am that we really can change things. A better world is possible and I think you will be a big reason for it. Thank you for the motivation to not give up on these ideas. A lot of the time it is hard to focus the energy when it is just you but knowing I am not alone is a weight off my shoulders," Scott assured.

"I want to escape the chaos here but I don't want there to be chaos anywhere. I want to help make change wherever I go and I can sense that in you too. Sorry for the tangent I know you just asked a pretty simple question," Zara tittered.

"I love your tangents. I have the same issue. Let's relax and watch a show," Scott said.

Zara laid back down and cuddled up next to Scott. She grabbed the remote and turned on the television.

"What were you thinking of watching?" Zara asked.

Scott hadn't thought of that but knew he wanted something to distract him and not think about the world. He would be doing enough of that over the next eight days leading up to his presentation.

"Something funny and light-hearted. Like The Theater," Scott replied.

"You like The Theater? I love The Theater!"

"It's my favorite show! My best friend Tim and I usually spend hours watching it when we can. I can't wait till you meet him. I think you guys will get along well."

"That is awesome! I probably haven't seen it as much as you, so we better get started!" Zara giggled.

Scott pulled Zara in closer as she turned the show on.

The episode focused on a big premiere night and the antics of the closing crew. Two of the managers were dragging a big gondola full of trash bags across the theater lobby and one of the characters dropped three huge bags of trash onto the tile flooring. The character dropped his shoulders and threw his phone down and it bounced several feet onto a carpet nearby.

Scott and Zara were laughing and enjoying the show when they heard a knock at the door. Zara looked down at her phone and realized it was their food. She opened the door to meet the android food delivery worker. In his hands were two bags from a local chicken wing restaurant.

"I have a delivery for Zara. Here you go!" said the android, handing her the bags.

"Thank you so much!"

She grabbed the food bags and shut the door.

"Ready for chicken wings?" asked Zara.

"Always ready."

He sat up as Zara brought the food over to the bed and got the boxes out of the bags. Scott opened up his box to reveal the most beautiful sight: chicken wings smothered in barbeque sauce with a side of french fries, flanked by a cup of ketchup.

"Thank you so much, this is wonderful," Scott said while giving Zara a kiss on the cheek.

"You're welcome. You're working hard so you deserve it."

The two shared a kiss then turned their attention back to the show. They scarfed down their food and enjoyed the night together.

Scott woke up to his mind racing. This was his last chance to interview Mashir and he knew that afterwards he would have to gather his things and head back home. His flight was booked for eight P.M., so it gave him time to make it back to the hotel to grab his things. Zara was still sleeping when he woke up so he decided to let her sleep until he was ready to leave. He took a long shower, double the time it normally took him. Most of it was spent talking to himself about the interview questions and how he would wrap this whole process up. Once he finished, he got dressed and started to organize his things. He wanted to make the process of checking out and leaving as easy on future Scott as possible. He put everything he needed by the chair and took with him just his satchel and camera drone. He walked over to Zara and tapped her shoulder to wake her. She stirred and rolled over towards him.

"Oh are you heading out already?" she asked sleepily, her eyes barely opening.

"Yeah, I wanna make sure I have time to prepare and get all my questions right. I packed my things and I'll head to the airport once I finish. I can meet you here if you want or we can check out and head straight there. If you need to grab anything else or wrap anything else up now would be the best time for that," Scott said.

"Okay sounds good. I'm gonna sleep for a while longer and then gather my things. Mostly everything is here or at the house. It shouldn't take long. Just message me when you are heading this way and I'll be ready. Give me a kiss before you go," Zara croaked and pursed her lips.

Scott leaned down and kissed her. They smiled at each other and Scott made his way out of the room. He requested a ride and headed down to the lobby. A sign with the words 'Free Breakfast' was strewn across the lobby. He stopped in his tracks and decided to grab something to eat. Today would be a long day and an empty stomach was not something he wanted to deal with. Three long tables were filled with breakfast foods including scrambled eggs, toast, sausage patties, waffles, pancakes, fruit bowls and oatmeal. Drinks including orange juice, coffee, milk, chocolate, and more filled up a smaller table near the end. Scott grabbed a plate and filled it with eggs, a few sausage patties, and three pieces of toast. He grabbed a glass and filled it with chocolate milk and took a seat near the door. He took only about four minutes to inhale his food as if he was a vacuum cleaner in a dirty room. He drank his glass in about three chugs and placed his dishes on a dirty dish cart. Right as he finished cleaning his space, his ride arrived. He made his way outside and was waved over by the driver.

"I'm here to pick up Scott, is that you?" asked the driver.

"Yes sir. Thank you," Scott replied.

Scott hopped inside of the car and stretched his legs while making himself comfortable. This trip seemed different than the last several he had taken there. He knew this would be the last time he would meet with Mashir, at least for a while, and that he had to make the most of it. He took a look at his notebook and saw hundreds of pages that he would need to sort through over the next week. This wasn't his first rodeo, so he knew he could do it, but the added importance of this case would weigh on him for the interim. A notification popped up on Scott's phone and he looked down to read it:.

Wildfires burn down forests throughout North America and Europe

California had been ablaze for almost an entire century at this point. Continuous wildfires were unable to be put out because they simply didn't have the resources required to offset the damage they had already done. Inept leadership that stretches back centuries have led to this damage being irreversible and something that we have to live with now.

Scott snapped back to reality and looked outside the window of his ride. Large crowds down the street blocked his normal route. Huge signs and bright flashes from police vehicles stood between them and the rest of the road.

"Hold on, we'll have to take the scenic route," said the driver, turning down a road to the right.

They continued their detour and Scott noticed that a lot of people were making their way towards the crowds. There were huge plumes of smoke coming from the other side of town, which concerned him. He really could not get out of here soon enough; Cairo was a powder keg ready to blow. The rest of the ride took a few minutes longer than normal but not enough to cause him to be late. As they arrived at the library, Scott's phone rang; George's contact was on full display.. Scott tapped the answer button and raised it up to his ear.

"Hey George what's up?" Scott asked.

"Scott! How's it going buddy?" George boomed.

Scott waved thanks to the driver and exited the vehicle as he started to respond.

"I'm actually about to head into my final interview session in a few minutes and once I wrap that up I'm headed back home," Scott replied.

"That's great! How are you feeling about what you've got so far? This speech is certain to have a huge impact on their final vote," George asked.

"I think I have a lot of good stuff to work with. I'll be ready once it's time." Scott boasted.

"Good. I have faith in you. I'll leave you to it just let me know once you're back in town. I'd love to go over some of your notes with you."

"Sounds good. I'll see you soon," Scott said before hanging up the phone.

The chilly air nipped at Scott so he quickly made his way inside of the library. He walked down the corridors for the final time and took a turn towards the library. Verona stood near the door to her office, looking in Scott's direction - he ignored her. He wanted to return his book before the final interview session started, mainly to just get it out of the way. The librarian stood by the front desk. He approached the desk as he pulled out the book.

"Hi, how can I help?" asked the librarian.

Scott placed the book on the counter.

"I wanted to return this," said Scott.

"Perfect, I was wondering if you'd bring it back on time," said the librarian, with a rare smile and giggle.

"Do I need to do anything else?" asked Scott.

"You're all set, have a great day!" replied the librarian.

Scott smiled and walked out of the library. He stopped to grab a drink of water from the fountain and then made his way towards the meeting room to set up. He still had a few minutes before Mashir and Yolen would arrive and used this to organize his notes and to make sure he would be able to hit every talking point he wanted to. It was just about noon. They should be here any minute. Scott took a seat and stretched. As he finished the door to the room opened and in entered the guests of honor.

"Scott, how are you doing today?" asked Mashir as he grabbed Scott's hand to shake.

"I'm doing well, and yourself?" replied Scott.

"I'm feeling better. I'm still coughing, but it's getting better. I'm also a little sad that this is our last time speaking for now. Here is my card, and feel free to contact me anytime," affirmed Mashir.

Mashir handed a small gray business card to Scott. It wasn't paper, more like a tiny tablet with a screen showing Mashir's contact information. Scott would be able to sync this up to his phone and save the information.

"Thank you, I'm looking forward to our next encounter already," Scott said.

Scott and Mashir shared a laugh and then they both turned to Yolen.

"Yolen, it's been a pleasure chatting with you and getting to know you. I appreciate your input and point of view," Scott said.

"The same to you, it's been interesting. Thank you for listening to me, not many humans give me a chance," Yolen replied.

Scott stuck his hand out and shook Yolen's. Yolen smiled and became slightly overwhelmed with emotion.

"I almost forgot, here is the book I wrote on the Great Collapse," said Mashir, grabbing the book from his bag and handing it to Scott.

"Thank you Mashir. I really appreciate this, it will be a ton of help," said Scott.

Mashir glanced over at Yolen and gave him a look of understanding and patted him on the back.

"Alright, we can cry it out after the interview wraps up. Let's get started," Mashir said.

The three took their seats and got comfortable. Scott pulled out his notes and turned to a page with a long list of points that he wanted to follow up on. Scott started with the first item on the list and began his final interview.

CHAPTER NINETEEN

Seven Days Later

Scott couldn't help but stare at a few interesting shapes in the steam from the shower. He took his hands and used them to wipe his face off and then grabbed a small towel to finish drying his face. The day has finally come and Scott was simultaneously ready and woefully unprepared. He walked out of the bathroom into his bedroom and started to get dressed. Zara had already left while he was in the shower. She would be meeting him at the headquarters but had to run a few errands first. Scott had been working non-stop for the past week making sure that his speech was exactly how he wanted it to be. Once he finished getting dressed, he checked the time and noticed that he was actually ahead of schedule. He had about two hours until the assembly would start and he only needed to be there an hour prior. He decided to use his free hour to check in on his favorite news channel.

"Breaking news! Fourteen children have gone missing in a coal mine in Argentina. Officials say that the children in question were 'not supposed to be there' and had snuck in while guards were not looking," the news anchor announced.

Unfortunately, this was the third such incident in the last year. Scott remembered hearing about this same thing happening right before he left for his vacation and here it was again. He decided to flip to a different station.

"War between India and China has intensified with rocket and artillery fire being levied against opposing cities and villages near the border zones of the two warring nations. The United Nations has declined to comment on whether they will step in to resolve these disputes diplomatically. Many are worried that this could be the start of World War Five and be the end of the global power structure as we know it. Back to you John," said the field reporter.

The reporter seemed to be near a warzone - the sound of distant gunfire was distinct. A sudden loud boom caused the reporter and cameraman to fall to the ground. A loud scream pierced the air before the feed was cut.

"Greta? Can you hear me? Guys can we get her back? Get them back!" John demanded, trying to hide his fear.

The feed cut to a commercial and Scott decided to try a third and final news channel. He clicked to what could be an even less optimistic report.

"Thousands gather outside the U.N. headquarters today as a special hearing will be held to discuss options and solutions to handle the Nilleon refugee crisis. A vocal portion of activists have taken to the streets to demand that the U.N. refuse a path to safety. Supporters of anti-alien extremist groups have been spotted in the crowds and have threatened violence online. No comments were given by the local or federal police in response to these threats. Others in the crowd are more supportive and wish to see the world governments be more accommodating."

Scott turned off the television realizing that no matter what channel he went to, something more sad and disturbing would appear. The vicious cycle that the news media perfected resulted in becoming increasingly more upset and more worried about what the future would hold. Scott got off the couch and grabbed his satchel that sat by the door. He double checked to make sure he had everything he would need before leaving. There was still some time before he needed to get to work so he pulled out his phone to call Tim. The phone only rang three times before he got an answer.

"Hey man, how's it going?" Scott asked once Tim picked up.

Tim cleared his throat.

"I'm good, just woke up a little bit ago. How are you feeling about your speech?" Tim asked.

"I feel pretty confident. I've gone over my notes about twelve times at this point so I think I should knock it out of the park."

"That's awesome man. I'll be rooting for you all the way from here. Just remember to speak from your heart and tell it like it is," Tim affirmed.

"Oh absolutely. No worries about that. I appreciate it, Tim."

"That's what I'm here for. I have your back always. I have to get going. I don't wanna be late for work, but let me know how it goes!"

"I will for sure. Talk to you later."

Scott hung up, did a final check of his bag, and made his way outside as he called for a ride. He took his time walking towards the road and noticed a few birds chirping on one of the trees in the yard. They built a nest and looked to be talking between themselves. Scott smiled and kept walking. He got to the edge of the driveway and checked his phone - still about eight minutes before his ride would get here.

He sat his bag down and laid down in the grass. All the air escaped his lungs as he rested his arms down to his sides. The blades of grass tickled his skin. He hadn't done this in years, perhaps since he was a child. Something about laying in the grass reminded him of his grandmother's house. Scott gazed at the clouds. Today was a lucky day, because there were a few white clouds still floating high. Greenish-orange clouds dominated the majority of the skyline. His entire body relaxed as he shut his eyes.. He spent the next several minutes resting in the grass and letting himself feel connected to the Earth. A small shred of beauty in a world that had fallen into ugliness. His mind rolled and rotated as if the earth moved with it.

After only thirty seconds, he got too dizzy and felt sick to his stomach. The ride was about to arrive so he sat up, fixed his hair, and stood up off the ground. He grabbed his bag and made his way out to the street. The ride pulled up right to him and rolled the driver side window down.

"Scott, how are you doing today?" asked the driver.

"I'm good Jason. Nice to see you again," Scott said.

Jason was the same driver who drove Scott and Zara home from the airport a week ago; this was now the third time he had gotten him as a driver. Scott hopped inside the ride and took a deep breath.

"Are you doing alright sir?" Jason asked, with a slight amount of concern.

"Just a big day," Scott replied.

Scott relaxed and stared out of his window for most of the ride. The city hadn't changed much in the short time he was away, but a lot of the same issues seemed to persist: protests for multiple social justice issues, fighting amongst local officials regarding election controversies, and demands that the energy companies stop toxic practices that are harming the environment.

A notification rang on his phone - Haladi was giving a speech to his nation regarding the U.N. vote. Scott clicked the link and pulled up the livestream. Haladi stood on a stage overlooking the square filled with tens if not hundreds of thousands of his supporters. They waved Haladi and Egyptian flags and cheered for him as he waved back. Haladi wore a long black coat with a red tie and black gloves. A dozen flags were placed behind his podium. He stood straight and crossed his arms while peering out into the crowd. A smug grin painted his face. He raised his hand to indicate he was beginning to speak.

"The media will not show the magnitude of this crowd. Our crowd. They don't want to show that there are hundreds of thousands of you here today. I want them recognized and I want them heard. I set out with one goal and one purpose. To make Egypt great again. I think I have done it. I think we have done that! Our nation has been under attack by a vicious enemy unwilling to compromise and wanting to see our country fall apart. The bad things that have happened are because of those who betrayed our country. They stabbed us in the back when we were our most vulnerable. I have not forgotten and we will never forget what they have done. The United Nations thinks it can decide what is best for us and who we allow in our country. No matter what their vote is, we will continue down the path I have laid out. We want one nation for our people, our Egyptian people. They want to take that away from you and I won't let that happen. I have fought for you and I expect you to fight for me. If you don't fight like hell you're not going to have a country anymore. We won't take back our country with weakness, you have to show strength! The criminals of last November tried to take this great country from us and I stopped that from happening. We remain undefeated on the battlefield, free from any foreign influence or entanglements. One is either the hammer or the anvil. We confess that it is our purpose to prepare the Egyptian people again for the role of the hammer. The battle beginning today will decide the fate of the Egyptian nation for the next thousand years. We are a nation built upon the strength of our will and our commonly held beliefs. Service is our freedom! Obedience is our power! Your sacrifice is necessary, to ensure our victory is forever! I could not have done that without the support of you. Together we will make... Egypt... great again!" proclaimed Haladi, pounding his fist on the podium as a pair of fighter jets flew by overhead.

The crowd roared in applause, throwing their hands in the air.

"One People, One Empire, One Leader! Haladi Forever!" chanted the crowd in complete unison.

Scott turned the stream off as Haladi continued to ramble. This was enough fascist rhetoric for one day. He looked forward to getting through today and going back home with Zara. He planned to show Zara around the town for the next few nights. It was going to be a surprise and he hoped that he could tell her about it after knocking the speech and presentation out of the park.

The rest of the ride was smooth and he arrived at his office building. The building itself is connected to the U.N. Headquarters through a system of bridges between multiple buildings. He thanked Jason with a generous tip and made his way inside the office. A few people in the lobby waved, but he was focused on getting up to the office. He walked over towards the elevators and entered the closest one. Both of the other occupants were strangers to Scott but he still smiled and nodded anyway; the pair responded in kind. The elevator stopped at floor eight and floor eleven. Two tall men in black suits entered the elevator with one carrying a briefcase. Scott smiled and laughed to himself.

Some things never change.

The ride up to floor thirteen was quick and Scott entered the lobby area of his office. Kevin shuffled down the hall towards his office with several tablets in his arms. They made eye contact as Kevin made his way over to Scott.

"Hey Scott, it's great to have you back. How was the trip?" Kevin beamed.

"It's great to see you too Kevin. All in all, it was a wonderful time man. A few minor bumps in the road but nothing too unusual," responded Scott.

"I'm really glad to hear that. I'm looking forward to your speech, good luck!" said Kevin, offering Scott a fist bump.

Scott returned the fist bump.

"I really appreciate that, Kevin. I'll see you later," Scott said, returning the fist bump.

He walked up to Stacy's desk. She locked eyes with him and jumped out of her chair.

"Well, look who's back! We missed you Scott. How're you feeling? Are you ready to go?" Stacy hollered as she ran around the desk to hug Scott.

Scott returned the hug with a smirk.

"I missed you all too. Cairo was nice but something about home is just too alluring. And I'm ready as I'll ever be," Scott responded.

"Well good. I'll be watching you live while it happens so I'll root for ya," Stacy said as she sat back down.

"I appreciate it. Is George in his office?" Scott asked.

"Go right ahead, he's expecting you," Stacy said.

Scott nodded and walked towards George's office. He made his way inside and shut the door behind him. George's office remained unaltered. He couldn't explain why, but he had missed it. He looked at the globe and noticed it had been spun a few times. It was now pointed at Eastern Europe specifically with Saint Petersburg pointing up. Scott smirked and turned towards George who was seated behind his desk.

"Fascinated with the globe still?" George smiled.

"It's pointed at Saint Petersburg. I just thought that was interesting," Scott replied.

"Why's that?" asked George.

"If this globe was a couple decades older, it would say Petrograd. A few more after that and it would say Leningrad and then St. Petersburg. And after that it would be as it stands today once more, Leningrad. This globe being accurate today is just something I find interesting," Scott said.

George had a big grin on his face and stood.

"That's why I know you'll be great in your new role. You care about that kind of thing when almost no one else does. Most people wouldn't see that, but you do."

"Thanks George. I appreciate that."

George shook Scott's hand and chuckled

"So, are you ready for today?" George asked.

"I kind of have to be, don't I?" Scott cracked.

"You know what I mean," said George as he walked back over to his desk.

"I've got my slides ready to go. I've got my notes memorized and my speech is gonna cap it off."

"I knew you would be ready. You're always ready. That's why I told them you were the man for the job. Today's the last day you have to report to me. After this meeting and your speech, we are co-workers. On the same level. I'm looking forward to it. I think maybe you'll be less of a kiss ass," George declared.

Scott smiled and couldn't help himself from laughing.

"I'm also looking forward to that. You've been a great boss and I'll always appreciate what you've taught me. I just hope I can make a difference with this speech." Scott said.

George looked out the window out towards the city, admiring the clear sky and flocks of birds flying in between the skyscrapers. The bright sun shone into the room and started to impair Scott and George's vision.

"Let me close the blinds," George offered.

He got up and ended the sun's reign on the throne of light sources.

"Mashir was nice enough to provide stock footage of thousands of years of Nilleon's history. Hundreds of hours of documentaries covering almost any topic you could think of. It made it easy to find the footage for the presentation," Scott gloated.

"That's kind of him. I hope that helps his case. I still don't know how the council will vote. I can't believe that the head of the library wanted you to use their propaganda footage. Did you look at what they gave you?" asked George.

"I did. It painted Haladi as the savior of the nation, like he was some sort of god. One People, One Empire, One Leader, Haladi Forever is what they would chant. It was chilling," responded Scott.

"Do you still have the hard drive?" George asked.

"Yes, my plan was to make a copy and give a report about Ms. Kampf's request to the U.N., " replied Scott.

"Good idea. Can't let them get away with threatening you like that. I knew it was getting rough in Cairo, but Ivan never has this much trouble," said George.

"I just hope the council will listen to what I have to say with an open mind," Scott said.

"Me too, Scott. Me too," George sighed.

Scott looked over at the clock on the wall - 12:25 P.M.

"Alright, I'm gonna gather my things and start heading that way. I want to be ready to go. See you out there?" Scott said, pointing a finger at George.

"See you out there," George replied, pointing back at Scott.

Scott left the room and made his way towards the exit, spotting Larry walking around the corner.

"Scott, I wanted to catch you before you went on. How're you feeling?" Larry asked.

"I'm feeling good. Have to get through this, so I'm ready."

"Any nerves at all? I know you've done this before, but this seems like a big one," Larry cautioned.

"A few for sure. I just know the best way to get over them is to just go out there and say what I have to say."

"I know we don't see eye to eye on everything, even on this topic at times, but I wanted you to know I hope they vote yes. This clearly means a lot to you and I don't think you would be on the wrong side of this. I was only looking at things from what I've known in my own life, not from anyone else's perspective."

"I appreciate that Larry. I know it can be tough getting outside of our own bubbles and seeing what others are experiencing but it's an important step in the process. I'm going to give it my best and I hope they listen to me," Scott sympathized.

"That's good buddy. I'll be watching you. Good luck!" Larry said as he patted Scott's shoulder.

Larry walked off and Scott continued his way out of the office. Around the corner came Uyanmas dressed in a blue suit and carrying two small boxes.

"Hey Scott! It's about time for your speech isn't it? asked Uyanmas.

"Yes sir. Getting ready to head over that way. Do you need any help with those boxes?" offered Scott.

"I've got it! It's just a few things for my office. How do you think the presentation is going to go?" Uyanmas asked.

"I'm as prepared as I can be. I'm just hoping that the council will do the right thing," replied Scott.

"I hope they do too, Scott. I'm just not so sure they will. Even here, we see hatred and oppression against aliens. We're one of the more progressive countries and yet we still let the police attack them with impunity and no consequences," sighed Uyanmas.

"That's true, but I still have this feeling that things can change. It's inevitable we just have to steer it in the right direction. Open our eyes and see the world for what it really is and seize the world that we want," Scott insisted.

"I don't know anyone besides you that could convince me of that. Best of luck to you man. I know you'll do great," said Uyanmas.

The two shook hands and parted ways. Scott heard a news broadcast coming from the break room and went to check it out. He walked in on Brittney and Hila sitting at the table, chatting and watching the news.

"Scott! Just in time, I wanted to tell you good luck before the speech," said Brittney with a soft wave.

"I know you'll do your best, are you nervous at all?" asked Hila.

"A little for sure. I'm ready to say what I've got to and see how the council responds," said Scott.

"I can't imagine them not siding with you. We can't just abandon these people and leave them to die," Hila stressed.

"There are plenty of people who feel the way we do, but I saw a lot of the opposite first-hand in Cairo. They are going down a dark path and I don't know what that is going to mean for everyone else," Scott advised.

"It seems like so many countries are facing these kinds of struggles. I don't know what I would even do if I was an alien. I wouldn't be able to live where I do or work here even," said Brittney.

"Yeah, in the rule book it still states that you have to be a human being to work at the United Nations. It was added back in the 30's and all these decades later they haven't even touched it," noted Hila.

"Aesthetics and names change, but nothing ever really changes. It's the same core with a new skin," said Scott.

"I hope things can change for the better. I don't see why people want to keep going backward. We've gotten to this point for a reason, right?" asked Brittney.

"I agree, but I think that's just the way of the world. Things remain peaceful for too long, and someone is going to rock the boat," replied Scott.

" I'm going to miss these conversations once you leave. I never stop thinking when I'm talking to you," Hila complimented.

"I will miss them too, Hila. I need to get to the hall so I'll talk with you guys later," Scott said as he made his way to the door.

"Talk to you later! Break a leg!" yelled Brittney.

"You've got this!" exclaimed Hila.

Scott smiled and exited the room. He turned around the corner and made his way towards the first bridge he would need to take. The sun peeked through windows alongside the ceiling and walls of the bridges. Scott peered out at the city as he walked along the path. A huge crowd gathered near the central portion of the city near an old war monument. It looked like police had surrounded the area. He looked over to the other side to see a few bustling streets with cars flying amongst themselves. Scott pulled out his phone and checked the time - 12:33 P.M. He had plenty of time to get there and get ready. He went to Zara's contact image and pressed call. A few moments passed and then they were connected.

"Hey babe, I'm about to go on. Just wanted to see if you were here yet?" Scott inquired.

"Hey you! I'm just outside of the presentation hall, waiting for them to seat us. Are you feeling okay?" she asked, biting her lip.

"Okay good. I'm doing alright. Just trying to calm some nerves. I hope you like the speech," Scott said. His nerves intensified and he began to slightly shake.

"I know you're going to do a great job babe. Don't worry yourself too much. Just speak from your heart," Zara encouraged.

Scott smiled and took a second to catch his breath.

"Thank you, that means a lot. I can't wait to get through this and be in your arms again."

"You're welcome, that's what I'm here for. You'll do amazing. I'll let you go so you can get ready," Zara said.

"Okay sounds good. I'll see you afterwards."

Scott ended the call and put his phone in his pocket. He continued on turning three or four different directions before finally arriving at the central building. He noticed a guardpost stationed at the end of the hallway manned by two guards in U.N. fatigues. One was checking papers and the other was standing perfectly straight with an assault rifle in hand. His index finger laid across the trigger guard.

"Hello officers," Scott greeted..

"How're you doing Scott? Big day right?" the guard without the gun asked.

"I'm doing well and yes it's an exciting day," Scott nodded.

The officer looked him up and down and used a device to scan Scott's bag.

"You're good. Good luck!" he said, while patting Scott's shoulder.

Scott thanked him and continued into the building. He made his way into the main lobby area with a service desk, seating areas, and a ton of people looking for which conference hall to funnel into. Scott was overwhelmed and a man in a blue suit walked up to him, taking notice of his sudden anxiety.

"Scott! It seems I must have missed you in Cairo," said the man, with a thick eastern European accent.

"Ivan! Nice to see you man. Yeah, we just never crossed paths. I got caught up in a few things so I didn't have a ton of free time," Scott replied.

Ivan stared at Scott blankly for a few moments, causing Scott's cheeks to flush with unease. Ivan relented and laughed. Scott laughed along with him once he realized Ivan was teasing.

"A lot of unrest in Cairo the past week, wasn't there?" Ivan raised his brow.

"Quite a lot. The police gave me a hard time at a diner and I still can't figure out why," Scott grumbled.

"Haladi has an issue with aliens and you interviewing one probably aroused some suspicion. I'd be more wary about where I conduct those kinds of interviews," stated Ivan.

"I just don't know how they even found out about the interview."

"I'm just glad you made it back in one piece. Haladi is known for being violent towards journalists and other intellectuals. I'm really looking forward to your presentation."

"Thanks, Ivan. That means a lot. I think I'm ready to go. I need to meet them in the west hall meeting room. Do you know where that's at?" asked Scott.

Ivan smirked and pointed down the hall to the sign that said "West Hall Meeting Room".

"Fair enough, thank you. See you there," Scott said.

Scott walked towards the room and tapped on his leg to an old song he used to listen to as a kid. While he enjoyed his walk to the room he pulled out his phone to check the time - 12:50 P.M. Right on time. Scott knocked on the door before entering. A group of about a dozen people were running around and screaming at each other. A tall, sharply dressed woman with dark brown eyes and bright blonde hair spotted Scott and made her way over to him.

"Scott It's nice to meet you. I'm Hailey Poff. The Executive Assistant of the Head of the Galactic Relations Council for the United Nations," said Hailey.

Scott knew the name and was impressed.

"Hailey, nice to meet you. I've been looking forward to working with you," said Scott.

"As have I. I've read your work and thought you would make a great addition to the team," Hailey responded.

Hailey waved her arm at Scott and darted off as Scott trailed behind. They made their way through two other rooms. Scott paused to admire the large window looking out at the General Assembly hall.

"Come on, hurry," Hailey snapped.

Scott picked up his pace. They made their way down a flight of stairs that led to the Assembly Hall's main staging room. Hailey turned around once they were in the middle of the room and looked at him.

"Your presentation is loaded up and ready to go. Here's the clicker for the slides," said Hailey, handing Scott a black remote.

"Thanks," Scott said.

"How're you feeling?" asked Hailey.

She paused in the hectic frenzy that was the meeting room and focused all of her attention on Scott.

"I'm working through it. Cairo wasn't exactly the most pleasant experience, and there is a lot riding on the results of this vote," Scott said in between short breaths.

"Okay, before we head out there. Do you have any other questions for me?" asked Hailey.

"Not that I can think of right now," said Scott.

Scott checked the time again - 12:55 P.M.

"We still have a few minutes, I need to take a second," Scott said.

He found the closest chair and took a seat. He took long, deep breaths to attempt to slow his breathing. His shaking slowed as well.

"Are you okay?" Hailey hesitated.

"Yeah, I just need a moment. I'll be out in a minute," said Scott.

Hailey nodded and collected herself before making her way out to the hall. Scott could hear the crowd chatting amongst themselves. Through a large glass window, he saw crowds forming outside of the building. Activists in support of Nilleon rights and those who wished to kick them off the planet shared the street and drowned out the sounds inside the hallway. Flags were waved; some positive, some hateful. Pro and anti alien flags flew amongst android rights and other activists flags.

One individual waved a large, black and red Haladi flag. Scott's stomach sank.

Why would supporters of the Egyptian president be here halfway across the world?

The roars of the crowd were deafening. He knew the hall itself would have the proper sound proofing material, but the noise overwhelmed Scott. He was curious what the reaction from the crowd would be, regardless of the vote. He snapped back into reality before going down a rabbit hole. Representatives from every major nation on the planet and members of over a hundred other alien worlds would also be present today.

Scott stood up and walked over to the mirror on the wall, observing himself. He reflected on the hard work that led to this moment before taking one final, cleansing breath. He walked through the door and out to the hall.

CHAPTER TWENTY

Hundreds of people were seated and waiting for the presentation. Journalists and media personnel sat near the back and a group of Nill refugees, who were guests of the council, sat over to the side.Zara was near the back of the crowd. Time froze as their eyes locked and Zara smiled proudly. That energy would power him through these next several hours. Members of the General Assembly would sit on the main floor of the hall. The Security Council sat on the stage with a podium on the other side.

Scott was ready. He walked over towards the center of the floor and spotted Hailey.

"Where should I go?" he asked.

"We'll sit right over here. When the speaker calls for you to come up, that's when it's on you," Hailey guided.

"Sounds good to me," said Scott.

The two of them took their places. The speaker who would introduce Scott was seated and watched as the crowd chatted amongst themselves. After a good minute of observation, he stood and made his way over to the podium. The leaders in the first few rows took their seats and stopped talking.

The speaker tapped the mic. The sound ricocheted across the hall and the room silenced. The representatives took their seats as the speaker cleared his throat into the microphone.

"The United Nations General Assembly and Security Council have gathered today to hold a vote on the issue of refugee status for members of the Nill race of the planet Nilleon. The United Nations Galactic Relations Council has asked to speak today to weigh in on this issue," announced the speaker.

"We will now welcome the representative of the council to the podium to present on this issue. Thank you," said the speaker as he walked off and waved Scott on.

. The crowd clapped to welcome Scott. He waved modestly and smiled when he spotted George.. They made eye contact and George winked at him.

You got this.

Scott replied the same and stood behind the podium. Scott exhaled as he admired the crowd and gathered his thoughts. He leaned into the mic, finally ready to speak.

"Representatives of the United Nations and our fellow allied planets: I am honored and humbled to be speaking with you today. My name is Scott and I work for the United Nations as an advisory Historian. I was recently promoted to serve on the Galactic Relations Council for the U.N.," Scott said, pausing for a crowd response.

The crowd clapped for a few moments at the mentions of the U.N.

"I am here today to speak on the state of the Nill refugee crisis and address what we must do as a planet to ensure continued existence for their species. I had the pleasure of sitting down with Mashir Khan and Yolen Babtir, two surviving members of the Nill population, who fled their home prior to the conclusion of what has now been referred to as The Great Collapse. This was a series of events that took place over the course of two hundred and fifty years that directly led to the collapse of their society and ability to continue inhabiting their planet. This led to a mass exodus of their people and now they are in need of help.

"The Nill have seeked peace, shelter and asylum on worlds throughout the known galaxy. This is a crisis all too familiar for the nations of Earth. Looking through time, no matter how far back you go, we have always had people fleeing oppression for freedom. We have never really acted on that promise, instead only slowly lifting the pressure when forced by more progressive members of our species. We in the last few hundred years have been fortunate to discover other life in the universe and have our societies interact for the betterment of both. We have learned a lot from our allies and our foes. We have not always acted in the best ways and have ultimately caused more harm than good just as we have on Earth," Scott waved his hands in frustration.

"There are certain truths we must go by. We have brains and we have hearts; and far too often the two conflict with each other. How some of those in this room live with themselves is something that keeps me up at night. In our long history as a species, Humans have used religion, myth, and tall tales to explain the unexplainable and the unknowable about the world around us. These serve a purpose and connect with a very real part of ourselves as humans that seek a bond on another level beyond personal or familial. The spirituality or religiousness inside all of us manifests in countless ways and remains necessary beyond explanatory methods of use. As humans developed the scientific method, different cultures used these methods to begin understanding the world around them better. Religion and myth took on a new role that could be further exploited and used to help entrench those in power and maintain the status quo. We have ignored crisis after crisis and pushed it further down the road for our children to handle. We are those children now and we must act.

"The survivors of Nilleon share many traits, characteristics, and experiences that those of us on Earth can relate to. They had given far too much power to strongmen who did not share the best interests of their people and they pushed aside issues that had real consequences to be handled by the next generations. They oppressed their own because of differences that were entirely inconsequential. They fought wars over resources, faith and flags," Scott pointed to the United Nations flag hanging on the wall.

"We must continue to adapt to the situation in front of us. We have fought countless wars in the name of one religion or another where so much of what was believed about the other side was misinformation and scare propaganda. I find religion and spirituality to be a crucial aspect of an individual's personal life. When we begin talking about the state or government level, then we must look at the material conditions around us. Of course, not every individual will agree on the truth to religion, god, spirituality, and similar theological questions, so we must require a state that enforces free expression as well as a true separation of religion from the operation of the state. If we want to succeed in our goals, then we must utilize the sciences to make our decisions without a mindset stuck centuries in the past."

Tension filled the air as Scott took a moment to breathe.

"We have advanced so far from the wheel to horse and buggy to cars and planes. We explored our lands, explored our oceans and set out to explore the galaxy. We have developed technologies that allowed us to communicate across countries, continents, and worlds. I can get in contact with someone a solar system away within a few moments!" Scott said, his powerful voice echoing across the chamber.

Scott turned to the security council and looked them deep in their eyes. They looked displeased, but making the council happy was not his priority. He wanted them to live up to the ideas they represent.

"We have built systems that are designed to oppress and not allow change. It builds on top of itself until it's unrecognizable. We have the resources, we have the money, we have the ability to do more and to do better. I think we owe it to ourselves and to any and everyone that comes to the Earth seeking a better life. We should not turn our backs on those who are so willing to share their technology, their knowledge and their history with us. We learn about the consequences of our actions and decisions through history and history loves to echo itself because humans are opposed to change. They want to keep trying the same thing over and over, because they might be able to get away with it one more time before it's too late. The Nill people are similar in so many ways to our own with similar systems of belief, government and social interaction. We would be wise to study their history as carefully as we do our own. We cannot let our ego get in the way of what is right..." Scott paused, letting pure silence saturate the room.

"Not anymore," he finished his thought. He then used the clicker to point at the screen behind him.

A presentation screen appeared with images of Nills wearing rags for clothes, carrying all of their possessions in their hands and bags. They looked starved and ready to die. Numbers and letters were tattooed on their skin with blood coming out of gashes. Many audience members looked away to avoid the graphic images. Even Scott had to take a moment to collect himself. "What I am showing you today includes interview footage between Mashir, Yolen, and I. Mashir was also kind enough to allow me access to archives spanning thousands of years of Nilleon's history. These images here were taken in the last three months of refugees who were denied immediate asylum and have to live in a self-described 'assimilation center' for refugees. Calling something a different name does not change the true nature of what that something is. A concentration camp is a concentration camp whether you call it an assimilation center, a detention facility, a labor camp, a death camp, a re-education center, whatever nonsensical term you want to call it. The purpose of these camps is to temporarily hold these refugees until you have the legal and presumed moral authority at that point to dispose of them as you wish. We are treating sentient life as if it was an old school farm animal."

Scott pressed a button on the clicker and the screen scrolled through a series of images.

"The world is at yet another crossroads. A phrase often repeated during our remarkably defiant existence. We continue to beat the odds. We continue to allow the fate of the world to be put into hands that we cannot trust and we continue to do irreversible damage to our planet and way of life. Some would see this as a cute story on the ability of humans to persevere. While that conclusion can be drawn and has certain roots of truth it misses the bigger picture that we have continued these disastrous and ultimately harmful policies that only serve to divide us further. How can we ever truly expect to have a long lasting and respectable standing in the galaxy, let alone in the universe!

"We have seen throughout our time on this planet that we can achieve what is believed to be impossible if we work with each other instead of against. We all have our differences and we all have our own ideas, norms, culture, experiences and values that guide how we live our lives. I'm suggesting that for the first time in our history we put those aside and finally come together to tackle the threats that are rapidly approaching us.

I want to show a few clips from my interview with Mashir and some footage showcasing events he speaks of," Scott gestured to the screen.

The lights in the room dimmed to show a clip of Mashir speaking with Scott. The video's setting was of the meeting room of the library in Cairo where they first met. Scott could instantly recall how he felt sitting down with Mashir for the first time, knowing that it would lead to the moment he was in right now.

"How would you describe to Earth and to humans what The Great Collapse is and the role it played in the downfall of Nill society?" Scott asked in the video.

"Well, I would say that the first misconception I want to tackle is the idea that it happened suddenly or that we didn't see it coming. We did see this coming. We knew for centuries and we had activists fighting to do something about it for the majority of that time. Our leaders ignored the crisis that was brewing and put it off to the side. They expected our children to handle the problem and that worked for the first few generations but what about when it came time to reckon with the storm? We had the ability, we had the funds, and we had the knowledge to combat these problems with real, feasible results and yet we didn't do that. We would squabble over petty differences, enact changes that had no substantial impact and then pat ourselves on the back. We waged wars against our own species, we enslaved members of our own species, we oppressed our own species because it made some feel superior to others. In the end we all face the same result, no matter how much money, influence, or power we have," Mashir replied.

Footage played over these words ranging from combat footage showing Nills marching victoriously through destroyed cities, starving Nills begging on the streets for food, water, clothing, or anything of value to barter. The images were chilling and many in the crowd were unable to watch. The interview continued.

"So give us a brief rundown of the events. What amount of time does 'The Great Collapse' refer to?" asked Scott.

"It is an era more than anything. It spans roughly two hundred and fifty years or so with events that took place building on top of each other and snowballing into each other. No one event truly encapsulates the impact of 'The Great Collapse'. Endless wars, poverty, greed, oppression, systemic and systematic racism and bigotry, ignoring scientists, expanding the use of dangerous fuel sources and the sheer disdain for those who seek higher knowledge. Strongmen who make promises, lie, cheat and steal their way to power will never give what they say they will. They are liars through and through. All of us fall for a lie whether it's a big lie or a small one. The difference is at what point do you realize that that's all it is, a lie. Our planet didn't fall because of outside influence or because we were naturally weak. We collapsed because those in power ensured that their riches and themselves were safe while the majority of the population suffered in effective silence. The economic system was not sustainable and was going to collapse unless it was artificially propped up or overthrown by the workers themselves. That proved to be an enormous challenge that seems to be the requirement necessary to tackle the challenge we faced. Without that we could not enact enough change that would allow us to survive. We failed to meet history at the gates and let it pass us by. I see many of these same problems on Earth and ultimately I hope to work with anyone willing to listen to help prevent your planet from walking on a road that we know the destination of," replied Mashir.

The video continued to play, showcasing more disturbing images, striking the nerves of several in attendance. A clip came on with the camera focused on Yolen.

"This question is for you Yolen, how was your experience as an orange Nill and what about that experience has led to how you feel now?"

Yolen took a moment to gather his thoughts.

"I am an orange Nill, and I will not and have not ever apologized for being so. My group was oppressed and punished for the pigment in our skin. It's a beautiful color with a proud legacy steeped in stories that date back seven thousand years. We didn't choose to be who we are and yet we were punished as if it was a choice we made in defiance. We were locked away in camps, unfairly charged under the law, paid lower wages to work the same jobs and were never given adequate representation in our governments. They spent so much time, effort, money and energy to keep us down because they didn't want us to seek revenge. I can't speak for everyone, but the majority of us did not want 'revenge'. We wanted to be treated the same as everyone else. We didn't want better treatment, nor did we want more privileges. Consequences were of no concern either and we just sought equal treatment. We were seen as foreigners and as outsiders to our own communities. We were pushed out and, if not for the brave heroes who recognized this injustice and stood with us, we would never have gotten back the modicum of freedom that they allowed us to attain. They slowly gave us more freedom and yet continued to obstruct our ability to be fully equal. They changed the names, changed the protocols, and changed the standards to make it even harder for us to attain the things we fought so hard for. I am just so tired of fighting this fight because I knew then that it won't end in my lifetime and I know now for certain that it won't end in my children's lifetime." answered Yolen

The audience tensed =and looked appalled by the words they were hearing. The clip continued.

"I came with Mashir to Earth in part because of the relationships he had formed during his time as an advisor with our government collaboration efforts. I trusted what he said about Earth and about humans," said Yolen.

"How do you feel now?"

"I trust Mashir with my life and I still trust his judgment. I think humanity at its best can offer a lot for itself and for other species. You're not the first species to make these mistakes or these achievements but your spirit is admirable. I have unfortunately seen a dark part of humanity in my time here and I ultimately hope to push those memories into the past and welcome brighter memories that I wish to make on this planet. I hope the humans making the decisions will ultimately find value in adding us to the so-called melting pot," Yolen responded.

The video played for another ten to fifteen minutes, showcasing more footage of Nilleon's history from their early days exploring and settling the planet, to more recent clips of their first contact with humanity and cooperation of the two planets. It also showed the drone footage Scott recorded around Cairo. He managed to compile plenty of b-roll, but had to cut much of it out to fit Mashir's interview footage in.

"When you look at our planet, what do you see? What are the similarities and differences of our planets?" asked Scott in another interview clip.

"We certainly both have a habit of causing our own problems," Mashir laughed and Scott joined in.

"I see many of both. Our species have evolved over thousands and thousands of years, ultimately conquering our planets and becoming the rulers of the planet. We both abused this power to strip the planet of its resources for our own personal consumption. We have allowed the very worst of ourselves to become the norm and to become the standard against which we try to judge ourselves. It's okay to not be perfect and it's okay to realize when you're the problem. Nilleon and Earth suffer many of the same issues that can cause long-term planetary catastrophes. From my studying of Earth history and the culture I have noticed a distinct sense of resolve to not let the odds defeat you. Humanity seems to be convinced of its own self-appointed responsibility to be the leaders in anything they do. A moral superiority that could very well be unfounded depending on who you ask, but this is not always a bad thing. Like most things, especially concerning living beings, it is about how you utilize these beliefs and how you act on them that truly represent what makes you who you are. I do not blame humanity for feeling it has a right to the planet it came from and that those who don't come from there stay away. I simply ask that you stop looking at the differences between our species but look at what we have in common. Not just the good things and not just the bad things; look at everything. Look at our history and tell me what you see. Tell me what you would say if instead of the word NilII said human. I have a feeling that most humans would feel differently about us if they started to look at us as something like themselves and not just aliens who are devoid of what some would call a soul," stated Mashir.

Scott felt the mood shift in the room with more and more of the audience paying closer attention to what was being shown and said. Once the video concluded, the lights were raised up. Scott turned back towards the audience and took a deep breath.

"I hope the clips shown and statements made by Mashir and Yolen have made you uncomfortable, saddened, and retrospective. I believe that what they articulated should be seen as a sign that we move to continue the acceptance of and the expansion of the asylum program allowing Nills seeking safe passage and shelter to remain and continue to come to Earth. I was witness to a hate crime committed against Mashir and

Yolen - human police officers intimidating, harassing, and assaulting refugees seeking a home. Looking at our own history and seeing the parallels in Nilleon's own collapse should not be a surprise, but a return to logical thinking. We can't continue to make the same mistakes we have been making and we can't continue down the same road that they went down because we know how it ends. The collapse of their entire society twenty years ago was the result of a more than two hundred and fifty year process that looks shockingly similar to our own. If we don't seek their knowledge and learn from their mistakes, we are doomed to repeat them because we have already made so many of those same mistakes ourselves," Scott peered into the crowd. He spotted an android waiter bringing a bottle to someone in the audience.

"Humanity has a long history of oppressing and dividing ourselves over issues that ultimately only showcase the amazing diversity of our people. We are all different and all have things that make us unique, and yet that is what makes us who we are as a species - that conflicting paradoxical philosophy that we are all unique just like everybody else. Some interpret this in a more somber tone and reject it. I see it as the thing that made us the dominant life form on this planet and the thing that ultimately makes us different from other animals. We have the ability to process and understand our role in the universe and to continue the same barbaric, animalistic endeavors that we have carried out - for millennia only serves to lock us out of progress.

"If we are truly to expand our influence and explore the cosmos, we have to sort out our differences on Earth. This not only applies to our own issues, but issues that have sprung up from our own inventions. Android life has become a major issue for some on this planet with the debate ranging from whether these beings are property, whether they deserve any rights at all, or if they even have a soul. This ultimately boils down to the question of how we treat these beings that we created ourselves. I have had the

pleasure to meet many, many fine androids in my life and, while not all of them are

perfect, they are all living. They have sentience and awareness that they exist just like we

do. I met a waitress at a restaurant in Cairo named Emma who was very sweet and kind

in the short time I got to know her. I wanted to interview her and gain her insight on the

struggles faced by androids in our modern world, but sadly she was slain before her time.

I found her dead in the dumpster behind her restaurant after having been yelled at by her

boss for fighting for her rights as a worker. The conditions we have allowed androids to

live in has become entirely cruel and something we must look to correct if we are going

to coexist and continue to live in peace. If we don't, they will rise up just as we would. I

witnessed a protest by androids turn violent due to the police responding to their words

with terror. Whether alien, android, or human, all those who fought back against the

regime and its ideas were attacked by the state and its police force.

"I met with many android workers during my stay in Cairo and one whose

words will always stick with me will be those of Marius. He told me that not mistreating

them was not good enough anymore and that not speaking up was unacceptable. He told

me that things had gotten worse, but that they had always been terrible. It won't be a

quick or small change to restructure our world. We must be committed to a complete

overhaul of how people and beings see each other. While being driven by him, I asked

him some questions about his life and what he had seen. He told me that he had no more

rights than he had seventy years prior when he was fresh out of the academy. He has lived

a storied life, and I don't think his thoughts and his actions mean any less because of how

he came to be alive. A massive campaign of propaganda has been utilized to turn the

citizens of Cairo and Egypt itself anti-Nill and spread false stories because of the cult surrounding their leader Abdel Haladi. Many aliens are suffering with a specific and focused hatred of the Nills being central to their ideology. Some humans subscribe to the idea of a creator that designed us to be the way we are. I would argue that there is no difference in that sense between an android and a human. The only difference would be whether they were made by man or by a deity. With that thinking, then we essentially have been playing god by creating a sentient life form," Scott paused for both effect and a breath.

"For those who do not adhere to an ideology of creation by a third party, then the logical and moral response to the question is even more clear. We are no more than beings who are alive and realize our place in the grand scheme of all things. These life forms may be made by us but that doesn't make them any less real. They don't feel less emotions, they don't feel like they are any less real than us, and they just want to be treated the same as humans. They deserve the rights and opportunities that all living beings are given. If we as a planet allow any of us to be in bondage, or to be oppressed, or to be denied the same rights as anyone else then we are all in danger of losing the very same.

"Earth is fast approaching a reckoning with our own disregard for the planet and its health. The best time to act would have been two hundred years ago, but the second best time is now. We have the ability, the resources, and the power to make real change on this planet and in the galaxy. We can save the planet, we can guarantee basic, inalienable rights to everyone living on this planet and make sure that we treat all beings with the respect that they deserve. No one should be in camps and no one should be denied service or access to necessary amenities. We have been repeating these same mistakes for centuries. Many of those in power would tell us it has always been like this, but that is not the case. Just like the aristocrats before them, the capitalists will be replaced one day by the working class who seek to fully utilize the forces of production for the betterment of society. I know the doomers out there want to say that things are better now than they ever have been. I would say that this might be true for the very wealthy and those in power, but not for the majority of us. The majority of us live our lives as simple cogs in the wheel of the larger system that has no care or regard for our well being. We didn't choose to be born on this planet and we didn't choose where we were born or who our parents are. The capitalist organization of the economy forced upon us has led to an immense suffering the likes of which is unparalleled in the Earth's history. We align ourselves with nation states that are barely a few generations old and ideologies that don't care about our own self-worth but only to continue their own self-preservation. We need a system that works for the people and ensures the rights of everyone are protected. I ask that we as a species come together and tackle the ruling elite who aggrieve us and to not repeat the mistakes of the Nill people. I know change can be scary and can take an incredible effort but without change, we soon won't have a planet anymore. There won't be a city, or a nation, or anything to call home. We will find ourselves in the same crisis that we find the refugees of Nilleon in."

Scott caught his breath and cleared his throat..

"I ask that the United Nations vote to continue this program and allow more Nilleon refugees to seek asylum on Earth. I, and hopefully many others in this chamber can see ourselves in their situation because we face the very same issues today on our planet. Refugees from war-torn, oppressed, and poverty stricken nations have been flooding into other nations seeking a better life for all of our existence and we still take issue with that! Our own policies have led to this crisis and we berate and belittle the victims as if they are something alien to our own way of life. Our own species on their own planet seeks safety and we want to persecute the victims instead. In a world where we now have communication with and access to other planets and sentient life forms, we owe it to ourselves and to our universe that we seek to improve everyone's lives, not just those in power and with money. The most humane thing we can ever do is to look at our mistakes and grow from them. It is never too late to do the right thing and it is never too late to guarantee that every sentient being on this planet and in the galaxy is able to freely explore and live on the Earth. If we don't and we find ourselves in the very same predicament, then all we can do is hope that they are more human than we have become. Has Capitalism fully driven it from us? Or is it still inside of us burning on despite the darkness enveloping us every day?

"Let's give ourselves, our galactic friends, and all life in the universe no reason to question whether humanity stands on the side of dignity and respect for life or on the side of tyranny, oppression, and hate. We can be better together and there is nothing too difficult for us to overcome. Our own version of what Nilleon experienced is fast approaching and likely has already started. I believe that with the proper response, we can make sure that our planet lives to tell another generation the story of how this all transpired. The majority of us here on the planet are workers - we create the very things that give society its essence and its signature form. The processes that we all partake in and benefit from could be made more efficient and more reliable if we democratized the workplaces and allowed a less authoritarian style as we see in Haladi's Egypt and our very own American Union. We cannot sacrifice the lives of billions of our people for billions in profits for fuel industry CEO's and tech billionaires. Their oligarchic rule must come to an end and in every nation on the planet, a government ruled by a party made up of workers must come to pass and overthrow the economic shackles we find ourselves in. The truly violent and abhorrent atrocities that are afflicting the people are caused by our current system and are largely ignored due to their systemic form and nature. Systemic violence is seen as natural. Existing itself without the influence of any bad actors and ignoring the very design of the machine. Individuality has blinded our conception of how this affects whole populations of people. If you oppress and attack someone long enough, they will fight back and you will be responsible for the acts of resistance required to bring change and facilitate peace. Capitalism can no longer be the economic system we operate on. It must come to an end. It is destroying the world and our species. This is a matter of survival. It is truly Revolution or Extinction! Drastic measures must take place and we have to be sure to defend any gains made. This will be used to demonize us and our cause but we must hold strong! We don't ask for any apologies for the countless crimes perpetrated on the working people of the planet by the ruling elites, for when it is our turn we won't apologize for the terror!"

Scott's words hung in the air as he prepared himself for his final statement.

"I hope that this will be remembered as the moment where we put aside the issues that make us so different and where we decide that humanity will not go quietly into the void. We have so many opportunities to build a better world because it is possible. It will be a long battle and it will be a struggle but we must fight. We don't seek this better society for the far distant future because we have to build this society ourselves. It will not just form from nothing! We must teach the people we know around us as much as we can about the state of things and how they truly function and we must lift the blindfolds and the walls that separate us. This includes humans, our androids brothers and sisters, as well as our alien comrades. Sentient life is the bond that forms our collective will. It shapes our collective humanity and gives our movement strength. This vote will be remembered as the start of the course correction of Earth and our species history. We will stand united as one species determined to continue our existence on this planet for as long as it allows us - proudly facing and tackling the greatest threat we have faced in almost 100,000 years. With the power of the peoples of the world behind us, we will achieve unity, freedom and peace in our time!" Scott concluded proudly.

Every member of the security council and almost half of the representatives stood and applauded. Many in the room had been moved to tears as they cheered. The representative of Egypt scowled at Scott,lifting his thumb and pointing it down. Scott didn't even care as he scanned the crowd for Zara. She was standing and clapping harder and louder than anyone else. He walked back over to his seat and sat down next to Hailey, who was still cheering for him.

"How'd I do?" asked Scott.

Hailey sat down as Scott did.

"It was better than I could have imagined," she replied in awe.

Scott and Hailey watched as the audience and council members finished clapping and took their seats. The speaker sat up from his spot and walked over to the podium.

"The representatives will take a short break and when they reconvene will hold a vote on the issue at hand. Thank you."

CHAPTER TWENTY-ONE

Hailey led Scott out of the assembly hall as the rest of the audience dispersed. The short break could range from five to fifteen minutes or longer. They returned to the room that they had been in prior to the speech. The formerly hectic environment was now occupied by caution and optimism. People who were previously frantic were now waiting on pins and needles for the results. Scott's optimism was overshadowed by his previous experiences working with government officials. He was seated at a table with Hailey next to him along with other group members. A news channel was displayed on the television, showing the crowd and police in front of the headquarters. Those with signs and who were the loudest were being rounded up by officers and being detained - out in the open, with no attempt at covering it up. Rubber bullets discharged, tear gas canisters were thrown at protesters, and media personnel reported the event. The cracks from the shots were deafening. Scott tried to focus on his speech and what the council's vote would mean going forward.

"How are you feeling?" asked Hailey.

Scott turned to Hailey and let out a loud sigh.

"I feel much better after having finally finished that. I have been dreading that moment for over two weeks now and to finally wrap it up felt great. I hope I covered everything that I wanted to," he said.

"And how do you think they will vote?" she hesitated.

"I can only hope that I was able to convince them to look at things from my perspective. I can't force them to do anything, but I can show them a point of view they hadn't considered before. I hope the words of Mashir and Yolen had as much of an impact on them as it did to me when I interviewed them."

Hailey smiled and patted his back reassuringly. They were now patiently awaiting the decision's fate and what that would mean going forward. A woman entered the room after knocking lightly.

"They've reconvened, let's head back in now," she said urgently.

Scott and Hailey exchanged a glance, saying 'well, here we go!' with their eyes.

"Let's do this," Scott smirked.

They made their way back to the general assembly hall as others filed back in. The two of them took their seats to the side of the stage. Scott looked towards the security council's seats and looked for any noticeable sign of their decision. The crowd was a melting pot of joy and worries.

"I can't gather a consensus from all of these faces," said Scott.

"You and me both," Hailey laughed, the sound of her voice tapering off.

After a few more moments of everyone gathering back into the hall, the speaker walked over to the podium.

"The Assembly and Security Council will now cast their votes via tablet. The council acknowledges the President of the Security Council, Viktor Pohl, to count the votes."

Viktor Pohl reared his ugly face again. The same maniacal politician running for chancellor of Germany served on the Security Council. If it were up to him, the resolution would be dead in the water. The crowd applauded as Viktor rose from his seat and began to make his way over to the podium. He was a man of average height, with facial hair you'd need a magnifying glass to see. His light blond hair and sharp facial features gave him that extra charm. He arrived at the podium and gripped the edges of it with both hands. As the applause died down, he began to speak.

"Thank you, thank you very much. Representatives, please begin voting. The timer will count down from five minutes or until all the votes have been received," barked Viktor.

A large screen sat behind Viktor, split in half with the silhouettes of each nation's flag on the bottom. A few started to switch to the top as more representatives placed their vote. Victor read each vote out loud as they appeared.

"Ethiopia, Yes. Oman, No."

The tension in the room could be cut with a knife.

"New Zealand, Yes. Russia, No. The Islamic Caliphate, No. Mongolia, Yes."

Viktor would continue this process for every nation that would vote. India had voted no. Germany had voted no. Egypt, France, Turkey, Argentina, Southern Confederation, all no votes.

India, No.

Germany, No.

Egypt, France, Turkey, Argentina, and the Southern Confederation all voted no.

Slowly, the number of yes votes increased. Sweden, Italy, Montenegro, Brazil, Cuba, Australia, First Nation, and the Inuit. The numbers kept climbing and soon were both in the fifties.

Ireland.

New Al-Andalus.

The Terolu Confederation.

Scott tensed and the adrenaline overwhelmed him. Viktor's voice got dryer and dryer, his momentary water breaks barely relieving him.

The final vote was in.

"Tuva. Yes!"

Viktor took a moment to catch his breath and gazed over his tablet holding the voting information. His eyes grew large as his face grew red.

"The final count is 100 yes and 100 no," growled Viktor, stepping back from the podium and pointing to the screen showing the tied vote count.

Chatter began amongst representatives, journalists, and others in attendance.

What did this mean?

The speaker walked up to the podium and ushered Viktor next to him.

"In the event of a tie vote, the President of the Security Council reserves the right to cast the tie-breaking vote. The council acknowledges the President and awaits his vote," said the speaker, returning back to his seat.

Viktor stepped up to the podium and wiped a few beads of sweat from his forehead.

"I vote Yes!" yelled Viktor, displaying peace signs with his fingers.

The hall erupted into euphoria. The group of Nill to the side jumped from their seats and danced. Scott and Hailey stood and hugged each other, overwhelmed by the news.

"You did it!" Hailey cried, throwing up a hand to high five Scott.

Scott high fived her back but could barely speak. He could only smile. The utter shock engulfed him..The speaker walked over to the podium.

"This will conclude the assembly meeting," the speaker announced over the piercing cheers of the auditorium.

"How are you feeling?" Hailey shouted over the noise.

"I don't really know. We were this close to a no vote and I honestly expected Pohl to vote no. I'm a bit overwhelmed by everything," Scott yelled back as his breathing slowed..

The council and representatives made their way out of the hall followed by Hailey and Scott. Scott and Hailey grabbed their things from the meeting room while Scott greeted the other members of the team.

"Today was a great start to our work but we have a lot more to do if we are going to make a real difference. I can go over more of the basics of our work and responsibilities tomorrow, I think we should take the rest of the day to relax and celebrate the win," Hailey suggested.

Scott let out a large sigh of relief.

"I'm going to need that, that's for sure. Should we meet here going forward or do we have another area?" he asked.

"This is just our meeting prep room for any council assemblies or votes. Our actual office is on the fourth floor, suite 8891. It's hard to miss. You can always call me if you can't find it at first," she said with a light laugh.

She handed him a digital card with all of her contact information.

"Thank you. I guess I will see you and the rest of the team tomorrow. Can't wait to meet everyone else," Scott said.

"We can't wait either, Scott. I'll see you," she said as she made her way out.

Scott followed her and spotted Zara just outside the audience exit of the hall. The smile encompassing her face could be seen from the moon. Zara ran full speed in his direction once they locked eyes.

"You did it babe! You really did it! I'm so proud of you," said Zara, with the biggest smile on her face and a few tears running down her face.

Scott grabbed Zara's face, tasting the saltiness of her tears as he kissed her passionately. The exhaustion overwhelmed him but he fully enjoyed the moment. He wiped the tears from her face.

"I couldn't have done it without you. Thank you so much Zara," Scott professed.

The pair embraced and shared a tender kiss, not wanting to separate for even a second .

"So, what now babe?" Zara asked into Scott's neck.

"If you want, I can see if Tim wants to have us over. He mentioned that he has a new friend he wants us to meet," Scott suggested, still refusing to let Zara out of his grasp.

"Sounds perfect."

Scott pulled away and grabbed Zara's hand, holding it in his tightly before leading her towards the exit. Outside, a large crowd of protesters were being encircled by riot-geared police officers. The writing on their signs indicated that they were pro-nilleon, so Scott couldn't understand why they were being attacked by the police. Across the street, a crowd of seemingly anti-nilleon protesters brandished signs demanding "Death To All Foreign Aliens!" and "End The Nill Race".

A large wooden effigy of a Nill was lit on fire as the crowd chanted around it. The police stayed silent while cracking down on those trying to shake the status quo. It's as if they were almost protecting the anti's by separating the two groups. A few of the representatives left the building, walking opposite of the anti-nilleon protesters. Viktor Pohl was among them and was waving to the crowd. A protester wearing a "Death to Nill" shirt threw up a fist and Viktor threw up his fist in solidarity. When the Egyptian representatives passed the crowd, those carrying Haladi flags cheered. The group of Nill refugees made their way out, not going unnoticed by the protesters . A few started to throw shoes and rocks at them, causing them to sprint towards the bus that had ferried them here. Concern enveloped Scott and Zara.

"Let's take the side street and avoid all of that. I don't think it's going to end well," Scott cautioned.

"Good idea," Zara agreed. "Lead the way."

They found the exit to the side street. Scott noticed a poster for Silvius Johnson's campaign on a nearby building - a human with a hammer and a pitchfork stood on top of a platform being carried by two androids and two aliens. The center featured big, bold letters reading HUMANITY FIRST! Everything one needed to know about that man was displayed.

The chants grew louder. Sirens blared and popping noises began. . Loud bangs reverberated, mocking the deployment of flashbang grenades. Scott called for a ride and they only spent a few minutes waiting before the driver arrived. They ran up to the window right as the driver rolled it down.

"Scott?" the driver asked

"Yes, sir," confirmed Scott.

"Hop in, I'm ready when you guys are."

Scott opened the door for Zara before following her inside. He stretched his legs out and then his arms. The weather was beautiful despite the ongoing rage of the people. It was a smooth seventy degrees and the sun beat down with minimal aggression. Scott let the sunlight absorb into his skin. He wrapped his arm around Zara, who immediately relaxed into his chest. He decided to give Tim a call to check in while they had some time.

"Tim, we did it! They continued the program!" Scott celebrated the second Tim answered, barely giving him the chance to speak.

"Wow! That's fantastic man! I knew you could do it," Tim praised, choking back tears.

"Zara and I were going to celebrate. Would you want to hang out and celebrate?" Scott suggested.

"You already know man. Let's do it, I'll host!"

"Perfect, I'll let you know once we get there." said Scott before ending the call.

Scott checked his phone to review the notifications referring to the U.N. vote. He usually wasn't personally tied to breaking news, so this was an entirely new experience for him. The ride didn't take too much longer before arriving back at their home. Scott hopped out of the car, opened Zara's door, and paused to thank the driver.

"Thank you for the ride, I appreciate the work your people do for us. It doesn't go unnoticed," Scott complimented.

The driver seemed taken aback, his voice slightly cracking when trying to respond. Likely an audio motor issue.

"Of.. ofcourse anytime. Thank you, it isn't always the easiest job," said the driver.

"I'm sure it isn't, hopefully you have a great rest of your day," Scott said, waving to the driver as he walked away.

Scott approached his house and headed inside.

"So, we've got a little bit of time before we have to be there, right?" she asked, looking in his eyes and motioning towards the bedroom.
"I always have time for you," Scott smirked. Scott carried Zara into the bedroom where the pair celebrated Scott's victory.

Once their private celebratory ceremony concluded, Scott and Zara got dressed and ready to leave for Tim's. Scott changed into something a bit more casual, styling a pair of jeans, sneakers, and his new t-shirt he had bought in Cairo. Zara wore jeans and sneakers as well, but added a frilly pink top. The two of them made sure they had everything they needed before making their way outside. They sat on their patio chairs to wait for their ride.

"Should be here in about five minutes," Scott said.

"Perfect, just enough time to lay in the grass!" Zara sang as she grabbed Scott's hand.

She pulled him out of his seat and the two of them ran out into the yard, laying side-by-side. The feeling of the grass overwhelmed their senses as they gazed out into the sky. Scott saw two satellites shooting past his view. Zara noticed a huge flock of birds making their way across the sky.

"Look at the bird over there!" Zara giggled.

"Wow I haven't seen a flock like that in months. Hopefully they'll keep showing up! It was sad to not see them for so long," he replied.

The two of them enjoyed feeling at one with the planet and enjoyed the remainder of the time before their ride showed up. Once it did, they hopped up and ran to greet the driver. The driver rolled his window down to introduce himself before unlocking the doors. They hopped in and made themselves comfortable in the back. A bird landed on the mirror of the ride, providing Scott and Zara some mild entertainment. The rest of the ride was mostly uneventful, with Zara pointing out cool sights on the route and Scott answering questions about the history of the town. Once they arrived at Tim's house, they hopped out and ran up to the door. Tim opened it just before they managed to hit the doorbell and he looked like he couldn't be happier.

"Scott! Zara! Great to see you guys again!" Tim beamed.

Tim went in to hug the two of them and they reciprocated.

"It's great to see you, man," Scott choked.

"How's it felt to be back home, instead of halfway across the globe?"

"It feels really good, but it was worth it to meet her," Scott replied as he pulled Zara by the waist, closer to him.

"That is beautiful, Scott," Tim said, eying Scott's shirt at the same time. "I love the shirt man, where'd you get that?"

"I got it in Cairo! I saw it and knew I had to have it," Scott chuckled. Tim always did have an eye for clothing.

"Now I want one for myself," Tim winked.

"Thank you for having us, it means a lot for you to accept me so quickly," Zara said.

"Absolutely. Anyone that cares about Scott is a friend of mine," Tim said, ushering them into the house.

He shut the door behind them and they made their way over to the living room. The television already had an episode of 'The Theater' on and a bowl of chips and dip.

"Looks like the party is ready to start!" laughed Scott.

"Absolutely. John should be here any minute now," said Tim.

"Is John your new friend you wanted us to meet?" Scott smirked.

"Yeah! He's sweet, funny and he's also a great cook. He made us steak and potatoes the other night and it was amazing," Tim blushed.

"That's wonderful, man. I'm glad you've found someone who wants to be with you. Are you two exclusive yet or are you taking it slow?" Scott asked.

"We're taking it one step at a time, but I think I'm ready to take that step further. I hope you guys like him."

"I'll like anyone that makes you happy, man. That's all I want for you," replied Scott.

"I'm excited to meet him, everyone deserves to be happy," said Zara, smiling and putting her hand on Tim's shoulder.

"That means a lot guys, thank you," Tim said through teary eyes.

The three of them took seats on the couch and started to dig into the chips. Tim pressed play on the remote. The scene began with a customer talking with a manager about getting a refund.

"So, that new Christmas movie? Awful, just awful," the customer complained.

"Oh, wow, really? I thought the trailers looked funny at least. That's a shame," said the manager.

The customer stared blankly at the manager before speaking up.

"So, what are you going to do for me?" he asked slyly.

The manager looked puzzled as he held back his laughter.

"I'm sorry, what do you mean?" the manager asked.

"Well I didn't like the movie. I'd like a refund, it's me and these eight people in my party," he responded.

The manager smirked,shocked by what he was asked to do.

"I'm sorry, we don't give refunds after you have watched the whole movie. We don't make the movies, we just show them," said the manager.

The customer was shocked, quickly growing angry.

"Well, I want you to take care of me. Where's your boss, let me talk to him!" the customer demanded.

"Okay," replied the manager.

He went into a back office room and grabbed his superior, Dean, and explained the situation. He followed Dean out to meet the customer and listened while he explained the policy in the exact same way he did. The customer grew angrier and stormed off with his party. The other manager, Robert, who was also his superior, approached them with a look of uncertainty.

"What was that about?" asked Robert.

"He watched the movie and didn't like it, so he wanted a refund for himself and his entire party," said the manager.

"And you didn't give him anything right?" Robert said.

"Nope, nothing," said the manager.

"Good, fuck that guy!" said Robert.

Scott, Zara and Tim laughed. This happened to be their favorite scene.

"I'll go ahead and order pizza, what should we get?" asked Scott.

"Go ahead and get three pizzas and two orders of breadsticks. I like the works and whatever else you guys want too," said Tim, handing Scott his card.

"Are you sure? I can cover it!" Scott offered.

"This is your day man, don't worry about it."

Scott grabbed the card and began selecting what he wanted from the pizza place. Once he finished, he scanned the card with his phone to pay for the order.

"Should be here in about forty minutes or so."

"Perfect," Zara said, wrapping around his arm and holding tight.

The three of them continued watching television until someone knocked on the door.

"Sounds like John, let me grab it," said Tim, hopping out of his seat with haste.

He walked over to a mirror and fixed his hair before opening the door, revealing John. John was slightly taller than Tim, with tan skin and dark brown hair. He smiled once he saw Tim and the two of them hugged and kissed.

"Nice to see you again, as always," John smiled.

"You as well, you look great tonight," Tim complimented with a wink.

"Thank you, you look pretty great yourself," replied John, returning the wink.

Scott and Zara stood up and walked over to greet him.

"John, let me introduce my best friend, Scott and his girlfriend Zara."

"It's nice to meet you guys!I'm glad I can finally put a face to your name, Scott. Tim always talks about you, which started to make me jealous until he brought up Zara," said John.

"Nice to meet you too," said Scott and Zara, only slightly off sync.

"Well, we've got pizza ordered and 'The Theater' on, let's get to it," said Scott.

The four of them made their way over to the couch and made themselves comfortable as they began chatting about their days and what was going on in their lives. Tim disappeared to his room for a few minutes before returning with an armful of goods.

"You guys wanna smoke?" said Tim, tools in hand.

"Always," said Scott.

"You already know," John replied.

Tim sat down next to John and started to prepare everything for them. They continued watching the show until Tim handed the first piece to Zara.

"I haven't had a hit all day," Zara said before inhaling deeply. She held the smoke in for a few seconds before exhaling.

"I haven't had one in hours," said John, taking the piece from Zara and inhaling for eight seconds.

"I hit my pen right before you got here," Tim laughed before taking a much larger hit.

Scott grabbed it and attempted to take a larger hit than Tim. He needed to relax and wanted to make sure he would enjoy the night. The stress of the last few weeks was finally starting to subside and he realized that his new job might have a lot of opportunities that he hadn't expected to have. He let out the smoke and then sank back into the couch, letting all of his emotions boil up to the top.

"You okay, babe?" Zara fretted, resting her hand gently on his thigh.

Scott sat back up with a big grin.

"I'm good, I just need pizza and this will be a perfect night," said Scott.

They continued to party, smoke, enjoy the show and then enjoy the pizza once it arrived. Scott did his best to enjoy his time with his friends, even though at some moments he felt overwhelmed by the social interaction.

"Oh I almost forgot, listen to what happened at the coffee shop today!" said Tim.

John sat up and raised his brow.

"What happened?" asked Scott.

"John and I were grabbing something to drink on our lunch break and we were holding hands in line of course and some person started yelling at us! Said that we were indoctrinating people and that we should be ashamed of our agenda," Tim explained.

"The dude was a total lunatic," added John.

"Sounds like it! I can't believe people are still like that," replied Zara as she rolled her eyes.

Scott's pen made its way around the room, starting with John. By the end of the night, everyone felt complete euphoria. By midnight, the four of them were falling asleep.

"It's getting late, babe. Should we head back home?" Zara yawned.

Scott looked over at Tim, who he knew would continue to hang out as long as he wanted, but Scott was about ready to sleep himself.

"It's about that time, we should start heading home. I really appreciate everything Tim, thanks for doing this, I needed it," he said sincerely.

"Absolutely man, that's what best friends are for. I'll walk you guys out," Tim stood.

"It was great to meet you, John. I hope we see you more often," said Scott while glancing at the pair.

"Likewise, I'm sure you'll be seeing plenty of me," said John with a wink.

The four of them slowly made their way towards the door, continuing their conversations for another ten or fifteen minutes. Finally, they said goodbyes and Scott and Zara walked out of the house. A ride waited for them on the street. They got inside and started the journey back towards their home. On the way home, Scott checked his notifications and timelines, noticing several breaking news stories: a new terrorist attack in Japan, a dam bursting in Ethiopia, and a large protest in Chicago about police violence and brutality. It seemed like things never changed, no matter the year, decade, or century. He put his phone down and held onto Zara who was halfway asleep in his arms.

Scott carried Zara inside before setting her on the bed and tucking her in. He walked back outside to his patio to take a quick smoke break. He continued to check on the news and respond to a few messages from family and friends. A live feed of a speech by Anna Patsch regarding alien immigration popped on his screen. Standing in front of a crowd of her supporters, she was addressing the aliens seeking asylum in her country. She said 'Do not come here', noting that they should not make the dangerous journey. They should stay home and presumably continue being oppressed by other governments. This was a shock considering her yes vote earlier in the day. Good to know that governments on both sides of the issue would do what they wanted regardless of the vote. He saw a story from an Egyptian media outlet about his speech, calling into question what his motivations were. He hesitantly clicked on the article. They questioned the legitimacy of the footage he used in his presentation, the testimony from Mashir and Yolen, and his own legitimacy as a historian. They even interviewed Verona about what my business in Cairo was and she stated that he was altering footage to make Egypt look bad. She called him a fake historian and ordered that the library of Cairo never carry another work by him again.

Scott didn't care all that much, but the critique was still weird to read. This was clearly a hit piece written by someone angry that Scott didn't follow what Verona wanted him to do. They were trying to normalize this position against the U.N. decision. They were trying to quell any thought that was anti-government. Anti-Haladi sentiments were a crime. A specific line near the end of the article made him laugh. It questioned whether the U.N. had planted Scott in Cairo to rile up the Egyptians and give the American Union a reason to go to war with Egypt. This was, of course, just a conspiracy theory but it was getting shared by hundreds of thousands of people. So, many more people would soon enough read this and believe it to be true; or at least let the thought simmer in their minds until they didn't know what the reality was.

Scott continued to scroll, but was mentally and physically exhausted. He would certainly need to rest before taking on any future assignments. He did look forward to working with Hailey and wondered who else he would get to work with. He took one last hit and held it in for as long as he could, coughing the smoke out. The warm feeling that overtook him caused him to immediately relax. He walked back inside, took his spot next to Zara, and shut his eyes.

Tomorrow is a new day.

Scott woke up at about seven in the morning, before Zara had even moved from her spot in the bed. He picked up his phone from his nightstand and took a look at his notifications. He had three missed calls from Hailey, which was odd.

Why was she calling him this early in the morning?

He grumbled and maneuvered his way out of his bed. He walked outside to the patio to call her back.

"Hey sorry I missed your calls, it is seven in the morning," Scott chuckled.

"Sorry to wake you but we've got something big going on. Can you make it in? Like, as soon as possible? We have to meet with the Security Council. They asked for seven and I told them we could possibly do eight," Hailey yakked, barely taking a breath.

Scott was taken off guard, not one hundred percent ready to go to work, but this was clearly important.

"Yeah, I can be there. I'll be there as soon as possible, the same meeting spot as yesterday?" asked Scott, suddenly more awake.

"That works, see you there," said Hailey.

Scott ended the call and looked down at his phone. His timeline and notifications were starting to blow up, with multiple breaking news reports flying in every few moments. Scott hurried back inside and started up the shower. He walked into the bedroom and lightly tapped Zara on the shoulder.

"Hey, I have to go to work. It's unexpected but it seems like it's really important," Scott whispered.

Zara was fighting through the haze of sleepiness and smiled.

"It's okay, babe. Be careful and let me know what's going on," said Zara, who leaned up and kissed Scott's cheek.

Scott took one of the fastest showers he has ever taken. He threw a set of clothes on, making for a very business casual outfit before grabbing his satchel and phone. Scott pulled out his phone while waiting for his ride and turned to his newsfeeds to catch any clue of what was happening - lots of domestic issues, a couple new conflicts brewing, and a violent response to the protest in Chicago. Seemed like another day on the planet Earth, but nothing that seemed to point towards the Security Council meeting, especially not this suddenly. The front door opened and out came Zara in her morning robe.

"I figured while you wait, I would sit with you," said Zara, holding Scott's pen.

"You know me so well," Scott said as he grabbed it..

"Do you know what's going on?" she asked.

"No. Nothing on the news seems like it would be important enough to take a vote on, or meet with the Galactic Relations council. It could have something to do with my speech?" Scott guessed.

Zara grabbed the pen and took a hit for herself.

"Whatever it is, I know you're up for the challenge. They won't be able to hold you back from achieving what you want. You took a major risk to speak from the heart and anyone who has a problem with that isn't worth the energy," Zara encouraged, making direct eye contact.

She kissed him lightly, pulling him close. Scott took one last hit from his pen as his ride pulled up.

"Wish me luck," Scott said as he stood.

"Hey!"

Scott stopped in his tracks and turned around.

"I believe in you!" Zara shouted.

Scott smiled and continued on to tackle his newest challenge. He had nothing to lose and a world to win.

The End

ABOUT THE AUTHOR

Bobby Hutchinson 3 was born in 1998 in Indianapolis, Indiana. Son of Bobby Hutchinson Jr. and Grandson of Bobby Hutchinson Sr., he was named after his father's love of Dale Earnhardt and his signature #3. Growing up, his favorite subject in school was history, specifically the time period of World War II. He was inspired by the work of George Lucas and started writing stories and comics at the age of six. Motivated by a chaotic and changing world in the year 2020, he decided it was time to put his thoughts to paper and began writing. In Our Time is Bobby's first book.

www.ingramcontent.com/pod-product-compliance
Lightning Source LLC
Chambersburg PA
CBHW071218300726
48975CB00002B/269